IN CONCERT

A That's Entertainment Novel

By Christine Harvey

That's Entertainment Series
Take Two
In Concert
Tasty Dish
Rising Stars: a Prequel Novella

IN
CONCERT

A That's Entertainment Novel

Christine Harvey

MVP
Meadow View Press

Published in the United States by Meadow View Press

Copyright © 2015 by Christine Harvey

Second Edition 2020

ISBN: 978-0-9963152-4-1

Meadow View Press
www.meadowviewpress.com

DEDICATION

For Jim Harvey
He loved music and words, especially the made up kind
I miss you, Dad

ACKNOWLEDGMENTS

As always, boundless thanks to my writing partners. Tammy Kaehler, Cary Sparks, Tracy Tandy, and Wendy Young Howard: I couldn't get through my life, much less a book, without you all. Thank you for your opinions, laughter, love sandwiches—and for sharing and celebrating every step of this process with me.

For Josh, who gave me the time, space, food, and encouragement to finish this book. You're my country music song without the heartbreak and hound dogs.

I'm especially appreciative to Tav Sparks for sharing so much information about Georgia and a musician's lifestyle, and for giving me the inspiration for Luke's "spiritual-sleepy-cool" speech.

CHAPTER ONE

It's a *dive*."

Victoria Clausen stood staring up at the windowless brick building. "This is beautiful. If it weren't a cliché, I'd rub my hands together in glee." As producer of two successful reality TV shows, she dreamed of settings like this one, a neighborhood in Potrero Hill with stunning views of San Francisco's skyline. And a stereotypical bar in its midst.

Earlier that day at Reality Strikes Studios, her assistant Teresa raved about Tyler Landry, the country western band she'd seen the night before at Tony's Tavern. Victoria grilled her for all pertinent details, sent her off to do more research, then took the band's flyer to her boss and slapped it down on his desk. "Buzz Taylor's son," she said, pointing to the cowboy in the middle.

With the city in the background, the band members posed in a semi-circle at the north end of the Golden Gate Bridge, arms folded, and wearing the requisite country gear: hats, boots, jeans, western shirts. But Luke Tyler caught the eye. He stood with his legs set far apart, all in black, tight shirt hugging the planes of his chest. And he'd rolled up the sleeves to enhance his biceps, one wrist turned just enough to show the line of muscle running up his forearm. Victoria couldn't tell what color his eyes were, but dark, wavy hair peeked out from the hat, and a half smile quirked his lips. Her contract forbid her dating the talent, but that expression alone promised perpetual relationship drama for the show.

"The Buzz Taylor," she continued, as Jerry studied the poster. "Biggest womanizing, partying, country singer this side of Johnny

Cash. His son is in a band in San Francisco. Four guys," she told him, pointing to each band member in turn. "Two local, two from Georgia. Kenny Chesney's label is showing some interest. No manager, recording contract or strong social media presence. The exposure from a reality show could shoot them into the stratosphere."

After her recent promotion to supervising producer for the two programs she'd created—Hairdressers for Hire and Dress My Best— she'd recruited junior field producers to cover them, and was searching for a new show to develop. The thought of bringing Tyler Landry's story to the screen gave her a tingle up the spine that either meant she was onto something big or about to have sex. Since she couldn't remember the last time she'd had sex, she must be sensing a winner.

Jerry sat back in his overstuffed chair and watched her in silence. He'd tried this tactic with Victoria when she first interviewed for a job at the station eight years earlier, testing if she'd hang herself with babble to fill the silence. It didn't work then, and it didn't work now, but she let him have his moment. He hated saying "yes" immediately; she hated having to play his game. But she'd do it for this project.

After Jerry watched her for a solid minute without speaking, he leaned forward and steepled his hands under his chin. "Why the different last names?"

"Celebrity kids do it all the time, go by mom's maiden name, use a middle name. They want to be accepted on their own merits." She didn't know if this applied to Luke Tyler, but she'd find out. "Strong conflict," she added.

"They good?"

"Yes." She trusted Teresa's judgment.

"Heard them yet?"

That one was harder to hedge. "Teresa has. The two of us are going tonight on recon."

He went silent again, his black eyebrows the only animation on his face as he raised them a miniscule amount, which meant, "I don't want to hear an idea until it's fully researched." It was a long-standing argument between the two of them, but she knew her track record gave her an advantage. She'd created two of the top ten shows in the Bay Area; she had a winning streak, and she knew it.

Unable to wait him out this time, Victoria laid her palms on the huge desk. "Buzz. Taylor's. Son," she repeated. "Instant audience." She straightened and crossed her arms over her chest. "And we currently don't have a docu-series in the lineup."

When Jerry leaned back, she knew she'd won even before he said, "Determine their interest level. I want potential viewership data, marketing strategy, a thirteen episode story outline, and a one-sheet for the network on my desk first thing tomorrow."

To Victoria, that was a yes. She picked up the poster and did a little dance backward out of the office. "You're the best."

She worked on the reports between meetings, phone calls, texts and tweeting promotions for her other shows. Her last meeting of the day kept her at the office until eight o'clock, so she had only a few minutes to gulp down a Dr. Pepper and a turkey sandwich from the downstairs vending machine, brush her teeth and touch up her makeup before she had to leave for the tavern.

Teresa had gone home to change, but Victoria wanted the impact of a suit. She felt authoritative in her gray blazer and trousers, tailored to add the illusion of height to her five-foot-three-inch frame, a blouse in soft dove, and red platform pumps with a peek-a-boo toe. As always, she'd pulled back her thick auburn hair in a low, sleek ponytail.

Teresa wore a long denim skirt, purple cowboy boots and a batik top in shades of deep orange and russet that complimented her skin. She'd let down her braids for the evening, and they hung like jewelry around her shoulders. If Victoria had any envy she'd ever admit to, it was that she knew she could never look as casually, comfortably gorgeous as Teresa.

Victoria pulled at the dark wood door of the tavern, the handle sticky under her fingers, and, with a smile, gestured Teresa ahead of her. As they headed to a bar that ran along one side of the building, Victoria made a rapid-fire assessment of the setting, a full list of possible shots downloading in her head: dark wood paneling, typical etched-glass mirror behind the bar. An open doorway straight ahead leading to pay phones and restrooms. Carrie Underwood playing on a jukebox in the corner. Against the wall a semi-circle stage that didn't look big enough to hold a band—especially with the drum set and keyboards already in place—and framed pictures everywhere. Victoria slowed to peer at some of them in the dim light. Celebrities. Sports figures. Famous musicians. Harrison Ford, Jerry Rice, Mick

Jagger. It was a dive with a celebrity-loving owner. And it smelled like stale beer and fried food.

Her grin grew to epic proportions.

She noticed groups of chattering women already crowding most of the small, round tables by the stage: big hair, low tops and short skirts. Except for one, who didn't look old enough to drink. She sat on a stool at the end of the room, wearing jeans and a sweater, face lowered to a copy of *Gone Girl.* She didn't fit in with the other patrons, and Victoria made a mental note to keep an eye on her. It paid to watch out for the quiet ones.

A few customers sitting at the bar observed her progress with Teresa, and Victoria also mentally logged them for possible inclusion in the show as she approached the bartender at the far end. He stood with a towel slung over one shoulder, hands on his hips, watching the Giants beat the Rockies. She smiled, noting his Basset-hound eyes when he turned to her, his expression unchanged. He would look great on camera: the curmudgeonly barkeep.

He gave her a nod. "Get you something?"

"A Tanqueray and tonic, please."

"And beer on tap," Teresa said from behind her.

As the bartender turned to his tasks, Victoria directed her first question to him. "Would the owner happen to be here? I'd like to speak to him or her."

The bartender didn't look at her or respond right away. He set cardboard coasters on the bar and placed their drinks on top. "Ten bucks."

Teresa dug into her purse and Victoria tried again. "The owner? I have some questions about—"

Still not acknowledging Victoria, the bartender focused his attention on Teresa, taking payment for the drinks and giving her change. While Victoria was still forming her next question, the bartender turned back to her.

"Built in 1898," he said without preamble. It took Victoria a moment to realize he was talking about the building. "The 1906 tumbled it, that owner rebuilt, used the same bricks, no windows in front on account of a construction glitch, always been a tavern, not for sale."

"I'm not interested in buying it." Victoria laughed at the thought. "But I am interested in giving it some publicity."

Those Basset-hound eyes narrowed, but she ignored that. She held her card out, but he didn't take it or look at it, so she set it in front of him on the dark glossy wood and tapped it with one fingernail. "I'll be filming Tyler Landry here for a reality TV show, and you'll have so much PR, those guys will want to hang out here on a regular basis." She nodded at the baseball players on the television screen. "Not to mention an increase in bar sales."

The eyes widened. Yep, he was the owner.

"You can call the number on the back," she continued. "He's the executive producer and he'll vouch for me." With a smile she picked up their drinks and headed to the stage.

"I'll get the next round," she said to Teresa, scanning the area again. Tables full of chattering women in the middle, one reader to the right, one blue door to the left with an "Employees Only" sign. That must lead backstage. Two giggling blondes sitting side-by-side, heads close, thumbs tapping out texts, occupied a table directly in front of the stage.

Victoria headed for them, set the drinks down and leaned forward. "Hello, ladies, how would you like to be on television?"

They looked around, fluffing their hair, as if expecting to see cameras pointed at them with the red light on. When none appeared, they turned back to Victoria with hopeful looks.

"My associate, Teresa Steplowski, will fill you in on the details," she told them.

With a pang, Victoria set her Blackberry to vibrate so she wouldn't be disturbed, leaned toward Teresa and said, "When I get back, I'll have another show in production."

Teresa glanced at the door. "You're going backstage now? They might be...busy or something."

"I'm going to change their lives, T. They'll be busy figuring out how to thank me."

Without a backward glance, she straightened her jacket and strode forward, ready for any challenge.

CHAPTER TWO

Luke Tyler sat on a stool, eyes closed, shoulders pressed to the wall, guitar held upright and close to his chest. Around him, his band mates performed their pre-show routines in the storage room—turned "backstage."

Luke didn't need to open his eyes to know Tyler Landry's newest member Marty sat on a box labeled "green olives," drumsticks in hand, beating a rhythm in the air. Or that Parker, also with his eyes closed, meditated in the narrow aisle, legs crossed Indian style. Cort would be sitting in a chair he'd brought in from the bar, listening to Shooter Jennings on his iPod, head rocking up and down in time with the song.

Cort often joked Luke must be imagining crowds of screaming girls throwing their panties at the stage. But that was *Cort's* dream; the plain truth was Luke sat quiet like this before each show to pray. He and God didn't converse much, not since Luke discovered at seven that praying for God to help Daddy stop drinking didn't work real good. But he'd found that, like music, praying helped hold him together.

He kept it real simple: Please, God, let me do my best.

He knew he took everything too serious, but it was his way. He believed if Tyler Landry worked hard enough, they'd get somewhere. Simple again, and maybe naïve, but life was better kept to the basics. And Tyler Landry was getting somewhere. Just a few days earlier, a BNA rep had asked for a demo disc. They had one, but Luke wasn't happy with it, so they were re-recording a couple songs at the Barn tomorrow. He didn't want to think too far on it, to jinx anything, but this could be their break.

So he prayed for that, for some good to come out of the bad, for the band he and Cort had started as kids in Georgia to go somewhere. During a lean period, they'd signed on to be the house band at Tony's for a year, and had renewed the contract eight months ago. Tony appreciated the additional customers, but the pay was low, they had to do their own advertising, and it tied them to one venue more than Luke liked.

He also snuck a prayer in there for his mama back in Georgia, because she'd always been a big part of his strength, of what kept him going, and she deserved some of that in return.

His father, one of America's favorite country music stars—up there with Johnny Cash, Hank Williams, and Merle Haggard—the man who made "You're My Prayer" famous, didn't get a prayer from his son.

Buzz Taylor didn't deserve one.

Luke shifted on the stool, not wanting to go that direction right now. As a rebellious eighteen-year-old, he'd thought changing his last name from Taylor to Tyler would be enough to distance himself from Buzz. He'd learned it wasn't that easy, especially since he stayed in such close contact with his mama, and she took every chance to remind him Buzz would always be part of his life. As he took a deep breath to re-focus, shuffling feet distracted him again.

Cort's voice boomed out, "Just a few minutes, boys, and I predict some panty-throwing tonight," before the laces of his boots clattered on the floor.

Luke opened his eyes. Cort hardly ever tied his shoes, and he could barely keep still more than a few minutes at a time. Once he started on the panty-throwing, they could say goodbye to quiet. That was all right. When thoughts of Buzz crept in, Luke's concentration went sidewise anyway, so he needed a diversion.

Marty kept air drumming, although a smile stayed on his face as he watched Cort striding up and down the narrow aisle between boxes. Parker still sat cross legged on the floor with a dreamy look, as if he'd figured out how to bring about world peace, but Luke and the boys all knew that was a good sign. It meant Parker was ready to play. And even on his bad nights, Parker could play their boots off.

Cort strolled by and knocked lightly on the side of Luke's head with his knuckles. "Time to wake up, son, and give the crowd what it wants."

"We got some time," Luke told him.

Cort pulled one work boot off, then the other, and tossed both to the side before tugging on his cowboy boots. "Then let's us go out and mingle, work up the crowd."

"I could go see Miranda," Marty said, easing to a standing position.

Cort put an arm around Marty. "Son, out there with her book, she's happy as a coon dog on the scent."

"How do you know?" Marty asked, his eyes wide. "Did you go out there?"

"Nope," Cort said, with a hearty clap to Marty's shoulder. "I'm just familiar with your girl."

Marty pulled away. "What's that supposed to mean?"

Luke moved his guitar to the side and leapt down from the stool in a smooth motion. "It means that Cortland pays attention to women." He gave Marty a smile. "All of them."

He was about to tell Marty not to mind Cort when someone rapped sharply on the door. It swung open to reveal a woman in the doorway, and groups of women sitting at tables in the main room behind her, all staring into the small storage space. Luke froze at the unexpected interruption and noticed the boys did the same.

"Hello, gentlemen." The woman barely reached Luke's shoulder, even in some real high heels, but she marched in like she owned the place, and shut the door on the prying eyes to look at each of the band members in turn.

Smooth and commanding in a sexy gray suit, sleek hair, and red lipstick, Luke thought she'd be right at home on the streets of Manhattan. During his and Cort's short stay in New York, he'd found the women there always made him feel second-rate and warm under the collar at the same time. Warm turned to hot once he'd learned firsthand that under their all-business outfits they often wore all-play underthings. Considering the lipstick and shoes, he figured her color of choice was red. His hands tightened on his guitar.

"Am I in the right place, or what?" she asked.

Luke shook his head. He didn't know what she wanted, but if they let one woman in, the rest would follow and then he'd never get Cort to focus. Of course, if they were all like this one, he'd be in trouble, too.

"Wrong door," he finally said. "Ladies is by the bar." Moving his guitar to the side, he reached around her for the doorknob, but she held a hand out. Pressed it to his chest.

Lowering her voice, she said, "I don't want the ladies." She peered up at him through thick lashes.

Luke inspected her up and down again. He couldn't see it, but this was San Francisco. His gaze lingered on her hand, which generated a light pressure and delicate warmth through his thin shirt. A darn shame. "Gents is right next to it."

She tossed her head back and laughed, finally dropping her hand. "No. Not that, either. I'm here for you."

The others had recovered themselves by now and crowded around Luke to look at the woman. She was so short, even in those shoes, any other woman might've felt threatened, but she didn't give an inch. Luke thought she might even be having a good time.

He was about to say this was the wrong door for groupies, too—that had been one of his father's downfalls, and Luke wouldn't have it—when Cort cut in.

"'You' as in all of us or one in particular?"

"All of you."

Cort sidled around in front of Luke. "Well, now, wouldn't you rather have—"

Luke raised his guitar in front of Cort's face. "It's nice of you to come here, darlin', but we've got a no visitors policy before shows. We're just about to get ready, so you need to run along."

She tilted her head at him, and the corners of that tart-red mouth lifted up, surprising him. This declaration usually earned him a frown from the many women who snuck into the backstage area.

From behind him, Cort said, "Now, Lucas, I been meaning to bring up that policy..." but he trailed off when the corners of her lips lifted higher.

"You guys are going to look amazing on camera."

"Beg pardon?" Luke asked.

"Cam-er-a," she repeated, as if he were slow. She glided around him to set herself directly in the middle of the group, and inspected them, one by one.

"Dazzling," she said. "So photogenic. I can see the personalities already. Rebel. Scene Stealer. Innocent, and..." She appraised Parker, pausing, but instead of finishing the sentence, clapped her hands together and spun on her heel to face Luke again. "My name is Victoria Clausen, I'm a producer for Reality Strikes Studios, and I'm here to make you all famous."

"How's that?" Cort asked.

She turned to him and smoothed her hands over her hair so the neck of her silky blouse shifted to one side, giving Luke a glimpse over her shoulder of what he'd guessed at earlier. He'd been wrong, but he liked the truth better.

Pink. Her underthings were pale pink.

His ears rang, and he let out a harsh breath. In the next moment, the boys were in an uproar, Cort hooting, the others talking all at once. He realized he'd missed what Victoria Clausen, TV producer, had said.

"Beg pardon?" he repeated.

"Your own reality show." She spread her hands in an arc. "Tyler Landry, filmed 24/7. You'll be in households across the country, and eventually the world. Getting PR like you never imagined. Album deals. Gigs. We can call it...*Tyler Landry: In Concert.*" She tilted her head away from him for a moment, smiling as if to herself. "It's brilliant."

Before any of them could respond, she pressed business cards into their hands. "I know you have a show to do now, so we can chat afterward."

She reached Luke last. With the card held between the first two fingers of her left hand, like a femme fatale in an old movie looking for a light, she tilted it toward him.

He didn't move, staring at the card as if it might burst into flame if he touched it. Her sexy, authoritative appearance had already made him hot under the collar.

Up came the corners of that mouth again. She flicked the card away and tucked it into her cleavage. "Come find me when you're ready."

Then she was gone.

CHAPTER THREE

Victoria wanted to lean against the storeroom door behind her and take a moment, but all of the giggling patrons had stilled and shifted in her direction when she came out, so she produced a well-practiced "I'm in control" smile. Her heart beat so hard against her chest, she felt it might jolt her forward and back in an awkward dance, but she just added extra swing to her hips as she made her way to a seat next to Teresa. She figured only T would notice any inconsistency, and this wasn't the place to discuss it. She took a big gulp of her drink to settle her body and mind.

She hated using sex to close a deal. It felt nasty and implied she would fulfill her part of the bargain as long as the other party did the same, which was a big lie. And despite her often creative use of language, she didn't lie.

But pressing her hand to Luke Tyler's firm chest, feeling the strong, steady rhythm there, had sent a tingle through her entire body. For a moment, she imagined his long, tanned fingers sliding along her collarbone to her breasts, rough and warm against her smooth and cool, as he retrieved the business card.

She took a deep breath and let the tavern's activity fill her senses. Soon talk, clinking glasses, and laughter replaced the fantasy. Teresa was watching her, but she was saved from having to explain herself by one of the blondes trilling, "So how'd it go?"

"Round One successful," Victoria replied, thinking she sounded her usual assured self. And yet, the slightly quizzical expression remained on Teresa's face.

Her heart was beating too hard, and her fingers still prickled where she'd touched Luke Tyler's shirt. She checked her phone; no texts, no e-mails, Facebook or Twitter notifications. Damn. Just when she could use the distraction. To break the spell, Victoria asked, "You ready for the whirlwind next week?"

Teresa took a sip of her beer, looked about to say something, then seemed to change her mind. "Sure. It'll be nice to finally meet your sister."

After a short visit last year Kristen decided the Universe wanted her to be in San Francisco. Victoria knew easygoing Teresa and friendly Kristen would get along. She wasn't so certain how *she'd* do living in the same flat with her sister. Victoria lived corporate, driven, and no-nonsense, while Kristen radiated carefree, spontaneous, and relaxed. And that was just the beginning of their differences.

"She promised she'd only be here until she found her own place—two months, max—and I'll hold her to that."

"I'm not worried," Teresa said.

"Well, I am. Longer than two months and she'll turn our place into an Age of Aquarius yoga meditating ashram Buddhist colony or something."

Teresa laughed. "She can't be that bad."

"She doesn't believe in *TV*." Victoria clutched her drink, leaning toward Teresa to emphasize her point. "Or *meat*. She's a strict vegan, did I tell you that?"

"Well, now, that is a problem." Teresa leaned back and signaled the waitress for more drinks. Teresa had dreams of being a star chef, and Victoria reaped the benefits of her culinary creations. "It's a drag to cook for that. It's all tofu and bean sprouts."

"So two months, right?"

"Damn straight."

The blonde girls sharing their table pulled their heads apart and stopped laughing and texting long enough for one to say, "So will we still be on TV?"

Victoria gave them her full attention. "Do you come here on a regular basis?"

They nodded. "We come to every show," one said.

"They know our names," the other added.

Victoria smiled. "What are your names?"

In unison they said, "Candy and Mandy," then did double jazz hands and announced, "Twins!"

"*Really*," Victoria said, as if they'd charmed her socks off. She'd already noticed that one wore a melon halter top and raspberry miniskirt, while the other's top was raspberry and the skirt melon; both revealed toned and tanned legs and midriffs. Victoria itched to get them on camera. She'd already figured them for best friends; twins was even better.

"Oh, we know," the one Victoria decided to call Candy said. "We're not identical."

"But we've pulled off a successful switcheroo in our time," Mandy said.

Victoria rested her chin in her palm. Now she *was* charmed. "Do tell."

"Well..." they said together. "There was that time with Cort Landry..." They shared a glance and a giggle.

The waitress came by with their drinks then. Victoria grabbed her bag to pay and gestured for the twins to continue their enticing story, but looked up from her wallet when Tony's Tavern erupted into high-pitched cheers and clapping. Without introduction, the band walked out the blue door and headed for the stage, settling behind the drum set and keyboards and microphone stands. The half circle stage, with a faded maroon drape behind it, looked even smaller than before with four men crowded on it. She blinked up at them, a shiver going up her spine.

Teresa elbowed her in the ribs. "I told you they're prettier in person."

"Mmm hmm." Victoria had seen that in the "backstage" room, and she now stared up at Luke Tyler, waiting impatiently to hear how he sounded. In one respect, it didn't matter. All four were striking enough and had plenty of groupies to bring in an initial TV audience, but if they played badly, it could just add to the drama. People loved to watch attractive people screw up.

When the applause finally died down, the tall blonde in jeans, a white western shirt and white cowboy hat spoke first. Cort Landry, he of the famous switcheroo story with the twins, had seemed enthusiastic when Victoria came in. Luke, all in black, had tried to get rid of her immediately. Were they Good Cowboy, Bad Cowboy?

"Evenin'," Good Cowboy said, speaking to the crowd in general, then winked in Victoria's direction. "We're Tyler Landry," he continued, but stopped when vigorous applause broke out again.

He pointed at Candy and Mandy and said with a grin, "My girls!" over the cheering audience. The twins waved their hands in the air.

Cort continued. "We may not sing 'Can't Get Over You, So Why Don't You Get Under Me,' but we've still got some fun music for y'all." Then he strummed his guitar and shouted, "Yee-dawgies!" into the microphone before the rest of the band broke into the theme from *Smokey and the Bandit*.

Victoria clutched her phone, then put a hand over her mouth to hide her grin. She had to keep her edge, and that meant not revealing too much enthusiasm before the band signed on the dotted line. In the meantime, she would revel in every one of the upcoming songs about girlfriends leaving, dogs dying, and trucks breaking down.

She sent a quick text to Rebecca in Legal, asking about any covers Tyler Landry might want to play on air; getting rights could be tricky. Another text to Wen in the Art Department; she would need country accessories in their shooting locales. Or should they accentuate the San Francisco vibe as a contrast to the music? As she set up digital tasks for herself and replied to a few e-mails, her thoughts wandered to filming the show. Run-and-gun style with handhelds? Maybe. She didn't see *In Concert* as an edgy show, but she wanted to capture their uniqueness along with a younger audience, and handheld footage simulating home videos was hot right now. No, she decided, she'd attract an older demographic with these boys, too, especially anyone interested in Buzz Taylor, so a combination of camera styles might work better. She should be able to get some crossover with both the MTV and *The Bachelor* audiences. And if she could get one of the band members involved with an older woman, some of the *Real Housewives* viewers might tune in. She made another note on her phone, then glanced up at the stage.

Luke Tyler had lead singer written all over him, so why was Cort Landry singing? Could she finagle a switch for the show? What about installing Pelco cameras in the band members' homes? Originally designed for surveillance and with night-vision capability, they were expensive, but often resulted in some great, unexpected footage. She'd been wanting to develop a less structured show for awhile now, and this group could provide the perfect material. More organic, and with less producer interference, it would mean additional work on the editing side. But she loved that aspect of the business, too. Another note, and she bit her lower lip, considering other options.

A new voice through the microphone startled Victoria out of her thoughts. She looked up as Luke Tyler introduced the next song. Their eyes met, and she didn't know how to interpret his slow grin. She adjusted the collar of her shirt, feeling the sharp edges of the business card still tucked into her bra, and his gaze shifted downward.

Teresa leaned close to Victoria. "It just got warm in here," she said, fanning her face. "He's more cowboy than I've seen in a long time."

Victoria had to admit he looked the part. Lean legs, broad shoulders, tight black shirt buttoned halfway up, revealing the perfect amount of chest hair to run your fingers through, dark skin, and his eyes overshadowed by the hat. He didn't seem the tanning salon type, so how in the world did he keep so tan in San Francisco?

"Very Tim McGraw," Teresa noted.

Only bigger in the chest, with a football player's breadth, Victoria thought, trying to figure out if he was actually watching her or just looking in her general direction. She wanted to peek under that hat and find out the color of his eyes. How had she missed that when she went backstage?

The first strains of the song drifted from the electric fiddle, matched by the bass and drums, then joined by Luke's guitar. Head still turned in her direction, he opened his mouth, and sang, "Well, baby, when you talk like that..." and Victoria felt as if she'd been dropped hard onto her seat. A nice tenor that leaned toward a baritone on certain notes; a shiver skated up her spine and she let out a gasp. Truly, the prep for a new show was better than sex.

She surveyed the rest of the crowd, mostly women, a few men, everyone mesmerized. Teresa swayed in rhythm with the music, and tried to catch the eye of Cort Landry, who looked like a Marine in country duds. Marty Jacobsen, the drummer, had a sweet quality to him, with his shaggy brown hair and wide eyes, and barely looked out of his teens. Parker Guinto's black hair and angular features spoke of an Asian heritage, but his bright blue eyes startled her. She hadn't lied when she said the camera would love them.

Luke Tyler faced her again, and he ducked his head as soon as her eyes met his, shadowing them under his hat. Sweat slid from under the hat at his temples, and his mouth tilted up on one side before he turned that intense gaze on his adoring fans, leaning toward them during the more impassioned moments of the song. He definitely had the "it" factor.

The song ended, and as the applause died down, Parker at the keyboards and Marty on drums both lowered their hands and Cort settled his bass guitar alongside his body. All of them looked at Luke, who stood straight, eyes closed. Victoria felt the general hum in the room dip down until it eased into stillness as everyone focused on the man at center stage. Even the waitresses stilled and glasses stopped clinking at the bar. Luke leaned into the mic and sang one word, "Down..." extending it for a moment before adding, "...by the river."

Victoria stared at his face with such intensity, she jumped when he opened his eyes and held her gaze before resuming the song. He kept his eyes on her as he sang.

"I saw you...
Down by the river
I saw truth..."

He continued to sing a capella, and his voice carried such a draw, the stage might as well have been completely dark except for a spotlight on him. It sounded more like a hymn than a song, a prayer of thanks for what he'd found, and the lyrics kept that discovery unclear, letting the listeners make up their own minds whether it was God, a woman, or maybe even the singer himself.

Luke straightened his guitar right before the second chorus, strummed a few chords at the same time the rest of the band began to play, and they all joined in on the harmony, singing about their experience, there by the river.

As the song ended, there was a moment of silence, the intensity drifting through the crowd, and then the audience roared. Luke winked at Victoria. She came out of her own trance, picked up her glass, raised it to him in salute to the unspoken challenge, and took a sip.

Handsome, talented, son of a country legend, and a little rebellious.

She was going to get an Emmy for this one.

CHAPTER FOUR

After "Folsom Prison Blues," Victoria lifted her head from her phone to see Cort Landry shove back his hat with one thumb. "It's that time, folks," he growled into the mic.

"'Turn to Me!'" Candy and Mandy announced, making what Victoria already considered their signature move: arms straight up in the air and fingers wiggling. They shoved their chairs back at the same time, and gestured for Victoria and Teresa to join them. All through the bar, people pushed chairs and tables to the side.

Teresa started to rise, but Victoria, hearing the buzz of another text, shook her head. "No, thanks. I don't dance."

"Oh, but you have to." Candy tossed wavy blonde hair over her left shoulder.

"No, I don't, really."

"But everyone does." Mandy tilted her head so her long blonde hair fell over her right shoulder. "If you don't—" she gestured at the band "—you have to get on stage and sing a song by yourself."

"It's 'I'm My Own Grandpa'," Candy said. "You don't want to have to sing that."

"No one does." Mandy gave a shudder.

"No one does," Teresa repeated with a grin, crooking her finger at Victoria.

Victoria shook her head, this time in resignation, and followed Teresa into the crowd. She'd suffered worse indignities for a show than dancing, although she couldn't recall singing a crude country song. As she let Mandy and Candy position her and Teresa between them she wondered if she would go that far. She restrained an eye roll. *Line dancing*. But she noticed that even the little bookworm in the corner had joined them. Teresa beamed at Victoria, kicking one booted foot out and back.

"Oh." Candy leaned forward as the music started. "One more thing."

Mandy leaned in from the other side. "You have to do what they say in the song. Sometimes they change things up."

The music exploded, Cort began to sing, and the dancers let out a cheer.

"What?!" Victoria shouted over the noise, but didn't get an answer because first Candy, and then Teresa linked their arms in hers and did a sashaying two-step to the right. She looked down the line and saw that all the others had linked arms and were now stepping to the left.

"You broke my heart," Cort sang from the stage, "now turn around and get outta my life…"

Victoria's arms were dropped and with a hand now on her shoulders, Candy gently guided her to a 180 degree turn. She twisted her head and watched as Luke shouted from behind them: "But wait!" All of the women and the few men pumped their hands in the air as if swinging a lasso and spun back around on one foot. Victoria wobbled, but righted herself after the spin. Luke had one hand up, too, his other on the guitar he'd slid to one side.

Pointing to the crowd, he rumbled, "No leavin' with my heart, darlin'."

"What do you want for it?" they shouted in unison. Victoria stared around at them in awe.

"What do I want for it?" he called back. "I'll tell y'all what I want for it."

He slung his guitar forward and as he strummed his fingers along the strings, he sang, "Well, I want you to jump back, turn around, say you're sorry and you done me wrong."

The ladies did as they were told, then broke into a more traditional line dance through the rest of the song, which Victoria still couldn't keep up with. She saw her Blackberry light up on the table and figured she could sit down now without being punished with cowboy karaoke; she'd played her part in this mad dance, and needed to type up some notes for Jerry's episode outline. As she turned on one spike to sneak sideways through the line, her heel slipped on a wet spot.

One foot slid out from under her, and she collided with a table, knocking a glass over, which shattered on the concrete floor. Trying to avoid the shards, she shifted as she fell, but was beyond regaining her balance and stepped on the hem of her pants, feeling the material tear. Her ankle twisted painfully one direction as her body turned in another, and she felt the jagged glass points dig into her shin and knee and palm when she hit the floor.

On hands and knees, she cried out, the sound lost in the music, and fell back hard on her butt to relieve the sharp, stinging pain. She stared at her outstretched palms, then looked past them to her leg, where dark drops of blood bloomed in a random pattern on her lower pants leg. Teresa crouched by her side, then Candy and Mandy grasped her shoulders, and before she knew it, all of the big-haired, short-skirted patrons seemed to be surrounding her, leaving a wide space around the broken glass and overturned table.

The music stopped with a discordant jangle, and she closed her eyes against the pain creeping deeper into her cuts, but still felt tears welling at the shock, and blinked them back.

Strong hands pulled her up into a chair, and her twisted ankle shrieked and her banged knee shouted. She bent over, trying to hold back the pain, but the stinging in her palm overshadowed both and she ended up leaning over with her lower arms wrapped around the knee, her hands held out. Cold sweat broke out on her forehead and upper lip, and she panted slightly. Someone set a glass of water next to her and another brushed her hair out of her face. So many bodies and faces and voices pressed against her, asking if she was all right, if they could get her anything, did she need a doctor, but the only voice she heard was the one directly in front of her, suggesting she might need some room.

Startled, she raised her head to look up into Luke Tyler's dark green eyes; everything else drifted into the background. She barely registered Teresa's hand on her shoulder, Cort Landry's command to, "Shove back now, y'all, she needs some breathin' space, but don't go too far, 'cause we'll be playin' again real soon," as he got the crowd to back up. Most of them did. Luke Tyler didn't.

"You all right?" He crouched in front of her, one hand on the edge of the seat, the other resting on the arm she held over her knee.

Her mouth opened, but no words emerged. She couldn't believe the band had stopped playing; she'd never seen that happen for a disruption in a club. She was slightly charmed, probably in shock, and mildly embarrassed, a novel feeling. She shut her mouth and just nodded. Her leg and palms throbbed in time to the beat of her heart.

Luke pushed his hat up higher on his forehead as he nodded back, holding her gaze. "We want to get people dancing," he said. "Not falling."

The bartender rushed over with a first aid kit. "You sure you don't want me to call a doc?" he asked, holding it out.

Luke broke eye contact when he twisted to reach up and take the kit. Swallowing hard, still bent over, Victoria shook her head; she'd forgotten how to speak, all of her senses suddenly focused on the burning in her knee, ankle and hands.

Teresa leaned close. "Are you sure, Victoria?"

She nodded again, her attention on the man hunkered in front of her. She watched his lips form her name. He didn't say it out loud, just mouthed it while looking into her eyes, as if testing it out. She felt his breath on her skin when he did it, and her lips parted slightly as a shiver worked its way down her spine.

He cleared his throat suddenly and said, "Well, Miss Victoria, I got to tell you..." Twirling his index finger in a circle, he pointed at her cleavage. "Your card's showing."

"My what?" She looked to where he pointed; her top button had popped off, and her crouched position forced her breasts up, revealing both the card tucked into her bra and the bra itself. "Oh." If she ever blushed, this might have been the moment. Instead, she reached up for the card, then hissed in a breath as her palm contracted around a tiny shard of glass.

A flush swept up Luke's tanned cheeks and he grasped her wrist in one hand to stop her movement, his gaze moving from her hand to her leg. "You're bleeding."

Victoria heard gasps behind her and thought one might have come from Teresa, but they sounded far away. For all she knew, it could have been Candy. Or Mandy. Or the entire bar. She tried to wave away the concern on Luke's face, but he still held one arm, and she had the other firmly wrapped around her leg, covering the blood there. "I'm fine."

"You're not," he countered, turning her arm to expose her palm. This time, he hissed in a breath and stared at her, a surprised expression on his face. "Glass," he said, shaking his head. "Tony, could you get this mess cleaned up, and clear these folks away?" He lifted his chin at Cort Landry, who stood at his side. "Right that table, would you?" When Cort had done so, Luke rested Victoria's hand on it, palm up, then looked into her face again. "How's the other one?" She held out her good hand, and he nodded. "Now let's see your leg."

She shook her head; her ears had started to ring. "It's fine, really. Just a little cut."

"Foolish little..." He shook his head, too, then shifted to stand. "Have it your way."

Luke stood and Victoria felt like she could breathe again; he'd been so close, so warm, she hadn't been able to think. She really was fine, just a few glass splinters. She lifted her hand and peered down to look at her knee through the hole in the fabric, then felt swimmy at the sight of all that blood on her Versace pants.

"Looks a little less than fine," Luke said. Crouching down again, he slipped the first two fingers of each hand inside the rip, and pulled, widening it with a harsh tearing sound.

"What are you doing?" The fuzz in Victoria's head cleared at the sight of her ruined trousers. "These are two hundred dollar pants."

Luke paused and peered up at her. "Well, maybe you'll think twice about spending so much on your next pair."

Victoria was so surprised she could only make an indignant noise, which turned into a squeak when he completely ripped off the bottom section of material. He slid one hand along the side of her shoe to the heel and lifted her foot. His thumb grazed her ankle and she jumped.

"I think it's twisted," she said by way of explanation, still feeling the brush of his rough skin on hers.

"My apologies." He gently lowered her foot back to the ground.

She made a noncommittal sound and waved him on.

He offered no apology when he reached for the remaining material of her ruined pants and rolled it up out of the way over her knee, his fingers warm on the skin of her thigh. They both leaned forward to look at the damage. The skin there had swollen and turned a pinkish-purple. A long, shallow cut in the middle had begun to coagulate from Victoria holding her arm over it for so long; many smaller cuts from the glass shards surrounded it.

"Ooh," she said, looking down at the slash and feeling slightly queasy. Maybe it wasn't nothing.

"Doesn't look so bad. Just needs to be cleaned a bit." Luke smiled up at her, and her breath stopped. He reached in the first aid kit and tore open a packet of disinfectant. Holding the pad by one corner with a thumb and forefinger, he held out his other hand. "Here."

"What?" She looked down at the long, supple fingers, wondering what he could possibly want.

"Squeeze if it hurts."

She had a wild thought that if she grabbed hold of that hand, she'd never be able to let go, so she shook her head. She sat back, bumping into Teresa, and braced herself for the sting. She scrunched her face up tightly and gripped the edge of the chair with one hand while Teresa put both hands on her shoulders. She was still unprepared for the pain when he first pressed the pad to her cut, and her leg tensed, then kicked out, colliding with his shin and throwing him off balance so he fell on his butt.

"Oh!" she cried out. "I'm sorry." She leaned forward, disengaging herself from Teresa's grasp, and held out her good hand. "Squeeze if it hurts."

CHAPTER FIVE

I need that band, T," Victoria said.

"I know, honey, but they're not going anywhere." Teresa held the car door open while Victoria struggled out with her bandaged hand and booted ankle. Not fashionable footwear, either, but a walking boot she had to wear during waking hours for her second-degree ankle sprain. Who even knew sprains had degrees? She'd debated this with the doctor until he'd moved on to the next emergency.

Teresa had insisted on taking her to the ER when they found more glass fragments and her ankle swelled. They sat for hours while hospital staff treated car crash victims, a heart attack and a broken arm. It was now past four a.m. and Victoria couldn't stop thinking about Luke and Tyler Landry.

She needed to talk to them soon; timing was critical with any new show, and she knew with deep certainty that *In Concert* would be her next. She would have to get filming started ASAP if she wanted to slot the show in by June.

Shoes in one hand, Victoria put her other arm around Teresa's shoulders for help up the steep sidewalk and front stairs. As she limped forward, Victoria stared down at the hideous boot. Physically exhausted, and mushy from painkillers, ideas still careened around her brain on how next to approach the band. Direct had worked with three of them, but she instinctively knew they wouldn't agree without Luke Tyler's buy-in. Him, she would have to finesse.

She stumbled when Teresa stopped suddenly at the foot of the stairs. "What?"

"I didn't leave a light on inside when we left."

Victoria looked up at the double bay windows that faced the street. Soft light shone out, filtered through the closed blinds. Who could be in the flat? She didn't know, she couldn't think. The cold concrete seeped through the hospital sock on her good foot, and her head felt as foggy as the pre-dawn air.

"Maybe you forgot," she said, and shuffled forward again. She was ready for her big soft bed and this day to be over.

"I never forget."

"Maybe Adele put it on for us," Victoria said, although she couldn't imagine their upstairs neighbor and landlady leaving her window to do something like that. "I need sleep, T. I have morning meetings. It's freezing. I may have to pee. Let's just go check it out together."

Victoria galumphed up the stairs and onto the small porch, where she gingerly set her booted foot on the cement and held onto the iron railing for support, as Teresa pressed her face to the door, which hadn't been completely closed. Teresa blinked a few times, then straightened.

"It sounds like someone's humming."

"Our burglar is humming?"

"Or our serial killer." Teresa glanced at the door.

"Maybe we'll get a singing detective," Victoria said, and snorted out a laugh. She covered her mouth with her hand and looked up at Teresa. "I've got to get inside, burglar or not. The meds are knocking me out."

"Okay, but we're not going in unarmed." Teresa set down the bag of Victoria's items the hospital staff had given her, and got a grip on the cane they'd told Victoria to use as needed.

"If they get me," Teresa said, "you scream bloody murder and run…" Her eyes dropped to the boot. "Um. No." She dug in her purse and pulled out her cell, then tapped three numbers and handed it to Victoria. "Hit Send if they attack."

Victoria clutched the phone. "This is feeling a little too Lucy and Ethel. Can we just go in?" She was convinced Teresa had just forgotten and left the lights on.

"Here we go." Teresa gripped the door handle with one hand, and raised the cane in the other. She threw the door open, and jumped inside with an "A-ha! We've got you—" then stopped dead and said,

"Are we in the Haight?"

Victoria peered around T's shoulder into the room. Her younger sister sat in the lotus pose, a serene expression on her face, and beamed up at them. Overhead, incense hung in a haze, floating in lazy patterns from the draft created by the open door. Victoria saw Kristen there, smelled the sweetened smoke, even saw it drift about as she waved her hand, but she couldn't quite believe it. Maybe the painkillers were messing with her head more than she'd thought. "Kristen?"

"Hi, big sis," Kristen said, and laughed at the old joke. Victoria was older by five years, but Kristen had been "bigger" for at least the last fourteen, when some recessive Viking gene emerged. She towered over everyone in the family, overwhelmed men with her voluptuous figure and wild tangle of strawberry blonde curls and eventually charmed one and all with her charismatic personality. At her own puberty, Victoria had been short and round with a reddish tint to her brown hair. Round had turned to curvy, but not much else had physically changed for her. She and Kristen shared the same body type, but Kristen's was stretched out by about eight inches.

"What are you doing here?" Victoria sputtered. She hobbled into the room as Teresa stepped aside and shut the door.

"Yoga," Kristen said, holding her arms out from her sides, palms up. "Actually, I'm almost finished. I had a nice long session while I waited for you." She pressed her palms together, bowed her head over them, said, "Namasté," then rose straight up out of her pose like someone had pulled an invisible string on her head.

Teresa looked up at her. "Man, you're tall."

Kristen smiled. "It must be the California air. It makes me feel so expansive." She pulled Teresa to her chest in a huge hug. "You must be Teresa. Victoria told me how radiant you are. It's such a blessing to meet you."

She let go, and at the confused look on Teresa's face, Victoria wondered how to explain. She'd never used the word "radiant" when describing T; that had been Kristen's interpretation. But her thoughts remained muddled and she had more pressing subjects to deal with.

"You weren't supposed to be here until next week. How did you get inside the flat?" Victoria asked before Kristen could reach out to hug her.

"Robbie and Dad were driving me nuts. 'Why do you have to

leave? Isn't it bad enough your sister abandoned us?"' She put her hands on her hips and lowered her voice. "'We're Illinois born and bred, we got no reason to leave.'" She peered down at Victoria, her serene expression gone. "I had to get out of there. After Delhi, I needed a city, people, movement, excitement. A *life*. I thought I could make it work, that I could change them for what I needed, that I could make my own little India in Illinois on the strength of my will alone. But they're just too them, and I'm just too me for that."

Victoria limped to the couch and collapsed on it, dropping her head back; it felt so heavy. "Well, you're here now…"

"Hey, what happened to your foot?" Kristen asked, sitting next to her.

"Sprained my ankle," Victoria muttered, staring at it. She wanted to talk more about Tyler Landry and their show, to review and analyze the evening as she always did with Teresa, but the words wouldn't come.

"I've got some Rescue Remedy," Kristen offered. "It helps in stressful situations."

Victoria had tried some of Kristen's "remedies" before. "No. I just need sleep."

Silence descended, sleepy for Victoria, apparently serene for Kristen.

"So, welcome to San Francisco," Teresa finally said. She set the bag and cane down. "Ah…"

Victoria gave her what she was sure looked like a grim smile; maybe she hadn't given Teresa enough warning about Kristen.

"Thanks," Kristen said to Teresa, then turned to Victoria. "I know I'm early, and I tried to call you from the airport, but I couldn't remember your number, and I didn't know where else to go and your landlady is really nice—" Victoria ignored a snort from Teresa and nodded at Kristen to continue. "She let me in to wait for you, so here I am." She held up a hand. "But I already promised I wouldn't impose on you longer than necessary. I've got money for a down payment on a place, I've got that job starting next week. I don't expect you to take care of me, I just need a place to stay until I get settled. And I'm so glad to see you."

Victoria let her head drop against the back of the couch again, noticing that during this speech, Teresa had moved over to the chair by the sixty-inch television set and sat down, watching the two of them like they were her own TV show.

"Kristen…it's fine." Victoria felt like she'd drunk too much and was trying to convince those around her she was sober enough to drive; sentences came out with difficulty and she wasn't entirely certain the words from her mouth matched those in her brain. "The couch is yours. I'm fine with it, T's fine with it."

"Thank you." Kristen headed to the door. "So let's go out. What are the best dance places?"

Victoria and Teresa stared at Kristen and then at each other. Victoria realized she didn't have the energy to fully explain her sister to Teresa; she shook her head. "They're probably closed," she said, pushing herself up and stumping toward the hallway. "You'd do better getting some breakfast at The Plant at Pier 3. Live it up. I'm going to bed."

CHAPTER SIX

Luke drove the band's van past the roll-up door into the Barn, hit the brakes, killed the lights and sat staring at the concrete wall in front of him. Victoria Clausen had insisted she was fine and set herself down right in the front row again, her hand wrapped, and her bare leg and foot resting on a chair, covered with a towel full of ice. But partway through "Rodeo Nights," her friend had signaled a waitress and Luke watched while they helped Victoria hop out, Candy and Mandy following with their gear. The twins had returned, the boys finished their set, and as everyone cleared out, the waitresses set chairs up on tables and swept the floor.

He'd started to slip his guitar strap over his head and step off the stage when Rhonda straightened with a rectangular object in her hand. "Another one," she said to Eileen. "Slipped under the stage." She made to toss the cell phone to the other woman but Luke stepped in front of her.

He swung the guitar to his back instead. "I got that," he said. "Belongs to the woman who fell," he added, when Rhonda turned to him. He'd noticed Victoria could barely keep her eyes off the damn thing during their first few songs.

Still holding the phone, Rhonda crossed her arms over her chest, looking him up and down. "What'd she want with you guys? I saw her go backstage."

"Nothing much." He held out his hand. Behind him, he heard Marty and Parker talking as they carried gear to the van parked in the alley. "I can get it back to her."

Rhonda lifted her arm, and Cort stepped between them and snaked the phone out of her hand. He slid an arm around Rhonda's shoulders and held the phone up. "Now don't you worry about this, Rhonda darlin'. We'll get it back to its rightful owner."

Rhonda snorted and slid out from under Cort's arm. "Sure. Probably in person wearing just a hat and a smile," she said, then grabbed her broom from where she'd rested it against a table and swatted Cort in the butt with it. Cort roared with laughter. She tossed a smile over her shoulder and went to sweep the other end of the room.

"She knows me too well," he said to Luke.

Luke shook his head. "She should, on account you've given her the hat and smile treatment a few times." He smacked Cort's shoulder with the back of his hand. "Give the phone here."

"What for?"

"So I can get it back to that producer."

Cort looked at the phone as he turned it over a few times in his palm. "Well, now, I'm not so sure about that. She may be happier to get it from me."

Luke tilted his head back, then rested his hands on his hips; one elbow brushed the body of his guitar. "Now why's that?"

"Because you want to say no to her, and I want to say yes." He leaned closer and said, "I'm thinkin' she's not a woman you say no to."

Luke ignored the suggestion behind Cort's words. "You want the show."

Cort straightened. "And you don't."

"I do not." Luke held out his hand again. "Just give me the phone back and I'll let her down easy."

"The show isn't just for you, Lucas." Cort gestured at the blue door, then ambled toward it. "This oughta be a group decision." Cort stepped through the doorway and stopped in the middle of the small room, before turning to Luke. "Why don't you want it?"

"Those shows are all setups. They make you look as foolish as possible for good ratings."

Cort made a skeptical face. "Well, I know I won't look a fool. Your mug might not translate so well on screen."

Luke snorted, slipping his guitar to the front and ducking under the strap. He flicked the case top up and set the Fender inside. "They take advantage, Cort. More harm than good." He snapped the latches and turned back to his best friend. "I don't see the gain." All he saw was manipulation ahead; imagined them sneaking Buzz onto the show for ratings, and dragging his mama's personal pain into the limelight. He crossed his arms over his chest.

"Exposure," Cort said, copying his pose.

"Exactly," Luke replied. "The bad kind."

"The free kind." Cort pointed at Luke's chest. "And I bet they actually pay us. Even better."

"Worse." Luke pointed back. "Then they own us. No one owns me." He felt his back going up, saw the fire in Cort's eyes as he prepared for one of their "wrassles." Ever since they were kids, they'd wind each other up as a way of settling quarrels. It usually worked for them, but tonight Luke felt too tired and distracted to play.

Cort slapped his hands against his thighs. "Dammit, Luke, your pride could cost us big," he said, his voice rising.

Marty and Parker rushed through the side door from loading the van. Parker said, "Now, gentlemen—" but Marty stepped right in between them, forcing each man to take a step back.

"You fighting?" Marty looked at each of them in turn, but neither said a word. "What about?"

"Not fighting," Cort said. "Wrassling. I say we do that reality show." He lifted his chin at Luke. "Lucas says otherwise."

Parker brushed his hair out of his eyes and moved his gaze from Cort to Luke. "Are we voting on that already? Should we not discuss it first, meet with that producer?"

"You, too?" Cort demanded. He looked at Marty. "What about you? You want to do it?"

Marty shrugged, moving from between Luke and Cort to stand next to Parker. "Seems like a good opportunity."

Cort looked at Luke again. "Two against two."

"My statement wasn't a no. But I don't believe in pitting us against each other. We're a team." Parker cocked his head when Luke turned to him. "I think it's a fine idea. But I don't believe we should make any decisions until we've talked it through, learned all it entails. Discussed it with the producer."

Luke was about to object, thinking he'd talk to Cort later about how he didn't want his mama's business dragged through the mud, when Mandy and Candy peered around the doorway. "You ready, Cort?"

Cort turned to them. "My darlings, I am always ready for you." He pointed at their tight tank tops and bare middles. "I can see you're both mighty cold and might need some warming up…"

Luke stopped him with a hand on his arm. Cort looked pointedly at his arm, then in Luke's eyes.

"The phone," Luke said. "I'll set up an appointment." His eyes flicked to the doorway. "Since you'll be busy."

Cort flipped the phone up and Luke caught it without taking his eyes from Cort's. He held it against his chest; it buzzed twice, then subsided.

Cort grinned at him, but it didn't quite reach his eyes. "I'm not changing my mind."

"Neither am I."

"We'll see, Lucas." Cort put an arm around each girl and headed for the door. "We'll see," he called over his shoulder.

Luke helped Parker and Marty finish loading the van, remaining silent during their attempts to talk about being on the show. Marty and Miranda offered Parker a ride home, so Luke drove around the city for awhile, attempting but not quite able to resist images of that gap in Victoria Clausen's blouse when she'd lifted her arms to smooth back her hair. He tried to banish thoughts of her round blue eyes, full upper lip, and that lacy pink bra. He cranked the window down, and the cold, foggy night air roused him. He could have brought someone home—among others, Patsy, one of the bartenders, had offered—but he'd been too preoccupied. By the time he got home to the converted garage on Folsom that he and Cort had dubbed the Barn, the cool air had chilled his face and hands. But not the rest of him.

He didn't know how long he sat in the van, staring at the wall in front of him, but after Victoria Clausen's phone buzzed again, he finally gave himself a shake, and jumped to the concrete floor. He stuffed the phone in his breast pocket before closing the pull-up door, then grabbed his guitar case and bounded up the stairs to his apartment.

When Cort's daddy died a couple years earlier, he'd left his son money enough to bankroll him for years. Cort bought the old garage with two apartments above it, and a small sports bar called Blitz for an investment. It wasn't until Luke asked what his rent would be, and what sort of work he'd do at the bar, that he learned Cort had bought the two buildings for them. He'd been offended at Luke's suggestion, but Luke hated the idea of someone else taking care of him. So he worked at the bar for a paycheck, and on the first of the month, he slid a rent check under Cort's door, even if it meant he ate Top Ramen for the next thirty days.

Inside his apartment, he tossed his hat on the coffee table and collapsed onto the couch without turning on the lights or removing his boots. Frog meowed from a corner, then leapt up to land on his stomach, turning in circles and kneading his shirt. He petted her automatically while he looked out the window at the buildings across the way. Not a pretty view—an appliance store and dental office— but he didn't care. He loved his space above the garage: one big room, with a small kitchen and bathroom, a partition to hide the bed, the long couch he actually fit on, a comfortable recliner, and a table where he ate breakfast. Cort was just next door down a short hall and their rehearsal space was downstairs, next to where they parked the van. He'd have bought the place, too, if he'd had the money, and he wouldn't have charged Cort rent, either. And Cort might've joked about the easy life, but he'd have paid his share.

He'd do anything for Cort, and vice versa, but he couldn't imagine being on a reality show. He'd seen those programs, edited to show the worst in everyone, playing up the smallest issues to make folks look ugly, and engineering fights, romances and dramas. He had enough of that in his life; he didn't need some brassy producer manipulating things in the background to exaggerate them. Tyler Landry had built up too much here to risk having a television show portray them as country bumpkins, or worse. He'd just have to find a way to convince the boys this wasn't in their best interest.

Still. He slipped the phone out of his pocket and cradled it in his palm while Frog purred on his belly. The woman would undoubtedly want her phone back. He'd give her a call at work and drop it off. Then he'd go on with his life the way it was meant to be: without a bossy woman trying to control him.

CHAPTER SEVEN

Victoria clomped past a row of redbrick office buildings on Battery Street and into the lobby of Reality Strikes Studios. She juggled shoulder bag, files, memos, mail, clipboard, and an extra-hot triple-shot espresso with one good hand and one bandaged one as she headed to the elevator.

Teresa had dropped her off with an offer of help, but Victoria needed her to sit in on a meeting with Chastity, the new field producer of *Hairdressers for Hire*, and report back. The show's stars, LaTanya and LaKenya were having fits over their next assignment: clipping and dyeing billionaire Cookie Shaw and her poodle to match. Proficiently conflict-averse, Teresa could help smooth things over, and Victoria needed to be in the studio, finishing *In Concert's* prospective story outline for Jerry and putting out feelers for a crew. Once in the lobby, she ran through her mental contact list on possible team members for storylines, camera and sound, editing, and a director.

She reached her bandaged hand out to push the "up" button, but froze when the door to her left opened and the frequent star of her romantic daydreams emerged. Her stomach dropped. Of all people to see her in this state: Brett Soloway, associate producer on *Man vs. Machine* and *Temptation Station*, lanky and handsome in his Armani suit.

Never rumpled or wrinkled, he still managed a boyish charm with a lock of hair that fell seductively across his forehead and a tendency to wink without looking smarmy. She'd been trying to get him alone for months to ask him out, believing with their common interests they would make great partners.

He smiled at sight of her, but his expression sobered when he glanced at her feet. Since all her shoes had heels, she'd been forced to wear a skirt and one of Teresa's flats along with the hideous boot. She turned to the side so he wouldn't see her bandaged hand, counter-balancing a stack of folders threatening to slide from her arms.

"Hey, what'd you do?" Brett asked.

"Oh, just a little mishap while doing some scouting." She would never confess to crashing into a table while line dancing. "The boot is more precaution than anything else." She tilted her chin up, wanting his gaze focused on her face and away from her feet.

He bent close, and she smelled his John Varvatos cologne, like a combination of Moroccan spices and leather. "Well, I won't insult your feminist sensibilities by offering to carry your bag," he said with a wink, "but I can get this for you."

He pressed the "up" button and the back of his hand brushed hers. Her throat went dry and she took a sip of scalding coffee to try to clear it, then had to hold back a gasp over her burned tongue.

"Thank you," she coughed out. He was one of the few men she'd met who seemed to appreciate the difficulties she experienced as a strong woman in their business. Brett Soloway knew that taking her bag from her would be offensive, as if she couldn't handle some small thing like a twisted ankle. Getting the elevator was the perfect touch.

The door dinged open and he ushered her inside, waiting until she'd moved to the rear before stepping in himself and pressing the buttons for floors five and six. He settled back, elbows on the railing. "Hey, congratulations on *Dress My Best* getting final approval for a new time slot right after *Temptation Station*."

She beamed. "Isn't it great?" Their shows would be running back to back. It had taken a lot of serious maneuvering on her part to convince the Powers that Be, AKA everyone from Jerry on up to the network executives, that it was their idea to make the change.

"I've got ideas for ads for both shows, do some crossover, convince viewers to watch both." The elevator dinged and the door slid open. Brett eased one arm out to hold it, then turned to her. "We should get together some time, discuss the mutually beneficial ways we can capitalize on these time slots. I'll text you."

She could only nod as he walked out, giving her a jaunty salute, and the door slid shut. Victoria clutched her folders to her chest.

"Damn," she said. "Damn, damn, damn." She had wanted to be the one to ask *him* out, not the other way around. It was always better to have and keep the upper hand in a relationship. Still, she had an opening now, and *she* would text *him*.

The elevator opened on the sixth floor lobby and she thumped out with a little more spring in her step. Well, metaphorically anyway, she thought with a bitter glance at the boot.

Jenna, the receptionist, raised her brows so high they reached her ruler-straight bangs. "Wow, what happened to you?"

Her words were such an echo of Brett's that Victoria almost forgave Jenna for being such a remorseless tattletale most of the time. She shrugged, feigning casualness, then swore as her bag slipped again. She caught it in the crook of her elbow, but its weight threw her off balance enough to jolt her arm and make coffee splash through the lid, down her hand and onto the carpet.

"Ow, son of a—" Victoria stuck the side of her thumb in her mouth, almost hitting herself in the face with the cup. She released her thumb and said, "Jenna, could you—"

"I got it," Jenna sighed, opening a desk drawer and bringing out some paper napkins. She crouched to sop up the spill and Victoria barely resisted the urge to drip hot coffee right along the part of that perfect blonde bob.

"I meant the door." Victoria tried to keep from clenching her teeth. "Since you're up?"

"I don't want this to stain," Jenna said, not looking up. "Jerry would kill me."

Victoria stood in front of the double glass doors as people in the other room popped out of their cubicles and moved from desk to desk. Once they caught sight of her, each one bent a head to their co-workers'. She could just imagine the gossip.

She was about to thump her cup on Jenna's desk and get the door herself when Jenna straightened, glided to the wastebasket on three-inch platforms, dropped the napkins, watched as they fell, performed a graceful pirouette on the balls of her feet, and sashayed to the doors.

"Let me get that for you," she said, and held it open long enough for Victoria to clump through and Jenna to trill after her, "Have a nice day."

Taking a sip of her remaining espresso, Victoria scanned the cubicles for possible assistance to her office at the back. Heads turned away as she passed. Only mousy Rita Zelenstein, passing by on her way to deliver some inter-office memos, met Victoria's eye and agreed to shift Victoria's purse back up on her shoulder and carry some soggy folders.

Victoria let out a sigh as she finally reached the end of the aisle and made a slight right toward the row of doors at the back. Rita returned the folders and other items to her and swept around the corner to deliver her memos. With Victoria's office now in reach, her demon bag slithered down again and a stray lock of hair came loose from her ponytail to flop in her eyes. Blowing it away, she lifted her head and stopped short as Frank Littleton, executive producer of the low-rated *Morality Squad*, stepped out of nowhere and blocked access to her door.

"So close," she muttered.

"Hey, Clausen, heard you had a run-in with a drunk down in the Tenderloin last night. Crazy stuff." He tilted his head to look at her foot, and she opened her mouth to blast him, but his next words made her shut it with a snap. "Too bad about *Dress My Best*. Crappy to have to follow any of Soloway's shows." He flicked a rolled up memo against her upper arm with a "See ya, Rambo," and ambled away, whistling.

Muttering about little pissants trying to rile her up, and ignoring the memos in her inbox by the door, she went inside, set everything on her desk, and sat down heavily in her chair. Then she gave into a rare indulgence: she dropped her arms on the desk and her head on her arms, and devoted two minutes to feeling sorry for herself.

She'd gone to bed after her reunion with Kristen, but between her throbbing ankle and Kristen "ohming" until after six a.m., she hadn't been able to sleep. Kristen had finally slipped out after her extended meditation session, and Victoria dozed fitfully, to dream about facing a gunfighter in black at high noon and wake with a start, heart beating fast. She saw the time, jumped out of bed, landed on her bad foot and pitched sideways while spouting a few choice swear words.

Victoria had spent many sleepless hours on location to ensure a smooth production, balanced a twenty pound camera on her shoulder when camera operators called in sick, and personally found food, clothing and any requested item for her casts and crews as needed. Often she'd done all three in inclement weather. But she hadn't felt as tired as she did just now, considering her aching ankle, vivacious sister and vicious co-workers.

And her little unfinished business with Tyler Landry.

She straightened, took a deep breath, and reached for her bag. She told herself the reason she hadn't felt so tired at other times was because she'd kept moving. Exhaustion and depression can't catch up with you if you're on the go.

Her fingers slid around the specially constructed cell phone pocket for awhile before her brain shifted from thoughts of Tyler Landry and *In Concert* to the fact the pocket was empty. So maybe she'd put it in the main compartment. She pulled the bag closer and peered inside. No Blackberry. She fished around in there, but when her fingers still hadn't found the phone's smooth contours, she dumped the bag's contents onto her desk and sifted through pens, business cards, wallet, brush, hairclips and mints with an ever-increasing panic. It had to be here. It just had to be.

But it wasn't.

She sucked in a breath so hard and fast, it made her choke. She drank down the last of her coffee, now tepid, then took a few breaths. It would be fine. She would find it. She had to.

She picked up her office phone, tucked it between shoulder and cheek, and dialed the Blackberry's number with shaking fingers.

It rang far too long, and she expected it to go to voice-mail, when the ringing stopped and silence came on the line. Then a faraway sound, like throat clearing, a few beeps as someone pushed random buttons, and, "Hello?" The voice sounded morning-gruff, and slightly hesitant.

"Who is this and how did you get my phone?"

A pause, then, "Good morning, Ms. Clausen. I figured on calling you first, at a more decent hour, but you beat me to it."

She was so surprised, she didn't know what to respond to first: the relaxed tone or the salutation suggesting it was a man who knew her, but not well, and that he had been planning to call her later.

"Nine-thirty *is* a decent hour, for most people." And horrifically late for her; she usually got into the office no later than seven. "Now, would you like to inform me who and where you are so I can come retrieve my phone?"

"I do like the way you talk," he said, as if to himself. "But I'm real surprised you don't remember me, considering all we shared last night."

She dropped her face to her palm. One of her cowboys. How could she not know? The twang could belong to either of them, the teasing sounded more like Cort Landry, but he hadn't touched her bare leg with his callused palms, or squeezed her hand when she offered it. Something like that stayed with a woman.

"Mr. Tyler." She raised her head, smiling now. She had a captive audience. She opened her mouth to deliver a spiel about how much the show could do for him and the band, when he spoke again.

"It's Luke. How you feeling this morning?"

"I'm sorry?"

"Your hand, your foot?" he asked, as if she were a little slow. "How they doing?"

She grimaced, glancing at the white bandage wrapped around her palm. She'd almost forgotten about the hated boot, too. "Fine." She waved her hand through the air, dismissing the injury, even though he couldn't see the gesture. "Just a little twist and some cuts, easily bandaged. Now—"

"Your ankle looked real swollen when you left last night."

"Yes, well, that went down—"

"And you had a mighty lot of hurt on your face."

She shut her mouth, blinking. She'd had what? She shook her head. Never mind trying to translate; she needed to get this man on camera. "Mr. Tyler—"

"Luke," he said. "And I apologize about your trousers. I'm happy to pay you back for them."

"My trousers?"

"I ruined them, fixing you up."

"Yes, I know," she said, distracted by something, but unable to figure out just what. Her voice drifted off, and she didn't say anything else, trying to figure out what had preoccupied her in their conversation. She *never* allowed herself to be distracted. This odd conversation had to be due to her bizarre evening and lack of sleep. Or maybe, she considered…she'd never met anyone quite like him.

"I suppose you'd like to meet, then?" Luke asked, breaking into her contemplation.

She brightened. Oh, hallelujah. He was going to do the show. "I would. Just let me know where you are, and I'll be right over. This is going to be wonderful."

He sounded puzzled, but agreed with her. "Yes, ma'am," he said slowly. "I confess I can't wait to hand this thing over."

"I'm sorry?"

"You mind if I shut it off when we hang up? I turned it on, in case you called, but it's been ringing and beeping and vibrating to beat the band, and I'm likely to toss it right into the street, you don't get here soon."

Victoria's heart stopped. "No! Don't do that!" She held out a hand, as if to prevent him tossing the phone. "What's your address? I'll be right there."

CHAPTER EIGHT

As soon as Luke hung up with Victoria Clausen, he pressed END on her phone and dropped the damn thing on the couch. Then his own phone rang, startling him, but a glance at the caller ID had him smiling.

He swung the receiver up and tucked it against his shoulder. "Hey, Mama, how you doin'?"

"I'm above ground and mobile, and that's always good," she replied. "Mamie Sanderson down the way broke her hip in a fall the other day. She's doing fine, I brought her some of my famous cobbler. But did you know, she's actually five years younger than me? Makes a woman think. And makes me grateful." They spent the next few minutes discussing old neighbors and friends before she asked, "So how was your show last night?"

That was his Mama, rambling along, then changing course right in the middle. He paused, not sure where to start. "Real good," he finally said.

He leaned against the back of the couch, and Frog jumped up, butting her little head against his arm. He'd found her as a tiny kitten in a dumpster when they first moved to the city. And while she'd gotten rounder, she hadn't grown much bigger. "The regular crowd at Tony's, everyone singin' along," he continued, rubbing a finger against Frog's cheek, but seeing Victoria Clausen spinning around on the dance floor on them real high heels. He cleared his throat. "We did 'Rodeo Nights' for the first time. It was good..."

She must've heard the pause in his voice. "And?"

"I told you about that record producer showed up last week? The one from Kenny Chesney's label?"

"You did. Is there news?"

"No. Not yet. But another producer came by. From TV." He wandered to the kitchen, fiddled with a wooden spoon on the counter, gave it a spin and watched its wobbly rotation. "She wants to do a show about us, about Tyler Landry."

"Like a documentary?"

"No, like one of those reality shows, where the cameras follow you around all day and show...what you do." He realized he didn't want to get into the details of what some reality TV depicted. Not with his mama, anyway.

"And is what you do during the day all that interesting?" Then she laughed that beautiful, hearty laugh that had gotten them through many bad times.

He laughed, too, but briefly, his mind still too full to be distracted. "I don't think so, but the producer thinks it could help make us famous."

"Doesn't she know you're already famous?"

He let out a breath, holding the phone away from his face, and stared up at the ceiling. A spider crawled along it on its way to the window. He glanced down, saw Frog tracking it. "Not in my own right, Mama. But I will be," he added, before she could say it. Or give him another lecture about changing his last name. She hated that he'd done it, and regularly informed him how much it pained her.

"Well, your daddy'll be real proud to hear it," she said. "When will it be on the TV?"

Luke wandered to the windows overlooking the street, watching for long auburn hair and high heels. "It won't," he said, ignoring the comment about Buzz. "We're not doing it."

"Why not?"

"It's not the right...it's not...those shows don't represent folks right."

"Well, I can't say I've seen a lot of 'em, although that Simon Cowell does get me all worked up."

Luke pressed his forehead against the glass, cringing. "Mama..."

She laughed again. "Don't you worry. I'm not leaving your daddy, not even for a slick British gentleman. You want to talk to him?"

For a moment, Luke thought she was asking if he wanted to talk to Simon Cowell. By the time he realized she meant Buzz, he couldn't pull it together fast enough to deflect her. The thought made him tired. He straightened, rubbing at his forehead. "Mama…"

"He's been wanting to talk to you lately. Now that he's going through the steps again…" Her voice drifted off, and she sounded as hopeful as she always did when she brought up Buzz's supposed sobriety and a 12-step program.

Unable to think of yet another way to say "no," he didn't fill in the silence. Although it might be good practice, considering he'd be declining Ms. Clausen's offer. And like Cort said, she didn't seem the type of woman you turned down. He ran a hand along Frog's back, and she arched up, purring, and gazed at him in adoration. He gazed back in an attempt to ease his frustration.

"He's up to step eight," his mother continued. "Making amends. He wants to do that with you, Lucas. Soon."

Luke's hand froze on Frog's back and she bumped her face against his thumb. He automatically started petting her again, but he barely noticed. Buzz wanting to "make amends" was bigger than just wanting to talk, Luke had to admit; avoiding his father would be harder this time around.

"It's going to stick," Dot continued. "I feel it in my bones."

Luke loved his mama, but he hated when she lied to herself, falling into denial about Buzz's drinking, abuse and eventual turnaround. The further Buzz went each time he got sober, the more she believed in his success, and the further she fell when he messed up again. Luke didn't want that for her.

As gently as possible, he said, "We've been through this before, Mama."

"He hasn't gone this long before, honey. He's done community work, gone to a meeting every day for ninety days. He's been tracking down all of the people he's wronged, and making amends where he can, just like the step says."

"Tracking down…"

"Including you, Lucas. He'd give up finding all those others if you'd let him make it up to you."

"No." Relief rushed through him; he was still capable of refusal. "He can't ever make up what he did…" *To us*, he almost added, but kept silent on that. He'd heard from his Mama how she felt on this subject, and she believed in forgiveness. Luke didn't. At least not where Buzz was concerned. While a childish part of him wanted her to take his side, just one damn time, he knew being in the middle hurt her. It would tear her apart if faced with the decision: Buzz or Luke. "I don't want to talk to him. Ever."

"We won't always be here, honey. I was talking to little Suzy Westner down the way, lost her parents in a car crash few years ago now, says she's real sorry she had a big fight with them and didn't make it up—"

"Don't." Blood rushed in his ears.

"Every day, rest of her life, she says she regrets those nasty words she said to them. Now, your daddy—"

"I've got to go. I got to meet that producer. I love you, Mama."

He hung up.

Then he slammed the phone on the counter, felt the handset crack, and swore loudly.

Frog shot across the room to hide under the coffee table, and Luke dropped on the couch, throwing his head back. That conversation held a shade of new with the familiar, some devil leaning in too close for comfort and whispering in his ear: maybe Buzz could really stay sober this time. And that opened the door in Luke's heart by a small crack, just enough to let in some hope. He'd allowed that too many times growing up, and Buzz always smashed that hope. Luke wouldn't allow it to happen again.

A knock sounded on his door before Cort popped his head in and said, "Must be Thursday."

"Wouldn't be otherwise without a broken phone," Luke told him. He hunkered down at the coffee table to coax Frog out. She wouldn't have any of it, so he left her alone and flopped back onto the couch, sticking his booted feet off to the side. He closed his eyes and rested his forearm over them. "What you want?"

"Fifty million albums sold and the same number of women throwing themselves at me," Cort replied, sauntering to the window to look out over the street. "Since that won't happen in the next couple hours, I thought I'd tell you I'd be late for practice. Gotta fill in for Doug. Hour or so. He got some flu bug and we got a delivery this morning."

Cort worked most days at the bar, which were quieter, and left him free to perform at night. Luke worked late afternoon shifts, and two additional employees filled in the other times. Luke figured Cort never actually slept; he didn't when they were kids, and the pattern continued into their adulthood.

"Fine," Luke said, unmoving, his eyes still closed and covered. His heart beat hard in his chest, though, and he wanted another phone in his hand, to throw at the window this time. Shattering glass would be real satisfying right now.

"Dandy," Cort replied.

Luke heard boots and laces clattering on the floor as Cort headed out and knew he needed to tell him about Victoria Clausen. "That producer's coming over soon."

The boots thudded, the laces clacked once, and Luke felt Cort's silence, heavy and ominous. "Dammit, Luke. Were you going to invite the rest of us to your little meeting?"

Luke dropped his arm and looked at Cort, who stood in the doorway, one hand gripping the jam. "She's just fetching her phone," he said. "I was going to drop it off to her, but she can't wait to get the damn thing, so she's coming over." He didn't add that he'd hoped to have a chance to talk to her about the show, put a bug in her ear that it might not be something she'd want to pursue with them.

"And you were just going to say 'howdy, here you go,' and nothing else?"

"No. I might say 'nice to see you again, how's the leg?'" Luke pushed himself upright on the couch. "What d'you think? I was going to set up an appointment, just like we talked about, see when she was available."

Cort crossed his arms over his chest, and leaned against the doorframe. He studied Luke before one corner of his mouth curled up. "I'll do you better," he said. "Keep her here, I'll round up the boys, and we'll get this settled today. I'll find someone else to cover at the bar."

Luke clenched his teeth at being found out. He'd never go behind the boys' backs on purpose, but he had wanted to talk to the producer alone.

He fell back again and closed his eyes in surrender. "Fine," he said.

"Dandy," Cort repeated, and headed out.

Luke let his hand dangle to the floor. With a little "mew," Frog snuck out from under the table and rubbed against Luke's fingers. He turned to look at her and she peered up at him with big, golden eyes.

"I'm sorry, Frog. You know I'd never hurt you."

She gave another meow, then sat down to clean her front paw. Luke took that as absolution, got up, reached for his hat and guitar case, and headed downstairs. Belting out a few songs might lower his blood pressure.

By the time he'd gotten to the Barn's studio space, he'd pushed back some of his anger and frustration. He settled his hat, got his acoustic guitar out of its battered case, and gave it a quick cleanup as usual, caressing the fretboard with a cotton cloth. It was the first guitar he'd bought for himself after winning grand prize for singing "Blue Moon of Kentucky" at a county fair. That money plus his savings from a summer job had been enough to buy the Martin. Buzz had bought him guitars before, first to let Luke know that if the father did it, so should the son, and then as encouragement when he found out Luke and Cort had been secretly playing music for years.

Luke found a way to destroy each guitar, either by bonfire or pretending to be a rock star and smashing them on the ground. He'd even shot one with a rifle. He'd since bought others for himself, but this one, the Martin, the one he'd earned on his own, would always be his favorite.

He perched on a stool in the middle of the practice space, and hooked the heels of his black boots over the rungs. He looked out over the room, but didn't really see the battered table and old easy chairs in the corner at the far end of the converted garage, the roll-up doors, or the red door next to it that once led into the garage's office space. He didn't imagine Cort's panty throwers, either; instead, he saw the crowd at the Ryman Auditorium, Nashville's "Mother Church of Country Music," waiting in anticipation for Tyler Landry's first song.

Luke adjusted the guitar on his lap, tucking it under his right arm as he recalled a melody he'd had in his head a few days ago. Occasionally Luke wrote an entire song before previewing it for the band, but for the most part he composed the melodies while Parker wrote lyrics. Together, they added in drums, bass and keyboard along with the harmonies.

Cort had convinced him to start the band in the first place. He'd known Marty from various construction jobs they'd worked together, and they found Parker through a Craigslist ad. His e-mail response had been, "It's in the cards and the stars that I become a valued member of your group, and the heavens don't deceive." Cort thought he might be one twist short of a Slinky, but he had good credentials, so they interviewed him. When Luke asked why he wanted to play country music, Parker said, "You are aware it tells a story? There's a richness to it, an earthiness, something that insinuates itself into your very marrow." Marty's audition had been a nice surprise considering he'd never played professionally before, but Parker's trumped it. He could make a small keyboard sound like bagpipes, a symphony, or a rock band all the while with a look on his face that suggested he was communing with beings on another planet.

Luke smiled at the thought as he bowed his head over the guitar and did a few warm ups. He ran through a simple boom-chuck chord pattern before moving on to an RH arpeggio and a reverse arpeggio, which he always screwed up, but doggedly tried before each practice. He was waiting impatiently for that time when he stopped thinking, and just started feeling the music, through his fingers, his mind, his entire body. He strummed a few chords to work out the new song, throwing out possible lyrics as he went, but nothing clicked.

Luke loved working with the boys, despite their differences, but he also loved his moments alone in the Barn, absorbed in making music. But right now, too many things rolled around in his head, and the melody couldn't materialize. He huffed out a breath, re-settled the Martin, and ran through the scales.

Nothing. Damn. He couldn't stop thinking on what Dot had said about Buzz. Or about Victoria Clausen and how to convince her they weren't right for her reality TV show. About all the details that needed to be worked out for the demo disc. Then Buzz again, a constant presence, no matter how hard Luke tried to push the bastard out.

Luke would never throw his guitar against the wall, but he was mighty tempted.

To distract himself, he sang a Johnny Cash song, "Get Rhythm." He was working hard, rocking on the stool, eyes closed and one foot kicking out when the door slammed against the far wall. Jarred out of the song, he almost lost his balance. His head whipped up toward the sound and his fingers lost their place with a discordant jangle. He pressed his palm to the strings to quiet them and took a breath to settle his rapidly beating heart.

He grinned at the beautiful woman before him. "Ms. Clausen, you make quite an entrance."

CHAPTER NINE

Victoria smiled at Luke. Let him think she'd meant to announce herself boldly, when actually no one had answered her knock and the wind gusted when she opened the door. She hoped it would distract both from her inability to stride right in and take charge, and from the stupid boot.

But when he jumped down from the stool and set his guitar aside, she knew it hadn't worked. His concerned look as he took her elbow and gestured toward a grouping of ratty easy chairs told her as much before he even said, "You should sit."

She stood firm, raising her eyebrow at him and tilting her head at the chairs. "No, thank you. I'll stand." She held out her hand. "May I have my phone?"

His fingers tightened on her elbow a moment before he released her to fish in his pocket. He held the Blackberry out as if it were coated in slime. "Happy to be rid of it," he said when she grasped it and clutched it to her chest.

"It's my lifeline," she told him. "I couldn't do all I do without it."

A corner of his mouth twitched up and he pushed his hat back on his head with one thumb. "And what-all is it that you do?"

"The short story is I entertain people," she said, thinking that Luke Tyler didn't have a good understanding about personal space; he stood so close she could feel the heat from his upper body and caught a hint of his soap, one of those natural ones without perfume.

He pressed his fingertips to a spot just over his heart. "Well, now, I myself like a long story."

She smiled at his attempt to charm her. She had to admit he excelled at it, and with his country twang and dark, chiseled appearance, women probably swooned at his feet on a regular basis. She spent a lot of time around good-looking men, but had only to think of Brett Soloway as a reminder of her most suitable type of man. Polished, driven, and her business equal. Thinking of Brett helped keep her immune to the charmers. "I've changed my mind, Mr. Tyler. I'd like to sit after all." She turned and shuffled toward the furniture.

"Luke," he said.

She stopped and glanced back at him. "I beg your pardon?"

"My name is Luke. Calling me Mr. Tyler makes me feel like a schoolteacher or something."

"All right." She headed for the chairs again, but he stopped her with a hand on her upper arm. His fingers felt warm and firm through the material of her silk georgette blouse. She looked first at his hand, and then his at face. "Yes?"

"Got a leaf in your hair." When he tugged it out, a lock of hair pulled free from her clip. "I apologize," he said.

She heard the rustle of the leaf as he crumbled it, felt the warmth from his skin, and suppressed a shiver. "It's fine," she said, tucking the hair behind her ear with her good hand.

"Now, you've got that bum hand. Let me fix this..." He stepped so close she had to raise her head to avoid staring at his chest in its snug red t-shirt.

He curved his upper body around hers, located the clip at her neck and released it with a soft *snick* so her hair fell in heavy waves around her face and shoulders. He stepped back, holding the clip out to her. "Much improved."

She blinked at him, not sure if she should be offended. His smile seemed genuine. "But impractical," she said, taking the clip after a glance into his deep green eyes. She reached to pull her hair back with her left hand, but grimaced as the bandage tightened around her palm and the small cuts twinged; Teresa had put her hair up this morning.

"Here," Luke said, pressing his hand over hers. He stepped behind her, smoothed her hair from her face, and replaced the clip with efficiency. It was tight, and she gave it a tug to loosen it, then ran a palm over her head to convince herself her hands weren't shaking. Ridiculous.

"Nicely done, Mr. Tyler. Thank you," she said, unsure why his casual touch should distract her to such a degree. With her crew and the talent, she'd pat an arm, give a light hug, so they'd feel comfortable with her, lean on her if needed. It built a trusting atmosphere, and she encouraged it while skillfully maintaining control and emotional distance.

She couldn't ever remember feeling such *heat* coming off of one, though, or allowing someone to let her hair down and rearrange it, beyond her hairdressers for hire. The only tugs then had come from her scalp when they demonstrated micro braids, not from her stomach, which did a lazy flip and then jumped up through her breastbone as Luke Tyler ran his hands through her hair. *Brett Soloway*, she said to herself in a kind of mantra. *Brett Soloway...*

Breathing deeply through her nose, she straightened and raised her head to meet Luke Tyler's gaze. Time to take control here.

"Well," she said, as if she'd never gotten off track. "We should really talk about—" She turned slightly to the side and began to stride away, her usual practice when discussing business; she couldn't keep still. But one foot moved, the booted one didn't, she got tangled on the latter and stumbled, her bag thumping to the floor.

Luke grabbed for her arm but missed, one hand closing on the fabric of her shirt instead. She heard and felt buttons pop, material rip and one bra strap wrench to the side before Luke caught hold of her with his other hand and pulled her against him to keep her from falling farther.

She gasped as her body slammed up hard against his, but she instinctively wrapped her arms around his back to keep her balance. His palms pressed just below her shoulder blades, holding her close, and she would've pulled away with a decisive tug if not for a possible repeat tripping performance and the fact that her breasts had been exposed by a torn shirt and skewed bra. His t-shirt felt soft against her cheek and the tops of her breasts. For one exquisite moment, she relaxed into the firmness of his chest and thighs.

Still, there was no way around it. At some point, they would have to separate, and she wasn't one to linger over embarrassment or uncomfortable situations.

"Mr. Tyler," she began, but the rumble of laughter moving up from his belly to his throat stopped her.

"If anything qualifies us to be on a first name basis, I'd say this is it." Before she could respond, he continued. "Are you feeling steady now?"

"Yes." *No. Not with you holding me so firmly against your far too solid body.*

He relaxed his arms and moved smoothly away from her, dropping his hat to the floor before grasping the bottom of his t-shirt and pulling it over his head.

"Rate I'm going, I'll owe you a full wardrobe soon." He turned the shirt right side out and presented it to her without moving his head.

Victoria held the edges of her own shirt closed with one hand, staring at the smooth line of muscle running in a curve from his back, indenting at his shoulder and continuing along the back of his arm. His naturally dark olive skin went all the way up and all the way down; definitely not the tanning parlor type.

"I beg your pardon?" she said, still staring at his back. She'd never seen such smooth, warm-toned skin up close; she'd always dated businessmen, pale under their suits. Many had preferred sex in the dark, or under the covers.

He twitched the shirt at her. "Best put it on. I don't like talking with my back to people. 'Sides that, the boys are on their way and may be here soon."

She let her blouse slide from her shoulders and to the floor, then pushed her lacy blue bra back in place before grabbing the tee from him and hastily donning it. It fell to her knees, almost as long as the skirt she wore. Looking down, she figured she could make it work with a big belt and platform boots.

"I'm modestly attired now," she said, not avoiding any irony in her tone. "It's safe to turn around."

To keep from staring at his bare upper body, she bent to retrieve her torn shirt. She worried he might try to play the white knight and pick it up for her, resulting in them bumping heads and falling over like bowling pins, but he stayed in place, watching as she dropped the blouse in her bag.

"Well," she said in a firm voice, determined to get the two of them on task and help regain her equilibrium. "When will your band mates be here?"

"They're here," said a voice behind her. "And just in time to stop some shenanigans, I'd say."

Victoria turned—slowly—to see Cort Landry standing in the doorway with the other band members on either side of him. The two had their mouths open like fish, but Cort pushed a pair of sunglasses to the top of his head and grinned as if he witnessed moments like this every day. Perhaps he did. And if all was right in the world and Victoria got her way, she'd be capturing those moments on camera. Only it would be some other woman standing in a t-shirt next to this beautiful half-naked man.

"How did this come about?" Parker Guinto asked, strolling over. He studied her face. "Ah. The assertive television producer from the previous evening." He glanced at her feet, then back up at her face. "Your hand and ankle?"

"Better, thank you."

"Shorter women often heal faster," Parker said, and wandered away, hands in the pockets of his loose pants, his sandals making a shushing noise on the concrete. Without looking at her, he said, "Please enlighten us on this situation."

Victoria almost swayed with desire; oh, to get them on film. "I had a tear in my blouse and Luke was gracious enough to loan me his shirt so we can continue our negotiations." She addressed the situation directly to avert any more suggestive comments. It was difficult enough to keep from being distracted by the dark hair on Luke Tyler's chest and the trail it made to his taut stomach before it disappeared past the waistband of his jeans. Or the line of muscle along his forearms as he crossed his arms over his firmly rounded pectorals. And stared at her.

She glanced at each man in turn, stopping at Cort. "Are you all ready to be famous?"

"Honey, I've been ready since I was knee high to a pig's eye," Cort told her, stepping inside with Marty behind him and shutting the door.

Victoria laughed. "I need to get you boys on television, and soon."

"That sounds real good," Cort began, but stopped when Luke cleared his throat.

"We haven't had a chance to discuss your...proposition," he said.

"And of course you'll have questions," Victoria replied, ignoring his suggestion that because they hadn't discussed it the offer was off the table. She headed for the ratty chairs, moving with caution this time, and Cort rushed to put a hand under her elbow and walk with her. She let him get her settled in one of them, then formally introduced her to Marty Jacobsen and Parker Guinto. She already knew their last names from Teresa's research, but shook hands and gave each a "nice to meet you."

"We will film a one-hour pilot, which I will sell to a network for the summer season," she said, getting right to business. "For the pilot and any subsequent episodes, you will each be on camera twenty-four hours a day." She'd already decided her first impulse had been right: with a reluctant "star," it was better to have less producer interference and capture as much spontaneity as possible, adding structure back in through the editing process. "Two to three cameras will film you, along with stationary cameras installed in your cars, your homes, this studio, and what we call the Confession Booth, the location of which will be determined.

"You'll go to the Booth once a week to discuss the events of the past few days, and you may be called in individually for extra footage. After the pilot has been accepted and the series airs, we will promote your concerts, give you a page on our website, and link to samples of your songs." She leaned forward, hands on her knees. "We may be able to help in getting an album produced, maybe a single on iTunes, but that's not guaranteed. What is guaranteed is outrageous publicity. People will love you. You *will* be famous."

She sat back, smiling at them.

No one said anything. Cort stared at his boots, which seemed to have come untied, Marty and Parker exchanged glances, then looked at Luke. Luke, balanced on a metal stool, stared at her, but didn't seem to see her. Just as she asked if any of them had questions, Luke slapped his palms against his thighs and stood up to pace.

Cort glanced at Luke then turned back to Victoria. "I got plenty of questions. How much do we get paid? Do the cameras come in the toilet? What if we have a lady friend over? Can I promote my bar? And when do we start?"

Victoria focused on Cort, knowing instinctively if she got him, Marty and Parker would follow and Luke would eventually go with the majority. Probably after some struggle. She'd seen it before, and didn't expect this situation to be any different.

"I'm authorized to offer you a thousand dollars for the pilot, and thereafter fifteen hundred dollars per episode." She let that settle for a beat, then added, "Each." She overrode their murmured responses.

"Ozzy Osbourne was paid five thousand each episode for the first season of *The Osbournes*. And he was already famous. The cameras do not follow you into the bathroom, and for obvious reasons we would not air any blatant sex, but everything else is open for filming. If your…lady friends wish to be on camera, they'll have to sign a release, just like anyone else." She smiled at Cort. "You own a bar?"

"Lucas and I do," he responded.

"It's Cort's," Luke added. "I work there."

Victoria caught the tension between the two men, and filed it away for later; some definite conflict there. "I can't guarantee bar promotion," she said, keeping her focus on Cort, "but since it's part of your life and you will be filmed working there, we can most likely include some form of promo.

"As for when we can begin filming, one or two weeks after the contracts are signed."

"Well, let's get going," Cort said.

"Perhaps we should—" Parker began.

"I was wondering—" Marty said at the same time.

They both stopped when Luke stepped back into the circle and stood in front of Victoria's chair.

"Ms. Clausen, we'll be needing to discuss this together. Alone."

"Oh, take your time." She waved a hand at him. "I can check my messages." She averted her gaze from the distracting perfection of his naked upper body and reached for her phone. She knew he wanted her to leave so he could discuss the offer privately with the others, but if she left, the decision could get deferred indefinitely. Her presence insured a quick response and if any questions came up, she could easily sell the answer, leaving them no chance for doubt.

"This is a big decision," he said.

"Indeed it is," she replied, giving him a quick look from under her lashes before turning her phone on. "Please let me know if I can answer any questions. I want you to be completely comfortable with your decision."

"We'd prefer—" he began.

"Some privacy? Of course." She placed her phone back in her bag, set the bag on the floor, then scooted forward until her feet reached the ground. She began to push up from the deep, soft chair, fell back once, and tried again. She straightened, wobbling, and smiled at him.

He stood with his hands on his hips and his bare chest begging for further study, taking up her field of vision. She averted her eyes. "Is there some other place I can go so I won't disturb you?"

When he didn't respond, she finally looked back in his eyes but couldn't read the expression on his face. Possibly, he was warring with himself. Southern hospitality versus self-preservation. The former won, but with poor grace. He let out a sigh, dropped his arms, and gestured toward the chair.

"Stay. We'll be right back."

As he retreated, she studied the long lean muscles of his bare back, his firm butt in black Wranglers, and repeated grimly to herself, *Brett Soloway, Brett Soloway...*

CHAPTER TEN

Luke led the boys to the other side of the studio by the van. His back to Victoria, he leaned against the front bumper and crossed his arms.

Cort said, "You want to get yourself a shirt there, son, or do you need to flash the sexy producer some more?"

Luke gave him a glare, but ignored the comment. "So what do y'all think?"

"I'm in," Cort said without hesitation.

Parker glanced upward as he said, "It seems remarkably synchronistic that this producer has found us at a time when we've begun to blossom and expand out to the world, like dandelion fronds blown on the wind."

Luke let out a breath through his nose, bowing his head a moment. "So you're in, too," he said, and turned to Marty. "You?"

"I'm not too sure about being on camera so much." Marty glanced around at the others before staring at the floor. "Being followed. It seems kinda weird, and what if they catch us at stupid stuff?" He peeked at Luke, and then away. "But we could get some promotion, maybe get an album, and isn't that what we want? Plus..." He shuffled his feet. "I could use the money. I'm thinking...I was thinking about maybe...asking if...asking Miranda if she'd marry me."

Luke thought he heard a squeak from the other side of the garage, but kept his eyes on Marty until the other man looked at him. Then Luke gave him a smile and said, "That's real good, Marty."

Both Cort and Parker patted Marty on the back and offered him congratulations. Marty turned pink and shoved his hands in his pockets, his shoulders hunched.

"So Marty's in," Cort said to Luke. "Me'n Parker, too. What's your vote?"

Luke's first thought was to give an immediate "No." He didn't want this invasion in his life, he didn't want the potential humiliation for himself, his band, or his mother. He didn't want that good-looking, smart-alecky woman with amazing breasts—he'd looked; he wasn't stupid—calling any shots in his life. He also knew he couldn't let a likely opportunity go by without at least giving it a chance. And he wasn't asking anyone to marry him, but he sure as hell could use the money, too.

"I'm not in, but I'm not out, either. We need to be real careful about this, get a lawyer to look over the contracts, make some demands for ourselves. Just because she said how it's going to be doesn't mean that's the final say."

"Do you want this, Luke?" Cort asked.

In all the fussing over what he didn't want, Luke hadn't considered what he did want. He glanced over his shoulder at Victoria, her head bowed over her phone, fingers flashing on the tiny buttons, her whole body focused on it. Did it matter if he wanted to or not? She would be their producer. More than anything, he needed to trust her, and to know they had some say in their participation on the show. Could they turn this into something positive, without any damaging fallout?

Instead of answering Cort's question, he turned back to the boys and said, "Let's do this, but just like with anything else, we do it right."

He waited for a nod from each of them, then asked them to share any conflicts they might have. Marty didn't want so many cameras on them all the time. Cort didn't mind the cameras, but thought they should get more money. Parker wanted to be certain that all rights to any music they played on the show stayed with them. Luke added a few of his own, then raised his eyes up in a little request for help, and strode back to stand in front of Victoria, the boys lining up on either side of him. She pushed a few more buttons before raising her head.

"Have you reached a decision?"

Luke nodded. "We have some conditions."

"Of course. We want our stars to be happy. I'll assist you with whatever you need to feel comfortable with your decision."

Luke laid out their requirements, and Victoria wrote them all down. She agreed to pass them along to her folks at the station, but paused when he said they could meet again once he'd found a lawyer for the band.

She stopped writing, and gave him a brilliant smile. He couldn't help smiling back at the sight of her keeping real professional in his t-shirt, and with that boot. She'd rested one little foot on top of it. "I always recommend legal representation to my stars," she said. "Once you've signed with us, our team will be your team. Until then, having good legal counsel is crucial." She glanced at her phone. "It's ten-thirty now. I'll call you at three o'clock to confirm your attorney's information and I'll set up a meeting with all of you and our people." She gave them that charming smile and started setting her things in her bag. All except that damn phone. That she kept tight in one hand.

"Now, I'll just call a cab and be on my way so you gentlemen can get to the rest of your day."

Luke reached out a hand to help her up, but Cort beat him to it, slipping his big fingers around Victoria's slim ones, putting the other hand on her shoulder, and holding on once she'd gotten to a standing position.

"Now, we can't have you going off in a cab, fending for yourself with that bum ankle," Cort said to her, and Luke hid his smile at the slight narrowing of Victoria's eyes. He could've told Cort that coddling Ms. Clausen was no way to get on her romantic side. Or any side but the one that could claw his eyes out before he'd even known she'd done it. But it was more fun to watch Victoria pass that information along herself.

She pressed a hand to Cort's, then let hers drop. "That's very nice of you, but I have a multitude of stops to make on the way, and I wouldn't want to interfere with your own work." She waved the hand with the phone in it at them. "You've got a lawyer to hire."

They saw her into the cab, and Luke realized he didn't care that she'd gone off with no mention of giving his shirt back. They needed to keep things on a business level, and he would've felt uncomfortable with any reference to the fact that she wore his shirt, even though it was obvious for all to see, and nothing had happened between them. He appreciated her professionalism, tact and willingness to negotiate. He felt more in control.

He should've known better.

CHAPTER ELEVEN

This time when Victoria walked up the aisle to her office, she still couldn't stride, but she felt less like a clod and more like her true self: accomplished. On the drive back, she'd asked the cabbie to detour to Neiman Marcus and wait outside while she bought a new blouse and a pair of tall chocolate brown boots with four inch heels. She rolled up Luke Tyler's shirt and stuffed it in her bag; she'd have it laundered before returning it. And she'd wear those boots as soon as her ankle healed.

She couldn't wait to get in her office and start writing up notes for Jerry. He might dislike some of the demands the boys had—no cameras in their living spaces would never fly; not with the production she had laid out—but she knew they could come to an agreement. The hardest part was getting any subject to say yes to a show in the first place; the rest was all negotiation. The network execs wouldn't give on the demand for no residential cameras, but there might be something they could offer to make up for it. She considered the idea of a concert in Golden Gate Park, maybe as a season closer, to dangle at them to overcome any sticking points.

She was picturing the opening credits, an OK Corral-type walk, four abreast—could she get them in leather dusters?—when she walked into her office and saw Teresa there, wandering back and forth in front of the desk and chewing on a thumbnail. She wore a rumpled gray western shirt and skinny jeans, her braids pulled back.

"Hey," Victoria said. "Great news, I got Tyler Landry." She dumped her bag on the desk. "It took some finessing but I knew I had it when Luke Tyler gave me his shirt, which is a whole story in itself. We have to get him on camera sans shirt, by the way. He's picture-perfect." She flopped in her chair, ignoring her throbbing ankle. "We have got *so* much work to do." She waved Teresa to the chair in front of her desk and pulled a yellow legal pad closer. "Before I forget, how did things go with Chastity and the hairdressers?" Despite her sweet name, Victoria knew Chastity was tough, which was one of the many reasons she'd hired her to take over day to day operations on *Hairdressers for Hire*.

"Fine. They're fine."

Victoria nodded, adding a note in the corner of her pad to move up her meetings with both field producers; they were each relatively new to the business, and it wouldn't hurt to have more regular check ins.

"Now I need to train Maurice to contact Jésus and not me if he and Francesca are butting heads." Maurice and Francesca were the hosts of her other show, *Dress My Best*, and they adored each other. On screen. Away from the cameras, they were like gas and kerosene, with a lit match hanging over them. "I must've gotten twenty texts from each of them this morning. But we can go over that later. I want to get the preliminaries for Tyler Landry down first." She pulled out a pen and wrote *"Tyler Landry: In Concert"* at the top. "I still think the name's good," she began, staring at the words on the page.

"I got that catering gig," Teresa said.

"—And I've got this great idea for the opener. Very Kurt Russell and Val Kilmer in *Tombstone*." Victoria stopped, her head shooting up as Teresa's words sunk in. "What? Oh, T, that's great. I know how much you want to do the cooking thing. I'd get up and hug you, but this damn boot…"

Teresa waved that away after a pause and Victoria said, "We'll have to celebrate. Let's go for drinks tonight. Maybe to that new place in the Marina. They've got a bartender there begging to be on film, and I've been toying with a *Cheers*-type show, but with everyone so PC these days about drinking, it might be a tough sell." She pointed her pen at Teresa, who had a funny look on her face; maybe she was overwhelmed by the catering thing since she wanted it so badly. T often got bemused when confronted with the object of her desire.

"Anyway," Victoria continued, "we're going to celebrate you.

Now, for *In Concert*, I really want Jamie Ferrand to direct, so let's see if he's available. We're going to need a lot of releases, starting with Tony's Tavern. The owner, the waitresses, obviously we have to do a standard wide area release with the corresponding shots of the signs for legal. I want to avoid pixilating as much as possible, since this is going to be an expensive shoot as it is, which reminds me that I have to get a preliminary budget set up." She paused to scratch some notes.

"This is a big dream," Teresa said.

"What?" Victoria made another note. "No, it'll work. This show is going to be amazing."

"Not the *show*." Teresa pressed her lips into a thin line. "The catering. It's a big dream of mine."

"I know. You've been talking about it for years. Oh! The father. Buzz Taylor. I've got to call him and get him to make a special appearance, but the timing needs to be perfect. Luke Tyler doesn't quite trust me yet, and you know how I hate that." She slid her Blackberry closer to tap in a reminder to get contact information for Buzz.

"I quit," Teresa said.

"So I'm going to need you to—" Victoria's hand froze and she stared at Teresa. "I'm—what?"

"I quit," Teresa repeated, clasping her hands in her lap. "I thought I could do the station and catering both, but I can't." Her gaze slid to the floor.

"But, it's only one event…I don't understand."

"I know." Her face softened, then closed up, unreadable. "You don't. You're so wrapped up in your job. In this…" Teresa stood up fast, almost knocking over her chair. She grabbed her bag and darted to the door. "I have to go."

Victoria stared at Teresa as she almost ran from the room. "But…" she said, her voice barely above a whisper. "I can't chase you."

She picked up her phone and hit Teresa's number. It went straight to voice mail and she left a message. "T, it's V. I don't know what just happened, but let's talk. We can get you whatever you need, negotiate. Call me."

She hung up, then sent a similar text, and sat staring at the Blackberry as if it would buzz right away with Teresa's response. She had no idea what just happened. She knew Teresa wanted to be a chef, but that was far in the future, and this was just one catering job. Victoria couldn't believe Teresa actually meant to quit. Why would she want to give all of this up?

While she waited for Teresa's call, she continued her notes. They would need to set up a photographer for publicity photos, run background checks and do psychological testing, get friends and family names for potential on-camera interviews. She sat back, smiling and tapping her pen against the legal pad. And Buzz Taylor? He lived in Georgia with his long-suffering wife—Luke's mother. Victoria remembered hearing about a few drunken brawls and some dalliances, but nothing recently, and she knew nothing about Buzz's relationship with his son.

Except...Buzz Taylor loved being in the spotlight. He'd been in the news for something or other as long as Victoria could remember, breaking concert attendance records, escorting a starlet to a Hollywood premiere in his trademark red leather vest and hat, crashing his car and getting arrested for DUI on multiple occasions. He'd even smiled for his mug shot.

But his son, eye-catching Luke Tyler, had a slightly different last name, and as spokesman for his band, clearly did not want to be on camera. At least not for a reality television show. What was he hiding? She called Research and requested information on all of the band members, Tony's Tavern, Cort's bar Blitz, and holding a concert at Golden Gate Park.

Just as Victoria hung up, her cell phone rang. She glanced at the readout: Maurice Donnelly, the *Dress My Best* co-host who had been griping to her all morning via text.

"Darling," he said without preamble, "this time I really am going to strangle Francesca with her entire Hermès scarf collection."

"Maurice, where's Jésus ?"

"She wants our plus-size makeover gal to wear pleats. Pleats!" he shrieked, as if he hadn't heard her, and Victoria held the phone away from her ear. "A short sailor skirt just above her dear chubby knees."

Victoria reminded Maurice of the protocol about contacting Jésus instead of her with general production issues, got on a conference call with him, Francesca and the new producer to smooth things over, then went on to five meetings, thirty more phone calls and texts and a preliminary with Jerry and their legal counsel for the Tyler Landry contracts. She also called Luke Tyler to confirm he'd found a lawyer, but got his answering machine instead. She left a brisk message, leaving all of her various contact information, and wondered if he had a cell or even owned a computer. Somehow she doubted it.

She thumped out of a cab and up the stairs to her flat at nine-seventeen that night. Teresa hadn't called, wasn't home and had left no note. Victoria's sister, however, greeted her while doing a shoulder stand against the far living room wall.

Victoria closed the front door and said, "I'm fairly certain you were adopted."

Kristen gave her a serene upside-down smile. "I could say the same about you. Hi honey, how was your day?"

"Triumphant and confusing. Have you seen Teresa?" Victoria collapsed on the couch and picked up her basket of remotes from a side table. Her sixty-inch TV had picture within picture and she opened up four windows.

Kristen looked surprised and lowered first one foot, then the other to the floor in slow, graceful motions. She sat cross-legged by the coffee table and said, "We had lunch to celebrate her getting the catering job. I thought you'd be out tonight, doing more celebrating."

Victoria stared at the screen. "Did Teresa say anything to you about quitting?" She turned on a DVR and began scrolling through the saved programs. She started *Duck Dynasty* and *Keeping up with the Kardashians* playing; she would keep the sound down, taking notes on camera angles, costumes and sets, unless something looked interesting. She pressed Play on *Dance Moms* and turned the volume up on that one. She wasn't sure how much time had passed before she realized Kristen hadn't answered her. She turned and saw her younger sister watching her as if she were an unusual animal in the zoo. "So did she say anything to you about quitting?"

Kristen blinked a few times. "Would you please turn those off or mute them or something? They're awful."

"It's my job, Kristen."

"Are you wondering why Teresa quit?"

"So she did say something to you."

Kristen shook her head, her hair bouncing loose around her shoulders. "No, but it's not too hard to figure."

Victoria pressed play on *Sister Wives*. "How's that?"

Kristen stood in a fluid motion. "You should talk to Teresa."

"I've tried. I can't find her."

"Maybe you need to try a different way." Kristen headed for the door. "I've got a date."

"Dressed in that?"

Kristen picked up a yellow sweater from the chair near the door; it fell to mid-thigh, covering her yellow spandex shorts and bra top, but not much else. She grabbed a huge orange macramé bag, and stepped into a pair of thong sandals. "No. In this," she said with a smile, and left.

"Wait," Victoria said to the door. "What do you mean try a different way? And how do you already have a date?" she yelled. "You just got here." She let out a sigh. "I can't chase you, either." Why did people keep walking out on her?

She knew she wouldn't get an answer, but stared at the door a few moments anyway before falling back against the couch. Letting out a big sigh, she hit a few buttons on the remote, then pulled out a legal pad and began making notes.

Thank God *she* didn't have a date, she told herself. She didn't have *time* for one. Occasionally, she'd ask someone out, but often felt restless after a few dates, uninspired, and would move on. But now she had Brett Soloway to pursue. And with three shows in production, she would barely have time for *him*. At least they were in the same business; he would understand the pressures on her.

She leaned back and tried to focus on the television, but found herself picturing Brett out of his suit and wondering if he had any kind of tan all the up and all the way down.

CHAPTER TWELVE

Luke stood at the foot of the stairs, looking across the Barn. It was empty now, but in about ten minutes, Victoria Clausen and her crew would arrive to set up cameras for preliminary filming. The band's lawyer had reviewed the contract, there had been some negotiating, and it was done. He and the boys were going to be on a damn reality TV show. The cameramen would only be around on weekdays, but the stationary cameras in the Barn, their apartments and cars would film continuously.

Luke had partly hoped there'd be something too big in the contract for them to agree to, but it had been a passing thought. He'd promised to do this—for the band, for his career—and he didn't go back on his word. After signing page after page of agreements, they'd had interviews, psychological testing, physical exams and two rounds of photo shoots for publicity stills. Then they'd each sat in the new Confession Booth in one corner of the Barn for about two hours, talking into space at a camera they couldn't see. Instead of talking, Luke had sung a couple songs until Victoria stepped in and asked him a few questions, which he reluctantly answered. He reminded himself if Tyler Landry had a recording contract, they'd be the subject of a lot more cameras and potential gossip, so he'd better get over his reluctance.

Looking around the room, with the van nearby, the Lounge across the far side, and their playing area in the middle, lit only by the wide plastic windows in the pull-up doors, Luke figured it was his last chance for some quiet. Everything was going to change, he just didn't know how. He sent a little prayer up asking for it to go to the good.

Upstairs, he heard a door slam, booted feet clomp down the hall, and Cort's voice boom out. Parker's mellow one responded, followed by Marty's more sedate tone. Luke smiled. He had a good crew, and they always came through for him. Now he'd do the same. He plucked his hat from its peg on the wall, and flipped the light switches, readying himself for whatever Ms. Victoria Clausen, Producer, could dish out.

As the first set of boots hit the top of the stairs, someone knocked on the red door, then pushed it open, and Victoria came in, followed by a line of people all carrying equipment. Victoria wore a black skirt and blazer with a dark red blouse, and Luke wondered if this time she had matching red underthings. He'd really liked that blue bra from a couple weeks ago when her shirt had ripped. She still had the walking boot and he thought it might be the only thing allowing anyone to keep up with her. A huge bag hung from one shoulder, a fat black binder was in the crook of one arm and the cord of a white earpiece and microphone dangled between her breasts. He watched her lips move and looked for the ever-present phone. She had one hand curled around it.

She glanced up, saw him, and waved when he tipped his hat. She dumped her gear and gestured at the crew, directing them to different areas of the room with some complicated sign language. Luke had time to shake hands with each person, and introduce himself and the boys before the team spread out and began setting up as if they knew the place.

Cort headed to the Lounge and collapsed into one of the easy chairs like he'd been awake for forty-eight hours and couldn't hold himself upright anymore, and Parker and Marty followed him, watching as someone put a tripod in place near the chairs and set a camera on it.

Continuing her conversation, Victoria headed toward Luke, her eyes still on his as she said, "Well, it had better be resolved in the next ten minutes, or we're walking." Luke didn't know if that smile was in greeting or if she enjoyed making demands.

Something to think about.

She disconnected and removed the earpiece, her full lips still curved in a smile. "Good morning, Mr. Tyler."

"Ms. Clausen."

"The set-up shouldn't take more than an hour, then I'll do some quick interviews, and we'll be on our way. A short day for your initiation. Let me introduce you to Jamie Ferrand, our director."

"We met." Luke glanced at the tall, thin African-American man talking to one of the camera operators.

"What's he directing?" Cort called from the Lounge. "We're not actors."

Victoria turned her smile to him. "Jamie directs the shots and the cameramen, to assure we get the required footage. I'm here to make sure you're all taken care of. I'm your liaison between the crew and the studio. You just be yourselves."

From his cross-legged seat on the floor, Parker said, "Might we not alter our behaviors based on the very fact that we are aware of cameras in our presence?"

"Some do at first," Victoria said, and Luke respected her for not faltering or dismissing Parker for his odd language. "But people's core selves can't be changed, and they eventually get used to the cameras and behave as usual."

Victoria moved closer to the Lounge and glanced at Luke. She had her hair pulled back as customary and he couldn't decipher the look in her round, blue eyes. He watched as she settled on one of the old easy chairs, and continued to explain reality TV as she saw it. The crew kept bustling around, positioning cameras and setting up tall sheets of what looked like projector screens. He rested a hip against the side of Marty's chair and crossed his arms, watching her.

Victoria opened the huge binder on her lap and leafed through it. "I've got some questionnaires here that should have been passed around earlier, just a formality." She flipped a few pages forward, then back. "Normally, I have an assistant. Teresa. But she…switched careers recently." She turned to the last section. "Here they are." She pulled the binder rings apart and took out a few stapled packets. "I'll let you look them over while I talk to the crew." Each of the boys took one, and when she held the last one out to Luke, he wanted to shake his head no, but instead, leaned forward and took it from her.

He offered his other hand to help her up, and she tilted her head at him with a blank look. He figured she didn't often take help from men, but it wasn't in him to ignore a woman in need, and he waited patiently. She nodded, took his hand for just long enough to get on her feet, and made her way across the room to huddle with Jamie and one of the sound techs, Ray, a short, thickset guy slurping something pink from a McCafé cup.

Luke rolled the thick questionnaire into a tube and stared at it, wondering what he'd gotten himself into. Victoria Clausen's slim fingers had felt soft and cool, smooth as they'd slipped from his. He let the paper unroll and dropped it on the table before settling into the chair Victoria had just vacated; some fruity scent lingered, like mangoes, and he closed his eyes, breathing it in and giving himself a minute to unwind from the effect she had on him.

Leaning forward, hands between his knees, he flipped to the last question, numbered 532, with a capital T and F at next to it. He skimmed through a few more pages, not sure he was reading right, stopping to re-read the questions three or four times.

- I do not bathe often T/F
- When I am with people I am bothered by hearing very queer things T/F
- It would be better if almost all laws were thrown away T/F
- I more often introduce myself to strangers than strangers introduce themselves to me T/F
- I like architectural magazines T/F

Luke wondered if it was too early for a beer, because this surely made him want one. Victoria could call it a formality, but to Luke it felt like an intrusion on top of an invasion. It didn't seem a problem for Cort, who hollered out, "Hell, yeah, I have weird sex thoughts!" as he whipped through the pages. Or Marty, across from him, quietly circling. Or even Parker, who'd decided that essay answers were better and sat cross-legged on the floor, writing in the margins.

Luke reminded himself this was all for the best, but the whole enterprise still made him itch.

He glanced down at the page, saw "My father was a good man" and "No one seems to understand me" and stood up, muttering that he needed some air. Marty gave him a wave, Cort a grunt, Parker stayed in his little bubble, and Luke responded to none of them as he headed for the door.

On the way there, a lanky kid named Simon, couldn't have been more than eighteen, passed him carrying what looked like a big amp. Simon stumbled close to a propped up guitar case and Luke rushed forward, easing aside the case just in time to avoid a collision, and mentally scolded himself for not moving it out of the way earlier.

"Hey there, son," he told the startled kid, who hadn't seen him coming. "Let's just take care of that for you."

Simon apologized and moved on.

"Why do you do that?" Victoria asked from his side. He didn't know how she'd gotten there so quick, what with that boot and all.

"What's that?" he asked, not looking at her face.

"Call people 'son.' Wait." She threw up her arm, her hand inches from his chest. "Don't tell me yet. Save it for the camera."

The camera. The reminder that he'd be mechanically explaining his life to the world left him feeling like he didn't fit inside his skin. "It's from *Smokey and the Bandit*," he said, then turned away to find a safer place for the guitar, and maybe gather himself a bit.

"There's no need to be nervous," Victoria said, following him.

"No, ma'am." He pushed his hat back with a thumb. "I don't generally get nervous."

"Ever?"

He looked down at her, shaking his head and enjoying her surprised expression. He thought it might take a lot to surprise Victoria Clausen and couldn't help wondering what that might be like.

He shifted his gaze back to the workers. It was true, he didn't really get attacks of nerves. He could, however, be uncomfortable, have anxiety, or feel dread. He would follow through with this business because he had made a promise, but he didn't know how to *be* while it happened. The uncertainty of it all made him question himself too much, and he wasn't used to that.

He took a breath as he rounded the front of the van to a spot blessedly free of people. He set the guitar case between two shelving units that held band equipment and turned to find Victoria Clausen still at his side. He didn't think he reacted, but she must have read something in his face, because she said, "Better to get used to it now. The sooner you assimilate, the easier it will be to forget the camera is there."

He doubted that. "It's fine," he said, and made to move around her but she stood firm. Tough little character.

"It's a very positive thing," she told him.

"You're not telling me anything I don't already know."

Her big smile accentuated the curve of her cheekbones. "I love the way you talk."

He couldn't help but smile back; he felt the same about her. "Georgia meets Texas," he said, surprising himself with the admission; he rarely talked about his teen years.

"You lived in Texas?"

"Summers," he said, that one word recalling the dust and heat of those long days, the shift of muscles as his little Mustang swerved to return a cow to the herd, his body shifting with her. "From ten to seventeen, I went to my aunt and uncle's ranch to…"

His words drifted off, and her eyes widened at his pause, but she didn't ask him to continue.

"I need some air," he said, putting a hand on her shoulder. She swayed to the side to let him pass, and he felt her gaze as he grabbed his jacket and stepped out the rollup door past technicians carrying in still more equipment.

He tilted his hat against the sun and zipped the jacket against a brisk wind as he strode along Folsom to 19th, these surroundings worlds away from those summers in Texas, where his mama had sent him to get away from Buzz. He'd been a scrawny kid that first year, angry at the world, at his mother for abandoning him, and at the cowpokes who kicked his rich, spoiled ass until he fought back, then gave in, at which point they started to respect him. He merged his Georgia drawl with their Texas twang, creating his own language, and felt he'd earned the right to wear his boots and hat beyond any sort of fashion sense. In a way, he hated stark, hard Texas, but he also appreciated it for how it had shaped him.

He strode past the Chinese Food & Donuts place, the deli and the wine bar, taking longer strides and faster steps to drive out his thoughts, looking for a clear space to help him regroup. They hadn't even started filming, and the Barn no longer felt like home. He and Cort had laughed when they first found the old brick building with a garage on the ground floor and apartments above.

"How can we go wrong, son?" Cort clapped him on the back. "We can sing Folsom Prison Blues right here on Folsom."

They'd already been in the City over a year at that point, and experienced a wide variety of San Francisco's offerings: cable cars, Fisherman's Wharf, walking across the Golden Gate Bridge, The Fillmore, The Stud—an understandable mistake, but they'd ended up playing a good round of pool—pickpockets, amazing food, and great music. They'd also lived at the edge of the Mission and the Castro and been hit on by men and women alike, sometimes at the same time.

They felt and talked like country boys, but they'd grown up on the outskirts of Atlanta, and San Francisco felt like more of a fit than they'd've thought. So when Cort's inheritance came in, they decided to stay, and drove around in Cort's beat up Ford Ranger looking for a permanent place, saying, "Turn right here," or "I'm going to drive two blocks, take two rights, then a left, and see what we see."

What they'd seen was an old brick building with a garage downstairs, two roll-up doors, one red entrance door to an office in between, two apartments up top with lots of big windows across the front, a small parking lot in back and a flat roof to hang out on. It had taken almost all of Cort's money, but they'd gutted the downstairs themselves, lived upstairs during the renovation, christened it the Barn, and used the equity to buy the sports bar.

It had all come together, finding a place to live, settling in, booking gigs. But it took time, and they'd had to supplement their incomes for the first few years until Blitz took off. Both he and Cort worked construction, made deliveries, and bussed tables, which took away from performing. He'd once planned to have a record and be in the Top 10 by the time he turned nineteen, a foolish notion he knew now. He'd just turned twenty-seven, and until a few weeks ago hadn't felt any closer to fulfilling that dream, despite their dedicated fans at Tony's.

He kept telling himself he'd made a promise and he always kept his word, but he realized that hadn't been enough to convince him to give his all. He owed it to himself and the boys to man up, take advantage of this opportunity and run with it. Settling his hat more firmly on his head, he turned in the middle of the block and headed back to the Barn.

CHAPTER THIRTEEN

Victoria was relieved when Luke returned not long after he'd walked out of the Barn. She made a snap decision, calling out to Jamie at the same time she clumped toward Luke. She held a hand up to Luke's chest to stop him before he got too comfortable, and turned to Jamie. "Go through my list of questions with the boys, give me two camera angles, plus the stationaries on the wall, and…" She paused as Luke moved so close her hand pressed against his chest and warmed her fingertips. She made a concerted effort not to look at him. "And," she finished, "about fifty percent close-ups in case we need them for filler in confessionals. I need to discuss something with Mr. Tyler offsite."

Jamie nodded and moved away, assigning directions to the techs and camera men.

Victoria took a steadying breath and turned to Luke, very aware of his presence, her fingertips still absorbing his chest's solid warmth. He glanced down at her hand, but made no comment. She held it there a moment longer, then dropped it to her side and watched him, waiting. He could test her, but she had no hesitation about giving it right back.

"What do we need to discuss?" he finally asked.

"Your interview. I don't want to do it here." She wished she could see his eyes better under the shading of his hat. Even so, she knew his gaze remained on her.

"Too hectic," she added, when he didn't respond. "I need some air, too." She tilted her head toward the door and turned away, walking with care, but deliberately not looking back. She held her breath until the sound of his boots echoed behind her, then let it out slowly. Step one.

She commandeered a handheld and one of the studio's vans, ousting her tech Elmore, who blinked against the sunlight but made no complaint, and managed to get Luke to join her. She realized Luke still didn't trust her, but his curiosity won out. And maybe the Barn had become uncomfortable enough that he preferred being anywhere else. He struck her as someone who liked his personal life low key, and this filming was going to be a major disruption.

She drove along 17th through Cole Valley just beside the Haight-Ashbury, that enclave of the Summer of Love. She'd always wanted to do a show based in the area, but thought it might be too cliché. She glanced at Luke, silent in the passenger seat. For now, she had another cliché to occupy her time. It could be a long shot, but she figured a former Texas boy might miss being around horses. When she turned onto Frederick and drove past Kezar Stadium, she caught Luke turning his head to look between the black wrought iron fencing and hedges to the former home of the San Francisco 49ers. As they continued on Lincoln Way at the edge of Golden Gate Park, Luke kept his gaze on the greenery on their right. She wished she knew if his silence signified calm or annoyance.

At a red light, a small group of schoolchildren wearing matching t-shirts and holding hands clustered at the corner. Giggling and walking so close they formed a large clump of bright orange, they were hustled across the street by their teachers. Victoria caught Luke watching them, his normally sober expression gone soft around the eyes and mouth.

She desperately wanted to ask if he liked children, or if the antics of the orange-clad group amused him, but she knew it was too soon. Pose too many questions now, and he might close up before she could capture anything on camera.

They crossed 19th Avenue, one of the city's main thoroughfares, and continued along the park's edge in silence. Just a few blocks from the ocean, she turned into the park itself, drove a short way and stopped at a small parking lot near the fenced field. A trio of women led two saddled horses around the ring and over low jumps. It looked like a training session and Victoria wished she could ask them about their routine; one of the many joys of her job revolved around the inherent necessity of unearthing endless data about other people's lives. In other words, she could be a snoop and get away with it.

Victoria reached for the case with the handheld and its tripod, and hopped to the ground on her good foot, heading for the set of low stands painted forest green to match the field's fencing. Luke rounded the front of the van and held out a hand.

"Help you with that?"

She waved him away. "Go ahead and watch the horses."

He looked tempted, but instead fell in step beside her, matching his gait to her hobbling one. He shoved his hands in his front pockets and lowered his head. "I like these spots, some balance to the city streets."

"They give you breathing room," she agreed, although, she confessed aloud, she rarely came to Golden Gate Park, unless it was used during filming.

They settled on the second bench from the top and leaned back, Victoria with one booted foot resting on the next seat down, Luke with both boots there. They watched the horses, one bay and one black, put through their paces for a few minutes before Luke spoke.

"You been in this business long?"

"Behind the camera for eight years, and in front of it for a few before that."

He tilted his head. "You were on one of these shows?"

She laughed, not so much at the idea of being on a reality television show, but at the reality of her life before production. "I wanted to be an actress," she admitted.

"Can't imagine you taking direction," he said, but his tone was kind. "Only giving it."

"It's true. I thought I'd be the next big thing." She undid her hair clip, wrapped her hands around her hair to make a big ponytail, then clipped it back, enjoying the caress of the strands over her fingers, hyper aware of Luke's gaze on her.

Luke nodded, turning away to watch the black horse toss its head and snort, balking at one of the taller jumps. "We here for you to soften me up?"

She'd meant it when she said she loved the way he talked, that fascinating combination of country boy and street smart, all with a smooth resonant tone. "Is it working?"

"A bit."

"Then yes." He laughed, his eyes crinkling, and she added, "Do you mind if I set up the camera?"

His features hardened at that, less from resistance, she thought, than a need to convince himself to fulfill his contract. "Tell me about being an actress while you do it."

Using the stands' seats as steps, she made her way down and positioned herself in front and slightly to the left of where Luke sat. Instead of following the action in the ring, he watched her movements. That was all right; whatever he needed to feel relaxed around her.

"I was the good girl growing up," she told him as she removed her gear from its bag and set the pieces on the bench in front of her. "Behaved myself, got good grades, followed the rules. Between high school and coming to San Francisco, I made two impulsive decisions. One was to follow my best friend Alice to L.A. after we graduated, and the other was to come here."

"What happened to the best friend?" Luke asked from his perch in the stands.

"She went blonde, got blue contacts and a boob job, and changed her name to Harmony. She was already five-ten, so at least she didn't have to spend rent money trying to elongate herself, which, believe it or not, was offered in some places down there. She modeled for auto tools calendars, did some commercials, but her big break came when she played a cancer patient on *ER*."

Luke leaned forward, resting his hands between his knees. "How'd that work?"

"She started dating George Clooney." He laughed with her, and she attached the camera to the tripod. "I met some good people that I'm still in touch with. But I also waitressed at Roscoe's House of Chicken and Waffles and got tired of hearing that I had the looks, but I was too short and too dark. So I got out a map, closed my eyes and pointed. Guess where it landed?" She stopped, her finger above the ON button.

"Not San Francisco."

"Redding, California."

"Huh." His mouth turned up at one corner.

"Exactly. I decided not to trust fate to that one, and looked more closely at the map. San Francisco is one of those places you come to start over, right?" She gave a shrug, then looked at him. "You ready?"

"Not so much, but you go ahead and do your job."

Step two, she thought, in getting Luke Tyler to trust her. She turned the camera on and focused, using the viewfinder. Head bent, only looking at him through the camera, she asked, "What's in your wallet?"

He squinted at her. "Was thinking you'd ask me how I got involved with the band."

She watched his smile in the small screen and couldn't help a little smile herself. Just as she'd thought, he wasn't going to make it easy on her. And it would be a sweet reward when he opened up.

She straightened, looking at Luke in person. "Why would I ask you that?"

He shrugged. "Seems like something you'd want to know."

"This is just to start us off in a casual way, get you comfortable with the camera." She looked at him through the viewfinder again. "Your wallet?" she repeated.

"Well, now," he began, glancing up as if mentally reviewing the contents. "Nope, no other way." He shifted to his left hip and reached into a back pocket with his right hand, pulling out and opening a billfold. "Driver's license," he finally said. "Expires next year. Credit card. Paid off." He pulled it out and waved it at her before returning it to its slot. "Let's see. Membership card for Rednecks R Us, library card, Triple A and Kaiser. Oh," he added, peeking inside, "and a bit of cash. The amount of which I'm not saying on camera." He gave her a wink, folded the wallet, and replaced it in his back pocket.

"You're kidding, right?"

"No, ma'am. There are talented pickpockets in this city. I'd be asking for trouble if I announced any amount of cash in my pocket."

She straightened and finally looked him in the eye. "Rednecks R Us?"

"I drive a truck. I own a gun. My hound dog's in Georgia, but I do have one. According to the rules and regulations, I qualify."

Victoria's heart leapt. Oh, what the editors could do with those sound bites. "You have a gun?"

"I do. And I'm not saying where I keep it."

Victoria didn't know which to tackle first: the rednecks thing, the gun, or some hound dog in Georgia. She decided to go with the most unusual. "There's no such thing as Rednecks R Us."

"Are you sure?"

"Of course I'm sure." She wasn't. She'd never been to the South, but there was no backing down now; she wanted him to talk about it.

"Do I need to prove it?" he asked, and she felt his energy pick up for the first time that day.

"I don't think you can," she challenged. Step three.

He leaned over onto that hip again, but didn't move to take out his wallet. "Well, now, I can show you the card, can't I?"

"Anyone can make up a card on a computer these days."

He rolled back, then stood up, all long, lean grace, and stepped down to her. She made no attempt to adjust the camera, especially since he walked directly at it and soon blocked the lens. With his crotch. He leaned forward, looking down with a little smile. She breathed in his scent—pure male—without being too obvious.

"Are we going to have to call my Mama, then, and ask her?"

Oh, yes, please, she thought. But would he actually do it, or was he bluffing? Victoria crossed her arms. "I think we are. And I want it on camera."

"I'll call her, but no camera."

Victoria considered. Getting Luke on film talking to his mother, even without Dorothy Taylor's side of the exchange, would be great for ratings. But Luke wouldn't have offered to call his mother if he didn't have some trust in Victoria. Either that or he was testing her. Again, she pushed. They weren't here just for the fun of it.

"Sound, no picture."

"No sound, no picture."

She glanced at where the camera now recorded the shifting of his hips as they negotiated. "I'll focus the camera on the ground, but the sound stays on."

He inclined his head, following her gaze, then pointed at the camera. "Go ahead then."

She pursed her lips, and could swear she caught a spark of deviltry in his eyes. She tilted the camera all the way down, and watched Luke pull a slim cell phone out of his left pocket, noting the incongruity of the cowboy with the modern gadget. She liked it. And she had to laugh to herself at his fake fussing over her Blackberry. He turned away while the phone rang, and she studied the pull of his t-shirt across his shoulders, hips slightly forward, chest back, denim tight over his butt.

She pulled her top away from her front and fanned herself while his gaze was averted. She'd dropped her hands by the time he put his phone to his ear and looked at her. They exchanged smiles, and Victoria heard a voice through the speaker. "Afternoon, Taylor residence."

"Hey, Mama."

"Lucas..."

Before she could say anything else, Luke said, "I know it's not Thursday, Mama. Everything's fine. You remember that producer I told you about, with the reality show?"

"Sure do," Victoria heard. "And I'm real proud, honey. You're gonna be a star, just like—"

Luke interrupted her again, but with a tone of urgency in his voice this time. "Well, she'd like to talk to you, got a question about Rednecks R Us."

Victoria heard the laughter on the other end, getting louder as Luke handed the phone over. "Her name's Dorothy Taylor."

Victoria already knew about the different last names, but before she could use the opportunity to ask why, Luke pressed the phone to her ear, forcing her to take hold of it when he let go. "Hello? Mrs....Taylor?"

"Hi, honey," said a lovely, rich voice. "Lucas didn't tell me your name."

"It's Victoria Clausen, ma'am."

Luke rolled his eyes and Victoria made a face while his mother laughed again, one of those throaty, *Cat on a Hot Tin Roof* types of laughs. Victoria already liked Luke's Mama.

"Oh, honey, don't call me ma'am. It makes me feel old. You call me Dot, I'll call you Vic, and the world will be a good place." Victoria couldn't help smiling at that, and looked up to see Luke watching her, an unreadable expression on his face. "Now, Lucas tells me you want to know about Rednecks R Us. It's a real thing. He and Cortland started it," she continued, even as Victoria wondered why Dorothy was Dot and Victoria was Vic, but Luke and Cort were Lucas and Cortland. "Talked some printing company into making up cards, conned the neighbor boys out of ten dollars a year in dues, held monthly meetings to find a way to make the South rise again, and even talked me into baking my thumbprint cookies for their lemonade stand. They made a lot of money that day. I still don't know what all they did with it, and I don't think I want to know. So

77

where are your people, honey?"

Victoria had been lulled into the story, wanting to settle onto a bench and listen to Dot talk for days, but that last question threw her off. "My people?"

"You parents, your family, brothers and sisters."

Victoria glanced at Luke again, who was still watching her, and looked like he was enjoying himself for the first time during this process. She was sure he could hear his mother's side of the conversation just as well as she could, since the speaker carried so far. "My younger sister lives here, with me. My father and brother live in a small town in Illinois."

"Hard working folk?"

"Yes, ma—um, yes, they are."

"And your mama?"

"She died when I was seven," Victoria said, turning away from Luke's surprised look. She wouldn't lie to Dorothy Taylor, but she felt as if she'd let Luke down by not telling him about her mother's death. She had asked him to reveal everything about himself, but she'd held a piece of her own life back. As a bonding tactic, she often confessed something about her life in Los Angeles to her new cast members, but she never talked about her mother. She didn't owe him anything, but still...

"Well, honey, now that's a shame. Your father managing okay?"

"He has...a lady friend," she said, feeling funny about calling Margaret Ames a "girlfriend."

"Well, now, that's good, real good. How old are you, honey?"

"Thirty-one."

Dot made a tsking sound. "Just a few years older than my Lucas. Too bad you're not from the South."

"Why's that?" Victoria asked, but was caught off guard when Luke swooped in and grabbed the phone.

"No matchmaking, Mama," he said.

"She's pretty, isn't she?" Victoria heard Dot say.

"Beautiful as a Southern morning, Mama," Luke said, looking directly at Victoria. "But she's a professional, making a TV show, not looking for a husband."

"Any young woman from a good family is looking for a husband," Dot replied. "And she sounds like a good girl. Your mama's never wrong."

"I'm going now," Luke said. "I love you, and I'll call you Thursday." He hung up, and stood clutching the cell, smiling. "Mama thinks I should've been married years ago."

"But you're only twenty-seven," Victoria said, ignoring for the moment his comment comparing her to a Southern morning. He could have agreed she was pretty and moved on, but he hadn't. Thinking about that gave her a pleasant quiver in her middle.

"It's *already* twenty-seven to her, and without even one grandbaby for her to cuddle."

"Oh, she wants you married so she can have grandkids."

"She wants me happy," Luke said, sliding the phone back in his pocket. "You convinced now about Rednecks R Us?"

Victoria gestured back to the benches, and Luke sat without a word as she eased the camera into position and focused on him again. "How old were you when you and Cort started Rednecks R Us?"

He propped his legs straight out and crossed one boot over the other at the ankle. "About ten or so."

"So you and Cort have been friends a long time?"

Instead of answering, he cocked his head and paused, seeming to ponder something. Then he gestured toward her before dropping the hand to his lap. "I'm sorry about your mama."

Caught off guard, she froze, then stuttered, "It was a long time ago."

"Doesn't change the fact you lost her."

"I..." She swallowed. She'd been very young, Kristen even younger, and their brother Robbie just a baby. Still, it had been twenty-four years ago, and people often became so uncomfortable when it came up, the subject was generally changed, so she rarely spoke of it.

His voice soft, as if not wanting to startle her, Luke asked, "What was her name?"

"Anna. She was Danish," she added, confused by her own admission. "Her parents came from Denmark when she was seven. The same age I was..." Her voice drifted off as she suddenly remembered sitting in the rocking chair on her mother's lap, listening to the lilt of her voice, still with a touch of an accent, while she read *The Mouse and the Motorcycle*, Victoria's favorite book. She suddenly felt comforted and alone at the same time, and bit her lip, blinking fast.

Luke raised up from his lounging position and jumped to the ground in front of her. He stood close, his hands out as if to put them on her shoulders or hug her. "Hey, I didn't mean—"

"No, no, it's fine." She raised her hands as well, to reassure him, but also took a couple steps back, heel and boot sinking in the dirt, to put some space between them. She took a deep breath and straightened, finding her way to regaining control of this interview, but still he hovered. Too close. But if she stepped back again, she might as well fling herself forward and let him comfort her. Either way, she appeared vulnerable, and she preferred strong.

Before lowering her hands, she moved them farther apart, reminded how large he was. If her arms went around his waist, she thought, if he pressed against her, he would be so...solid. Was that the lure for so many women, to lose themselves in that strength, to not have to hold it together because someone like Luke could capably do it for them?

Well, she didn't need that. She could keep herself together just fine, thank you. She also didn't need the pity in his big green eyes as his head tilted toward hers. She clapped her hands together hard, and he straightened.

"We're losing the light," she said with a nod at the benches.

"You're all right?"

"Of course." She gave him a bright smile. "I'm always all right."

"No one can be all right all the time," he said, but settled himself back on the bench as if their little interlude had never occurred.

And it wouldn't, at least as far as the film went. That footage would be gone from the camera before it reached the editors. She couldn't use a lot of it anyway, since they were mainly here to get him more comfortable with the camera. She'd be asking more detailed questions during his next interview.

"You and Cort," she said, getting them back on track. "Friends for a long time?"

"Since the cradle."

"And..." She gritted her teeth; she hated feeling rattled. "Have you been playing together as musicians for a long time?"

"Long as I can remember," he said. "My...his daddy was a musician, too, played guitar, and since I spent a lot of time at Cort's house, we both picked it up."

Victoria wondered about that glitch. He must know she was aware his father was Buzz Taylor. So he wasn't that relaxed yet. Or could he be rattled, too?

"So how did you get to play guitar, while Cort went with the bass?"

"We wanted to start a band, but didn't want two lead guitars, so we played for it."

"Played for it?" She felt herself settling back into the rhythm of interviewing.

"A hand of poker. He won, decided he'd rather be a bassist anyway."

Victoria laughed. "The whims of fate."

"It worked out. Cort thinks bass players get more girls."

"Do they?"

"Don't make me make a joke about musicians and their instruments."

She held up a hand. "Fair enough. Why country music?"

"I'm from the South. Couldn't avoid it."

"I wouldn't think every musician from the South automatically leans toward country western music."

"No," he said, and he seemed more relaxed now, too. He leaned back against the bench, keeping his head forward so his hat wouldn't bump. "But music in general surrounds you in the South, with the roots to blues, jazz, rock-n-roll. And the air…it's humid, fertile." His eyelids lowered, as if he could feel the sultry heat lulling him into its embrace. Victoria felt the pull of it herself, even as the fog crept toward them from the ocean.

"The air gets in your blood," Luke continued in his seductive voice, "along with the music. Cort calls it spiritual-sleepy-cool. You can't hide from it and you don't want to once it takes hold of you. You think it's going to be the hardest thing you've ever done, until you give in to it. Then you wonder why it took you so long to get there in the first place."

Victoria's skin felt too tight after that speech, her body filled with a restless tension. How could one misplaced cowboy affect her so much?

CHAPTER FOURTEEN

Victoria made her way up the stairs to her flat, cursing her boot but smiling over the day's events. Not only had the initial shooting gone well with Luke and Tyler Landry, but she'd gotten a text from Brett Soloway: "coffee nxt wk for mktg re our shows?" She hadn't been able to hide her grin, but forced herself to wait ten minutes, then half an hour, and another twenty minutes after that, rehearsing how best to respond, before she'd typed: "caffe greco next mon at 6?"

He'd confirmed back a "c u then" and she e-mailed the exchange to herself, basking in some adolescent infatuation for five minutes before returning to work.

Just as she reached out to fit her key in the lock, the door swung open and Teresa froze in the doorway, one foot hanging over the threshold. She wore a long, multicolored skirt in blues and purples, a dark blue three-quarter sleeve top, and her purple cowboy boots.

"Hey," she said. "Thought you'd be working late."

"My hot sheets took longer than usual, and I did have to log some footage tonight, and get the call sheets ready for tomorrow. Then I met with Jane, who's going to be the story producer, and the editors. I got Harlan and JP, and you know how great they are. I also had to set up some catering and expand the storyline, since it might go longer than thirteen episodes. But the shoot went better than I thought." As she reported these details, she realized she missed sharing the ups and downs of her work with T. Very few people understood the particulars of reality TV production, but Teresa had been at her side for five shows, not including *In Concert*.

Teresa looked at her feet. "Great. That's great." She finally put her boot on the doorsill. "Well, I'm heading out." She made to step out onto the landing, but Victoria didn't move.

"Where you headed?" She shook her head. She'd been around Luke Tyler too long; she was starting to sound like him. "Where are you going?" she tried again.

"Oh." Teresa glanced at her, then away. "Just the culinary school. I may want to start taking classes. They have a great library there, all sorts of, you know, cooking...things..." Her words drifted off and she licked her lips.

A voice from inside the flat said, "Oh, for the love of the goddess, would you two get inside?"

Victoria started, surprised at the vehemence in her sister's voice. Forgetting the awkwardness between them, she said to Teresa, "What's her deal?"

"Um," Teresa began, then turned and went back inside.

Victoria followed, closed the door behind her and dropped all of her gear nearby.

Kristen sat in a lotus position in the middle of the couch, wearing a long yellow batik top and forest green leggings. She'd piled her hair on top of her head, making her appear even taller than usual. "Normally, I let people travel along their own spiritual path in whatever fashion they need to in order to learn their lessons, but I get cranky if I have to live with two people whose paths are connected but will do anything to avoid each other because of...of...well, I don't even know what."

"Parker would love you," Victoria muttered.

"What?"

Victoria shook her head. "I think I might need a Dr. Pepper for this." She walked through the living room to the small kitchen at the back of the flat, poured her favorite drink in a glass over ice, and returned, anticipating with great pleasure that first cold, fizzy sip.

Kristen wrinkled her nose at the glass. "So sit. Talk."

"About what?" Victoria asked, but she sat in the chair at one end of the couch, just as Teresa took the chair opposite. She indulged in a long swallow, then reluctantly set the glass on a coaster, and looked at T.

"Why it's been more than two weeks and you aren't talking,"

Kristen said. "Why Teresa quit without any explanation or long-term prospects. Why you haven't tried to find out why."

Victoria crossed her arms over her chest. "I texted. Called her. She didn't call back." It sounded petulant, even to her.

"She didn't want a relationship with your Blackberry." Kristen stood up. "Okay, I've started you off." She scooted around the coffee table and headed for the door. "You can take it from here."

Victoria looked at Teresa, who sat staring at the floor, clicking the toes of her boots together. "I can't believe you left in the middle of pre-prod."

Teresa raised her head. "Pre-production isn't the be-all."

Kristen took her hand from the doorknob and headed back. "Clearly you still need me."

As Kristen settled back on the couch between them, Teresa looked at her and said, "This is what I was talking about."

Victoria took in T's sullen expression and Kristen's nod. "What? What were you talking about?"

Kristen said, "Teresa feels that..." Her voice drifted off. "Sorry, T. You should be the one telling her this."

Teresa shoved her braids behind her ears with a loud clinking, then tucked the ends into her collar. "I know."

Victoria shifted in her chair; she hated slow negotiations, and she didn't handle slow-starting conversations much better. "So what do you need to tell me?"

"You—" Teresa began, then stopped.

In a loud whisper, and drawing out the word, Kristen said, "Iiii..." then rolled one hand in a "you can do it" gesture.

"Right." Teresa licked her lips. "I...feel like your job is always so important..."

"Of course it is," Victoria said, wishing one of them would get to the point. "It's what I do. It's my life."

Kristen sighed, and Victoria shot her a look.

"Are you saying you think I put my job before you?" Victoria asked.

"In a word," Teresa said, "yes."

"Oh, thank goodness." Kristen threw up her hands, then slapped her thighs. "That was much easier than I thought it would be." She looked at Victoria. "I thought it would take you much longer to get that."

Nonplussed, Victoria stared at her sister, then decided the easiest course would be to ignore her. She turned to Teresa instead. "I would never do that."

"Not on purpose," Teresa said, "but you have. Had. Lately. A lot." She stared at her boots again.

"Teresa hates conflict," Kristen told Victoria.

"I know that," Victoria shot back; she herself loved conflict, but she knew Teresa avoided it with great proficiency. "I haven't been so caught up in my job that I don't know anything about my best friend." She got up and sat on the end of the couch closest to Teresa's chair. "T, I'm sorry. You know how involved I get. It's what I *do*. I'm good at this." She made an expansive gesture, indicating the importance of every aspect of her work. She held a hand out to Teresa. "But that's no excuse for ignoring you and treating you second."

Teresa gave her a smile, but didn't take the proffered hand. "I know. I'm sorry I quit like that. It was unprofessional and I should've told you what was bothering me."

"But you were afraid I was too absorbed in the show to hear it." Victoria felt ashamed she hadn't recognized Teresa's discomfort.

Teresa nodded.

"And you want to come back?"

Teresa's shoulders dropped. "Could I? It was stupidly impulsive of me. I don't have any other income right now. But...just part time? I may get more gigs with the catering company, and I want to try to get into culinary school."

Victoria nodded. "I'm sure we can work something out."

Teresa released a breath as if she'd been holding it in for a minute, and smiled for the first time. "Thank you." She stood up. "I really have to go now." She turned to Kristen. "And we're still on for dinner at my parents' tomorrow?"

Kristen nodded. "Looking forward to it."

Victoria blinked at that, but stood up, too, and hugged Teresa.

"You'll tell me if I'm getting too caught up again?" she asked.

Teresa nodded and headed down the stairs. Victoria closed the door and reached for the basket of remotes, ready to dip into some research and finish her Dr. Pepper. But something nagged at her.

Before turning anything on, she asked, "You're going to her parents?"

From her spot on the couch, Kristen said, "Yeah. They have their family over once a week. She has older brothers and sisters galore, and they're all crazy successful like her parents. There's a lot of pressure for T to succeed."

Victoria nodded. She knew all of that, but she'd never gone over to the Steplowski's house herself. She thought she might have met one of the sisters, but couldn't recall a name.

Kristen tilted her head toward the door and said, "That was too easy."

"What do you mean?" Victoria shrugged out of her black blazer with a sigh and tossed it over the arm of the couch. Then she took another long, satisfying drink of Dr. Pepper.

"For Teresa to quit the way she did, something must've been building up. She'll explode again unless it continues to get addressed. Speaking of which, you really need some sex."

Victoria had undone the top button on her blouse, and was about to undo another, but stopped at her sister's words. She deliberately lowered her hands to her sides, and was about launch into a lecture on all of the reasons why she did not need any sex, and it wasn't Kristen's business anyway, but remembered her upcoming coffee with Brett Soloway on Monday at six and couldn't stop a smile.

"Uh oh," Kristen said with some glee, getting into a cross-legged position and grabbing her feet. She leaned forward on her knees. "You've had some, or it's on the horizon."

Sex on the horizon. With Brett. Something clenched in her stomach. Sure, she'd often fantasized about a romance with Brett: leisurely Sunday brunches, spirited discussions about their shows, clandestine kisses in the hallways of the Reality Strikes' offices. But she'd never been very skilled at sexual fantasies, so those remained vague: his hands on her body, undressing her, the two of them cuddling afterward. Would Luke Tyler be a cuddler? she wondered, and felt her face flush.

Flustered, she said, "It's not like that," and immediately felt like she and Kristen were ten and five years old again. Kristen's unique combination of easygoing and straightforward had often left Victoria feeling defensive, unable to respond in a satisfactory way. It had forced her to learn the art of a good comeback. She sat down, toying with one of the remotes.

"So which one is it?" Kristen asked.

"Which—?" Victoria stopped, confused. Which Reality Strikes Studios executive? Which co-worker? But Kristen didn't know about Brett Soloway, so why would she wonder which co-worker?

"It's got to be the lead singer," Kristen said. "That body, the olive skin, that outrageously sexy wavy hair you just burn to run your fingers through." She shivered, hugging herself. "Yum."

"The—what?"

"Not him? Okay, well, the blonde is hot, too, but I didn't think you liked blondes and he's a bit...frat boy, don't you think?"

Victoria had to consciously shut her mouth to keep her jaw from dropping. "Wait. You think I have the hots for someone in Tyler Landry?"

"If you don't, then you're potentially frigid and might want to get that checked out." Kristen tucked a loose section of hair back into her topknot.

Through clenched teeth, Victoria said, "I don't date the talent."

Kristen ran her hands down her neck and along her shoulders, then stretched her arms out from her sides. "You don't? Why not?"

"It's in the contract, for one thing. I would lose my job. And for another, it's not ethical."

"Why not?" Kristen repeated. "It's like dating a co-worker, isn't it? You just need to set some ground rules."

"No, it's not. It's nothing like that." But that reminded Victoria of the complexities of dating a co-worker; she and Brett would definitely have to set those ground rules. "It's more like dating a subordinate," she added, rubbing at her forehead. "But not that, either. I need my people to be themselves, and as the producer, I can't be swayed by any emotions. It could ruin the integrity of the work."

Kristen snorted. "Do you hear yourself? It's reality TV. It's like the antithesis of integrity."

"Are you questioning my integrity? You have no idea what I—"

Kristen pulled her feet up onto her thighs, then held out a hand. "Don't get your knickers in a knot. I know you have integrity. That's never been an issue." She waved the hand around, then leaned forward. "But the temptations must be extreme, having to twist things around to get the maximum dramatic effect. It's not normal. And then to talk about the integrity of the piece?"

"Some producers consider their shows to be a lab, like it's all a sociological experiment. I do not. I do as much as possible to keep what's filmed real." Victoria crossed her arms over her chest, feeling defensive and priggish. But she meant it: she wanted events and emotions on her shows to be as real as possible. And she would never risk her job—her *life*—on a date with one of her stars.

"But wouldn't it be more real to admit you like that handsome lead singer and—"

"Luke," Victoria interrupted. "And how do you know what they all look like?"

"Teresa showed me their picture." Kristen smiled. "Luke, huh? So admit you like him and film that. *That* would be real."

"And I would be fired. Besides," Victoria added, realizing how this must sound. "I don't like Luke. It's...someone else, and I don't want to talk about it." She tapped her foot against the floor, remembering that tight skin feeling earlier when interviewing Luke. It must be a sign of frustration, but she didn't want her sister to be right about the fact that she might need some sex.

"But you admit Luke is hot?"

"He's outrageously good-looking, yes." She flashed briefly on Luke telling his mother she was as beautiful as a Southern morning. "But I work with attractive people on a regular basis. It doesn't sway me."

"No? Maybe you *should* get that checked out."

"I am not frigid." She let her head drop against the back of the couch. Talking with Kristen could be so exhausting; a roundabout of nonsense half the time.

"So you like someone else, but you think Luke is good-looking, but you're not tempted because you want to maintain the integrity of your work."

"I might not put it exactly like that, but yes, that's the general idea." She pulled at her hair clip and it tangled at the base of her neck. She yanked it out with a wince and set it down. "I'm also not tempted because *I'm not tempted.*"

"Okay. Do you want to fix me up then?"

"No!"

"Why not? You keep your integrity, and I get some sex." Kristen raised her hands above her and stretched from side to side, wiggling her fingers.

"You had a date the other night."

"Dud." She dropped her hands into her lap. "Do you know how

hard it is to find a good straight man in this city?"

For the first time in this conversation, Victoria had to agree. Then she thought of Brett Soloway and smiled again. "Not impossible, though." She reached for the remote again. "Are we finished analyzing my love and work lives?"

Kristen shrugged, untwisted herself, and stood up. "For now," she said, wandering from the room.

Oh, good, thought Victoria. Something to look forward to.

CHAPTER FIFTEEN

L uke got up that morning and performed his usual routine: quick shower, teeth cleaned, brush through the hair, jeans and a tee. Then he headed to the kitchen to feed Frog and scramble eggs with green onions and bell pepper, home fries and bacon. He got the coffee brewing and just before it let out its final gurgle, he ambled to the door in his bare feet, the top two buttons of his jeans still undone. He opened the door to let the cooking smells be Cort's wake-up call.

Frog jumped to the back of the couch and Luke bent his nose to hers for their morning nuzzle, generating a loud rumble for such a small creature. When he straightened, he caught sight of the small black camera mounted in the corner, red light on during its first day of filming. He swore under his breath, turning his back on it.

Sound- and motion-activated, and state of the art, according to Ms. Victoria Clausen; it could probably pick up Frog's purr and the bacon's sizzle.

Or Cort, shirtless, scratching at his chest and yawning. "Morning comes too early," he said, wandering inside to grab one of the mugs Luke had set on the counter and fill it with coffee, cream and sugar.

He slumped onto a stool at the breakfast bar and yawned again. "I had me some nice dreams last night," he said, as Luke dished up the food. "That Victoria was dressed in some French maid's outfit and doing things with a feather duster that aren't recommended by the manufacturer."

Unable to stop himself from glancing at the camera again, Luke thumped the plate on the counter in front of Cort.

"We have company, don't forget," Luke said, before turning back to the stove to fill his own plate.

"What's that? Oh yeah, the cameras. Forgot all about that." With a grin, Cort turned around and waved at it. "Hey, y'all, how you doing this morning? No disrespect meant, Miss Victoria, you looked real fine in that outfit."

Luke bent his head low over the plate. "You aren't supposed to talk to them."

Cort turned back around. "Why not? She said just be ourselves. Myself talks to people, in person or behind a camera."

Luke said nothing, just shoveled in big bites of food. He rinsed his plate, set it in the sink and said, "You ready?"

Cort looked up, a fork full of eggs and potatoes hanging in the air in front of his mouth. "What's the hurry?"

"Just want to get going." Luke turned away. "I'll get my boots on."

"Take your time," Cort called after him. "We'll be fine out here."

Shaking his head, Luke went to the bedroom to pull on socks and boots. He ran his hands through his hair, then dropped his head in his palms. They were set to go over the books this morning before opening up the bar, and would be filmed by cameramen throughout the day. They didn't need the crew to cover any shenanigans here because of the in-house and in-car setups.

Victoria had promised coverage 24/7, and she meant it.

"You ready in there or what?" Cort bellowed from the other room.

Luke couldn't help laughing and shook his head as he rounded the partition to the living area. "Hold your horses, son," he said, and tossed a tee and flannel shirt to Cort.

Luke had planned to be as quiet and boring as possible during this process, keep his profile low, but that might not be possible with Cort around.

He grabbed his hat and keys from pegs by the open front door, checked that Frog lay sleeping on the back of the couch, and headed out with Cort clomping along behind him.

Cort drove them in the Ranger. Luke slumped in the seat and kept his hat low over his eyes while Cort waved at the tiny cameras mounted inside and near each side mirror, keeping up a running monologue.

"Once a quarter, see," he said, slamming to a stop at a red light,

"Lucas and myself go over the bar's books with our accountant, make sure we're not going into a hole, how many peanuts we can buy next month and suchlike." He shook his head and accelerated as the light changed. "Never thought I'd be a respectable businessman," he added.

Luke snorted.

Cort laughed. "Yeah, never thought I'd be a businessman." He glanced over at Luke. "You sleeping over there?"

"Nope."

"Meditating? Ruminating? Contemplating?" He addressed the camera again. "See, Lucas talks soft and like a redneck, but he's actually real smart and likes to think things over before taking action. Now, me, well..." He trailed off, making a hard turn that had Luke bracing his shoulder against the door. "Now, me," Cort continued, "I like to act before I think. Keeps life interesting." He socked Luke in the arm. "And makes us a real good team."

He pulled into the alley by the bar, and Luke noted the two unmarked white vans parked at the curb in front. Their camera crew, most likely. He slouched farther down in the seat while Cort straightened, pulling the key from the ignition.

"Definitely a good team," Cort continued, "but I'm still not real clear why he's so popular with the ladies."

Laughing, he angled out of the car just as Luke socked him in the shoulder.

INSIDE ONE OF the vans, Victoria and Teresa sat side by side and laughed while watching the live feed of Cort's dialogue with the camera.

"I really need to have him stop talking to the cameras," Victoria said, even as she chuckled over his last comment about Luke. She checked the time and made a note on her clipboard, then handed it to Elmore, her tech. He sat at the bank of machinery that served as their on-location production facility, drinking his fourth or fifth cup of Peet's that morning.

"Maybe we can use Cort's chatter in place of his confessionals." Victoria reached for the handle to the back door. "One thing's for sure, he's so garrulous, we won't have to Frankenbite him." This was the common practice of editing sound bites for maximum dramatic effect, sometimes completely changing the context of the original quotes.

Cort Landry addressing the cameras directly was hardly a problem, and in fact could be a novelty of the show, even if it was unplanned. No, her big concern was getting Luke Tyler to open up. He had so much promise—walking around with his jeans half undone, kissing his cat in greeting—but she needed those small moments magnified. Whether he realized it or not, Luke Tyler was larger than life.

All of Cort's mischief aside, he was too predictable, too one note. And while Parker offered quirkiness and Marty had a certain easygoing charm, those qualities could not carry a show. *In Concert* needed Luke's "it" factor, and the show might be doomed if he stayed in his shell. She'd broken through somewhat yesterday at the equestrian center, but he retreated whenever faced with a camera.

Luke and Cort stood just outside the door, talking to Carl Zabinski, a fairly new kid on her crew. A little overzealous, but a hard worker, he kept tousling his own mop of hair and rubbing a hand over his tiny goatee as he showed them how to hook a mic pack to their jeans. Neither man flinched as Carl trotted back and forth performing this procedure, lifting shirts, looping wires around, telling them if they were women, it would attach to a bra, then re-settling shirts. Talking the entire time about a disastrous date he had the night before with a burly guy named Harold.

"The hair this guy had, coming out the top of his shirt," Carl said, as he pressed tape to Luke's chest. "I could've braided it, it was so thick." He paused as he tugged Luke's shirt down. "I'm still deciding if I liked it. Of course, he was bald, talk about the irony..."

Victoria smiled at Luke when he turned her way and gave her a slight shrug. They were in San Francisco, after all, and they were Southern country music singers, but Victoria was glad to know she wouldn't have to worry about homophobia with these two. There were many things Victoria would encourage for ratings, but prejudice wasn't one of them.

She slid from the van to the ground, struggling with the boot, and Luke stepped forward to take her arm. She thanked him and gave him an appreciative look, noting his already familiar appearance, the jeans, boots and hat he wore so well.

He tipped his hat, then walked away, keys in hand, to unlock the bar's front door.

"Wait," Victoria called, and hobbled after him.

He turned, gave her a quick once-over. "I like you better in a skirt," he said.

She didn't, and she'd spent the previous afternoon shopping for pants with wide enough legs to fit over her hideous appliance. "Are you critiquing my wardrobe, Mr. Tyler?"

"No, ma'am, just being myself." He quirked one side of his mouth up, and turned away again.

"Wait," she repeated, contemplating ways to increase Luke's comfort level. He faced her, looking like he might be losing his patience. *So soon, Mr. Tyler?* she thought. "We want to film you driving in, parking, chatting as you open up the bar."

"I don't chat much."

I noticed, she wanted to say. Instead, she waved a hand and said, "Semantics. The important thing is to use it as an establishing shot, as a way to show your viewers what you're like, your day-to-day lives. Driving here together, opening up the bar, setting things up inside..." She refrained from mentioning moments like *making breakfast for your best friend* and *greeting your cat*; the viewers would eat up those tender exchanges, but she could tell from Luke's reaction when he spotted the camera that morning that reminding him it was installed in his home would not serve her current purpose. "Please?" she added, gesturing behind at her two cameramen and a boom operator who waited with the others.

He nodded. "Might be hard to tear Cort from your friend."

She turned as Luke strolled away from her. "Damn."

Teresa leaned back against the van while Cort stood with his head bent close to hers, clearly having taken lessons from Luke on misunderstanding the definition of personal space. Was it a Southern thing, or just confidence? Again, great on camera, not so much in real life.

She would have marched over if her boot had allowed it, but she did the best she could, thudding it against the pavement. She chose to forget the rules of personal space, too, and stepped neatly between Teresa and Cort, lifting her face up to the latter.

"Good morning, Mr. Landry," she said in a loud, clear voice. "I see you've got your mic and you're ready to go. We'd love to film you and Luke driving back in and opening up the bar."

Cort looked from her to Teresa and back. "But we just got here," he said, "and me and Tessa were having a fine conversation—"

Luke stepped over and hooked an arm around Cort's shoulders. "All part of the game, son. Let's go."

Cort allowed himself to be dragged back to the truck, grinning and giving Teresa the "call me" gesture with thumb to ear and pinky to mouth.

Victoria raised an eyebrow. "Tessa?"

Teresa held up both hands and walked away from the van, adjusting her multicolored tank top. "His name, not mine."

"But you like it."

Teresa stopped with her hand on the back door handle. "Yeah. I do," she said, then climbed inside to monitor the camera shots with Elmore.

Victoria stood staring at the dark opening at the back of the van, hands on hips. She could see Teresa's profile in the glow of the monitors. Beautiful, graceful, talented Teresa, who had had her heart broken too often by bad choices and felt she didn't have her best friend's support recently.

Victoria glanced over her shoulder at Cort and Luke, who now stood talking with her director, Jamie; the cameramen and boom operator lounged nearby. Jamie said something and Cort threw back his head, laughing. He'd put on a white hat, and now clapped a hand to it to keep it in place. He wore unlaced work boots, faded blue jeans, a flannel shirt with the sleeves rolled up tight to his biceps over a t-shirt, and had a smile that drew you in and made you want to be friends with him.

His antithesis, Luke, wore black cowboy boots and button flies, a dark green t-shirt and black cowboy hat tilted just far enough down to shield his eyes from the world. His entire demeanor shouted, "stay away," which meant women would be drawn right to him. He leaned against the truck, arms and ankles crossed.

Luke tilted his head up enough to catch her eye and flashed a smile that showed very white teeth. He waved a finger toward the ground and then lifted it up until it pointed to her legs, hung there, hovered at her chest, then lingered at her face before he tucked his hand in his pocket.

She felt herself flush at this, not sure why, or even what he was suggesting. That smile flashed again before his head tilted back down and the hat hid his eyes once more.

She looked around, feeling suddenly restless, and saw Teresa sitting with her long, brown legs hanging out the back of the van, watching. She swung her feet in small circles, clicking the heels of her sandals against the bottom of her feet.

In a mild tone, Teresa said, "We're in some trouble, aren't we?"

Victoria's throat tightened for a moment and she swallowed hard, then shook her head. "I don't know what you mean," she said, and walked as briskly as she could over to the cameramen to communicate some last-minute instruction.

After that, she went inside Blitz for a final review. It was small, pretty much one long room, with the bar running the length of it on one side, square tables on the other, restrooms in the back and television sets everywhere. Ray had said they'd need both the mic packs and his overhead boom to capture conversation over the noise of the televisions, but maybe she could convince the boys to turn them down a bit and have Elmore test the sound level and quality in the van.

She gave him a quick buzz on the walkie-talkie to have him check in with her if the audio was bad, then oversaw the filming of Luke and Cort's visit with their accountant. After that, she eased onto a stool next to a patron who called himself Lord Winston. Teresa had told her earlier he signed the release, but then demanded free drinks, since he was going to be starring in their show.

"I appreciate your cooperation with our production's interference in your day, Lord Winston, but Blitz' owners are the current stars of the show." Even though it was barely eleven in the morning and the offer made her queasy, she added, "Can I buy you a drink?"

He gave her a once-over and nodded, slamming down his current rum and coke and gesturing to Luke for another. She held up a hand for him to wait. "We'll start filming on that, okay?" she said to him, then turned to the rest of her crew. "Okay, gang, let's roll."

She edged out of the way and let her crew take over, Jamie capably setting up shots, keeping the production running smoothly, while Victoria logged each take and took notes about possible storylines for the bar. She'd filled about eleven handwritten pages when Cort's voice broke into her thoughts.

Cort had been addressing the camera throughout the morning, but now he was asking Ray about the merits of blondes versus brunettes versus twins. Jamie gave her a look and she slid a hand across her throat. Breaking the fourth wall by addressing the viewers could be charming. Engaging the crew broke one too many barriers.

"Cut!" Jamie called.

Everyone relaxed into a form of parade rest, and Victoria

clumped over to the bar, wishing for the hundredth time that she could charge, march, even just *walk* normally. "Mr. Landry," she said, leaning over the bar.

"Yes, ma'am," Cort replied with a smile, matching her pose, his face close to hers.

She gestured behind her to Ray, Sam with his camera, and the rest of the crew. "They're invisible."

He looked at her like she'd just suggested he put on a dress and dance on the bar. "Not so's I can see."

Luke, walking behind him, swatted at the brim of Cort's hat. "It's a suggestion, Cortland," he said, filling a glass with beer from the tap. "Pretend they're not there."

Cort shook his head. "I'm not sure I can do that." He gestured around. "They're all over the place, real close, with that microphone over my head all the time."

Victoria turned and signaled for Ray to go outside. "That's fine," she said to Cort, once the sound tech had gone. "Better?"

"They don't need to leave. I'm just not sure I can ignore them."

Luke sighed as he passed behind Cort again and set a drink in front of a patron.

Victoria glanced at her watch and saw it was almost two. No wonder her head was aching and the rest of the crew looked mutinous. "Why don't we break for lunch, and give it another try after that." She patted Cort's arm and said, "Just do your best."

"Yes, ma'am."

She sent Simon off to take food orders, then grabbed a folding chair and settled into it in the shade of the building, running through possible scenarios to fix the situation with Cort. She'd have to dig out another chair in a minute to prop up her foot. Her ankle throbbed in time with her heart and would need icing at whatever time she got home tonight. If Teresa hadn't already left for the culinary center, Victoria would text her and request some aspirin and cold water. She wasn't sure she had the energy to trudge to the van to root through her purse for her big bottle of acetaminophen and dig out a water from their stash. They'd agreed on Teresa coming back part time, but Victoria missed her already and wasn't sure how well this arrangement would work.

Something rattled and clinked nearby. She opened her eyes to see Luke Tyler standing over her with a glass of sparkling water with ice, lime, and a maraschino cherry. He'd set one of the bar's padded chairs in front of her and waved the glass so the ice tinkled invitingly. At some point that morning, he'd rolled up the sleeves of his tee-shirt.

"It's warmed up," he said.

She took the glass with a nod. "Thank you." The water soothed her throat, but something still nagged at her. "Why do you own a bar?" she asked, before she could stop herself. She knew it was too soon to get into why the son of a notorious alcoholic could serve booze to people on a regular basis, but she felt if she had an answer, she might understand him better.

"Cort owns it." He pulled a small tin from his pocket and held it out to her. "Tylenol," he said, and shrugged when she looked up at him. "I get a headache now and then."

She could imagine he did, with a friend like Cort and a father like Buzz. She took two Tylenol with more thanks, and downed them, then looked at him again, waiting.

He let out a long sigh and said, "You mean why's a boy with a drunken daddy want to be an enabler?" He gestured to the chair he'd brought out. "Put your foot up."

When she left her foot where it was, he sighed again, pushed away from the building and knelt in front of her. He held his hands out, then paused. "You're not going to kick me again, are you?"

She shook her head, gripping the edge of the chair tightly with one hand, like she had that night at Tony's Tavern after she'd fallen.

Luke cupped one hand under the ankle of her appliance and the other under her calf, and eased her leg onto the chair seat. Then he patted her knee and stood. "Much better," he said.

"Better than what?" she asked, pulling her mind back from that night with some effort. She'd taken her business card from her bra and slipped it down his shirt. He'd ripped away the torn material of her pants, and rolled up the rest, his callused fingers brushing against the bare skin of her thigh. She shivered at the memory, taking a long sip of water to cover it. The bubbles tickled.

"Better than falling on my keester," Luke said, and she couldn't help laughing.

"I'm sorry about that," she said. "Reflex."

"Reflex isn't a bad thing."

She tilted her head back to look at him; he'd taken his usual stance, leaning against the building, arms and ankles crossed, hat low.

Because of her chair's angle, however, she could see his eyes. They watched her. She looked back, unable to blink. Kristen was right: looking at Luke Tyler, you wanted to touch him, to compare your pale skin to his, to run your fingers through those thick curls that peeked out beneath the brim of his hat.

She blinked. Of course, *she* didn't want to do those things. But she could understand the appeal.

"In some ways, it's just a job," he said, finally answering her question. "They're not all alcoholics, and if they are, well…they'd get the booze one way or another. This way, at least I can get them a cab, keep 'em off the streets. Otherwise…" He shifted, appearing to consider his answer. "I never thought about it much, but I guess it makes me feel I got some control over it. The booze. It's all there in front of me, just waiting, but if I don't fall for its seduction, then I won't ever be like him."

She nodded. It made a certain type of sense. "Thank you for sharing that with me."

"You like what you do," Luke said instead of responding to her, and it wasn't a question.

"Yes," she agreed. "More than anything."

He nodded, propped one booted sole against the building, and looked out at the street.

"And you? With your music?" she asked, watching the pedestrians who passed by, some gawking, some accepting the presence of vans, cameras and sound equipment as perfectly normal on the streets of San Francisco.

He nodded again. "But not more than anything."

"No?" She couldn't imagine liking anything more than her job. So many people hated theirs; didn't that make her incredibly lucky? Surprised again, she asked, "Like what?"

Out came that enigmatic smile and he lowered his foot to the ground and uncrossed his arms. Exaggerating his accent, he said, "I don't rightly know if I'm acquainted with you well enough for that, Ms. Clausen." He pressed a hand to her shoulder and bent down to whisper in her ear, "Ask me again later," before turning on his heel and heading into the bar.

She downed the rest of her water and pressed the glass to her forehead.

CHAPTER SIXTEEN

When Luke got home Thursday afternoon, he set his keys and jacket on hooks, greeted Frog, and collapsed on the couch with his feet up and his hat over his eyes. From her perch on the back, Frog patted at his shoulder and he reached up with one hand to scratch under her chin.

They were set to practice in a couple hours, filmed, but he wasn't sure he could tolerate more cameras. And it had only been a few days.

Actually, if he were honest with himself, the filming hadn't been all that bad. He'd gone about his business as usual and pretty much ignored the cameras. If he kept his head down, the filming probably wouldn't be difficult. No, his dilemma was Victoria Clausen, or rather, her proximity, and how he wanted to touch her whenever he got within thirty feet of her.

It baffled him, since he leaned toward a softer, quieter woman, one who might remind him of a sweet Southern belle, magnolia-dripping accent not required. Victoria Clausen burned bright with confidence, her direct manner leaning real close to brash.

The women like that who threw themselves at the band after a show left him cold, and when he turned them down, they'd just shrug and turn to Cort or Parker. Marty had found his love, a sweet, quiet girl herself, and Luke envied him for it.

He sometimes wondered why he hadn't found something similar, or even a relationship lasting more than ten months. After leaving Georgia, he and Cort hadn't stayed in one place long enough for anything long-term, but since they'd settled here, nothing had stuck. There'd been a few one night stands he couldn't say he was proud of, a couple double dates Cort arranged—then Sandy showed up at Tony's Tavern. A leggy blonde, she'd started out sweet, luring him in with her big brown eyes and pouty lips, but she hadn't liked the attention other women gave him at their shows. Never mind he hadn't acted on any proposition, but she got more and more catty. One night, after picking yet another fight with him, she'd demanded they only book shows she could attend. He called her unreasonable and insecure, and she tore his place apart, throwing everything at him that wasn't nailed down. He was too busy ducking plates and mugs to get close enough to stop her.

Her well-aimed throws and screeching brought Cort on the run. He grabbed her from behind and carried her from the apartment over his shoulder, somehow getting her to her flat, where she'd hit on him and he'd refused. After putting a lot of space between them.

Besides breaking some of his dishes, Sandy also broke his heart. He found out later she'd approached more guys than Cort in the time they'd been together. Luke swore off women after that, which lasted all of a few weeks when he slept with doe-eyed Natalie, who immediately got clingy. Then curvy Summer, and a couple other girls whose names he'd never gotten. He didn't swear off women, then. He just plain gave up and stayed away. He did the math now, and realized that had been over a year ago.

So maybe his desire for Victoria Clausen was simple lust. She was a beautiful woman in his vicinity on a regular basis, and far too much time had passed since his last amorous encounter. Relieved at that reasoning, he nodded. That must be it. And if that was the problem, it was easily remedied.

He stood up. And remembered the camera in the corner. Maybe he should clean out the cat box or something. That would give them some real good footage.

Instead, he paced back and forth behind the couch, Frog's big green eyes following him a reminder of how Victoria watched him, her gaze unreadable as the cat's. How her shoulder had felt under his hand today, the weight of her leg in that boot, the silky skin of her thigh the night she fell.

He tossed his hat on the couch and ran his hands through his hair as he headed for the phone and his little black book. He needed a woman. He flipped rapidly through the pages, his heart pounding, until he got to the I's. Mmm. Isabelle. Slinky, flexible, no shame. Perfect. He picked up his new cordless phone and began to dial. Caught sight of the camera.

Hung up.

Swore loudly.

And stamped to the bathroom with the phone in his hand, turning on the shower before he dialed again.

Victoria hit END on the phone and put her head on her knees. Jamie's wife had been admitted to the hospital for an emergency appendectomy, and he didn't know when he would be available again. Sam, her main cameraman, had also canceled because of a daughter with stomach flu and a wife working late. Postponing tonight's shoot wasn't an option for Victoria. She had a tight deadline for the pilot and two of her best editors scheduled to start coordinating footage on Monday.

She straightened, blew out a breath, and scrolled through numbers on her Blackberry. Teresa had a date, so Victoria scanned her list of alternate directors, assistant directors, production assistants, and finally interns. Thursday night in the city and no one was available, except Carl, her new production assistant, and Tim, one of her rookie sound guys. As always, Elmore would be in the mobile production van. But still no director or qualified cameraman.

She'd started out making her calls on the couch, but ended up stamping up and down the living room carpet, cursing her boot and her co-workers in turn. She could *not* call off tonight's filming. "I'll just have to do it myself," she muttered, after the fifteenth call.

Kristen, on the floor in some indescribably improbable pose, asked, "Do what?"

Distracted, Victoria said, "My director and main camera guy canceled, I have a shoot tonight, and everyone else seems to have more important things to do."

"I can help."

Victoria stopped pacing and stared at her. Before she could reply, Kristen added, "Sure. I can schlep supplies, drive you wherever, get you a cappuccino, herd people as needed, lead them through a meditation to help them focus…"

Victoria held up a hand to stop her. "Can you use a video camera?"

"Not one of your big professional ones, but I can use a regular people one."

Victoria chewed on her lower lip. "I'll probably regret this..."

Kristen popped up from the floor. "Great! Where are we going?"

"The Barn," Victoria said, mentally reviewing all of the equipment she would need, and how best to replace Jamie without detracting from her regular duties.

"The Barn?"

Victoria opened a cabinet under the television set and pulled out a box of video equipment. "You'll have to follow my direction. No arguing."

"Arguing isn't conducive to my wellbeing," Kristen said, hanging over Victoria's shoulder. "What's the Barn?"

Victoria looked up from the box and took in Kristen's skintight black pants with the wide bottoms and purple halter top. "The Barn is where Tyler Landry has a rehearsal space and where Luke and Cort live." She pulled out an extra camera battery and memory disks and set them on the shelves. "You'll need to put on a bra."

Kristen looked down at herself. "I don't really need one."

Victoria straightened. "You know we both burst out of our tops without one. And what did I just say?"

"You're so easy." Kristen grinned at her and headed for the suitcase she'd stashed in a corner. "Don't worry, I won't go into the lion's den without proper protection."

Victoria shook her head and continued gathering supplies. After changing her outfit to a more sedate combination of a teal peasant dress and sandals, Kristen hauled everything to the car, and drove them to the Barn, parking in the small back lot.

Kristen looked up at the brick building and the old sign, "DePaetri's Garage," faded but intact, hanging between the bay doors. "Why do they call it the Barn?"

Victoria shook her head, still distracted by all of the details of the evening's shoot. "Some Southern thing. There's an area inside with decrepit easy chairs they call the Lounge." She picked up her bag and set it on her lap. "Carl should be here soon with the rest of the equipment and Tim will help do sound. I wanted to use the video camera to see if some rougher shots would work interspersed with the cleaner ones. I may need to hand it over to you at multiple points during the evening. Don't talk during the filming. Follow my instructions. And no flirting. Clear?" She opened her door and started the slow process of maneuvering out with the boot. "Don't forget those binders. I need to log the footage as we go. Oh, and I need you to sign a non-disclosure agreement before we start."

Victoria slung her bag over her shoulder and hobbled toward the red door. It opened before she reached it and Luke stood silhouetted in the opening. She recognized the broad shoulders, and hands-on-hips, wide-legged stance. If he'd been leaning against the doorway, both arms and ankles would be crossed. She smiled at the image.

"You look mighty cheerful, Ms. Clausen."

"I am, Mr. Tyler. Things have gone well this week, don't you think?"

"Hard to say, considering this is my first time."

He stepped aside for her to go in, but she stood where she was, waiting for Kristen. She wanted to introduce her sister to him first, well before the other band members caught sight of the Viking goddess she'd brought. She hoped he'd help her keep the boys at bay. Or, looking up into those perpetually shaded eyes, and considering Kristen's forthright manner, Victoria wondered if she might be setting up a situation best left alone.

"Wow," said Kristen, bounding up with her arms full. "You look like a real cowboy."

Best left alone, Victoria thought with an inward sigh. To save Luke struggling for a response, she said, "She may not look it, but this is my real sister, Kristen. Kristen, this is Luke Tyler."

"Sister?" Luke held out his hand for Kristen to shake, then took a few items from her grasp.

"Sister?" said a voice behind Luke.

Kristen eased right around Luke, and inside. "That's me. Hello!"

Luke and Victoria considered each other a moment. She didn't know what he might be thinking, but considered a few possible explanations before settling on, "Kristen is helping me tonight."

He took the hint that she'd decided to be businesslike and said, "I'm sure she'll do a real fine job," and ushered Victoria inside.

After prying Kristen away from Cort and Parker, and giving her some very detailed tasks, Victoria said, "All right, boys, tonight we'd like to film you rehearsing. Please be yourselves, as usual."

Victoria had Kristen watch the monitors for poor lighting or other issues, while Carl filmed with a shoulder camera and she recorded with her personal one. She wouldn't get much movement in due to her stupid boot, and she'd have to hand the camera over to Kristen eventually, but she'd capture as much as she could before she wore out.

She and Carl filmed the boys settling into place, and adjusting knobs and levels on their amplifiers. Accustomed to having a lot of equipment around, Victoria appreciated that the bass, keyboards and guitar all got their own amps. While they consulted with each other, Victoria hobbled to one of her many binders, flipping it open to add a note to ask each of them about their practice prep. Pulling anyone aside for on-the-fly interviews was out for tonight; she'd have to schedule formal interviews later due to time constraints. Then she settled back into place and focused on Luke, guitar hanging by a strap over his shoulder, standing in the middle with Cort just to his right.

Luke said over his shoulder, "Let's work on 'Wilderness.'" He lifted his chin at Parker, who stood behind the keyboard. "And add in that melody we talked about, right after the chorus."

Marty counted them in with taps of his drumsticks, and the song started with a slow drumbeat, then a bass line that matched it, before Luke and Parker joined on guitar and keyboard. Watching Luke tilt his hips back before leaning into the microphone, his entire body moving to the song's rhythm, Victoria marveled at how he came alive during a performance. She couldn't wait to film them at Tony's Tavern; the combination of the band's energy with the crowd's would create the magic she lived for.

She didn't want Kristen's crazy ideas to take hold in her mind, but certain things her sister said earlier in the week kept running through her head: *frigid...it's like dating a co-worker... need to set some boundaries*. Just because Victoria found a man attractive didn't give her the green light to ask him out. And Luke Tyler might be very attractive with a beautiful singing voice, but he was also brooding and cryptic. Really not her type. She would happily watch him seduce his pretend audience, dressed in black, hat low on his forehead, easing toward the microphone as if it were a reluctant woman, practically kissing it as he sang. And she would enjoy it, would film it, but that was all. She had other things to focus on, like completing the pilot, and coffee with Brett Soloway in four days. *He* was her type, not this reluctant star. She pondered scenarios for her date with Brett, letting her mind drift as she filmed.

Then Luke Tyler turned away from the ghost audience and switched his seduction to her, and it was as if someone had turned up the heat in the room. His gaze moved from out in the distance to focus on her face alone, his eyes dark on hers, one booted foot in front of the other and his upper body curved as if he'd stride forward and envelop her completely. She took an involuntary step back, stumbling and breaking the spell. He did take a step then, but she righted herself and kept filming.

Had he noticed her stumble, and wanted to help? Or was she reading too much into his motion? He was one of the more solicitous men she'd ever met, and she wondered if he behaved that way with all women, or just her. She had some thoughts along those lines, ways she might test out her theories. On camera, of course. She gave him a little smile and he inclined his head in response. She wasn't sure what the nod meant, but a shiver traveled from the base of her spine to her neck as he continued to watch her and sing.

In the wilderness
You pulled me free
Found me lost
Found me home...

The lyrics sounded like Parker's, but the song belonged to Luke; throaty, lonely, intense.

Holding the camera steady with one hand, she brushed a palm across her forehead with the other, then pushed a lock of hair behind her ear to break eye contact with Luke. She panned to the right to include Parker at the keyboards, then to the left to add Marty and Cort to the shot, but found herself centering on Luke. He closed his eyes and tossed his head back just before lowering it to the microphone to throw himself into the song's chorus.

Victoria zoomed out for a wide shot. The song ended on a long, mournful note; gripping the mic stand, Luke dropped his head, and Victoria let out the breath she'd been holding. She pulled the camera from her eye and watched through the LCD screen instead of the viewfinder as Luke straightened and Cort clapped him on the back. Luke looked dazed, not focusing on any one or thing for the moment, and Victoria got that spine tingle that meant she'd captured something the audience would love.

They were going to eat up Luke Tyler with a spoon.

She zoomed back in on him, his hat shadowing his eyes, shoulders slumped, not in resignation, but in satisfaction and relief. He looked like a man who'd just had great sex. He glanced in her direction, a small smile playing around his lips, and he nodded. Then his gaze cleared, and she felt like the one being filmed as he watched her, that smile still in place.

Her heart beat hard, then returned to its normal rhythm, and she lowered the camera, a tremor running through her fingers.

CHAPTER SEVENTEEN

After "Wilderness," they played for another hour before Luke finally stopped trying to use images of Isabelle to block thoughts of Victoria and decided to perform for the camera. That opened him up, and the boys followed suit. Cort layered some chord voicings with his bass while Parker and Marty's harmonies at the end of the chorus added dimension the piece had been missing.

The songs flowed, everything clicking, and like any time he got lost in the music, he didn't want it to end. But he had a woman waiting on him, and there wouldn't be any cameras at her place. So he declared "State of Mind" to be the last song of the night, and as Luke had known he would, Cort bitched about the title.

"Man, I hate that name," he said, lifting up his hat and rubbing his forehead against the sleeve of his t-shirt.

"It's fitting for the theme," Parker told him.

"Theme fleam," Cort said, replacing his hat. He turned to the girl Victoria had introduced as her sister, a fact Luke couldn't quite wrap his head around. "What d'you think, Sunshine?"

Luke saw Victoria signal for her cameraman to film the sister, while she kept her little portable on Cort. He supposed Victoria had found a way to make Cort's talking to the camera work for her.

The sister, Kristen, dimpled at Cort from her perch on one of the stools near the Lounge. She had wild hair, bright blue eyes and the longest legs he thought he'd ever seen. "It's a great title," she said, "but I haven't heard the song yet, and that might...change my state of mind."

Cort laughed, and Luke found himself smiling even as he watched Victoria for her response. She'd lowered the camera from her face, and while it still pointed at Cort, her eyes were turned to Luke. Next to her sister, he could now see the similarities, like the slightly upturned nose, big round eyes, and curly hair. Only Victoria Clausen didn't let hers free, and Luke wondered what might happen if she did. She and her sister shared similar full lips, too, the same size top and bottom, with a little dip in the middle of the top one. She wore an expression that said she was accustomed to her sister's quirkiness, but paired it with a smile. Luke wanted to jump off the stage and take a taste of that smile.

Cort continued, "State of mind just sounds..."

"Cliché?" Marty asked, tapping a cymbal for emphasis. He turned his ball cap backwards, glanced at the cameras, then cut his eyes away.

"Yeah." Cort waved a hand in Marty's direction. "Like that."

"But it's about a man's state of mind," Parker said.

"It's actually about hope," Luke said, forcing himself to stop staring.

"And hope can be a state of mind," Parker replied.

"Yeah, well..." Cort grumbled, but his expression changed in the next instant and he pointed at Kristen. "You listen real good, Sunshine. Let us know what you think."

She gave him a thumbs up, and Luke launched into the intro before any more discussion could take place. He didn't feel as loose as he had earlier because watching Victoria had tightened up his gut; he might've sounded natural to an outsider, but the tension in his vocal chords held him back.

At the end of the song, he stepped away from the microphone, keeping his guitar close, ready to clear the place so he could get the hell out of here without arousing suspicion. He knew if he gave any suggestion of a date, the boys would jump on it and Victoria would be chasing after him with a camera, boot and all.

Parker turned off his keyboard and reached for its cover. "An inspiring set," he said. "But I'm away. I must needs present myself to the world of booklovers tomorrow."

"Yeah." Marty shook his head. "If that means he has to work, me too."

Pulling his cell phone from his front pocket, Cort said, "I must needs present myself to the world of lovers." He glanced at Kristen. "Unless you need some company tonight, Sunshine?"

Luke turned from lifting his guitar strap over his shoulder, let it fall back into place. "Don't mess with the sister," he said.

Kristen laughed. "I don't mess with other women's men, but thanks for the offer."

Cort stepped closer to Kristen, hand to his heart. "I like to think of myself as a free agent," he began.

Victoria lowered her camera. "Cort, do you remember our discussion earlier?"

"Now, we've had quite a few, Miss Victoria, but I don't remember one about not flirting with your sister."

Luke saw Victoria's lips press into a thin line, and he brushed a hand over his face to cover a grin.

"My sister can take care of herself," Victoria said. "But right now, she's working for me, so she's part of the crew. The stars are not supposed to interact with the crew."

"Ever, or just when the cameras are rolling?"

"Ever." Victoria turned to Carl and Ray, the sound tech. "All right. We're done here."

Luke glanced around, eyeing the camera Victoria still held. How could he get everyone to clear out fast without her getting suspicious?

Victoria was still giving directions. He'd wait for her to finish, then say goodnight. "Go ahead and get everything to the van for the next location," she told the guys. "Kristen, would you help them with whatever they need, please?" She turned to the table where she'd set her binders while the crew lugged equipment outside.

Cort got on his phone and paced around the far corner of the Barn. Marty and Parker headed out together, waving goodnight to everyone. Luke gave them a distracted wave back and moved closer Victoria. "You filming another one of your shows tonight?"

She straightened up, pushing a loose lock of hair behind one ear. "No, not another show." She smiled at him. "This show. We'll be filming your date."

He felt a jolt through his gut. "My what?"

"Your date." She flipped through a few pages of the binder she held. "With the lovely Isabelle Cadwell." She closed the binder and pointed to his guitar. "You look like you've lived with that a long time."

"Since I was nine." Feeling like he was about to breathe fire, he lifted the strap over his shoulder and set the guitar in its case, snapping the locks shut with loud clacks. The distraction didn't work. He stomped over to her. "What do you mean, you're filming my date? How the hell do you know about my date?"

"You called her this afternoon."

"How do you know that?"

She tilted her head, looking confused. "The cameras."

"They could hear me?"

"Oh, yes." She pulled a notebook out of her bag and flipped a few pages. "We're going to have to put some bleeps in when we air it, but the audience will get the general idea." Ray came back in and she pulled a page from the notebook and handed it to him. "Here's the address. Head on over when you've got everything together and I'll meet you there. Kristen," she called over her shoulder, "would you please put the handheld into the van? I want to make sure it gets back to the station."

"Sure," she said, and loped outside on those long legs.

Luke stared at Victoria. Somewhere in the background he heard Cort call goodnight to everyone, but he barely responded. He couldn't believe she'd heard him dirty-talking Isabelle and planned to film their hookup like it was no never mind. "Call them off," he said.

She looked up from her notebook. "I beg your pardon?"

"Call them off. There's no date."

"It sounded pretty definite to me."

"And it felt pretty private to me."

Victoria closed the notebook with a thump and tossed it on the table next to her. "You have no privacy, Mr. Tyler. It's in your contract. I realize you've been reluctant to do this from the start, and I've tried to be patient, but it's wearing thin." She put her hands on her hips. "You're on a reality show about your life, and the lives of your band mates. The audience won't just want to see you practicing and playing at Tony's Tavern. They'll want to know what you eat for breakfast, what you wear, who you date, and everything in between. You've agreed to be filmed during all of these occasions, and you're just going to have to suck it up and let it happen."

Luke pointed in the direction of the door and the van outside. "You ever have that thing turned on you? You know what it's like?"

"I would imagine it's intrusive at first, and fine eventually." She reached for her bag and added, "Now, can we continue to the next segment?"

"That segment's been canceled," he said and turned for the stairs.

"Where are you going?" she called after him.

"To cancel my date."

"You can't do that." She sounded irritated, and a touch anxious.

He turned at the base of the stairs. "You need to film it before you'll believe it's true?"

Her lips compressed and she dropped her bag on the table next to the notebook. She hobbled closer with a pained expression on her face; it took some of the fire out of him. He'd rather she could charge right over and at least keep the disagreement equal; he could tell she liked to pace, to move when she was thinking. Or angry. He liked that about her. He liked too much about her. Except for her damn cameras.

Before she could say anything, he said, "Would those cameras follow you if *you* were my date?"

She stopped in front of him, her head jerking back. "What? Why?"

"Because whenever I'm around you, all I can think of doing is throwing you over my shoulder, carrying you upstairs, pushing you against a wall, and screwing you senseless," he said.

Her big eyes got bigger and he could see she'd lost her composure, but his speech had just made its way to his body, and his body took over. He stepped forward, took her face in his hands, tilted it up, and kissed her.

She held herself rigid at first, her mouth hard, but he ran his tongue along the seam and she gasped, her lips opening and softening under his. He pushed his hands into her hair, dislodging the clip and feeling the thick strands surrounding him, brushing against his skin, and he slipped his arms around her and pulled her up tight. Grabbing his belt loops, she moaned, and he darted his tongue in, brushing it against hers, tasting her, wanting more.

She pressed closer, her breasts crushed against his chest and he slid down, imagining her naked body sliding across his, kissing a path down his chest, her hair caressing his hips, her hands touching, grabbing, stroking. He groaned, kissing her harder, and wrapped his arms tighter to lift her up, get her as close as possible, bring her upstairs and—

"Victoria, we're ready to—whoopsy," said the sister from the doorway.

Victoria pulled away from him with a sharp inhalation, pushing her hands against his chest until he lowered her to the floor.

"What are you doing?"

"I reckon I'm kissing you."

"Well, that's obvious." She brushed her hair back from her face and wouldn't meet his gaze. "What I'd like to know is what you're about. I mean...you...you're..."

"I'm about frustrated to high heaven being attracted to you and not touching you, so I thought I'd see what that might be like."

"Oh." She stared at him, face flushed a pretty pink.

"And on my side, it was pretty damn nice. For both of us." He leaned close. "Would you disagree?"

Her eyes narrowed, and her fierce expression, meant to push him away, only made him want to haul her up against him again. She pointed a finger. "You're very attractive. I'm not attracted to you." She stopped, blew out a breath; he saw that her chest still rose and fell rapidly and her words came out in small rushes. "You could get me fired. I won't have that." She turned and hobbled away, telling Kristen to grab her things, they were going, and she went straight out the door, closing it behind her with a bang.

Kristen gave him an apologetic look as she gathered the big bag, notebook and binders and held them in her arms. "She's not really frigid, you know," she said, then turned and trotted out.

Luke bent and picked up the hair clip that had been dislodged during their kiss, running his fingers over its smooth surface, the way he wanted to do to Victoria's body. He shook his head. Her passion had never been in question.

CHAPTER EIGHTEEN

Heart pounding, Victoria stamped outside just in time to see the van moving away with Carl, Tim, Elmore and the footage of her kiss inside it. Her throat tightened up and she let out a gasping breath. "No," she wheezed out. "No, no, no, no, no."

Bright light spilled out from the doorway behind her, showing a shadow of herself, hands to mouth, one slim foot, one Frankenstein one. She wanted to curse everything. Why was Luke Tyler doing this to her?

"Well, that's an interesting development," said Kristen behind her, as the door closed and Victoria's shadow disappeared.

"Not now, Kristen." Victoria stomped to her Honda. "We need to get to Isabelle Cadwell's place in mid-Market. Now."

"Oh," Kristen said, setting everything into the back seat. "Are we still filming a date?" She got into the front and started the car once Victoria had put on her seatbelt. "Because back there it kind of looked like—"

"Not *now*," Victoria barked, and only spoke after that to give Kristen directions to Isabelle's. Normally, if a shoot were called off, Carl returned the van to the studio, but she couldn't risk that footage being seen and knew her skeleton crew would be too busy setting up equipment to review footage from cameras inside the Barn.

She gripped her seatbelt in both hands and tapped her foot against the floor as Kristen caught red light after red light on the way to Isabelle's. Her heart continued to beat hard and fast, and Luke Tyler's voice kept running through her head, no matter how much she tried to push it away: *Whenever I'm around you, all I can think about is pushing you against a wall, and screwing you senseless... I reckon I'm kissing you...I'm attracted to you...*

He'd said more, but that had been the gist. He was attracted to her, and he'd wanted to touch her, so he did. More than that, he'd kissed her, crushed her up against his chest, tasted her like she'd been dessert. And she'd tasted him back. And if she licked her lips right now, the lingering hint of warm, salty male skin would invade her senses, the way Luke Tyler had just done with his entire being.

It had been rough, and unsettling, and...She bit her lower lip, hard, tasting him. And *nothing*.

"Nothing," she announced out loud.

"What?"

"*Nothing,*" Victoria repeated.

"Right," Kristen said, double parking by the van. "Well, we're here."

Victoria fumbled her way out, greeted the guys who stood in front of a Pakistani restaurant, drinking steaming cups of coffee, said she needed to check on something and went into the back, locking the door behind her. Holding her breath, she deleted the last twenty minutes of the footage, letting out a sigh of relief after she saw the band just finishing their song on the monitor before it cut off.

"Thank you," she breathed. "Thank you, thank you, and it won't happen again."

She told the crew they could go home, since the event they were going to film had been canceled, and thumped upstairs to give Isabelle Cadwell the bad news.

Victoria knew Luke had already done so when Isabelle answered the door clutching a pink cell phone, dressed in a purple wraparound top, what looked like a white bandeau barely covering her hips and a pucker between her brows. Instead of looking at Victoria, her eyes flashed up and down the street, her long blonde hair swaying across her face as she moved.

"So no cameras at all?"

"Not this time," Victoria told her, although she had a feeling if it was up to Luke, the next time could be months away, if ever. "Luke called you?"

Isabelle finally focused on Victoria, her gaze lingering on the boot, before shifting to a point somewhere around Victoria's left ear. "He doesn't want the cameras to intrude on my life. Such a *gentleman*." She rolled her eyes. "He's hot, but that Southern gallantry shit could kill you. Do I look like I care about cameras?"

Victoria thought she looked very much like she cared about cameras, but didn't say so. "I'm sorry it didn't work out. We'll be filming some of their shows at Tony's Tavern. Cameras everywhere, and you've already signed the release." She edged back a step, as if about to leave. "So I'll have my assistant text you the show times?"

Isabelle straightened, shifting a shoulder so her hair slithered expertly behind her back, then forward again, to artfully drape over one eye. "Can I get a front table? All to myself?"

"You bet." Victoria dug out a card and handed it to her. "I produce the show. I'll see to it myself."

OVER THE NEXT few days, Victoria avoided direct contact with Luke. Most of the time, she sat in the production van with her taciturn tech Elmore and his endless cups of Peet's coffee, watching hours of live feed from the stationary cameras: of the boys practicing, at their jobs, making breakfast, and going on dates.

Well, she wasn't sure if she could officially call what Cort did a date. He met a girl at Blitz on Saturday afternoon and took her home. Victoria left Elmore inside the van to keep track of the feeds while she got dinner and coffee for the rest of the crew, who waited outside in the foggy cold for Cort and the young woman to emerge. They claimed they didn't want to disrespect Cort's date by listening to her protracted moans and squeals. After hearing an especially long session herself, Victoria suspected her team might feel inadequate if faced with such a task themselves.

Marty and Miranda definitely had a date. Victoria convinced Marty to hold off on his marriage proposal and directed him to take his girl for a walk by a jewelry store and linger there, point out the rings, and see what Miranda would do. Victoria filmed this herself, standing as far back as she could to keep from interfering, but still capture the event. Marty was a bit wooden, and pink in the cheeks, but the animated expression on Miranda's sweet face balanced it. Victoria could use that as the final shot in a future episode to lure viewers to tune in next week.

Victoria also did her best to avoid Kristen, which could have been difficult, considering they lived together. But Victoria often worked until late into the night anyway, and Kristen kept busy with her job at the yoga studio and dating what seemed like every eligible straight man in the city.

But tonight Victoria wouldn't be working late because she was meeting Brett Soloway at Caffé Greco. She'd had to postpone the time until seven-thirty, since her appointment with the editors and loggers ran longer than she'd planned. They'd all bemoaned Luke's reticence and had to review a lot more footage than usual to find any good segments for him. Luke shone in those moments, and she often had to look away from glimpses of him kicking a booted foot up slightly when he walked, his version of a swagger, or bending low, almost to a crouch, when he performed an especially moving section of a song. Those distinctive, intense movements made her think of the kiss. The way he'd pulled her so close she'd been crushed up against him, then lifted her as if she'd weighed nothing, and held her tight to his chest.

Her nipples still tingled at the memory, and she had to take a few shaky breaths before she could banish them and type a text to Brett, saying she needed to push their meeting up. He responded immediately, which she took as a good sign, and now she sat in a cab heading down Broadway past bars, pizza places and a triple-X bookstore to the coffee shop. She caught sight of City Lights Books where Parker worked, and typed a quick reminder in her phone to film some exterior shots there for their B-roll. Through the driver's open window, garlic wafted its way from the Stinking Rose restaurant. Now just a few blocks from the café, she ran her hands over her hair, checking for anything out of place, and thought about letting it down, and whether Brett would like it that way.

She stopped that line of thinking fast. Luke seemed to like it down, not Brett. Brett had always seen her with her hair pulled back, so she was leaving it. She typed another reminder into her phone, this one to ask Luke for her hair clip, one of her favorites, with its amber-colored stones and gold filigree. At the café, she looked across the street and saw Brett outside, a cappuccino on the small round table in front of him. He wore a pair of glasses and frowned at some papers, probably the latest ratings, which she'd also gotten and frowned at earlier.

She waited for her stomach to give a clench like it usually did when she saw a man she had a crush on, but maybe she was too tired and overwhelmed, because nothing happened. She paid the cab driver and made her way to the table.

"Hey," Brett said, pulling out a chair when she reached him. After she was settled, he took off his glasses and waved the stack of papers at her. "Can you believe these? Jerry can't be right that things are going downhill, especially not dating shows like *Temptation Station*. It must be some outside factor we haven't yet taken into consideration. People aren't tired of reality TV yet. It's just getting rolling."

That lock of hair fell over his forehead, and when he leaned closer she smelled the distinctive cologne he used. Its fragrance had always been both sweet and strong to her, but now it smelled stale, like dried sage.

"Of course not," she agreed. "Jerry always panics when the numbers shift down. He leans on us, we make some changes, and everything's fine. It's the slow time of the season. Shows are debuting at different times of the year now instead of the fall, which used to be standard. Now a reality show can premiere almost any time, depending on the length of its season. My new show, *In Concert*, will be—"

"Good point." He riffled through the papers. "I'll have to work the numbers a bit more, compare apples to apples." He nodded as if to himself, running one long finger down a column of figures. "Plus, there really aren't that many dating competition shows out like mine."

"So what are you drinking?" she asked, thinking he forgot to offer her anything because he'd been so involved with the numbers. Really, how many times had she gotten lost in the ratings herself and forgotten meetings and phone calls?

She frowned. Never, actually.

"Oh," Brett said, glancing up at her. "A cappuccino." He waved at it. "Sorry. Did you want something?"

"Please. A ristretto."

He stared at her a moment.

She cleared her throat. "A short shot."

He smiled. "Of course. Let me get that for you." He stood and she watched him walk inside. He was tall, but thinner than she'd always thought, although maybe that was just the cut of his suit. She gritted her teeth, shoving away the thought of Luke Tyler's wide shoulders and strong arms holding her against his hot, hard chest while his tongue plunged into her mouth. She would *not* compare Brett Soloway to Luke Tyler. They were nothing alike. Brett was sophisticated, smart and understood her world. He knew the rules and followed them; Luke was rough, fractious, and had no respect for the rules. To just grab her and kiss her like that, to stroke his tongue against hers as if—

She jumped when Brett set a cup in front of her and she forced a smile and her thanks.

He pressed his palms flat on the ratings printout. His long fingers and trim nails looked like they had regular manicures. He also looked like he habitually used sunscreen and gave himself a close shave, not missing a day and growing a five o'clock shadow that could brush roughly against a woman's tender skin. She lifted a hand to her cheek, remembering the slight abrasions left there by Luke's stubble.

No, she wasn't thinking of Luke. She was thinking of Brett. He took care of himself and she respected that.

"I have some strategies on cross-promotion for our shows, especially *Temptation Station* and *Dress My Best* since they run back to back. But I'm especially pleased about my plans for *Man vs. Machine*."

She pulled her bag into her lap. "I have some thoughts, too." She'd stayed up until three in the morning, carefully compiling data, creating charts and graphs, and typing up a general summary before assembling it all in a binder. She reached into her bag for it as he continued.

"I see Burl as a guest star on *Dress My Best*," he said, referring to the hulk of a man who starred on *Man vs. Machine*. He spent every week trying to outdo a machine, from an olive picker to a tug boat.

Victoria's hand froze on the binder. "You want my people to give Burl a makeover?"

"I want them to give all my stars a makeover." Brett had three shows in production, two dating programs and *Man vs. Machine*.

Having Maurice and Francesca from *Dress My Best* give all of Brett's people makeovers was a very clever idea. Crossovers were hot right now and she hated that she hadn't thought of it herself.

His hand punctuating his words, Brett continued laying out his plans, and Victoria set her bag back down without removing the binder. If he could expound on his ideas without notes, then so could she. She normally did well with off-the-cuff ideas, but she'd been so nervous about making the best impression with Brett that she'd gotten binder-happy.

She had concerns about Burl being the first makeover. Much like his name, Burl was large, fond of plaid checks and shooting small animals, and wore shaggy hair and a long beard. His program had a very defined, very male demographic in the 18-25 set and *Dress My Best* drew slightly older female viewers. It would be a challenge, and there was nothing like conflict to make good reality TV, but she thought maybe someone from *Temptation Station*, which set its dating contestants on a train in various locales, would be a better fit, especially since her makeover show followed it on Tuesday nights.

When Brett paused in his discourse to take a sip of coffee, Victoria mentioned this, then explained her reasoning. "It might be a better match to start with."

Brett set his cup down very slowly. "You don't like the idea."

"No," she countered. "It's a great idea." She put a hand on his forearm, felt the bones under his suit sleeve. "It just seems to be a better fit to have your bachelor go first. Ratchet up the competition among his ladies when they see his new look."

Brett moved his arm from under Victoria's hand to take another sip of coffee. "Rob is already well-coiffed and dressed. He's an underwear model who also spent two years in the outback learning to wrestle crocs. His hotness quotient is remarkably high. I was thinking of the ladies themselves getting makeovers. Ratchet up the difficult decisions for Rob."

"You want all of them to get makeovers?" *Temptation Station* always started out with thirteen female contestants.

"That wouldn't be efficient," he said with a shake of the head. "The first ones eliminated aren't on long enough to build a viewer relationship. Not enough to bring a viewer from one show to the next. I was thinking of the last three contestants." He looked at her and pushed out his lower lip.

Was that a pout? How adorable, she thought, studying his bottom lip. It looked sort of thin and she wondered what it would be like to nibble on it. Shouldn't a lower lip be fuller for a good nibble? She glanced at the side of his head; there was always his earlobe.

"You don't like my idea," he repeated when she didn't respond right away.

"I do," she said. "I just wasn't sure about all of the contestants."

He smiled, his teeth very white and straight. "We'll go with Burl first then." He reached across the table and brushed her ponytail over her shoulder so it fell down her back. "You have really beautiful eyes, Victoria," he said, and the tips of his fingers brushed against her cheek as if wiping away a smudge of dirt.

"Oh," she said, surprised, trying to figure out how they'd gone from Burl getting the first makeover to the last three *Temptation Station* contestants and back to Burl again. "Thank you."

He took her hand in both of his and rubbed her fingers one by one; the motion felt vaguely familiar but she was too distracted by the touch of his cool, smooth hands to identify it.

"I have a lot more ideas," Brett said, staring into her eyes. He ran the tips of his fingers between hers up to the webbing, then pulled back, still rubbing. "Let me tell you them in bed."

With a start, she realized he was giving her a manicurist's massage, and it took a few seconds for his last comment to penetrate. "I— what?"

He leaned over, lowering his lids and pushing out his lower lip again. "I want you," he said. "Come home with me."

She'd waited to hear those words from him for a long time. And wasn't it much more civilized to seduce a woman this way than to threaten to throw her over his shoulder and screw her against the wall? A shiver went down her spine, and Brett noticed.

He smiled, his nostrils flaring. "My car's around the corner."

Victoria barely remembered gathering her things and hobbling to the car, with Brett walking half a step ahead. When he noticed the boot, he said, "Can you...manage with that?" and seemed satisfied with her affirmative answer, whistling and jingling the keys in his pocket.

He drove his Volvo sedan just under the speed limit through the Marina to his small apartment on Bay Street, telling her about the trials and tribulations of his job as an associate producer, a subject she could fully understand.

She settled back into the beige seats, thinking this was how a relationship should be, smooth leather seats in a comfortable car, work in common, a civil seduction.

Brett's apartment met her approval, too: modern styling with black leather couches, chrome and glass tables, Ansel Adams prints and a fifty-inch flat screen TV above the non-working fireplace. All very sophisticated, spare, not a ripped Barcalounger in sight. Victoria walked in and set her bag by the couch.

Brett closed the door and leaned against it. "You look good in here," he said.

"I feel good in here," she said, although she actually felt a little shy, unsure what to do next. The feeling puzzled her.

He'd put his keys in his pocket and jingled them again, smiling at her. Would he come to her or was she supposed to go to him? His position against the door reminded her uncomfortably of Luke's promise to push her against a wall and screw her senseless.

And that reminded her that she didn't have any condoms. And why would she, considering she hadn't had sex in ages and hadn't planned to go home with Brett tonight.

"This was unexpected," she said. "I don't have any protection."

"That's all right," he told her, pushing away from the door, and walking toward her with a wide, toothy smile. His leather oxfords made no sound on the thick carpet. "I'm safe."

"Good," she said. "That's good." She still wanted condoms, though.

He rested his hands lightly on her shoulders, bent his head close, then stopped, craning his neck to look at her feet. "Uh, can you take that thing off or…"

"Sure, of course."

She had to lean against the arm of the couch to reach the buckles and Brett cleared his throat and said, "No, here, uhh…why don't you sit?" He guided her to the edge of the leather couch, then sat beside her. He reached for an oversized remote that she'd admired when they first came in, and ponderous bass jazz filled the room.

She undid the buckles, and tugged on the boot while trying not to look like she was removing Frankenstein's right leg. She wished she'd thought ahead, because all she wore under it was a white tube sock that went up to her knee. She'd managed a black pump with a low kitten heel on the other foot, even though wearing it made her lopsided, but the pump and the sock did not a sexy pair make.

"You're really beautiful," Brett said, pulling her attention away from the sock.

She looked up at him and he leaned in, hands on her shoulders again, puckered his thin lips, and kissed her. His mouth stayed in a tight little "O" and his tongue darted out between his lips like a snake's and touched one corner of her mouth, then the other, and finally the middle.

Startled, she pulled back, pushing her own lips more firmly together in response. The jazz thumped in the background, out of sync with the beat of her heart.

"Relax," Brett whispered, bending his head, the tip of his tongue now flitting to her earlobe and down her jaw line.

It felt like the time she and Kristen had spit watermelon seeds at each other as kids and one had landed on the side of her face. She shuddered and Brett murmured, "That's it, baby, just go with it," then eased her back into the corner of the couch, and continued his trail of wet watermelon seeds down her neck.

This wasn't how this was supposed to go. She'd had a crush on Brett Soloway for ages, ever since he'd complimented her on her ability to predict a show's success. He was sophisticated, smooth, her equal in business. He'd been her fantasy man for too long now, and she'd made sure she always said and did the right things around him so he too would recognize their suitability. Maybe she'd built up too much in her head. Fantasies could never match realities, could they? Or maybe he just needed some instruction. Only men in fantasies knew exactly where, when and how to touch a woman the first time they were together.

He was right. She just needed to relax. And give him some gentle guidance.

"Brett," she said, as his lips reached her top button and he nuzzled underneath her blouse while putting one hand on the side of her breast at the same time and squeezing it.

"Mmm..."

"Brett, could we...slow down a little?"

He lifted his head and looked at her, his eyes half-open, his cheeks dark pink. "I've wanted you here like this for so long," he said.

"Me, too," she said. "That's why I want it to be right."

"Sure, baby, whatever you want. But maybe we should get this first one out of the way and take the edge off. Then we can go low and slow all you want. I want you to be satisfied."

She swallowed. He bent his head and kissed just above the vee of her blouse; it felt less like a flicker and more like a proper kiss. He trailed kisses along the line of her clavicle, then back down, and she closed her eyes and let her head drop back.

"That's it," Brett whispered, the hand on her breast now kneading it and the other slipping up to release the top button of her blouse. He kissed her again and his lips felt warmer now, less puckered, and she kissed him back, but kept her tongue in her mouth, reminding him to go slow.

But he seemed to have fully unbuttoned her blouse while she focused on going slow, because his hand dove into her bra in a move she hadn't experienced since Mikey Forster had felt her up in a dark corner at Patty Prescott's fourteenth birthday party. Arm bent at an impossible angle, hand slipping down from the top to cup her entire breast, panting in her ear and rubbing his crotch against her.

Yep, just like Mikey Forster, who had later told all of his friends she had big boobies and was easy.

She grabbed his arm and said, "Brett" in a firm voice.

It took him a few seconds to stop panting and rubbing, but he finally did after she'd squeezed her nails into his wrist. "What?" he gasped. "What's wrong, baby?"

"Please, stop," she said, even though he'd already done so.

"I don't understand."

"This isn't...I'm not...Would you please take me home?"

He stared at her, and she tugged at his arm until he removed his hand from inside her bra. She straightened up on the couch and began buttoning her blouse.

"Wait," he said. "You don't want me?"

She glanced at him, then back down at her shirt, focusing on each button. Did she want him? She'd thought she did, but it had all gone wrong, felt wrong. She was embarrassed and confused. "It's just too soon. I'm sorry."

He straightened. "You came home with me."

"I know. And now I want to go home alone. I need more time."

"Are you kidding?" he said, his voice losing its breathy sound. "You said you've wanted me forever. What's wrong with you?"

"I'm sorry," she said again. She wiggled out from under him and off the couch, not caring that she had to land hard on her butt on the floor to get away. She reached for her boot and began to pull it over her sock.

"Wait." He reached down and put a hand over hers. "I'm the one who's sorry. You wanted to go slow, and there you were, so beautiful, writhing underneath me in pleasure. I lost my head." He closed his eyes and took a deep breath, made an inward sigh. "I just wanted you so badly. Don't go." He slid back on the couch and patted the spot next to him. "We can just sit here and be together. No pressure." He smiled and the corners of his eyes crinkled, and that lock of hair flopped over his forehead.

She hesitated. He seemed sincere, but still...

He held his hands up in surrender. "I won't even touch you if you don't want me to." He lowered his voice and said in a husky whisper, "I just want to be with you, Victoria."

Still, she hesitated. So he crossed his arms over his chest and leaned far back into the corner of the couch and gave her a boyish grin.

She set the boot aside and put a hand on the couch cushion to lift herself up next to him.

CHAPTER NINETEEN

With Toby Keith blaring from a boombox nearby and their flag football team down by three points, Luke armed the sweat off his forehead, then cupped his hands and turned them sideways under Carl Inger's butt to count off the snap. He looked left and right as he called out "Ninety-six double, ninety-six double," then "hut-hut," in rapid succession.

Carl snapped the ball and it shot into Luke's hands. Cort ran in front of Luke to help block him from DaVonn Washington, a six-foot-seven hulk in a Raiders jersey, who always grinned before he laid Luke flat. A loyal Georgia boy in his Dawgs jersey, Luke feinted to the right, throwing off DaVonn, then did a quick leap to the left before arcing the ball to his wide receiver, Andy Min. Andy jumped over two guys who'd crashed into each other trying to reach the ball, held it close to his chest and sprinted to a touchdown. Dancing in place at the end zone, Andy smashed the ball to the ground, and was joined by some of his team members in a chicken dance.

Once DaVonn Washington had let Cort up, they bumped knuckles and DaVonn pointed at Luke with one meaty finger. "Next time, white boy."

"If you can catch me," Luke called back, and they grinned at each other. DaVonn walked off the field still pointing at Luke. They called it flag football and they followed the rules, but there were up to nine guys on a side who sometimes got carried away with some straight arms, down-field blocking, and tackles. The guys all liked playing that way, and didn't get hurt beyond the usual bruises, scrapes and sore muscles. Well, except for Marty's first time when he fell on the ball after a fumble and about ten other guys fell on top of him, twisting his arm and knocking the wind out of him. But he bounced right back and kept playing.

Cort thumped Luke on the back. "Nice game. We might want to get the tapes from the guys to review that play in the third quarter." He gestured over his shoulder at the cameramen.

In four weeks, they'd played four games at Fort Scott Field in the Presidio, each one filmed. Cort had controlled some of his chatting with the crew while the cameras rolled, but he still treated them as if everyone knew they were there. Luke had stopped caring as much, though. He'd spent many hours jogging through the city streets and parks, often shirtless, in an attempt to distract his mind and cool his body. He couldn't reckon himself totally comfortable with the situation yet, but more so than he'd been at the beginning. And all four of them—five, if you counted Miranda—had developed tactics for dealing with the intrusion in their lives, including code words to use around the cameras and crew to discuss private matters.

There were some things he would never give the cameras, though, no matter how long the series lasted. That included being with a woman.

He'd gone upstairs that night after kissing Victoria and canceled with Isabelle, who'd sounded more disappointed over the crew not showing up than him breaking the date, and he hadn't called anyone since.

Not that he couldn't have enjoyed a woman, even if they just went for drinks and dancing, but he didn't feel up to it right now. Victoria had stirred something up in him that wouldn't settle. So he jogged. Wrote songs. Played them in the Confession Booth instead of talking. Dutifully called his Mama, but kept their conversations real short on account of her side sounding like a scratched record. And he played football. Cort and Marty joined him, with Miranda cheering at the sidelines and the cameramen running up and down the field. Parker claimed football too sweaty without much intellectual gain, and wasn't swayed when Cort told him that was the point.

Luke watched Gary turn his lens on Marty and Miranda, hands clasped as they walked across the grass to their car parked between the old barracks. Sam and Ray, with his ever-present boom mic, would follow the couple for the rest of the day. Luke gave them all a wave and headed to the cooler for some water and his towel. He skinned off his jersey, poured one bottle over his head, and drank half of the other in a few swallows. He shook his head to remove the excess and ran a towel over his face and hair.

"Well, hello, Sunshine," Cort said next to him.

Luke lowered the towel and looked out over the field past the guys standing around reviewing the game, to the camera crew huddled together, probably doing the same. His eyes caught Victoria's, and she crossed her arms over her chest as she talked to Jamie, their director, but held Luke's gaze for a few beats before turning away. As usual, he couldn't read her expression. Next to Victoria, Tessa collected equipment and handed it off. The nickname Cort gave Teresa had stuck, and now everyone referred to her as Tessa. Walking away from them all, and past the players who called rude but friendly things after her, was Victoria's sister, Kristen.

Her crazy hair flew free, her feet were bare, and she wore a pair of tie-dyed leggings with wide bottoms slit up to her ankles and a tiny matching top that looked more like a bikini than anything else and barely covered her tremendous breasts.

"I do like that girl," Cort said from next to him.

Luke moved the towel down to dry off his chest. "What about that other girl you like?"

Cort spared him a glance. "Which?"

Luke flicked his towel in the direction of the camera crew, at Victoria in her frilly blouse and skirt, and super high heels with a strap around the ankle, to Tessa, helping one of the cameramen carry a piece of equipment to the van.

"Tessa?" Cort said. "Well, I surely do like her, too. It's not a contest."

Luke sighed, and swigged the rest of his water. He was actually surprised to see Kristen here; she hadn't been around since the night he'd kissed Victoria. He supposed Ms. Clausen, producer, had banished her for being a witness to the crime.

"Hello, boys."

"Miss Kristen," Cort said, "you make me think of sunshine and summertime."

Kristen dimpled at him. "You're quite a charmer, Mr. Landry." She leaned forward as if sharing a secret and said, "Don't stop, I like it."

Cort tilted his head. "But it ain't enough, is it?"

She shook her head. "Not if someone else is interested in you."

Cort slung the towel around his neck. "Darlin', you're in for a long wait, then."

Kristen laughed, and Cort laughed with her, and Luke felt something tighten in his chest at their easy teasing. His gaze strayed to Victoria, and while he liked that she could wear those high heels now, he wondered how in hell she could walk anywhere in them, much less on the field. He also wondered what it would be like to see her in nothing but them shoes, her legs wrapped around his hips, holding on tight—

He shook his head, the fantasy dissolving when Cort socked him in the shoulder. "What?" he said, irritable at the interruption.

"Miss Victoria's sister wants a word with you. Why, I don't know," he said, shaking his head as if both Kristen and Luke were lost causes. He picked up his jersey and headed across the field to the guys, giving Kristen's backside a glance as he went past her.

"I apologize for his barbarics," Luke said.

"He's fine." Kristen waved a hand. "I know his type. Lots of bluster, attracts a certain kind of woman, probably really energetic in bed, fun to flirt with, not really my type."

Luke nodded, not sure what to make of her assessment. He'd say she was right about the bluster, but he wasn't going to delve into the rest of it.

"I actually want to apologize for my sister," she continued, with a glance over her shoulder. "She's doing her best to ignore the fact that your kiss knocked her sideways, so she's ignoring *you*, which means she probably won't charge over here, but..." She gave him a little smile, sweeter and more real than the one she'd given Cort. "You never know. She's sort of a force of one."

"I noticed." He thought the sister might not be too far from that herself, but kept quiet. His stomach had jumped at her words: *your kiss knocked her sideways...*

"She's really smart, but she's being extremely stupid about men right now. She's seeing this incredible moron who's going to use her and break her heart, and she refuses to accept that she likes you because you're on her show, and she doesn't date the talent." Kristen rolled her eyes, and crossed her arms under her breasts.

Luke's hands clenched around the damp towel and he took a step forward, his heart suddenly beating hard. "What did you say?"

"It's in your contract somewhere, but I'm sure there's a way around it, and anyway, the show won't go on forever. You could start dating after it ends. Either way, it's just bad for her spiritual center right now to be trying so hard to convince herself that she's attracted to this moron and not you."

"What?" He hadn't heard anything beyond Victoria liking some other guy. He growled, "What moron?"

One side of Kristen's mouth tilted up. "Oh, you like her more than I thought. That's good." She waved a hand around. "He's some executive type and she thinks that because they have so much in common and he respects her business acumen, that's why he's panting after her." Kristen pointed at him. "I think he's using her, and I don't like it. But she won't listen to me."

"You think she'll listen to me?" He crossed his arms over his chest.

Kristen shrugged. "She's gotten used to tuning out my energy. Yours is practically shouting whenever the two of you are in the same hemisphere. Putting up this front is exhausting her, and she doesn't even know she's doing it." Kristen's cheerful attitude disappeared and she stepped forward to put a light hand on his forearm. "I know you can help her."

Luke shook his head, stepping back, and Kristen's arm dropped to her side. "You've got the wrong guy."

"Oh, for the love of..." Kristen put her hands on her hips. "Are you serious? I can't believe I'm dealing with such blocked individuals—" She threw her hands up in the air, but dropped them when a voice behind them barked, "*Kristen.*"

Kristen froze. "Oh, shit." She gave him a pleading look with her eyes, but he didn't think he could save either of them from the wrath of Victoria Clausen, striding across the field.

The breeze blew the end of her ponytail to one side and her eyes sparked as they moved between Luke and Kristen. Her attitude didn't match her ruffled pink blouse and soft gray skirt, and that image of her in just those shoes flashed through his mind again. He grabbed another bottle from the cooler and upended it over his head before he could think, shutting his eyes and gasping as the ice cold water hit his neck and trickled down his chest and back. He opened his eyes and caught Victoria's gaze, unreadable as usual. Or so he thought.

As they continued to stare at each other, the expression on her face softened from anger to confusion, then her eyes followed a bead of water that rolled between his collarbone and pecs, down his stomach and caught in the hair at his navel. Its silky smooth movement made him shiver, and when he looked back at Victoria, he saw her do the same.

She took a step back just as he moved closer, his hand reaching for...for what, he didn't know. To brush the tips of his fingers across her face, to slide them down her collarbone and the vee of her shirt, to pull her against him in a rough embrace, and feel the coolness of her blouse against his heated skin? All of those things and more? He nodded and her eyes got big as she stood frozen on the grass in front of him.

He felt frozen, too, wanting her so badly he ached all over, knowing she wouldn't do anything about it, even if she could admit to him she felt the same way.

To the side, Kristen let out a low whistle and he was jolted out of his thoughts, although the ache didn't lessen. "Holy moly, you two, I'm surprised the earth hasn't scorched around your feet."

Victoria must have been jolted, too, because she pulled her gaze from his and turned it to Kristen. "I thought you had a class. What are you doing here?"

"Canceled. No one wanted to be inside doing yoga on such a gorgeous day. They wanted to be outside playing football, or watching gorgeous men play football." She smiled at Luke, and he almost forgave her for interrupting them. Almost.

"Well, we're done here," Victoria said.

"Not really," Kristen said.

"What do you mean?"

"Don't you have something to say to Luke?"

"Hey," Luke began, trying to stop her. It was pretty clear Victoria didn't have anything to say to him beyond "work" and probably never would.

"We got some good footage today," she said. "Your Tony's Tavern fans will enjoy it, I'm sure."

Luke nodded. "All for the ratings, right?"

Her lips compressed a moment before she nodded. "Right. There's a lot of buzz going on social media, and the five-minute teaser spots we've been showing on CMT have already garnered you a lot of fans."

He knew that. It had given him a hollow feeling in his stomach along with a swelling of pride to get a delivery of three boxes of fan letters and e-mail printouts. He'd read every one, and spent part of every day answering them.

Victoria continued, "And I'm expecting great ratings for the pilot tonight. Don't forget the launch party at Tony's."

"Wouldn't miss it," he said, not bothering to hide the bitter edge to his voice. His contract stated he attend, just like it stated he couldn't get involved in any sort of personal relationship with an *In Concert* crewmember, including its producer.

"Good. Great." Her gaze lingered on his face a moment before she turned to Kristen. "Can I give you a ride somewhere?"

Kristen shook her head. "I've got my car."

"You've got a car?"

"Yeah, a vintage Bug. I got it almost three weeks ago. Where have you been?" She shut her mouth with a snap of the teeth. "I forgot. In the state of denial."

Luke couldn't help snorting out a laugh, but Victoria looked appalled. "Kristen."

"Don't worry, I won't try to pull you out of it. I know enough about destiny and karmic relationships to know you've got to do it on your own time. But I'm heading out anyway. Since I can't unite two destined souls here, maybe I can do it somewhere else." She gave a little wave and skipped across the field, doing a cartwheel partway through.

Luke shook his head, smiling, and caught Victoria doing the same.

"She's pretty incorrigible," she said, shrugging. "She can be a challenge."

"Doesn't bother me none."

Victoria cocked her head. "Yes, well..." She gestured behind her. "I should get going."

Luke reached out toward her again. "Wait." He dropped his arm to his side. "I see you almost every day, but we're never alone together..." He suspected she had something to do with that, but when she didn't say anything, he plunged on. "We don't talk much, at least not past 'could you ask Cort about that girl he took home' or 'could you not turn your back on the camera so much'."

"Stage directions," Victoria said. "It's part of my job."

Luke took a step closer. "And what about the parts that aren't your job?"

"I don't know what you mean." She leaned back, but otherwise stayed in place.

He lowered his voice, even though there wasn't anyone around to hear them. "Yes, you do. You wear skirts more now your ankle's healed, and you look real pretty, but I haven't had a chance to tell you that. And that kiss—"

Victoria held up a hand, her bracelets jingling at the movement, but her cheeks had gone pink. "Shouldn't have happened."

Luke took another step closer. "But it did, and I'm not sorry. Are you?"

Her voice dipped down, too. "It seems I haven't been clear enough. My job is everything to me. *Everything*. And I won't do anything to put it at risk."

He wanted to say she already had when they kissed, but he knew it wouldn't come out right, and besides, he'd grabbed her, not the other way around.

"I'm also...seeing someone, a very good man, and you have too strong a moral center to interfere with another man's woman."

Even though Kristen had warned him, Victoria's declaration still hit him hard in the gut. At the same time, something clicked in place in his mind. "So that's it."

"What's it?"

"You know I don't care about the show, if I was kicked off, so that won't stop me pursuing you. But you do know I won't seduce a woman who's got another man."

Victoria gaped at him. "That's...you think I'm using Brett as a shield or something? I'm...that's..." She sputtered a little more, then spit out, "ridiculous." She gestured down the field, at Tessa talking to Cort. "I have to go," she said, turned on them crazy high heels, and stamped away.

Luke watched her, smiling. Victoria Clausen might think she had a man now, but he didn't believe that would hold up much longer.

CHAPTER TWENTY

Victoria reviewed her notes for the evening from a small table by the stage. The extra lighting her crew brought in hadn't improved the tavern much, but she'd call it atmosphere. They would only be filming the early part of the evening anyway, with the rest of the night reserved as a premiere celebration party, cast and crew mingling for the first time without cameras present. Despite almost a month of filming, she still detected tension from Luke and Marty around the crew and counted on tonight's break to increase their comfort level.

Tonight would also be her private celebration with Brett as her date. They hadn't slept together after their café rendezvous, and barely found time to squeeze in another two lunch meetings—their interactions mostly consisted of texting—so his agreeing to come tonight delighted her. He chatted at the bar with Ray now, wearing a charcoal gray pinstripe Armani suit with dark pink tie, and matching handkerchief in the pocket, his dark blonde hair brushed back from his forehead. She knew at some point that lock of hair would flop forward, maybe later in the evening when they were alone, and she could push it back up with a sweep of her hand.

No matter his protestations, Luke Tyler had no impact on her sex life with Brett. She wanted their first time to be exceptional, focusing only on each other. Their jobs consumed them right now; she didn't have the energy for a sexual relationship with him, and found it easier to concentrate on work. A show was never more vulnerable than during its pilot premiere and first few episodes and she needed to not only focus on *In Concert*, but also help Brett boost *Temptation Station*'s flagging ratings. They hadn't reached panic level yet, but Jerry hounded him on a daily basis, and she and Brett spent hours exchanging and reviewing strategies for improvement.

Brett glanced over from the bar and caught her eye, winking and raising his pinky from his appletini. She waved back and he returned to his conversation.

She looked up to see Teresa weaving through the tables toward her. "So. Brett Soloway."

"Brett Soloway," Victoria agreed.

"The stud you've had your eye on for so long."

Victoria blinked at her. Teresa's empire-waist bohemian dress, its amber top swirling into a beryl blue skirt and decorated with vines and fleur de lys, contrasted with her antagonistic attitude. "That doesn't sound very complimentary," Victoria said, feeling defensive.

One hand wrapped around her waist, Teresa chewed on her lower lip, then shrugged. "I don't know...Is he good to you?"

"He's very smart. And considerate. But just for the record, we're not public yet."

Teresa tilted her head. "Is it against company policy?"

Victoria wished she could read the expression on Teresa's face; T had been fairly impassive around her lately, and Victoria didn't know how to interpret it, but that reserve seemed to have turned into irritation without reason. "No," she replied. "We're working on boosting ratings for both of our shows, and with *In Concert* launching, we didn't want any accusations of collusion. You know I already get a lot of flack from the other producers."

"Hmm." Teresa scanned the room, then looked directly at Victoria. "Are you happy?"

Victoria waved at a chair. "Why don't you sit down?"

Teresa looked over her shoulder, glancing around the bar again. "No, I'm...I've got..."

"Do you have a date?"

"Something like that." She pulled out a chair as Tim and Carl walked by with a reflecting screen. Teresa waited until they passed, then leaned over and said, "I miss you."

"T..." Where was this coming from?

"You're...we haven't seen each other in awhile, you've been so busy with work and..." She waved a hand behind her, at the bar.

"Your new...Brett."

Victoria had softened when Teresa said she missed her, but she bristled now at T's abrupt change in attitude. "I have a lot going on, T. There's incredible pressure on me to make *In Concert* a success, and improve the ratings for my other shows. Chastity and Jésus are working out well for *Hairdressers* and *Best*, but they still need managing. I'm in a new relationship, and that always takes some work, you know how it is." She stopped, feeling odd about what she'd just said. She hadn't been in a long-term relationship for years. Wasn't a new one supposed to lift you off the ground with joy, float you along in its wake? Well, maybe for other people. She was just too damn *busy* for that. But from the look on Teresa's face, it appeared she'd been too busy for her best friend, too. "I'm sorry," she said, genuinely contrite. "I've been putting my work before you again."

Teresa smiled, but it looked strained. "No, honey, it's not that. I'm glad you're happy. I've got to help the guys out," she added, then stood up and was gone before Victoria could respond. She glanced at the clock above the bar, and started tapping her papers together. It was almost time to let their guests in, to be followed by the stars making their entrance, appropriately coming through the blue "Employees Only" door, the "backstage" at Tony's Tavern. Victoria had started calling it the blue room.

She frowned. They should all be here by now, though, and the only one who'd arrived was Marty and he sat in a corner, his head bent close to Miranda's as they talked. Their hands lay tangled together on the table and they didn't take their eyes from each other. Very sweet, she thought.

She tucked her notes in her bag and decided to stash it in the blue room before the party started. On her way, she saw Parker walk in, dressed in new Lee's with a crease down the front, a beige cowboy shirt complete with tan piping around the pockets and collar, and brown cowboy boots that looked slightly big for his feet. He'd also set a huge beige felt hat over his black hair, which he'd pulled back in a low ponytail. She'd asked all the boys to wear cowboy gear, and Parker had given that request its own definition. Cort strode in right after him, still looking like a Marine in cowboy duds, but more of a country western singer than Parker.

Parker presented himself to her and lifted her hand to his lips. He straightened and his hat slipped over his eyes. "I come prepared to appease the gods, and you, and perform my obligation to the Universe in service of the success of this show."

"You've met my sister, right?"

Cort gave her a shocked look over Parker's shoulder. "Now, hey there, Miss Victoria, if I can't flirt with your sister, neither can the P-man." He pushed his own straw cowboy hat back from his forehead with one thumb.

She smiled at Cort. "I wasn't setting them up. They're just very much alike." She turned back to Parker. "She's very, ahh...spiritual. Into being one with the Universe and all that."

Parker's face brightened. "Indeed, I remember her positive energy from a few weeks ago. Is she attending this evening?"

"She is." Victoria scanned the room. "She's talking to Tony."

Kristen stood leaning over the bar, wearing a burnt orange dress with sheer panels over the shoulders, a deep V in the back and a flirty skirt that fell mid-thigh, with another sheer panel at the bottom. She gestured wildly with her hands while she spoke, and Tony laughed, something Victoria had never witnessed before. She shook her head as Cort and Parker made a beeline for her sister, thinking she should just give up trying to keep anyone away from Kristen. She and Parker probably wouldn't do more than have a meeting of the minds, and she knew Kristen wouldn't take Cort up on his offers if any other women were interested in him. And that was a very long list.

In the blue room, she scanned the small area until she found a spot to tuck her purse behind some stacked jars of olives. She set it down and was heading back when the side door opened and Luke Tyler walked in from outside, the exact image of a singing cowboy she'd envisioned. Black boots and hat, well worn blue jeans slightly frayed at the bottom and around the pockets, and a dark gray shirt so tight it hugged his torso and she could see his nipples, hardened from the cold. The buttons were undone halfway down his chest, and he'd rolled the short, tight sleeves up to show off well-formed biceps.

Her breath caught in her throat and they both froze in place, she halfway turned toward the door to the bar, he with one hand still on the outside knob. She straightened, he lowered his arm.

"Hello," she said. "You're just in time."

"I said I'd be here." He sounded resigned.

"Because you had to be?"

He put his hands on his hips and let out a sigh, lowering his head a moment. "Yes," he said, then looked her full in the face. "But it's not the only reason."

"Oh?" She clapped her hands together once to break the spell he always seemed to cast over her. Watching that drop of water glide its way down his bare chest earlier today had made her want to rush over and lick a trail in its wake. He was ridiculously good-looking, utterly charming, and it was distracting. She needed to get a grip. "Well, whatever the reason, it's good that—"

"I wanted to see you," he interrupted.

"Did you have something you wanted to discuss with me about the show?" She took a step back. "I think it's going to be a big hit and—"

"Fuck the show," he growled. "I can't get you out of my head. Whenever you're around, I want to yank up your skirts and take you right there. I want to wrap your hair around my hand, pull your head back and kiss you senseless." As he spoke he stalked forward until he'd closed the gap between them. "No matter what you say about contracts and how you're not interested in me, you can't keep your eyes off me, you're undressing me just like I'm undressing you, and I'm about to go crazy from it all."

She held out her hands, as if to ward him off, but ended up pressing her palms to his chest, which pushed the material of his shirt aside, and she felt the hard muscle and thick curly hair, the heat stoking off of him. "Luke..."

He didn't let her finish, trapping her hands to his chest with his own, and lowering his mouth to hers. In some part of her mind she thought there might be a reason she shouldn't be doing this, and she pulled back at first. But his firm lips tasted of intensity and passion, and she couldn't resist, was so tired of resisting.

He let go of her hands and wrapped his arms tight around her shoulders, curving his body over her, enveloping her until she thought he'd sweep her up in his arms and carry her out into the fog. Instead, he eased her backward until her shoulders pressed against the door and she felt she'd slide right down it, her knees had gotten so shaky.

She had a quick image of doing just that, pulling him down to the floor so that he hovered over her, balanced on his hands, and letting his lips caress her entire body. Their mouths opened and tongues touched, sliding against each other, stroking and tasting, and Luke groaned, pressing his hips to hers, and wrapped her hair in his fist.

Someone shouted in the front room, and Victoria managed to break away from Luke with some effort and stood gasping with her hands on his chest, this time to keep him at bay for real. She felt the heat of him, his muscles tensed against her and had to drop her hands to her sides, then raise them directly in front of her without touching him when he leaned toward her again.

"You have to stop this," she said.

"What's that?"

"Trying to seduce me."

He resettled his hat as one side of his mouth lifted up. "I might've made the first move, but it seems to me the feeling was mutual."

"No," she said, and it sounded weak, even to her. "No," she repeated more firmly. "I will not risk the show. And," she threw out, when she saw the stubborn set of his jaw, "I won't let *you* risk the show. I will not let you use me as a way out."

Luke straightened as if he'd been slapped, let go of her hair, dropped his hands, and gaped at her. She took the opportunity to slide away and out the door to the bar.

CHAPTER TWENTY-ONE

Luke stared at the door, blood pounding in his ears. Is that what she thought? He kissed her so they'd get caught and he'd get kicked off the show? He might be unhappy doing *In Concert*, but he'd made a commitment and he'd stick to it.

"Damn it all," he said, stalking back outside to cool down. He took off his hat and rested his forehead against the rough brick wall. He hadn't kissed her to get himself out of *In Concert*, but he'd put them both at risk by doing it. And that was just damn selfish on his part. She'd said all along she didn't want to lose her job, that it was the most important thing to her, and he'd ignored every word. Well, he barely heard her objections because whenever she was around, everything tightened up. His ears buzzed, his throat went dry, and all he could think about was running his hands up her sides, feeling her soft curves under his palms.

The fresh May breeze didn't do a thing to cool the fire inside him, but he felt a touch more calm. He knew he'd need to back off, or at least get some self-restraint, if not for himself, then to respect her. Replacing his hat, he walked back inside just as Victoria charged into the room with Cort, Marty and Parker in tow.

Instead of avoiding him like usual when there'd been heat between them, she glared in his direction as if daring him to speak or make a move. What the hell was he going to say with all the boys there? And he couldn't make a move even if he wanted to. He was hard as a rock and it hurt just to stand there behind a box of drink napkins while his whole body throbbed. So he crossed his arms over his chest and glared back, unable to curb his frustration, despite the talking to he'd just given himself.

"Fine," she said, as if to him alone, then focused on the others, turning up her smile at the same time. "They're about to let in the guests. We have about seventy-five people coming, from Tony's regulars to Reality Strikes Studios executives, to that scout from BNA records."

Cort let out a whoop at that, but Victoria directed her next comment directly at Luke. "So be on your best behavior," she commanded.

"I'm always my best," Luke shot back. Parker gave him a look that he ignored, and Victoria gave no reply at all.

"I'll be making some introductory remarks," she continued, "while the four of you wait in here. I'll have a microphone, so you'll be able to hear me, and when I announce you, make your entrance and come stand next to me by the screen. You'll be seated at the front, the execs and scout behind you and the other guests behind them."

"Where will you be, Miss Victoria?" Cort asked. "And what about Sunshine and Tessa?"

"Teresa and I will be working, and Kristen will be with your other guests."

"What about your boyfriend?" Luke drawled.

"He's not my—" Victoria started, then closed her mouth.

Luke gave her a smile and her eyes narrowed. Baiting her was petty, but he was mad at her for not falling right into his arms, foolish as that was, and mad at himself for putting her in a bad position. Just plain mad.

Cort said, "You've got yourself a man?"

"You sound surprised, Cort."

"Not surprised that you could get one," Cort said, darting a glance at Luke, "but that we hadn't heard about this new beau." Cort leaned toward her. "He good enough for you?"

Victoria lifted her chin. "He'll be sitting with the other Reality Strikes Studios executives," she said, as if she hadn't heard Cort's question at all. "Any other questions?"

"So you're dating a co-worker?" Luke asked, and Cort shot him another look.

Luke had more interest in Victoria's look. Venomous hatred might be a good description. But underneath that he thought he saw pain, or hurt, and he could've kicked himself.

"The cameras will leave once the pilot begins," Victoria continued, and Luke had to admire her unflappability. It also made him want to flap her just a bit. "The crew will join us and the rest of the evening will be given over to the party."

"No cameras?" Marty asked.

Victoria smiled at him. "No cameras. For this evening, anyway. We already have a strong online fan base and preliminary numbers predict this show will be a hit. It's time to celebrate." She looked around at each of them, lingering least on Luke. "Is that all clear?"

They all agreed, except Luke, who kept quiet. It was clear. Real clear. She had a job to do, and he'd let her do it, but their discussion wasn't over. She walked out and he heard the noise level increase on the other side of the door as the guests came in. Luke had chosen the side door into the tavern to avoid those very crowds, while Cort and Parker went straight to the line of folks waiting in the cool night air and chatted them up, signing autographs and posing for cell phone pictures. Marty had been smart and gone in earlier with Miranda, avoiding the crowds all together.

Now the other three talked about how to approach the BNA scout, who else might be in the audience, and what ended up in the pilot. Luke tuned them out, listening instead to the ebb and flow of sound in the main room; he heard cheers, giggles, laughter, glasses clinking, people calling hello to each other. He wondered if Victoria was talking to her new beau. And he wondered why the hell he cared so much. Sure, he liked sparring with her, appreciated her smarts and her nerve. He loved kissing her, and he meant what he said about wanting to push her up against a wall and take her, hard, but he didn't know her well enough to be jealous of some other man.

He put his hands on his hips and dropped his head, letting out a sigh. Trouble was, he did know her pretty well, without them having to get coffee or go to the movies or hold hands across the table at Benuccio's. And he wasn't so sure he wanted her doing those things with someone else. But she'd drawn a line in the sand, and while he usually enjoyed tackling that kind of challenge, the look on her face right before she left gave him pause. She hadn't told him about this new guy as a challenge for Luke to steal her away, she'd done it to protect herself. But what from? Him? Or was her biggest fear really losing her job? He didn't know. But he didn't have to be kicked in the nuts more than once to get the point: he would give her some air.

He lifted his head as he heard Victoria's amplified voice. The voices outside the door died down, and his stomach knotted in anticipation. He loved this part, the frisson created in the moment between the hush of the crowd and breaking into that first song.

"...and I'd like to present to you...the stars of our show...Tyler Landry!"

The door opened and Tessa peeked around the corner, her smile inviting them out. Luke smiled back as he went past, then turned his grin on the crowd, a few faces standing out—Jamie and Tim from the film crew, Cort's twins Candy and Mandy, DaVonn Washington, some Tony's Tavern regulars. But for the most part, everything blurred as the four of them walked through the crowd to Victoria. She stood by a large screen in front of the stage, in a low-cut black dress with sexy polka dot heels and belt, beaming at them and clapping along with everyone else.

He and the boys reached her side, and after some wrangling, ended up with Cort and Marty on one side and Luke and Parker on the other. Victoria smiled all around without making any direct eye contact, then raised the microphone to her lips again.

"Ladies and gentlemen, let me introduce you to the stars of our new show, *Tyler Landry: In Concert*. Marty Jacobsen, Cort Landry, Luke Tyler and Parker Guinto." She waited for the cheering to die down before adding, "Take a good look, everyone, because these men are tomorrow's superstars, both on stage and screen. Now, if everyone will take their seats, we won't make you wait any longer for the premiere."

She gestured for the boys to sit in the front row, then Tessa and Kristen guided the others to their seats. After some shuffling and chatter, the lights over the main room dimmed and the show started. Luke sat straight, arms crossed over his chest, as the opening credits rolled. There they were, striding around the corner down the alleyway by the Barn, dressed *Tombstone*-style in the black trench coats Victoria had convinced them to wear, with cowboy boots and hats; Luke and Cort in the middle, Parker and Marty on either end. They tilted their heads up as they got closer to the camera, eyes squinted against the sun—which had really been a bright spotlight Victoria had brought in—ready for battle at the OK Corral.

They stopped in a line, crossed their arms over their chests in unison after a signal Victoria had given off camera, and stared ahead as the music from their song "Ride 'Em Cowboy" blasted out. Their names flashed across the screen, followed by the words "Tyler Landry: In Concert." Then a quick jump, and the boys were shown playing a rowdy number at Tony's, a few more credits rolled, and the show began. Luke nodded, surprised and pleased that it looked good.

He heard Cort's voice saying, "We've been Tyler Landry from birth," as Luke chased Cort across the field during a game of tag football on screen. "Born two days apart, me first, so I figured I'd give him a little somethin' and let his name be first."

On screen, Luke threw Cort to the ground in a spectacular tackle. Everyone in the room cheered, and Luke couldn't help grinning. The rest of the program moved fast, following their days: Luke making Cort breakfast; the two of them working in the bar; Parker meditating in the middle of City Lights Bookstore; Marty at his construction job; the practice session where they'd talked about "State of Mind"— what happened to the footage of their kiss, Luke wondered—then a final clip of them performing "Return to Me" with everyone dancing along. On screen, Marty and Miranda locked eyes at the end of the song. They heard Marty's voice saying, "I knew first time I saw her she was the girl for me."

In person, Candy and Mandy cheered at seeing themselves when Cort slung an arm around each girl and they walked out of Tony's together. The next shot showed Luke gazing toward the door, as if he were looking longingly at the three of them. Luke remembered the night that trio left together; he had waved them off and gone to the van, whistling from satisfaction over a good performance.

His voice, muffled by the shower running in the background, with text on screen so no one could miss what he was saying: "I'm a touch lonely, darlin', and looking for some company..."

Watching it, Luke clamped his jaw tight. The screen changed to Marty and Miranda standing in front of Delgado Jewelers, cut to an image of a diamond solitaire, then flashed to Miranda's glowing face, and froze there.

"Yee dawgies!" Cort's voice sounded as the screen faded to black.

The lights came up in the tavern and as Luke sat brooding, everyone around him clapped and cheered.

CHAPTER TWENTY-TWO

Victoria stood at the bar, looking up at Brett as he talked about camera angles, and wondered how best to ask him to change his cologne. She'd liked it at first, but it smelled stale to her now. Worse than the cologne, though, was her hesitance to ask him about it. Victoria Clausen did not second-guess herself, and she hated feeling this way around Brett.

And around Luke Tyler. She let her gaze drift around the room. It was no wonder she hadn't been involved with a man in so long. She turned into such a *mess*. She'd thought things would be different with Brett, they shared so many interests, but those stupid insecurities kept cropping up.

She could charge into a room of network executives and demand the moon—and get it—but she couldn't ask her boyfriend to change his cologne. Ridiculous. And ridiculous that Luke Tyler should make her swoon with a kiss or two. A contrived kiss, at that! She'd almost fallen for it, too. That rough talk about lifting her skirt up and taking her, the firm press of his lips against hers, their breath mingling, his heart beating hard under her palm. All as a way to get off the show. Well, it wasn't going to work. She would neither be distracted by his tactics, nor fall for them. Whether he liked it or not, Luke Tyler *was* the show.

She needed to take some control here. She laid a hand on Brett's arm just as he raised his second appletini glass for a sip. He'd been nursing them, and that got on her nerves, too. She had the desire to belt down a good ale right about now.

"May I cut in?" Luke Tyler asked, and both she and Brett turned to him, frozen in their pose.

"We're not dancing," Brett said, setting his glass on the bar.

Victoria dropped her hand to her side just as Luke held his out to Brett.

"Luke Tyler," he said. "Heard a lot about you."

"Brett Soloway, Associate Producer." Brett straightened and took Luke's hand. "All good, I hope."

Luke grinned. "All the truth."

Victoria saw him grip Brett's hand hard and a spasm pass over Brett's face before she stepped between them, forcing Luke to break his hold.

"Can I help you with something, Mr. Tyler?"

Luke kept his eyes on Brett. "Well, now," Luke drawled, pushing his hat back with one hand and hooking his other thumb around his belt buckle, "I was hoping to get a dance with your lady, if that would be all right with you?"

Brett shifted, looking from Luke to Victoria. "Oh, well, I—"

"Oh, for the love of—" Victoria grabbed Luke's arm and pulled him to the dance floor. "One dance," she said to Brett, trying to convey with a look that the topic of any man giving permission for her to dance would definitely be discussed later. She glared at Luke, too, before leading him to the middle of the room and putting her arms around his waist.

While Brett appeared confused at her look, Luke just chuckled and draped his hands over her shoulders. "I figured that was the only way to get you out here."

"You—" She stared at him, completely nonplussed.

"Was I wrong?" he asked, having the grace not to look smug.

"No." She couldn't hold back a smile. "You pay attention."

He didn't respond, just watched her with an unreadable expression, studying her. It took a lot of determination for her to keep her eyes on his, since it felt like that unwavering attention meant if he looked in her eyes long enough he could also read her thoughts. She continued to move her feet in a circle to Tim McGraw's "Watch the Wind Blow By" on the jukebox, but she wanted to run back to the bar and hide behind Brett.

Luke couldn't be right, could he?

"I feel like I'm in high school here," Luke said.

Victoria did, too, with her heart beating hard, her knees wobbly, and a blush creeping up her neck to her cheeks. The situation reminded her of high school, when the senior class bad boy almost kissed her right in front of her preppy boyfriend.

"Actually," Luke said, "I think I stopped dancing like this in *junior* high." He wrapped one arm around her shoulders, then took her hand from his waist and pressed it to his heart with his own hand curled over it.

Victoria looked at the floor. Dancing like nervous young kids, of course that was what he meant. She felt the steady beat of his heart under her palm, the warmth of his fingers entwined in hers and wanted both to flee from him and curl up against him. That kiss in the blue room had seared into her, and she couldn't push it away no matter how hard she tried.

At the same moment she said, "Okay, I give," Luke also spoke.

She blinked, caught off guard. "What?"

"I said you look beautiful tonight." He leaned down, tilting his head toward her, and his breath whispered against her face. "I'm sorry for pushing so hard. You look so beautiful it stopped my heart when you walked in the room. But that's no excuse. It wasn't respectful, and I apologize."

She made a sound in the back of her throat like a "mew" and swallowed to cover it. "Thank you," she whispered, unable to meet his gaze.

"And what was it you said?" he asked.

She shook her head, looking at the couple dancing next to them, and realized it was Cort and Teresa. T wore Cort's hat, and he held her so close she wondered how Teresa could breathe. That didn't seem to be an issue, though, because Cort whispered something and Teresa threw back her head with a laugh before settling her cheek next to his. Luke spun Victoria and she caught a glimpse of Brett at the bar, glass clutched in his hand and a glum expression on his face.

She wanted to tell him, "Don't worry, I'll be going home with you," but she wouldn't, would she? She didn't especially want to have sex with someone who kissed like he was spitting watermelon seeds, but she wanted to want to.

Luke stared down at her, waiting for an answer. "Nothing," she said, forcing a smile.

But she'd said, "I give," without meaning to voice it aloud. She gave up trying to fight the fact that she was attracted to Luke Tyler, but saying it aloud wouldn't make a difference because there was nothing she could *do* about it. The moment she gave in to temptation, she would be breaking her own code of ethics on top of risking her job, the thing that meant the most to her in the world.

The song switched to Luke Bryan's "Do I." Did he turn her on and on, indeed.

She dropped her arm from around his waist and pulled back. "I should go."

He held her tighter. "Don't."

Something in his voice made her look up. Instead of either the usual cocky or distant expression, he now looked almost sad, imploring. "Don't leave. This is real nice."

"You're too much of a temptation." She wished she could take the words back as soon as they came out; she'd now given him all the power.

He shook his head, still turning her in a circle. "I'm not the problem."

"What do you mean?" She put her arm around his waist again, taking a firm grip on his belt loop because she felt so off balance.

He lifted his chin toward the bar. "You're holding onto that boyfriend of yours for all the wrong reasons."

"Really," she said, furious at his audacity, tired of everyone suggesting she didn't belong with Brett. "And what would those be?"

He pressed his palm to the flat of her back, pulling her closer. Heat radiated from his fingers, and the base of her spine tingled. "Same reasons you won't admit you're attracted to me."

"Because I don't want to lose my job? That's ridiculous." He shook his head, but she went on before he could speak. "And for your information, I'm very attracted to you, so clearly I have no issues with admitting it, and thus, no issues with Brett. I just happen to know the difference between a smart relationship and a worthless one."

Luke stopped moving and dropped his hands, letting go of hers as well. He stared down at her, his eyes narrowed. "Let's hope you figure out which is which before it's too late."

He turned to push through the crowd, ignoring the well wishers, and stalked out the door.

LUKE DROVE AROUND the city for a long while, seething, before heading home. Victoria had finally admitted she was attracted to him. And that damn well lost its appeal after she claimed a relationship with him would be worthless.

He slammed the door, ripped off his shirt, which now smelled like her, and tossed it over the camera in the corner of the living room. Then he lay on the couch with his hat over his eyes and seethed some more until he heard Cort tromping up the stairs.

Tired of his own company, Luke got up and yanked open the door just in time to catch Cort reaching for the knob to his own place, his other arm tight around Tessa. They both froze, matching guilty looks on their faces. Cort recovered first.

"Hey there, son, we wondered where you'd got to. I figured you'd gone home with one of the lovelies at the party."

"You figured wrong," Luke snapped.

Cort gestured toward his apartment. "Well, you don't mind if—"

While the walls between their places weren't paper-thin, they weren't real soundproof, either. He and Cort had spent their budget for that on the downstairs.

"You won't bother me none," Luke said. "I was just going out."

Tessa, who hadn't been able to look at him for longer than half a second, stared at him now. "Without a shirt?"

"Damn right." He grabbed his jacket, slammed the door and stalked past them to the stairs.

He shoved his arms through the jacket sleeves as he headed away from the Barn, noting Tessa's little sports car in their small back lot. He got in his truck, slammed that door, too, and swore. Well, now what? He sure as hell didn't want to go back inside and listen to Cort and Tessa enjoying each other.

He started up the truck and just drove, a habit he'd gotten into when he and Cort first moved to the city and shared a derelict studio in the Mission. He hadn't been able to sleep much there from the noise on the street or Cort's snores from the next sleeping bag over.

They'd come far from there, with the Barn and Blitz, but it had all happened because Cort's daddy died and left him money. On a good day, Luke could argue that they'd both worked real hard for what they'd earned, including the band, but this sure as hell wasn't a good day and he was too angry to take any credit anywhere.

Besides, he was pretty much worthless, wasn't he? Damn Victoria Clausen and her declarations and denials. If she didn't have to keep defending her relationship with Soloway, they wouldn't be here. Damn her big blue eyes and slinky high heels, too.

He found himself driving around Russian Hill, wondering which place was hers. Tessa had once let slip that she and Victoria shared a flat there, admitting she could never afford to live in the area on her own. Luke stopped in the middle of Taylor Street, shaking his head. He was acting like a damn-fool lovesick teenager, and needed to stop.

He had to get over his lust for her. That's all it was, surely. He couldn't be feeling more than that for such a bossy, contrary woman. Maybe he'd been attracted by her assertiveness, but was that really what he wanted in a woman? Especially one who wouldn't, and couldn't, get involved with him? She was right about his ethics, but wrong about the way they worked. He'd step in in a heartbeat and steal her from that twit at the bar, but he wouldn't make her risk her true love: the job.

He put the truck in gear and revved it up the street. He took a right on Green and headed down the steep hill to the busy intersection at Columbus, finally ending up at The Watering Hole, one of his and Cort's favorite hangouts. He felt the chill of the night air on his bare chest as he headed up the sidewalk. Hell with it. He'd be there just long enough to play a couple rounds of pool and have a beer or two. Then maybe he'd drive around some more, hang out by the Marina to watch the lights of the Golden Gate Bridge, and head home.

The Watering Hole was a dive one step below Tony's, filled with dark wood, old pool tables, gilt mirrors behind the bar, regulars who never seemed to leave, and no one who knew your name. After greeting the bartender, he settled on a stool and ordered a beer on tap, wondering if Cort and Tessa would try to pull an all-nighter or if Cort was just sneaking her in for a quickie. He hoped for everyone's sake it was more than that, but as he took a nice long swallow of beer, closing his eyes as it went down, he realized Cort and Tessa were in the same place as he and Victoria, putting their jobs on the line by getting involved.

Damn.

Could they kick Cort off the show? Luke hadn't cared at first about getting himself kicked off, but wasn't sure how he felt right now. That ending had pissed him off, the suggestion that he was desperate for a woman, but the rest of it, he had to admit...he'd enjoyed it. He might not confess that right off to Ms. Victoria Clausen, but she and her team had done a fair job putting together all those hours of footage. And it wasn't like he'd given her much to work with in the Confession Booth.

Still, he worried about Cort. He didn't want his best friend in trouble. And he realized he hadn't really thought this through while he'd been panting after Victoria like a teenager, but if one of them got fired, would the show continue, or was it all or nothing? He didn't much look forward to interrupting Cort and Tessa, but he couldn't let Cort take the risk. As he threw some bills on the bar and gave a wave on his way out, he realized he couldn't take the risk for himself, either. Himself, or the boys.

CHAPTER TWENTY-THREE

Sitting on the edge of the bed in her party dress, Victoria tried to concentrate on a recorded episode of *Pawn Stars*, but she kept seeing Luke's face after her appalling pronouncement. *Worthless*. She hadn't meant to call him that, she'd just wanted the onslaught to stop. The warmth of his hands holding her so close, his heartbeat under her palm, the insane urge to have him kiss her silly again, her desire and his pressure that made her question whether she should be with Brett or not. It had all started to crowd in on her, and while she hadn't lied, she also hadn't intended to be so cold. She hadn't meant *he* was worthless, only that an attempted relationship wouldn't amount to anything—would, in fact, cause problems.

She'd have to talk to him. She didn't know how, but it was imperative for the show. And for herself. In the meantime, she was useless for any work tonight. With a sigh, she reached for the remote to turn off the DVR. Her phone rang, and she grabbed it, looking at the screen. Ray, her sound man.

"Victoria, it's Ray. Sorry to call so late. I couldn't reach anyone else..."

She waved that away, as if he could see her. "I'm always available. What's going on?"

"It's..." His voice died away. "Uhh..."

"Ray, is it the show?"

"Yes," he mumbled, but stopped once more.

She really wasn't in the mood. "Ray, spit it out."

All in one breath, he said, "Tessa's-gone-home-with-Cort-and-it's-on-camera."

Victoria froze, her heart stopping for a beat, then picking up again double time. "Stop the feed in the entire Barn. Immediately." She couldn't help but think of the footage she'd already deleted. No time to focus on that now, though.

"Aww, Victoria, you know we're not supposed to do that. Plus, Elmore's in the van, and he'd never let me get away with it." But she did know he, along with the majority of the crew, had a crush on Teresa and protected her in a variety of ways. Even Elmore would do anything for T.

"Equipment malfunction, spill coffee, drop a brick on it, just make it stop," she ordered. "I'll be right there."

Phone in one hand, she grabbed her shoes with the other, and raced into the living room and around Kristen, who sat in the lotus position. Victoria skidded to a stop by the door, dropped her phone to pick up her keys, and froze when Kristen spoke.

"Brett can't live without you?" she asked, her eyes still closed.

Victoria stared at her. "What?"

Kristen shrugged. "I'd only run out of the house without my shoes for sex, so I figured you were going to see Mr. Appletini."

"This is a work situation, and for your information, Brett—never mind. I don't have time for this!" She grabbed her bag and flew out of the flat without a jacket, shoes still dangling from one hand, barely feeling the wisps of fog on her bare arms or the cold concrete against the soles of her feet.

She drove automatically to the Barn, defending Brett to Kristen in her head. "Brett doesn't just drink appletinis, he has a very sophisticated palate. Tonight was a fun night, and his drink matched that. He's also above a midnight booty call, and for your information, so am I..." But then her voice drifted off and she realized what she was saying. You should never have to defend a good boyfriend to anyone. And that's exactly what she was doing. She'd even told Teresa that a new relationship always took work. She shook her head. That had been so wrong.

She wasn't ready to contemplate her relationship with Brett right now, so she turned to berating Teresa.

"What were you thinking?" she demanded, banging on the steering wheel. "You know better."

But then, she herself knew better, didn't she? And given a few slight changes in circumstance, she could be in Teresa's shoes. But it was one thing to bring on her own destruction, quite another when a friend set herself up. Was that why Teresa had been so evasive this evening, acting so strangely? Had she already slept with Cort, or did she know it was going to happen tonight?

Victoria pulled to a stop behind the white van parked across the street from the Barn, and opened her door to set her pumps on the ground and step into them. Then she reached for her bag on the seat next to her, and gave a small shriek.

She'd grabbed Kristen's bag by mistake. Kristen's orange macramé looked nothing like Victoria's black Marc Jacobs. Victoria pulled it on her lap and peered inside: scarves, hair ties, tarot cards showing the Fool and the Chariot, condoms, what looked like a cherry bomb firecracker, incense, a scented candle, and a Janis Joplin CD. Among other things.

But no phone. She'd dropped it on the table. How could she function without a phone?

A car door slammed, and Victoria looked up, disoriented. Ray got out of the van, looking disgruntled, a McCafé smoothie in his hand. Reminded of her purpose, she leaped out of the car, and automatically shoved the bag onto her shoulder. Under all those condoms, there might be something useful in there.

"I owe you one," she told Ray.

"I lied to Elmore. I don't like it, Victoria."

"Neither do I. Let me talk to Teresa, clear things up."

He crossed his arms over his chest. "I'm not deleting the footage. We already lost some awhile back and I got bitched at for it by the editors." He slurped coffee through a big red straw.

Victoria flinched, feeling guilty that Ray had gotten in trouble for her actions. Tonight would be her second transgression after wiping out the recording of their kiss, third if she counted the time she deleted the footage of her telling Luke about her mother at the equestrian center. "I'll talk to them. And I'll take responsibility for the filming being stopped. You won't be brought into this at all."

Ray stared at her, his nostrils flaring. "The crew like Tessa. That's why I called. But I'm not stopping the feed again after this," Ray continued. "Not for T, not for you. Jerry'd kick my ass, and then fire me."

She held up her hands. "Understood. I'm going up to talk to T now, make the situation clear to her." She stopped. "Why are you shaking your head?"

"You might not want to go up just now." He gestured behind him with the coffee cup, wiggling it side to side at the van. "They were just starting in on...stuff when I called you. I could hear 'em. Loud."

Victoria hesitated. She didn't want to be a part of this, but she needed to stop things *now*, before any potential problems escalated for Teresa. "It needs to be done, Ray. You and Elmore go on home. I'll call you in the morning." Once she'd gotten her phone back.

He shook his head again, clearly not satisfied, but said, "Yeah, will do," and headed back to the van.

Victoria crossed the street and marched around the side of the building to the door leading up to the apartments, muttering all of the things she'd like to say but knew she shouldn't. "What were you thinking, letting sex with a love 'em and leave 'em man get in the way of your career? Was it worth it, was one night in bed worth what you'll have to face tomorrow?" She reached for the buzzer to Cort's flat. "Really, is one night of sweaty gyrations worth losing your livelihood?"

"Depends on the gyrations," a voice drawled behind her.

Jumping, she shrieked again, pressing her hand to her chest. "You," she gasped, trying to get her breath back.

Luke pushed his hat back with a thumb. "Didn't mean to startle you."

"You snuck up on me."

"No, ma'am. I called out, but you were talking so loud you must not've heard me. I figured I'd let you run down, then announce myself."

"Well," she said, nonplussed. She looked him up and down, puzzled. "Are you not wearing a shirt?"

"No. Are we going up to stop those two being foolish?"

"Yes. Of course." She pulled her gaze from the curly, dark hairs exposed above his jacket's half done zipper.

He put his key in the lock and gestured her ahead of him. She marched up the stairs, her heels clicking loudly on the cement steps, and firmly pushed away all the naughty thoughts trying to creep in at sight of Luke's chest. She was here to do a job. That was all.

"You were wearing a shirt earlier." A nice one, too, she recalled; it had felt silky and thin under her fingers, as if she could tear if off with no effort. She wondered briefly where he'd been, why he'd removed his shirt there, and wished she'd had a camera following him. "What happened to it?"

"Took it off," he said as they reached the landing.

She stared at him, expecting him to crack a smile after that deadpan statement, but he looked as grim as she felt. With a start, she remembered her last words to him at Tony's and felt her face flush.

"Well," she said again, turning to the door. "Shall we?"

Without responding, he stepped forward and hammered on the door with the side of his fist. "Get your britches on, son, and get out here."

He dropped his hand and they waited, listening.

"I don't hear anything," Victoria said, slightly relieved. Teresa had brought boyfriends to the flat before, but they'd mostly been discreet— or Victoria had been out, working—and she didn't relish the thought of knowing what sex between Cort and her best friend sounded like.

Luke glanced at her. "I wouldn't expect them to jump right up and run to the door."

This time, Victoria knocked, but it didn't sound as authoritative as Luke.

"Teresa," she called, then didn't know what else to say. *Stop that sex right now and get out here, you bad girl?*

Suddenly she felt foolish, embarrassed, and very aware of Luke standing near, raising the temperature within a ten foot radius.

Why had she rushed over here like this? She certainly didn't have some teenage notion that Luke might be home, and she'd bump into him. She'd only wanted to help T. But she'd made Ray stop the feed. And standing here in the hallway, she realized the damage was done, and it wouldn't make any difference if she talked to Teresa and Cort now or later. And speaking of that...she turned from the door to ask Luke why he wanted to stop Cort and Teresa, but he stood so close, she bumped into him and wobbled on her heels.

Luke caught her by the arms to steady her, then immediately dropped his hands.

"I don't think they're coming out," Victoria said. "But since we're here, I owe you an apology. For earlier, when I said..." She stopped. Luke had started to walk down the hall. "Where are you going?"

"My place."

"I'm talking to you."

He stopped at his door, turning to her. "I don't want to do this out here."

"Do what?"

"Convince you I'm not worthless," he said, and walked inside.

Victoria stood staring at Luke's open door. She heard him hanging his keys on a peg and pictured him setting his hat on another, as she'd seen him do over and over on film. She knew so many of his routines now; at this point he'd probably be greeting Frog as she lay on her customary spot on the back of the couch.

Luke didn't have to do any convincing; she'd never thought of him as worthless and he deserved her apology and an explanation. She wasn't sure she wanted to go inside his flat to do so. She might be able to chastise Teresa for risking so much to be with a man for one night of sex, but going in there could turn her into a hypocrite.

She took a deep breath and sighed. This was ridiculous. She could be alone in the same room with Luke Tyler and not fall all over him. They could have a private conversation, she'd explain her thoughtless comment, let him know how sorry she was, and convince him it wouldn't have to interfere with their working relationship. In fact, it would be better to have this conversation without worry of being interrupted.

Taking another deep breath and straightening her spine, she clicked firmly down the hall and through the door.

And stopped dead with a gasp.

Luke stood with his back to her and had just shrugged out of his jacket and started sliding it down his shoulders when she came in. The muscles at his shoulders bunched up and dented into dimples partway down his back, begging for her fingers to trace them. She crossed her arms tightly around her middle, tucking her hands in. His film image had nothing over the man in the flesh.

He turned at her gasp, letting the jacket slide off the rest of the way, and caught it with one hand. Barely sparing her a glance, he walked past her and hung the jacket on the pegs by the door. Then, as she continued to stand immobile, he closed the door and stood in front of her.

She'd seen hours of his footage, but he'd been very careful to change in the bathroom, and always tossed a t-shirt over the camera in his bedroom. She'd given up trying to get him to stop, especially once she realized he probably wouldn't be bringing a woman home anyway. Up until today at Golden Gate Park, she'd seen him mostly clothed. That drop of water rolling down the indent between his stomach muscles had been devastating, but they'd been in public, and distracted by Kristen. Standing alone with Luke in his living room felt wonderfully audacious, complete with a pleasurable shiver up the spine. She didn't know if she wanted to stare at his rounded pecs and the lines of defined abs with their dark hair leading toward the waistband of his jeans, or to run away. Or do something more physical. To those abs.

"Make yourself comfortable," he said. "I'll just get a shirt and be right back."

"No!" she said, then bit her lower lip at his startled look. "I mean, of course. Whatever you need to do. I wasn't going to take much of your time. I owe you an apology. What I said earlier at Tony's was unconscionable, and I'm sorry."

He crossed his arms over his bare chest and stood watching her, not saying anything. She never squirmed in a staring contest; she usually won them. But she felt like squirming under Luke Tyler's gaze. She wouldn't, however, drop her eyes first.

Luke looked away before she did, at the camera in the corner. Victoria glanced at it, too, saw the shirt hanging over it and understood he thought the cameras were still rolling. She also understood the where and why of his shirt removal. She didn't yet know why he'd left the house with only his jacket, though.

"What's it going to take to stop you doing that?" she asked and pointed to the shirt.

He lowered his gaze to her lips and one side of his mouth quirked up, but he continued to remain silent. Victoria glanced at the covered camera again, realizing Luke would remain reticent as long as he thought the cameras were on. She wanted to talk to him about what she'd said earlier, wanted him to feel completely comfortable in whatever way he needed to discuss the situation.

She also knew, in both an intellectual and visceral way, that telling him the feed had been turned off provided more than just an opportunity to talk. She waited for her stomach to clench up, like it usually did in situations like this, and relaxed when it didn't occur. Her attraction to him was based solely on his physical appearance, then; surely she'd be able to have a rational discussion with him, state her position clearly, then leave to deal with the Teresa situation .

She nodded, mostly to herself, and said, "It's important to discuss this. If it helps any, the feed in the entire Barn has been turned off. It won't be turned back on until tomorrow morning."

Luke cocked his head at her with a smile. Then he walked to the camera and flicked his shirt down, pulling it on but not buttoning it after studying the camera long enough to determine that no red light glowed from its center.

He turned to face her. "Thank you."

She nodded, but it was her turn to be silent as she waited for more.

Instead, they ended up in another staring contest, and Victoria gave up with a loud sigh, slapping her palms against her thighs. "Really, Mr. Tyler, this isn't getting us anywhere."

"Since we're about to go to bed, maybe you can start calling me Luke."

Her jaw dropped. "I—"

He took a step, leaning in close enough for her to smell his warmth. "Since a relationship would be worthless, I figure we can just have hot, sweaty meaningless scx."

His words made her knees wobble and her mouth go dry, but she held her ground. "That's very presumptuous of you."

"Is it? Haven't we been heading toward this from the beginning?"

"And besides that, it's cruel to throw that in my face after I apologized to you." She took a deep breath and said, "I am sorry."

Hands on his hips, he sighed and looked at the floor. "I know you are."

"I don't want this to affect our working relationship."

He looked up at the ceiling, shaking his head. "You are a wonder, Victoria Clausen." He met her gaze again, his green eyes dark. "Don't worry, your comment won't affect the damn show."

"What do you mean? Why do you say it like that?"

"Anyone ever accuse you of being one-track?"

She opened her mouth to automatically refute his claim, but he was right. She didn't think anyone had ever had the nerve to say it to her face, though. "Not out loud," she said. "No."

He laughed as if she'd just said something charming, slipped his big hand around to cradle the back of her neck, and kissed her like the most natural response was to press his warm lips to hers. She stiffened, but he didn't move, other than to run the tips of his fingers up the base of her neck, and through her hair. She shivered, closing her eyes and gasping out a breath, but Luke kept his lips still and his fingers caressing. His thumb curved over the back of her ear, along her jaw line, brushed the corner of her mouth where it met his, and swept back across her cheek.

His other hand came up to cradle her face, and she raised a shaking hand to press her palm to the firm, flat plane of his upper chest. When she first saw that bit of exposed skin tonight at his neck, the dark curls peeking out, she wanted to run her fingers through them, slide the curls under her fingernails, smooth her fingertips over them, brush her nose against his skin there and breathe him in. So she did that now, stroking upward through the soft, curly hair with the pads of her fingers, then down, raking him lightly. He groaned, curving his body toward her, but still did not push himself on her beyond his tender kiss.

She tilted her head, parted her lips slightly under his, and traced his nipple with a thumbnail. His hands went to her shoulders and she felt him go rigid.

"Say it," he breathed into her mouth.

She went still as well, his words washing over her.

He tilted his head, moving his mouth closer to her ear, and in a hoarse voice whispered, "I won't go further unless you say so."

That was about the sexiest thing anyone had said to her in a long time and it turned her brain to mush. She lowered Kristen's purse from her shoulder and shoved it at him, blurting out, "I have condoms."

Luke caught the bag and gave her a slow smile before hanging it from a wooden peg. "Well, now, that's real—" he started, but Victoria stopped him by pushing to the tips of her stilettos, shoving his shirt aside, pushing it off his arms and letting it drop to the floor. Then she wrapped her arms around his neck, and pulled his face down to hers.

His pupils darkened and, wrapping his arms tight around her waist, he pulled her off her feet to kiss her. He held her so tight his belt buckle pressed into her belly and her breasts into his chest, but only his kiss filled her senses, his lips warm and soft and hard at the same time. His tongue brushed against hers, along the roof of her mouth, across the bow of her lips until her entire body quivered against him from the tingling his explorations created.

He made a noise in the back of his throat, and slipped one hand down to cup her rear and spread the other along her upper back.

Skirt riding up her thighs, she wrapped her legs around his waist and reveled in his strength, in the feel of his mouth tracing a line down her throat. She let her head fall back, her body held in his grip, pressed tight to his torso, and he nipped lightly at her neck before claiming her mouth again. She shifted her shoulders so first one sleeve, then the other of her wraparound dress slid down her arms. She lifted one arm out at a time, her other looped around Luke's neck, then pressed herself to him.

She stroked the length of him outside his jeans, and he muttered, "Ah, God," and pressed firm kisses on her temple and down the curve of her ear. She reached for his belt buckle just as he undid the hook on her bra. She felt uncharacteristically fumbling and awkward while Luke radiated smooth and confident, but she didn't want to stop, couldn't at this point. She wanted to feel him inside her, pushing her up against the door like he'd promised. And she wanted a whopper of an orgasm. She managed to unzip his jeans and ease him out, then froze with a gasp as Luke ran his tongue around her nipple, and sucked it into his mouth.

She ran her hands through his hair, held his head close, and panted out, "Purse. Condoms."

Still suckling her breast, pulling sensations from deep down inside her, Luke shuffled them to the pegs until her back was pressed against the door and she could reach into the macramé bag with one hand. She sighed in satisfaction, undid the packaging, then reached between them and slid the condom on, leaving her hand wrapped around him long enough to feel him pulse against her fingers, firm and ready.

He was right: she'd wanted this from the very beginning, from the moment he held his hand out to her after she fell at Tony's and said, "Squeeze if it hurts."

"Make it hard," she commanded, squeezing her legs tight around his waist. "Now. I don't want to wait."

"I've been waiting too long myself, darlin'," he breathed in her ear, then balanced her against the door, pushed her panties aside and slid into her, hard. They both stilled at the contact, then Luke grasped her hips, shifted her up, then down—slow, teasing—and she stopped knowing where he began and she ended. His scent mingled with hers, his breath warmed her neck and she shivered all the way down to her stilettos as he thrust into her, lifting, then pulling her hips down until the full length of him was inside her, and thrusting again. He kept the rhythm steady but hard, as she'd demanded, her back thumping against the door, her nipples tingling, a delicious pulsing between her legs.

He thrust faster, then reached between them and rubbed his thumb over her silken panties, pushing the damp material into her, rough and soft, rough and soft, the friction creating a small spark.

"Yes. *There*," she moaned as the ember burst into flame and her orgasm blazed and flared out, leaving her panting and breathless at the same time, helpless against its power.

As the rest of the world gradually returned, she heard Luke's harsh breath in her ear, the urgency for his own release. She encouraged him by tightening around him, digging her heels into his thighs, and while the movement rekindled her recent pleasure, it also spurred him on so he drove into her faster. She clung to him as another orgasm peaked, and he followed soon after with a shuddering groan that ran through his entire body, and they were both left limp and panting.

CHAPTER TWENTY-FOUR

Luke gave one last shudder, his thighs trembling with exertion, then rested his forehead on Victoria's shoulder, holding her tight to him as they caught their breath. Victoria murmured something in his ear and stirred in his arms.

"Shh," he said, pretending not to hear the words "need" and "leave."

He shifted, holding her tighter, and headed for the bedroom, snaking the bright orange bag from the wall peg along the way. He'd waited too long for this; he wasn't going to let her go after a quick, intense, screw against the door.

He briefly wondered why the bag made a strange clunk when he dropped it on the floor. He set Victoria at the foot of the bed, put his hands on her face, and kissed her before she could object, but instead, she grabbed his forearms and melted into him, kissing back as if they'd been separated for months. He pulled away with some difficulty, pressed his palms over her hands, said, "Don't go anywhere," and rushed to the bathroom to dispose of the condom. He gave a start when he saw the yellow smiley faces on a bright green background. Best they use his for the next round.

He'd tried to be quick, but when he got back, she'd fastened her polka dot bra and was pulling her dress up over her arms.

"Don't," he said, and she froze, one hand on her other arm, and looked up at him.

"I have to," she whispered, fixing the rest of her dress in place.

He knelt in front of her, his knees on either side of her legs, very aware of his bare chest and open fly. "Why?"

She wouldn't look him in the eye, just shook her head, staring at her lap, her eyelashes resting on her cheeks.

He brushed a thumb across one cheekbone, then dropped his hand to his thigh. He thought she might revert back to Ms. Victoria Clausen fairly quickly, that she'd pull away from him if he didn't keep her in the moment, but he wasn't sure what to make of this quiet withdrawal. "I didn't hurt you, did I?"

She shook her head.

"I'd like you to stay," he said, "but I won't make you."

He slid his hand along her forearm, then edged back to stand up and let her go. Her hand shot out and she grabbed his wrist. "Make me," she said fiercely.

Startled, he rocked back on his heels, but recovered quickly at the memory of her demanding he take her, hard. He shifted forward and said, "Be careful what you wish for, darlin'..."

"I'll go, otherwise," she said, gripping him tighter. "I'll have to."

He could tell from the look on her face that she expected him to toss her back on the bed and take her. He saw more in her expression than just the belief that he'd take her up on her offer. He also saw hesitation. Not fear, but some uncertainty, and he wasn't about to rough her up in that case.

He also wasn't going to let her go.

He reached for her hands and eased her to a standing position, then pressed his mouth to the inside of her wrist. She made the smallest of moans and he took that as encouragement, moving his lips to the center of her palm. This time she let out a sigh and her other hand relaxed in his.

When he sucked her index finger in his mouth, she tensed again, but leaned into him right after resting her forehead on his chest. Her breath warmed his bare skin, and made his stomach muscles jump and flex.

He released her finger and pressed a kiss to the top of her head. He brushed a lock of hair off her face, took her by the shoulders and breathed in her ear, "Stay..."

She slumped down and might have fallen back on the bed if he didn't already have a good hold on her.

"Is that a yes?"

She nodded and one side of her mouth curled up in a cat-that-ate-the-canary smile and his gut tightened at the sight. His feisty Victoria hadn't been swept away by an against-the-wall quickie. Or her own doubts.

"Good," he said, then undid the wide polka dot belt and let it drop to the floor. He reached around to unzip her dress and his stroking hands followed its slide down her arms until it lay on the floor. He crouched in front of her, cupping one calf as she lifted a foot to step out of the dress. She gestured down.

"My shoes…"

He held a hand out at that. "Leave them."

She stared at him. "You want me to leave my shoes on?"

He couldn't respond right away; his throat had closed up at the sight of her matching polka dot bra and panties, her rounded hips and stomach, the curve of neck and shoulder where a tendril of hair curled down toward her breasts. He tried to say, "Please God, leave the shoes on," but the words caught in his throat, so he pressed his lips to the satin ribbon of her panties while hugging her hips. Then he kissed his way up her body from belly, torso, breast, and neck to her lips, savoring each smooth, spicy, luscious portion. Cradling her with one arm, he lay her back on the bed.

Victoria Clausen's body was nothing like her personality. Soft, curvy and sweet, he found it easy to fall into, to run his hands and mouth over her bare skin, to explore all of her tender places, enjoying her response as she quivered under him, each gasp shooting through him like a thunderbolt.

With a sigh against his mouth, she pressed her hand to his belly, and his muscles jumped under her fingers. She slid her hand around his side to his back, spreading her fingers over his shoulder blades.

He pressed kisses along the side of her face and down her neck to her collarbone. She threw her head back, clutching at him, as he worked his way down, kissing her belly, his hands wrapped around her sides, holding her in place as she shivered. He turned his head and rested it on her stomach. She ran her hands through his hair, while his tongue glided over her hip bone, then across her stomach at her waistline and up her body. He caressed the side of her breast, cupped her face with his free hand, felt her nipples harden against his chest, and moaned against her mouth. He forced himself to pull back and look down at her; her hair lay spread across the pillow, her cheeks flushed, her lips parted.

"What do you want?" he whispered.

She looked surprised. "I don't..."

"This is for you," he said, brushing his fingertips over her hip. "What do you want?" he repeated, pressing kisses along her temple as he spoke.

After a pause, she said, "I want to undress you."

He nodded at that. "I've already liberated you of yours..."

She pressed against his chest until he sat up so she could remove his boots. The right one was tight, so she straddled his leg facing away from him, and pulled it off that way. Watching her bent over, her behind flashing at him in her satin polka dot underwear, he had to lay back on the bed with a groan, close his eyes and throw his forearm over them for good measure. He felt her tug his jeans off, heard them fall to the floor with the clunk of the buckle, then the bed depressed as she climbed next to him.

She laid her palm just above the waistband of his underwear and whispered in his ear, "I want to come first, before we..."

He lowered his arm and looked at her as she blushed pink, watching his reaction, and he vowed to do his best to grant her wish. He cleared his throat, but couldn't speak, just nodded.

Luke ran a hand along her stomach, up to her breasts, then back down to rest on one hip. She fell back as he pushed himself up and leaned over her. He bent to brush his lips against her cheek, and down along her jaw until he found her mouth. While exploring with his tongue, slow and easy, his hand on her hip moved south. He ran a finger across the line of her panties, then slipped beneath it and between her legs.

She clutched at his biceps as he studied her body, testing and tasting, waiting for her reaction before he moved on. He moved his fingers in slow, firm circles, and she pulled her legs up, arching her back.

"There," she whispered, then raised her head. He continued in that slow way, kissing her, pulling away to kiss her temple or the side of her neck, just below the ear, while she shivered against him.

She ran her hands along his sides, then up to his neck to press his face with her palms. She slid her fingers through the hair at the back of his neck, tugging at the ends. She gasped, and he intensified his movements until she pushed against the bed with her heels, indenting the mattress.

"There," she hissed, "right there."

She broke away from their kiss to let her head fall back, her breath ragged and rapid, and she arched her body even more as Luke flicked a tongue over one nipple.

"Oh!" she cried, her eyes flying open. "Yes, like that." She clutched him tighter with a soft cry. He took her breast in his mouth, increasing the pressure from his hand. He kissed his way to her other breast, teasing her nipple with the tip of his tongue, then brushed his palm against the side of her face and moved his hand under her neck until he had his arm under her shoulders and was holding her tight to him, just as tightly as she held onto him.

She moaned, clutching his arms, her body moving against his while he continued to intensify the heat. Then she cried out, shuddering, her muscles convulsing around his fingers, and collapsed back onto the bed.

Luke waited until she stilled, then fell next to her, one damp hand resting on her belly. "That what you had in mind?"

"Better," she gasped.

With a hand on his cheek, she turned and pulled him close for a kiss, her body pressed to his, his erection pressed against her soft, round thigh. "But we're not finished," she murmured, snaking a hand down his torso and easing his shorts from his hips.

When she reached for her shoes, Luke growled, "Leave them on," this time grabbing a condom from his nightstand. While he rolled it on, he watched her shimmy out of her panties.

He hovered over her, and looked into her face. In the dim light from the street lamp, she met his gaze, eyes wide in invitation, lips parted. He burrowed into the side of her neck, kissing his way down to her breasts and back up to her lips, where he stayed until she arched up to him.

His body bowed, he pushed into her slowly. She lifted her legs and pressed them against his thighs as he continued to kiss her and move with slow, even strokes until he was all the way inside. Then he stopped, pulled far back, and thrust into her with a groan. He planted his hands along the side of her head, and she wrapped her arms and legs around him, sliding her shoes up and down his thighs, the heels a sharp contrast to the silkiness of her that enveloped him. Everything moved in rhythm, her belly against his, their breath ragged and intense, until the pleasure rose again.

He felt her orgasm, her muscles clenching, and when she cried out, he let himself go, too, his pleasure so intense it felt like it shot out his fingertips. "Victoria," he whispered in her ear, before his shuddering increased, then gradually slowed.

With a sigh, he rested his forehead on hers, then rolled away, pulling her to his side to hold her close. She lay her face to his chest while their heartbeats returned to normal. He wrapped his arms around her, rested his face against the top of her head, and drifted off, feeling relaxed for the first time in weeks.

CHAPTER TWENTY-FIVE

Luke heard the front door slam. Still groggy, he didn't understand that Victoria no longer lay beside him, and it took him longer than he liked to stand and make his way to the living room. The sound of her heels clicking down the hall convinced him she really was leaving, and he rushed out the door after her.

She was fast, though, and he had a little something holding him back, mainly being naked as a jaybird. But he kept jogging along the hall, down the stairs and out the side door, wincing as the breeze chilled his privates. At the bottom step just past the door, he saw her car roaring through the darkened streets and away from the Barn, brake lights flashing once as she rounded a corner.

"Son of a bitch," he said.

He hadn't scared a woman away like that in...well, never. Usually they didn't want to leave and he had to give them a nudge. Luke sat down hard on the step, then leapt up with a yelp as the cold concrete met his bare butt. Rubbing it with his palms, he swore a few more times and headed back upstairs. Victoria wasn't coming back. But why the hell had she run in the first place?

He reached the open doorway to the hall and stopped short. He hadn't cursed this much in years. Cort stood at his own door, just undoing the lock. And he wasn't alone. At Luke's exclamation, Cort turned, and Tessa turned with him.

She let out a squawk and covered her face with one hand, but he caught her peeking at his goods through her fingers, and didn't do anything to hide the display. What the hell. She and Victoria would talk later and compare notes anyway. Cort didn't look down, but he didn't cover his eyes, either. In fact, he grinned and said, "Forget something there, partner?"

Luke snarled and stomped past them with as much dignity as he could muster, considering his parts were hanging out for all to see and the breeze to blow. "My sanity, I expect," he muttered as he went by.

He caught Tessa still watching, and he couldn't help saying, "Like what you see, darlin'? Tell your friend she's not getting any more of it."

Tessa dropped her hand and said, "I don't understand," but he'd already stalked by her and didn't answer or look back as he went inside and slammed the door behind him. He then stalked by the cat, who mewed at him, and into the bedroom, where he flopped face-first onto the jumbled bedclothes. Panting in anger, frustration and a bit of embarrassment—although he'd never admit that part out loud—he rolled over and tossed an arm over his eyes.

The bed smelled like Victoria, like the two of them together, lust and satisfying sex. He wanted to sink into it, but only if she was with him. Hell, he was going to have to sleep on the couch. Just as he pushed himself up, a knock sounded on the door, and someone opened it.

Victoria.

Luke almost tripped over his feet as he grabbed his jeans and stepped into them, heading for the door at the same time. Head bent, fixing up the buttons, he stopped at the voice. Deep and sarcastic. Not Victoria.

"You got your pants on yet, son?"

Luke glanced up to see Cort in the doorway, one hand on the knob, looking pointedly in the other direction.

"Still butt naked, you jackass."

Luke did up the last button and walked to stand in front of Cort. "You want a peek?"

"I need a horror show, I'll watch a Georgia Tech game."

Luke socked him on the arm and walked away, this time to collapse on the couch. "I'm decent," he said. "What the hell're you doing here? You've got a woman waiting on you."

Cort sauntered in and stood by the couch, looking down. "The woman sent me here."

Luke waved one hand at him and pinched at the bridge of his nose with the other. "I'm all right."

"Sure. All right folks usually stomp around nekkid in hallways in the middle of the night. But she's not worried about you, she's got some concern for Victoria. Wanted to make sure you didn't have her tied up in here or something."

Luke lifted his head and stared at Cort, who had perched on the arm of the couch and sat watching him. "You're serious."

Cort shrugged. "Tessa is, anyway. Took all I had to keep her from charging in here after you. I think you scarred her for life, son. Plus," he made a gesture as if tipping a bottle to his lips, "she's had a bit to drink tonight. There's a wild woman inside my girl Tessa."

Luke let out a snort, and dropped his head back. "Victoria's not here. Tied up or otherwise."

"But she was here?"

"Was."

"You scared her off?"

"Scared herself, I think." Luke pushed up from the couch, still restless. Had he scared her? She'd had that moment of hesitation earlier, but there hadn't been any fear. No, she was a very happy woman last he checked. He ran a hand through his hair, bent his head and sighed. He raised his head again when he realized something. "How come you didn't see her in the hall?" he asked Cort.

"We started our fun in the Barn, came up the inside stairs. Must've just missed her."

Luke nodded absently, then began to pace, staring at the floor. His head was starting to clear, even as he tried to puzzle out why Victoria left. "What the hell're you doing with Tessa anyway? Victoria came over here to stop you two, but you'd disappeared."

"So you decided to get nekkid with each other? I could ask you the same."

"It's different," Luke said, distracted. What the hell had happened?

"S'pose so," Cort said. "Tessa quit, so she's not part of the show anymore."

Luke's head shot up. "She did?"

"She did indeed."

Luke waved a hand at him, nonplussed. He didn't have enough

space in his head to deal with that information right now. "Well, what the hell you doing here?" he repeated. "You've got a woman waiting on you."

"I've also got a friend taken to running around naked as a jay bird."

Luke looked up at Cort and thought of the two of them as kids, so close his mama called them Siamese twins, and how in tough times, Cort had often chosen Luke's welfare first, even over his own pleasure.

Looking at Cort, even knowing Cort for awhile, one wouldn't think of him as a protective sort, but he had it in spades, especially when it came to Luke. And Luke realized it was time he started protecting himself more and cutting Cort loose from that responsibility.

He held out his right hand, and Cort automatically reached out with his own. They clasped wrists instead of hands, something they'd done since they were boys, a way of acknowledging they loved each other without having to sound like sissies and say it out loud. They pulled their hands back, letting the palms and fingers slide against each other, then dropped them to their sides.

"Tell Tessa that Victoria went home in one piece. No harm done."

"Couldn't stand looking at your ugly mug anymore?"

"Something like that, I expect." Luke clapped Cort on the back, and walked over to open the door.

He started at the sight of Tessa standing there, one fist raised to knock. "She went home," he said.

She put her hands to her hips. "If you've hurt her—"

One hand on the door, the other on the frame, Luke leaned forward, hanging over her. He was pleased to see she held her ground, despite swaying a little. "If she tells you it wasn't good, she's a liar," he said, then opened the door wider and gestured Cort out. "Now go put smiles on each other's faces and leave this poor bastard alone, would you?"

Tessa opened her mouth to say more, but Cort slid an arm around her shoulders and started leading her away. "She's fine, darlin'. She just ended the evening early."

Tessa shot Luke a look over her shoulder, but he closed the door on it. He leaned against it, staring into the room without seeing anything.

Jesus, but he was in trouble.

CHAPTER TWENTY-SIX

Man, she was in trouble. With a capital T.

She'd just run out on the best sex of her life. Among other complications.

She dropped Kristen's purse on the floor by the front door, let the keys fall beside it, then leaned against the door and put her hands over her face. What was *wrong* with her? Would it have been so difficult to stay there, to fall asleep in his arms, make love again in the morning, and leave like a grownup? Or maybe she shouldn't have gone inside in the first place.

"Was the sex that bad?"

Victoria jumped, dropping her hands, and stared at her sister, who'd materialized in the living room in tie-dyed bike shorts and a tight t-shirt that read "I Left My Dharma in San Francisco." She held a sesame seed bagel slathered in soy cream cheese in one hand and a steaming mug in the other.

"It was amazing," Victoria said, before realizing what she might be getting herself into with the admission. "Wait. How did you know?"

Kristen pointed with the bagel. "Bed head. Belt sticking out of the bag. General aura of lust. You've either started exotic dancing, or you had sex. The cowboy?"

Victoria pressed her lips together. After all of her protestations, how could she admit she'd had sex with Luke?

"I can't see Brett giving you that glazed look, so please tell me it was the cowboy."

A quick flash of Brett's stingy pecks gave way to Luke's

worshipful kisses traversing her body and she couldn't suppress a quiver. Victoria gave a tiny nod.

"Hallelujah." Kristen tilted her head. "So you're back home because...you went through all my condoms?"

Victoria let out a half-snort, half-groan and banged the back of her head against the door. "No. You still have some left."

"Then the sex couldn't have been *that* great." Kristen lowered herself onto the carpet and licked cream cheese from the edge of the bagel. She set the mug on the coffee table next to her and looked up at Victoria expectantly.

Given a choice, Victoria probably wouldn't have chosen free-wheeling Kristen as her confidante in this matter, but she couldn't call Teresa, who was AWOL. And she really needed to talk to someone. She took a few steps forward and sat on the carpet in front of Kristen.

"Believe me. The sex was great."

Kristen nodded. "He has that look about him," she said, then took a big bite of bagel.

"What look?" Victoria asked, then had to wait in frustrated silence while Kristen calmly chewed, swallowed, then took a sip of what smelled and looked like asparagus tea.

"Like he'd be an excellent lover." She took another bite, and Victoria wanted to throttle her. "Confidence combined with reverence. Great hands. You've seen the way he holds his guitar." She leaned forward, her eyes big.

Victoria sighed. "I have."

"Like he knows how to handle precious objects," Kristen added.

Victoria nodded, then held out her hand, gesturing at the bagel. When Kristen pulled the remainder in half and gave her a section, Victoria said, "Don't you have any chocolate around?"

"Nope. This is my vice." She stared at the tip of her forefinger, smudged with cheese, then licked it. "That and men and sex and dancing and loud clothes and talking too much and—" She stopped. "But we're talking about you. And Luke. You had sex, but you didn't stay." She stopped again, her eyes widening. "Was it on camera?"

Victoria shook her head. "I had the feed stopped." At Kristen's look, she added, "For Teresa. Because I thought she and Cort were going to get caught on camera."

A small crease appeared between Kristen's eyes. "But you're the one that ended up in bed."

Before she could either scream or figure out another response, Victoria's cell phone rang from the table by the door where she'd dropped it on her way out. She dove for it, and clutched it to her chest before checking the display: Teresa S. She might as well change it to "Tessa," she thought, feeling both a surge of gratitude that T had called her, and disappointment that it wasn't Luke.

But she'd run out on the man. Why would he call her?

She hit SEND and put the phone to her ear, but before she could say anything, Teresa said, "Juss 'bout t'have the sex, but couldn't 'till I knew you okay."

Victoria pulled the phone away and blinked at it before replacing it and saying, "That's...what? Where are you?"

"Where're *you*?"

"Home."

"Oh, thank God." Teresa let out a breath on the other end, then added, her words even more slurred, "Why hell'dja leave? The mansha god. Maaan," she said more slowly, clearly trying to enunciate, "is. A god."

Victoria was tempted to blink at the phone again but restrained herself. "Have you been drinking?" Kristen, who had been finishing her bagel half, set it on the table and looked at Victoria with an expectant expression. Victoria shook her head, hoping to convey that she didn't know what was going on, either.

"Loads," Teresa said. "Regret myself the morning, but when Luke said you wasn't getting any again, but *naked*, didn't sound like a threat, more like a...well, a shh...a shomething. But he sure was mad. But pretty," she sang out. "That boy is pretty, pretty, pretty..."

"Teresa," Victoria said very slowly, in her most patient voice. "When did you see Luke naked? And how is that connected to you about to have sex?"

Kristen's eyebrows shot up, but she kept quiet.

"Couldn't focus, and Luke not helpful, but Corrs was...Corrs was..." She giggled, then said to someone in the background, "Darlin', I can't say your name." Into the phone, she said, "But he's a friend, so a-course he'll believe *him*, but he so sensitive and said call and be sure, Tessa, Tessa, you be sure Vic's okay before we keep going, so I'm calling."

Victoria's head hurt. Kristen held out a hand and wiggled her fingers, and Victoria gratefully handed over the phone.

"Tessa. It's Kristen. Talk to me." She listened for awhile, nodding and saying, "Uh huh, huh, really?" at varying intervals. At one point, she said with a smile, "I knew he would," then continued listening for another minute. "Okay. I'll tell her." She ended the call, and handed the phone to Victoria.

"She went home with Cort after the party and they had too much to drink downstairs in the Barn, then ran into Luke, naked, coming back from chasing you after you'd left. She didn't get any reassurances from him that you were okay, so Cort told her to call you to make sure. He's a sweetie." She took a sip of tea and added, "Oh, and naked Luke is a sight to behold." She waved a hand around. "That's from Teresa, not me. Apparently I'm the only one who hasn't seen him naked yet. So do I get your side of the story now?"

Victoria sat for a moment, nonplussed. "I don't think I can put it as succinctly as you did."

"Don't feel like you have to." Kristen lay back on the floor and lifted her legs, pointing her toes straight at the ceiling.

"I hate that you can do that," Victoria told her.

"You could, too. Just takes some practice. So spill."

"I went to the Barn to—damn it," she said, remembering why she'd shown up there in the first place. She reached for her phone. "I was supposed to get Teresa out of there, not encourage her."

"Oh." Kristen held her hand out, blocking Victoria's access to the phone. "T said she needs to talk to you about that. It's really not up to me to say, but you don't have to worry about Tessa and Cort breaking their contract for the show. Plus, she's had a lot to drink, and now might not be a good time to go into everything."

Suddenly, lying on the floor seemed like a good idea, and she joined Kristen there, shimmying the skirt of her dress down as she snuggled next to her sister. "I slept with Luke." She knew she was stating the obvious, but she needed to start somewhere.

"And the cameras were off," Kristen said. "Or else you wouldn't have."

"Right." She liked to believe so. Thinking back, as they stood facing each other at his door, when he'd said it was inevitable, she wasn't so sure the cameras would have stopped her. The thought made her stomach hurt.

"But you left..." Kristen prompted.

"I got scared," Victoria admitted.

"Of what?" Kristen lowered her legs, and turned to look at Victoria.

Victoria shook her head. She didn't know how to narrow it down. "Too many things." She tried to imagine Luke, naked, running down the hallway and out to the street after her, and couldn't quite picture it. She felt even more guilty, knowing he'd heard her leave and had chased her down. "It's too complicated. The working relationship, the show..." She stared up at the ceiling. "I've never felt this way before, and I can't let it go any further. It's not fair to lead him on. I shouldn't have slept with him in the first place. If I stop now, it won't get any more complicated."

Kristen lifted herself on one elbow and stared at Victoria. "You really believe that?"

"It has to be that way," Victoria insisted.

Kristen flopped back onto the floor. "I think you're in love with him, and having sex brought out emotions you weren't ready for."

Victoria's spine tingled. "I can't be in love with him."

"Why not?"

"Because it would never work out."

"I don't think you have a choice. I think it was all predestined, that your souls agreed beforehand that when you came to earth, you'd be together at the right time. So it's kind of a done deal. The rest is just logistics, figuring out how to stay together."

Victoria gave a brief smile, once again looking up at the ceiling. She still didn't have anything concerning Luke figured out, and her entire world was turned upside down, but at least Kristen would always be Kristen. "So you're saying we're soul mates?"

"You've got all the classic signs."

"You make it sound like a disease. How can there be classic signs for soul mates?"

Kristen held up her hands and began ticking items off as she spoke. "One, instant attraction. Two, a constant awareness of the other person whenever they're in the room, like some kind of homing beacon. Three, an intense need to be with them, despite not knowing them well."

"That could just be lust, you know. Drunken Saturday night lust."

"It's Sunday now. Four," Kristen continued. "Fear."

"Why would soul mates be afraid of each other?" Victoria asked, even as her heart started pounding hard.

"Not of each other. Of messing up. You make a big commitment out there in the Universe as a soul or spirit or whatever, but you know when you get back down here, it's going to be confusing and you're not really going to remember your promise, even though it's embedded in you deep down, so there's always going to be something inside of you, going, 'Is it him? Is that him? Is he the one?' And then when you do find the one that you think is the one, well...what happens if you mess up?"

"But Luke can't be the one."

Kristen turned on her side and propped her head in her hand. "Why not?"

Victoria let out a frustrated sigh. "Have you not been listening? It's too complicated. It would never work. It would just end up ruining things for both of us."

"Sometimes the house of cards has to fall before you can rebuild something better," Kristen said. "And I don't think you have a choice," she repeated. "Not if he's the one."

Victoria stood up. "Stop saying that. He's not the one. My one can't be a cowboy on my show with a famous father and a chip on his shoulder a mile wide. No matter how many amazing orgasms he gives me." She picked up her phone and clutched it to her chest. "Thanks for the condoms, by the way," she said, then marched into her room.

CHAPTER TWENTY-SEVEN

On Monday morning, Victoria sat at her desk, head in hands, trying to avoid her life. She was also avoiding Brett, Jerry, and Luke Tyler. She'd sent her backup, Chris, to oversee the day's shoots for *In Concert*. After reviewing the social media responses, she noted the show was trending on Facebook, Twitter, BuzzFeed, The Huffington Post, and Salon. But the television ratings for *In Concert*'s premiere episode had gotten held up because of some glitch, and Jerry was having a snit, acting as if Victoria had personally sabotaged the computers.

The one person she wanted to talk to, usually the sanest one in the middle of any flurry of insanity, was apparently still in bed with Cort Landry. Teresa hadn't been home all weekend, and Victoria gave up on worrying about her best friend being filmed for the show. Even a few days ago, she would have gone to Brett and asked his opinion on the situation; she'd become accustomed to sharing her thoughts with him. But she couldn't do that now.

She knew she had to talk to him at some point, but her mind was in such a whirl, she wouldn't know how to begin. Plus, any thoughts of Brett were immediately replaced by visions of Luke—dark hairs curling on his bare chest, eyes closed, sucking her finger into his mouth. They overtook everything else, and her traitorous body tingled in all the places he'd touched her, begging for more.

Her office door banged open and Jerry demanded, "Have you got those ratings yet?" He yanked at his tie and brushed thinning hair back from his forehead.

Victoria glared at him, tired for once of being accountable. She didn't think Jerry would talk to Brett or Frank that way. "*I haven't.*" She hit refresh on the ratings site, then swiveled her computer screen to show him the error message. "But I'll be thrilled to rush right into your office with bells on to let you know when the ratings bureau gets their damn computers fixed and gets the damn numbers to me. In fact, I'll shout it out from here, text you and get you on speaker phone. Better yet—"

"Attitude," Jerry threatened, looking both surprised and angry. They'd had plenty of face-offs in the past, but she'd never been disrespectful. She'd even been about to say she'd let Jenna know, because the entire building would have the news in seconds. He met her gaze. She didn't blink.

A voice called over Jerry's shoulder, "We get Saturday's numbers in yet?" and not only did Victoria blink, but she shut her eyes tight.

When she opened them again, Brett stood next to Jerry, who said, "Apparently we'll get them when Victoria is good and ready."

Brett glanced between Victoria and Jerry, but neither of them moved or spoke. Finally, Jerry tossed a hand at Victoria and said, "Fix it, or you're in my office," then stormed out.

Brett closed the door behind him and stood looking at Victoria. "What was that all about?"

"Jerry being an ass." Victoria stared at her Blackberry, willing it to ring. She'd talk to anyone right now rather than have to face Brett.

"But that's not unusual." His voice rose, sounded almost girlish. "You gave him attitude?"

He sounded awed, and he must have been listening at the door because Jerry had accused her of giving attitude before Brett walked in. She felt like giving them both some attitude right now. She stood up, crossing her arms over her chest. "Your point?"

He came around the desk and had his hands on her shoulders before she could find a way to deflect. "Baby, what's wrong? I've been trying to get hold of you forever. You cut the premiere party short, you left without saying goodbye, you haven't answered your phone." He touched a fingertip to her nose with a wink, and tilted his head. He was trying for charming, but he just looked smarmy.

How had she not noticed before?

She shrugged away from him and his arms fell to his sides. "I hate when you touch my nose that way, like it's the button to turn me on." She closed her eyes and pressed her lips together; she hadn't meant the innuendo.

"It's not?" he teased, his voice gone husky. "I guess I've been pointed in the wrong direction all this time."

She felt him move closer to her again, and opened her eyes.

He tilted his head toward the door. "What say I lock that and you show me the right button?"

"This isn't the time."

His face hardened. "Really, Victoria? And when will that be? Because I've been pretty patient so far. But I've got to tell you, my patience is wearing a bit thin."

Did he always talk in clichés? When had he gotten so *wrong*?

She took a deep breath, trying not to get caught up in his anger, considering so many emotions were roiling around inside her. "Brett...I need to tell you something."

"Well, that's never a good beginning." He gave her a smile, one of the ones that used to feed her crush on him. What had happened?

When she didn't respond right away, he held his hands up in an "I surrender" gesture, and went around to sit on the chair across from her desk. She remained standing, her head down and her fingertips pressed to the desk blotter, trying to figure out what to tell him and how to say it. Everything sounded trite to her as well. *Brett, you're a great guy... we've grown apart..it's not you, it's me...*

"Whatever it is," Brett said, "I'm sure we can work it out."

Victoria held back a slightly hysterical laugh. Okay, they were going to play it with clichés, then. "Actually, I don't think we can. This is too big to—"

A knock sounded on the door and she gritted her teeth. What now? She just wanted to get this over with.

She heard him before she saw him, the thud of his boots on the floor, that rough-smooth voice with the pronounced Southern drawl, and she felt her knees give.

"Victoria? The receptionist said just come on in. I told Sam he didn't need to film this on account of I only wanted to ask about something in my contract." He edged around the door and smiled at the sight of her; because of the angle of her desk to the door, he hadn't yet seen Brett.

"Mr. Tyler," she said in a professional tone, hoping to head him off in case he said something inappropriate.

He ducked his head, hat shading his eyes. "So we're back to that, are we? After Saturday, I'd think..." His voice trailed off as he came fully into the office and in sight of Brett. He'd already reached behind him to push the door shut, and it clicked with a soft sound that seemed to ricochet around the room as everyone froze at Luke's words.

Brett stood up in a smooth motion, shot his cuffs and held out a hand. "Cort Tyler, is it?"

Luke pushed back his hat and gave Brett a slow smile, clearly picking up on the game: mess up a man's name, prove he's easy to dismiss. To Victoria, Luke's broad shoulders, thigh muscles accentuated by tight jeans, and added height from well-worn black hat and boots made Brett's trim silhouette look diminished and ineffectual. When had this happened? She refused to believe one episode of good sex could change her perspective on Brett that easily. Of course, it had technically been more than one session. And multiple orgasms.

Luke shook Brett's hand, this time without playing who's-the-stronger-caveman by trying to squeeze his hand to a pulp, and said, genially, "It's Luke Landry, actually."

Brett looked confused. Victoria shook her head. Brett knew perfectly well what Luke's name was; she always used the talent's full names because it was the best way to cement someone into another person's mind. She also did it to keep Brett from feeling threatened, as casually dropping four men's names—especially one who happened to be a sex god—into a conversation with your boyfriend could possibly be taken the wrong way.

Her boyfriend. She snorted, and both the "boyfriend" and the sex god turned to look at her.

She coughed to cover it, even though she knew it was too late. "Sorry." She cleared her throat. "So what can I do for you, Mr. Tyler? Did you need to ask me something about the show?"

"Indeed, I do, Ms. Clausen."

"Well," Brett said, a bit too brisk. "I can see I'm in the way here. Victoria..." He brushed against Luke on his way around the desk to give Victoria a too-long kiss she pursed her lips against, and a tap on the end of her nose. "We'll continue our conversation later, yes?" Without waiting for her answer, he headed for the door. "Mr. Landry."

Luke inclined his head, and Brett went out, shutting the door behind him with a stern thud. While Victoria pressed her hands to the desk again to regain her composure—at the same time wondering if she would *ever* regain it—Luke sprawled into the chair Brett had just vacated, his long legs out in front of him and his boots crossed at the ankles.

"I've a mind to give that pipsqueak a good thrashing," he said, crossing his arms over his chest.

"You will not," Victoria commanded.

"What happened to you?"

"Well, it was all a bit confusing, you know," she said, "you and Brett in here at the same time..."

He shook his head. "Saturday night. Why'd you leave?" He straightened up, shoving the chair forward, and leaned his elbows on the desk to reach for her hand. He held it between his palms, warming skin she hadn't even known was cold. "I wasn't finished."

"I need to sit down."

He let her hand go and came around to her side, pulling the chair out and resting his hands on her shoulders until she settled in. Then he spun the chair around and crouched in front of her, forcibly reminding her of their night together, when they sat facing each other half dressed on his bed, after having sex against his front door. Hard, pounding, satisfying sex.

"Are you all right?"

She didn't know how to answer that. "What are you doing here?"

"You can ask that after the other night?"

She looked at the door, as if all of her office mates were squashed together on the other side, trying to hear their conversation.

"You afraid your boyfriend might come back?"

"He's—" She stopped. She supposed Brett was technically still her boyfriend, but even if he wasn't, she didn't want to say that out loud to Luke. Even if she didn't have a boyfriend, nothing could come of their...their...she struggled for the right word. Their attraction.

"He's what?" Luke prompted.

"This isn't the place."

"Then where?"

She looked at his face, the deep green eyes, slightly crooked nose, and generous mouth, and didn't know whether to kiss him or push him away. They needed to talk—she owed him an explanation for why she left, among other things—but she didn't want to be alone with him. Just thinking about that made her body tingle; the way he looked at her now reminded her of his hands on her breasts, how he'd eased aside her panties, slid a finger deep inside...

She shook her head, completely at a loss for words.

He stared at the floor, then nodded, and stood up. "I get it. One-time thing." He took off his hat, ran a hand through his hair, resettled the hat and headed for the door, which once again opened. Victoria thought at this rate, she'd have a heart attack before the day was over.

Hannah, one of the station PAs, stood in the doorway holding a sheaf of papers to her chest. "They're in," she said, then caught sight of Luke and made a humming noise in the back of her throat, her gaze traveling from his boots up and up to the crown of his hat. "Oh my," she said. "You're Luke Tyler. I loved the premiere, but we haven't seen you with a woman. Please tell me you're not gay, married, or twisted."

Luke tipped his hat at her. "No, ma'am, none of the above."

"Excellent. That makes about seven of you in SF. I may not move back to Wisconsin just yet."

Victoria didn't even try to keep from rolling her eyes. "Did you have something for me, Hannah?"

"Oh, sure, the ratings finally came through." Hannah held the papers out, still smiling and batting her eyelashes at Luke.

With a sigh, Victoria took them and positioned herself in front of Hannah, knowing it wouldn't break her line of sight with Luke—Hannah was five-foot-eight, willowy and San Francisco chic—but at least it might distract her. "Thank you, Hannah," Victoria said in a loud, clear voice. "You can close the door on your way out."

Hannah didn't take her eyes off Luke. "Do I have to? Don't you want to show him off?"

"He's not a prize pony," Victoria said with disgust, the papers in her hands crying to be read.

"No, he's more like a sta—"

Victoria held a hand up in front of Hannah's face. "Don't," she commanded. "Now please excuse us."

After pretending to drop her pen to bend forward and give Luke a flash of her cleavage, Hannah finally made her way out of the office. And left the door open.

Victoria banged it closed and turned the lock for good measure.

Luke gave it a look but didn't say anything. Victoria set the sheaf of papers on her desk and stared at them. If she hadn't been so used to interpreting them, they'd have looked like a bunch of nothing, considering her current state. As it was, she'd trained herself to quickly find her shows and make rapid calculations. "*Duck Dynasty*, yeah, yeah, always high ratings," she muttered. "*Dress My Best*, good, *Hairdressers for Hire*, decent, I'd prefer higher...*here*." She slammed her palms on the desk and said, "Yes! Oh, yes! Three point seven rating and a twelve share."

"So that's good, then?"

She jumped. She'd been so lost in the numbers, she'd forgotten for a moment Luke was there.

She turned to him, beaming. "*In Concert* debuted at number one." In her joy, she reached up on her tiptoes and put her arms around his neck.

He tensed against her and she moved to let go, her cheeks warm, but he wrapped his arms around her waist and lifted her off her feet as if she were weightless.

Before she could squeak out her surprise, she found herself sitting on Luke's lap in her office chair, being kissed senseless. His warm lips covered hers, his tongue teased and stroked, and his hands caressed her face and pushed her hair back behind her ears.

"Your hair's down," he murmured in her ear.

She made a noise of agreement, clutching at his shoulders when he stroked a particularly delicate spot on her neck.

"I like it," he added.

"Mmm..."

"We should probably stop," he breathed against her cheek.

"Umm..."

Loud pounding on the door jerked her upright and she scrambled off Luke's lap. Patting her hair into place, she headed for the door, doing up two buttons she hadn't realized until now that he'd undone. She glanced back at Luke, waiting for his nod of assent before she opened the door.

"Oh, thank God you're here," Teresa said, almost falling into the room. "You didn't answer either of your phones and Chris said you weren't on the shoot today and—" She stopped when she caught sight of Luke, casually leaning back in Victoria's chair. "Luke," she said coolly.

He gave her a nod. "Tessa."

"I'm surprised to see you here." A pause. "Dressed."

While they faced off, Victoria lunged for her Blackberry. No signal? What the hell? Shaking it, she glanced at her office phone and saw the DND button activated. She'd set it on Do Not Disturb when she first got into the office at five-thirty that morning, having spent the night tossing and turning and finally getting up in disgust. With the parade of people in her office all morning, she'd forgotten to take it off.

"T, I think my Blackberry has a defective battery or something," she said, frowning at it.

When Teresa didn't reply, Victoria looked up to see her and Luke glaring at each other. It was one face-off too many today.

"Teresa, I really need to talk to you. Luke, the same, but this isn't the place. I will call you and set up a meeting time."

Luke gave a nod and stood up, brushed a hand down Victoria's hair, tipped his hat to Teresa, and strode out of the office to excited murmurs from the main room. Victoria was sure Hannah was lying in wait for Luke behind a potted palm.

Victoria closed the door behind him and leaned against it with a sigh. Teresa had lost her aggression and stood in the middle of the office, fussing with the zipper of her purse.

The ratings numbers had improved Victoria's mood, and she felt even better at the idea of setting things right with Teresa. At the same time, she was still angry with T for sleeping with Cort, at herself for sleeping with Luke, with Teresa for not talking to her about wanting to quit, and with herself again for not noticing that T was unhappy enough—or so caught up with Cort—that she felt she needed to leave her job *again*.

She collapsed in her chair, still warm from Luke's body heat, and gestured for Teresa to sit as well. Victoria couldn't help comparing this moment to the time six weeks ago when Teresa had come into her office in the same kind of agitated state, and she had quit.

Teresa sat in the chair with her head bowed, clutching her bag on her lap. Victoria didn't know what to bring up first: the job, Teresa sleeping with Cort, or what was going to happen next.

She finally settled on, "Are you all right?"

"I can't believe I slept with Cort Landry," Teresa replied. "He's like a drug. I can't even blame it on being drunk because we didn't start drinking until after we'd...well..." She smoothed her hands over her suede bag. "A couple times. Then we went downstairs and...well, you two must have come in then. I knew better. I *know* better, but he makes me feel like I'm the only woman in the world." She held up a hand. "I *know*. We're talking about Cort Landry here, the guy who might as well have 'womanizer' tattooed on his forehead, but I'm telling you..." Teresa finally looked at Victoria. "I can't get enough of him."

If this had happened a week ago, Victoria might not have been so sympathetic. As it was, she understood better than she wanted to. Even now, she wanted to jump up and call Luke back into her office.

"So you're quitting to go out with him?"

"No! No. I was going to quit before that. My catering gig has been great, and they offered me a job, and want to help me with culinary school. Doing this—" she waved her hand around "—was getting to be too much. Plus, I..." Her voice dropped. "Well, I think I wanted to get your attention."

"You're not blaming *me* for your sleeping with Cort, are you?"

"Oh no, that was all me." Teresa gave a little smile, but it disappeared quickly. "You were just so focused on *In Concert*, and that idiot, Brett. I am *so* glad you broke up with him, by the way."

Victoria bit her lower lip. "I haven't broken up with him. Technically."

Teresa clapped a hand to her mouth. "Technically? But I...but you...you don't cheat. I mean, I'd never think you'd sleep with someone else while you were dating..." Her eyes got big. "Or the show. You slept with someone on the *show*. I was ready for the cameras, but..."

"You were?" Victoria was fascinated. After briefly considering the possibilities the other night, she realized she could never be "in front of the camera" material on a reality show.

Teresa shrugged, although she didn't look completely indifferent. "Another part of my rebellion, I guess." She leaned forward. "But the *show*. Does Jerry know yet?"

Victoria shook her head. "I had Ray turn off the feed that night."

"Oh my God. You're shattering all of my long-standing beliefs about you. You had them turn off the feed so you could have sex with Luke?"

"No! I did it to save *you*. I went over there to stop you, but you must've already gone downstairs, because no one answered when we knocked."

Teresa scooted forward on her chair. "We?"

"Well, Luke lives there, of course. We...ran into each other." Victoria let out a long breath, relieved to finally be talking about this with her best friend.

Teresa leaned back. "I can't believe you went over there to stop me."

"I was trying to stop you from making a big mistake."

"But I was fine."

"*I* didn't know that." She reached across the desk, wiggling her fingers, and Teresa scooted her chair closer and grasped her hands. Victoria felt another layer of stress peeling away. It meant everything to still have her best girl at her side. "And I had a show to protect, too."

Teresa shook her head, but didn't release her hands. "Always the show."

"It's my—"

"Life," Teresa finished for her, and this time she did let go. "I know," she said, but not unkindly. "What about Luke?"

"What about him?"

Teresa gestured behind her at the closed door. "He was just here. Are you going to see him again?"

"Of course not." She blinked at that, surprised at her response. Was that true? But, how could she see him again, considering?

"Because of the show? Or because you don't like him?"

Victoria didn't want to say "because of the show"; she felt like a parrot in that regard lately, and it was starting to lose its impact. But she couldn't say she didn't like Luke, because that would be a lie. She finally settled on the uncharacteristic, "I don't know."

"Do you like him?"

"Yes."

"Would you keep seeing him if you weren't his producer?"

"T, we aren't exactly dating. We just had sex."

Teresa smiled. "That doesn't answer my question."

And Teresa was asking her all of the hard questions she should have been asking herself. "You've been hanging around Kristen too much."

Teresa laughed. "Who knew? That girl's actually been a help to me."

Victoria thought of the condoms in Kristen's purse, and the talk they'd had that night. Who knew, indeed? But then another thought struck. "You've had to get help from her because I haven't been around."

"Oh, V," Teresa said.

Victoria watched her friend struggling with a reply. She didn't want to make Teresa uncomfortable, but the two of them needed to stop dancing around certain subjects. And that meant letting Teresa speak her mind, even if it hurt to hear. It also meant finally being honest with herself.

"Yes, and no," Teresa said. "It's true you haven't been very available, but Kristen really has been great—in her own cuckoo sort of way. And part of me didn't want to have to fight for your attention. Between Brett, work..."

"Oh, T, I'm so sorry." Victoria got up and went around the desk just as Teresa stood, too. They hugged, both apologizing and saying it wouldn't happen again. They were still hugging and wiping at their faces when Hannah came in and said, "Jerry wants to see the damn numbers." She stared at Victoria. "And it's urgent that I get that hot cowboy's number."

CHAPTER TWENTY-EIGHT

Luke paced so much he thought he might wear a groove in the cement of the Barn floor. Victoria had stirred something up in him that first night they met, and it hadn't calmed any since; making love to her and kissing her at her office only charged him up again.

When she ran out on him late Saturday night, he felt like she'd kicked him in the balls with one of her spike heels, but he wasn't ready to give up on her. He'd barely been able to stop himself driving back to Russian Hill and shouting her name in the middle of every street until she came out, but Tessa's protectiveness held him back. He wanted her to stay all night, but there was some reason she'd raced out like a scared rabbit, and he could give her some time.

Some.

First thing this morning, he'd thought about trying to call her from Blitz or Tony's, but groupies now followed him along with the cameras. Cort had some in his wake when he left for the gym, and Luke took a few minutes for pictures and autographs, but more kept showing up. Time alone without a film crew or gaggle of girls nearby seemed impossible, but he figured he'd sneak a word in when Victoria got to the Barn. Then Chris showed up instead, saying Victoria had a scheduling conflict and he'd be producing for the next few days.

Luke had grabbed his keys and jacket and driven straight to the television studio, with Sam and groups of fans racing after him.

Then to find that pipsqueak with her in the office.

Now, Sam gave a loud sigh from the corner and said, "Dude, this is not great TV."

Jolted out of pleasant thoughts of pummeling Brett Soloway until he cried like a girl, Luke had to force his hands to relax at his sides. "Thought you weren't supposed to interact with us." He heard the edge in his voice, and didn't care.

Sam straightened, taking his eye from the viewfinder, and shifted his shoulder to adjust the camera. "I like your music, but I don't get paid enough for this kind of shit, following you around while you either do jack or get laid. Then we all have to sit around listening to it."

Luke froze. Did he know something?

Sam scratched at his belly. "Well, the other guys get some anyway. You must be—"

He stopped when Victoria clicked her way through the main door.

Luke watched Sam shrink back as Victoria drew herself up in front of him. "Sam," she said, and that one word carried so much disappointment and frustration that Luke found himself feeling bad for the guy. For himself, he wanted to shove Sam outside, lock the door, then bend Victoria over a chair and take her long, slow and deep.

He made an involuntary noise that he tried to cover with a cough, but she didn't turn away from Sam.

"Take the rest of the afternoon off," Victoria said. "And we'll talk tomorrow."

Her tone allowed no retort, but Sam still gave her a glare as he stomped outside. The door slammed behind him, but Victoria did not lower her shoulders. Instead, she rummaged in her bag, pulled out a date book and opened it to a blank page in the back. "I apologize for his attitude, Mr. Tyler. He'll be spoken to." Head bent, she wrote with a large marker, circling near the door until she hit a spot the cameras couldn't pick up.

She flipped the calendar up until he could read "Meet at Side Door," and closed it as soon as he gave a small nod.

"Appreciated, Ms. Clausen."

"Have a good afternoon," she called on her way out the door.

He didn't respond. He was already halfway up the stairs. He bounded up the hallway and down the other set of stairs that led into the alley. Victoria sat in her car and gestured for him to get in, which he did without hesitation. He leaned against the door and watched her profile, her sweet mouth, the curve of her cheek. He itched to touch her.

"We have about half an hour," she said, pulling away from the curb. "Forty-five minutes at the most."

"Before what?"

"Before..." Her voice trailed off. "Someone will most likely try to get in touch with me and it will be some sort of an emergency."

"And you're the only one who can take care of it?"

She gave him a quick look out of the corner of her eye before focusing on the road again. "Yes."

"And someone'll die if it's not handled in the next half hour?"

She shook her head. "This can't happen," she told him.

"What's that now?" He deliberately misunderstood her because they both deserved better than such an abrupt ending.

She pressed her lips together, but didn't answer.

He tried to wait her out, but he had little patience these days. "Do we have a destination or are we having this discussion driving?" he finally asked, as Victoria continued to make turns that seemed to result in them circling the city.

"Driving," she said as she signaled to make another right.

"That doesn't suit me."

"Well, it suits me." She stared through the windshield.

"Victoria..." he said, and saw her shoulders tense up and her hands tighten on the steering wheel. "We can't have a decent conversation like this. Pull over."

"There's no parking here."

Stubborn had just met stubborn. He pointed ahead. "Get into the right lane here, then up the hill. There should be more parking, and a pretty respectable view."

She glanced at him before easing the car into the right lane. "The reservoir," she said. "Not many people know this way up there."

"Been here awhile." He leaned back, more relaxed now that her tension had eased. He'd still have to go gentle with her, but that would be harder if they had to discuss things while she concentrated on the road.

As the car climbed the hill, the flats and businesses gave way to more greenery, large rocky outcroppings and eucalyptus trees.

"I did a lot of driving when we first got here," he continued as the hill grew steeper and the car shifted into a lower gear. "Wasn't real sure what two Southern boys were going to do in Frisco." He saw her look and laughed. "I don't call it that anymore. But at the time, I didn't know any better, and I kept trying to figure what the hell we were doing here. We'd failed everywhere else and I was just following Cort's lead, pretty sure we'd fall short in this city, too. And where would we go from here?"

They turned onto a street with houses on one side and low hedges on the other, which gave way to a view of the city below them and the East Bay across the water. Victoria pulled over at a curve in the road, so they could both look out at the rooftops, groupings of shrubbery, and distant hills. She turned to him. "I didn't know any of this. You didn't say anything in the interviews."

He shrugged. "We didn't fail. No sense revisiting all that."

"So why are you telling me now?"

He wanted to say, "Because you don't have a camera with you, and because I like you and want you to know me as a man and not a film subject." But that would just scare her off. Or make her mad. So he told her the other part of it. "It's how I got to know the city. For instance, the reservoir there is extra water for the fire department. I came up here one night, real frustrated about things, and had a fine conversation with a fireman who was checking things over." He faced her and his knee brushed hers. She pulled her legs back, but he pretended not to notice. "When we first got here, I was real restless, lonely, mad at Cort, who didn't seem to have any trouble sleeping or any worries about what was going to happen next."

"Does he ever?"

He smiled. "Not much. You know it's serious if he does."

"So you drove around while he was sleeping?"

"Drove. Walked. Took the Muni. Learned not to walk around in cowboy boots and a Stetson in some areas unless I wanted to get myself a boyfriend or two."

She laughed. "I'm sure you were popular. How did you feel about that?"

"Hard not to be flattered, really. Who better to know what's sexy in a man than another man?"

"I wish I had a camera right now," Victoria said with a soft exhalation.

Luke took her hand in both of his, stroking her palm when she tensed at his touch. "Life isn't all about what you can get on camera."

Victoria looked into his eyes. *"Mine* is."

"No, darlin', life is about moments. All strung together, some bad, hopefully more good, and sharing them with someone else."

"But that's what I do, capture those moments for people to share together."

She was so rooted in this life; could he help her break out of it? "They're talking about someone else's lives and experiences they've watched on a screen. What about their own experiences? What about yours?"

She looked genuinely confused. "Mine?"

He leaned forward. "What about ours?"

She didn't look away, didn't try to take her hands from his, but her fingers twitched slightly. "This is why I wanted to drive while we talked."

He ran a finger over her knuckles. "Why's that?"

"Because my brain stops functioning when you touch me."

He smiled. "And think of those experiences we've had when I've touched you." His fingers circled one small wrist, brushing against the slim bracelet she wore.

She shook her head.

"Victoria—"

"Don't call me that." He heard the edge in her voice, the way it cracked on a couple words.

"Why?" His fingers now slipped under the sleeve of her blazer and brushed the fine hairs on her forearms. Gentle, he reminded himself.

She shivered, but didn't pull back or look away. "You always call me Ms. Clausen or Victoria Clausen. When you call me Victoria, you're either being sweet or serious. Or both."

"Don't you think it's time to be serious?"

She sighed. "Yes."

"After Saturday night," he began, but stopped when she retreated more. He kept his hand on her arm, stroking the tender skin just above her wrist. "I thought it was all about lust on my part, that maybe if we had sex, I'd get you out of my system." She didn't say anything, but he had her attention, so he continued. "Turns out, I only want you more. And it's not just lust, it's...everything. Your smarts, your courage, the way you take charge. I got a taste, and it just made me hungrier." There. He'd laid it out. And still she stared at him like he might bite her. He leaned closer. "What about you?"

She pressed farther back, but still didn't try to take her hand away. "I want to get to know you better."

His heart clenched up. Was that all he was going to get? "We can't do that with the cameras rolling."

"No." She was practically braced against the door now. "Please don't ask me to make a choice."

So that was it. He glanced out the window behind her, the city unfolding below an unfocused blur to him, then back at her face. He read fear, worry that he'd demand a decision from her, but also noted the stubborn set of her features. So that really was it. "You've been real clear about what you'd choose. I'm not stupid." Persistent, maybe, when he wanted something. A touch blind. But not stupid.

Fear changed to sadness, but stubborn stayed. "I never said you were," she whispered.

He knew he shouldn't push, but he needed to hear it from her. "Am I wrong about your choice?"

She didn't say anything, just squeezed his fingers and hung her head.

His gut tightened, but he ignored it. He had to ignore all of those reactions from this point on, or he might break. And that wouldn't do either of them any good. Lifting her hand, he kissed the palm before setting it back in her lap. She looked up when he let go. The anguish in her eyes firmed his decision. He couldn't ask her to do this, so he'd take the option from her.

"You've got one less choice now," he said softly. He wanted to kiss her one last time, to press his lips to hers just for a moment, but knew that would do him in. Instead he opened the door and got out, striding down the hill without looking back. The wind gusted up from the ravine, sucking the breath from his lungs.

He forced himself to keep going, even after he heard a car door slam behind him. His stomach lurched at the thought of her following him. But it couldn't be her. Their conversation proved her job had won, and he'd lost.

But in between the clacking of his boots and the thudding of his heart, he heard tapping that sounded like them too-high heels, then her voice, her strong, clear voice.

"Luke! Wait!"

He didn't want to stop. God damn it, if he stopped now and let her in, he wouldn't be able to let her go again. He wouldn't. She had no idea that her choice was as difficult as his. Choose her, he made her unhappy and forced her to lose her livelihood. Let her go, and he might lose the woman he couldn't live without.

"Please," she called out.

He stopped. Hands on hips, he lowered his head, took a breath, and turned. She stood twenty feet above him, hair flying around her face in the breeze, a determined expression on her face.

"God damn it," he whispered to himself. To her, he said, "Don't make this harder, Victoria."

"It's too late for that." From the distance between them, she held out her hand.

She took a few steps down, he took a few up, and before he knew it, he'd bridged the gap and swung her off her feet, holding her tight to him and kissing her soft, full lips like there was no tomorrow. Everything fell away—the hill, traffic, honking cars, the fog coming in on the breeze—and the woman in his arms became his world.

CHAPTER TWENTY-NINE

Victoria lay in bed, staring at the ceiling. Beside her, Luke stirred, and she turned her head to look at him. His short, wavy hair didn't rumple easily, but with his face squashed into the pillow and one arm flung over her middle, he definitely looked like a man who'd just had great sex. And had given as good as he got.

She took a slow, deep breath and watched his arm rise up with her stomach and his fingers flex around her bare hip, then relax when she let the breath out. She smiled, seeing him drift back into deeper sleep. How had they gotten to this place? A jolt of energy shot through her and she had a strange desire to bounce around and yell her head off.

Not only was that very unlike her, nothing could tempt her to disturb Luke. So with a careful stretch, she reached for her Blackberry on the side table and shot off a few tweets and posts about *In Concert* debuting at number one. She answered some e-mails and texts and reminded her boss that they had a meeting the next morning with the story editor to discuss potential storylines for *In Concert*. With its rapid success, they needed to be absolutely certain her initial story outline could still be followed through. If not, she would have to move fast to get everyone going in the right direction.

She set down the phone after another peek at Luke. Moving fast sounded so unappealing right now. He'd been beautiful from the start, but she'd only seen him as someone pretty enough to light up the screen and make *In Concert* a hit; it embarrassed her she hadn't seen past that. She saw it now, though, saw *him*, a considerate, humorous, intelligent, sexy man.

A man on her show, in her care. A man she'd become involved with. Could she keep her perspective if she needed to move a plotline around that affected him? With the premiere episode, she'd set him up as the one yearning for love. Viewers would demand a resolution; first a few episodes focusing on his heartache, and ultimately finding his sweetheart. She'd been prepared to bring in a ringer for that, someone he couldn't resist, even with the cameras running.

Could she watch him have a relationship on film to satisfy the viewership? Would he even do it?

She shook her head. He wouldn't do it for himself, so how could she even think he'd risk what they had for *In Concert*? He was definitely too honorable to see her and date someone on the show at the same time, even for ratings.

She grabbed her phone again, navigating to the message boards. She scrolled through the thread titled "LUKE is Sooo freakin' HOT!!!!!" and her mood dipped and soared with each post. They loved him, they wanted more of him, he broke their hearts, they wanted to comfort him, was he gay or what? What was wrong with him that he didn't have a bunch of women throwing themselves at him?

"Absolutely nothing," she muttered to the screen.

"Are you naked texting?" Luke asked in a still-sleepy voice.

Startled, her hand jerked and the phone slipped, dropping onto her chest. "I guess so," she laughed.

He snagged the phone as it slid down the slope of one breast, his fingers gliding back up to brush over one nipple. She let out a shuddery breath at the contact. He shifted the phone to his other hand and continued to explore her bare skin. "Sexy..." he said. "Sexier if you were naked texting me, instead of..." Propped on one elbow, he glanced at the phone, and his hand stilled on her hip. Without a word, he turned the screen toward her. The rows of post subjects glared out from the phone's screen.

"I don't know what to do," she admitted. "I needed some help."

He pushed up higher and dropped the phone to the table with a clunk. "You needed help figuring how hot I was?"

"No." She didn't like him looming over her, so she sat up against the headboard, pulling the sheet to her breasts. He fell back on the pillows, a forearm over his eyes. "No," she repeated, studying the sharp line of tendon running from wrist to elbow, the long curve of his triceps down to the well-defined muscles along his side and over to the wide planes of his pectorals, all shadows and tempting brawn in the dim light. "No help needed there." She caught his smile, and gave him a nudge. "About the show."

His smile faded. "That damn show," he said.

"That damn *number one* show. I had everything planned out for it, and now none of it will work. I don't know what to do about it." She started pleating the sheet, unaccustomed to feeling so much at loose ends.

He lowered his arm and sat up, taking her hand in his to still her nervous fingers. "What you're really saying is you don't know what to do about us."

She nodded. "That, too."

"Well, not much we can do, is there? We're between a rock and a hard place, and we need to play it cool until filming's over."

She turned and found him watching her. "You'd do that? Keep things quiet until..."

"I'd do that for you, yes." He tugged at a curl that lay across her shoulder and she shivered as it brushed her bare skin.

She hesitated before replying, afraid he'd pounce on her idea as a viable option. But he needed to know it was a possibility, and she wouldn't lie to him. "I could back out, find another field producer."

"And end up resenting me for it? No, ma'am, that's not the answer. Besides," he added, pulling her close, his bare chest rubbing against her peaked nipples as he slid under the sheet with her, "then I wouldn't get to see you every day, pass you notes in class..."

He laid her back on the bed, and she accepted the distraction of his body until she fell into exhausted, satisfied oblivion.

While he dressed the next morning, she got out a metallic gray sweater, matching slacks, panties and a bra, and was pulling her sweater over her head before she realized how comfortable she felt with Luke.

With past lovers, despite her own confidence, she often felt they were silently critiquing her less than ideal body, reminding her of her short time in Hollywood, and how she'd never been quite right. Without saying a word, using his hands and mouth, Luke made her feel beautiful and desirable in a way no one else had been able to do in the past. She felt like a giddy teenager, and didn't know how to handle the highs and lows, sometimes within the same breath.

She slipped on a black platform pump and set her foot on a padded stool to fasten the ankle strap. Halfway through fastening the second one, she realized Luke had stopped moving, and stood staring at her foot.

"The shoes, huh?" she asked.

He nodded, letting out a long breath through his nose. "The shoes."

They spent more time kissing in the middle of her bedroom, with Luke holding her up as she wrapped her legs around his waist, only breaking apart when Victoria's phone rang again. She ignored it. When it buzzed twice more, she gave it a glance. Jerry. Demanding to see her. Now. Their meeting wasn't for another hour, but she'd stop by his office when she got to the studio.

Laughing quietly over nothing in particular, they headed down the hallway, and before reaching the living room, Luke put his hands on her shoulders, turned her and kissed her again, this one soft and sweet. She held tight to his belt loops and kissed him back, forgetting everything else for a few moments. When they separated, Luke took her hand and led her into the living room.

Where Kristen sat in the lotus pose, palms pressed together at her heart, a beatific smile on her face.

"You've completed the circle," she said.

"Three and a half times," Luke replied, without missing a beat or dropping Victoria's hand. "How you doing, Sunshine?"

"My world is always enchanting," she said. "I'm glad to hear my condoms helped yours to be as well."

Luke paused on the way past Kristen to the front door. "Well, now, that explains a few things."

Victoria pressed her palm to Kristen's mouth as she went past. "I'll deal with you later."

"I don't doubt it," Kristen said with a grin, once her mouth was freed. She bowed her head over her hands. "Namasté."

Luke's shoulders shook with silent laughter as they went down the steps to Victoria's car, and she couldn't help smiling, too. As they turned on California Street, she took a quick peek at the Top of the Mark, a San Francisco landmark with gorgeous views. Filming a segment there would be such a coup, but it didn't fit any of her shows at this point.

"Your sister is a caution," Luke said, still laughing and shaking his head.

"She's something, all right."

"I'm real relieved those smiley face condoms were hers and not yours."

Victoria laughed out loud. "Her condoms have smiley faces on them?"

"Gave me a start," he said, taking her free hand.

She sighed in pleasure at the warmth of his fingers on hers, the view of Grace Cathedral in all its French Gothic glory directly ahead, and general contentment of living in San Francisco. She loved this city and all it had to offer.

Luke stared up at Grace Cathedral's columns, turning his head to look at the entire building as they passed and she remembered the day she drove to the stables to film him, hoping to ease him into being comfortable talking on camera. He'd watched everything from the window then, too, as if it were all brand new to him.

Not wanting to break this new bond between them, Victoria took the indirect way back to the Barn. Luke kept quiet as she avoided yet another one way street, and drove past Civic Center Plaza and the Asian Art Museum, her palm and fingers tingling from Luke's caresses. When she got to Howard and neared 11th, she knew she couldn't delay anymore, and let out a real sigh this time as they stopped at a light a couple blocks from Folsom.

Luke said, "You can let me out any time."

Her happy daze interrupted, all Victoria could think to say was, "What?"

"Sam might be there. Or..." He made a face. "Groupies."

"Of course." She pulled over in front of a narrow driveway. "I guess I...still don't know what to do. About us. The show."

"I know." He squeezed her hand. "We'll make it work."

"I'll call you," she said, then pressed her lips together, realizing she couldn't even do that.

"Best if I call you," he said. "Or maybe text."

"Of course," she repeated.

He set her hand in her lap, then got out of the car and strolled up the street without looking back. Victoria watched until he'd turned the corner, then put the car in gear and headed for the studio, plugging her earphones into her Blackberry to listen to her messages. For the first time she could ever remember, she wasn't excited about going to the office.

CHAPTER THIRTY

Victoria tried to breeze past bitchy Jenna, but when the receptionist called out, "How's your boyfriend?" she had to stop.

She tried to arrange her features into neutral. "Excuse me?" she asked politely, thinking furiously. Jenna must mean Brett. He was currently so far off her radar as boyfriend material, she had trouble connecting Jenna's smarmy comment with Mr. Watermelon kisser. Shit. She still had to deal with him, and now, thanks to Jenna, the gossip would be around the entire building.

Jenna smiled up at her through her long blonde bangs. "I hear he's researching something really hot right now."

Willing her heart to stop beating so hard, Victoria said, "Well, we're always looking for the next big thing we can develop. I hope it pans out for him. If you'll excuse me, I have a meeting with Jerry." She heard the snobby tone to her voice, but didn't have the patience to deal with Jenna right now. She needed to meet with Jerry, discuss the direction she wanted to take *In Concert*, then find a way to see Luke again.

"Oh, he's not in at present," Jenna said in a cloying tone. "But feel free to wait. You won't be waiting long."

Victoria gave her a tight smile and headed to her office. Fine. If he wasn't there right now, she'd make a quick stop to see if she had anything in her inbox that needed her immediate attention. She didn't like Jenna's sticky sweetness, but there was nothing she could do about it right now. So she was the subject of some gossip. It wouldn't be the first time.

Rita Zelenstein popped out of her cubicle and greeted Victoria with a cheerful hello. Victoria cringed at how she'd thought of Rita as mousy, and Rita had been the only one to help her that day she'd struggled up the aisle with her sprained ankle.

"Hi, Rita, how are you?"

Rita went pink in the cheeks and laid a hand on Victoria's forearm. She glanced quickly around the room, then leaned close and whispered, "I wrote a play and it's being produced at Campo Santo."

Victoria grasped her hand. "Congratulations, that's so exciting. They're a very prestigious theatre."

Rita nodded over and over, her eyes huge, clearly overcome.

"Will you tell me when it opens? I'd love to go."

Rita nodded again, and Victoria gave her hand another squeeze before heading back up the aisle. She was truly happy for Rita, but a small pebble thunked to the bottom of her stomach when she realized she'd not only been standoffish with Rita, but with many other people at Reality Strikes. When Frank Littleton passed her with a smirk on his face and a "Hey, Clausen, hear Soloway's riding something hot—yee dawgies!" and made a sizzling sound with a finger against his cheek, she also realized her co-workers didn't respect her.

Or, she thought with chagrin, she didn't respect them. And treated them that way.

Distracted, and forgetting that she meant to stop at her office first, she turned left at the end of the aisle and walked to Jerry's office instead. Inside, she stopped short with a gasp.

Brett sat in one of the chairs across from Jerry's desk, an ankle crossed over his knee and a remote control in one hand.

That little bitch, Jenna. She knew Brett was in here. But what did that mean?

"Where's Jerry?"

Brett's knee bounced up and down, jiggling his propped foot. "On his way."

"Well, I'm glad you're here. We need to talk."

"Where've you been?"

She eyed him. Beyond the agitated leg jiggling, his hair looked messy instead of its usual deliberately tousled, his tie was loosened, and he had a grease stain on one sleeve. "Research," she said, trying to keep her voice neutral. Maybe this wasn't the time to tell him she didn't want to see him anymore. But if not now...? "You haven't been around, either. I..." She stopped, disturbed by Brett's attitude.

His gaze drifted down her body. "Nice shoes," he said. "Were those the ones you wore?" He stood up, took a few steps toward her, his eyes squinting. "The ones he wanted you to keep on?" His hand clenched around the remote, the fingers whitening. "While he fucked you?"

Victoria felt the blood drain from her head, staggered as if she'd been slapped. Her ears rang, and she clutched the back of a chair for support. He *couldn't*. He couldn't know.

Brett towered over her, his cheeks mottled. "Is that why you kept putting me off? You were saving it for your cowboy? And here I thought you were just playing hard to get or something. Good thing Ray knows his job and didn't turn off the *sound*, or we'd never know what a manipulative bitch you are."

Victoria's heart thundered in her chest. This wasn't happening. He couldn't be talking about her night with Luke. Ray had stopped the feed. She'd ordered him to. There was no way Brett could be talking about that night. He was guessing, mad at her for ignoring him, just making things up.

But the shoes. He knew about the shoes...

"You're over the line." She wanted it to come out strong, but it ended up in a whisper.

"I'm over the line? Not even close." He pointed the remote at the television on the wall of shelves behind him, not taking his eyes from her.

Her own voice filled the room, breathy and unfamiliar: "Make it hard." Then panting, the sound of her back thudding against the door. Moans. Hers, mingled with Luke's. Oh, God.

She stumbled back a few steps, one hand to her mouth, the other to her belly. Her stomach churned.

Brett sneered at her. "Ray's been working on *Man vs. Machine* with me. Guess he mixed up some footage, and I ended up with these little gems."

"You sorry son of a bitch," Victoria said when she could catch her breath. Then she stopped, realizing she'd given herself away. He hadn't known for sure it was her. Had he? She frantically tried to remember what she'd said to Luke that night, even as her moans of passion filled the office.

"That's pretty rich," Brett said, "you calling me names." He pressed a hand to his chest. "I'm the innocent party, patiently waiting for his woman. Being *gentle*. When the whole time she was spreading her legs for some hick and begging for it hard."

Without pausing to think, Victoria slapped him. The sound still rang in her ears and the sting reverberated in her fingers when Jerry walked in with a sheet of paper in his hand.

"You've just added to your list of crimes, Clausen," he said, rounding his desk and standing behind it. "Turn that crap off, Soloway," he ordered, and Victoria's moans stopped playing through the office. It didn't matter, though. The sounds echoed in Victoria's head.

"What's going on, Jerry?" she asked.

"Breach of contract." Jerry put the tips of his fingers on the desk on either side of the document he'd laid there.

"According to whom?" she asked, desperate to regain some control, despite the evidence she'd just overheard. She refused to look at Brett, who had at least backed away after Jerry came in.

"Yourself, Clausen." He gave her a withering look, one she would have been able to deflect, even to challenge, just ten minutes earlier. "It's on tape."

Her stomach dropped. Of course Jerry had heard it all, too. They were in his office. He and Brett had been listening to it before she showed up, hearing her private conversation with Luke, her very personal moment.

"You don't know that's me," she said, bluffing. "It's just a voice...sounds..."

Jerry reached for the remote, which was always on the corner of his desk, and Brett gave him a dismissive wave. "I got that."

He pressed a button and Victoria's cries filled the room. She wanted to slap him again, get her hands all the way around his scrawny neck and squeeze. Hard.

"That's enough, Soloway. Yesterday afternoon's tape."

Yesterday? Victoria's mind raced, shifted into paranoid mode; she suddenly felt like there must be cameras everywhere. Had they also filmed her time in bed with Luke at her own house?

"My bad," Brett said and hit another remote. A small TV on one of the shelves to the side of Jerry's desk lit up and Victoria saw herself from the back, looking very small, standing on Sutro Terrace, and looking down at Luke, who had just turned around. She couldn't hear what he said to her, just the sounds of traffic, but it didn't matter; she recalled every word.

"Don't make this harder, Victoria."

And she had replied, *"It's too late for that."*

She remembered taking a few steps down and holding out her hand, which had been enough for him to rush to her, lift her off her feet and kiss her breathless. It had been a lovely moment.

Now it felt ugly, violated.

Staying on the defensive, her mind whirling and her insides in turmoil, she said, "Why was I being filmed?" She knew she was done, but she wasn't going out without a fight. Or finding out how this had happened.

"Research," Brett said in a snide voice. "Just happened to be scouting some locations with Sam yesterday around Twin Peaks."

"Scouting, my ass, you little pissant. You had me followed." And she had pissed off Sam when she sent him home from the Barn. And Ray, the night of the premiere.

"You begged for it," he sneered at her. "Just like you begged your cowboy to make it harder."

"That's enough, Soloway," Jerry cut in. "Clausen, as of today, Soloway is taking over your shows. You'll hand over all your files to him—"

"Like hell I will." Shaking, she crossed her arms tightly around herself.

Jerry looked pained. "It's not a request."

"Let's talk about this, Jerry."

Brett cut in. "You got caught fucking a client on tape, Victoria. There's no negotiating."

Victoria wheeled on him and got some satisfaction in seeing him flinch, but Jerry intervened.

"Out, Soloway. And mind your manners. We'll talk later."

After Brett slammed the door, Victoria said, "Mind your manners? I always knew this was a boys' club, but that's too much."

Jerry didn't say anything.

"He'll ruin my shows, Jerry."

He sighed. "Have a seat."

Her knees shook and she quivered all over. "I'll stand."

"Soloway's an ass, but he's a good producer."

Victoria tightened her hold on herself. "I'm better." And he hated that, didn't he? That she knew just how good she was, and used it to push him every time. One of the cardinal rules in reality TV was to make your Executive Producer happy. She certainly hadn't done that. She pressed her lips together to keep them from trembling. She wasn't sorry.

"We know you deleted some earlier footage, too."

She flinched at that, but didn't say anything. Who had ratted on her? Elmore? Ray again?

"You screwed up," Jerry said. "I know you step on toes, you do half of everyone else's job." At her look, he added, "Sometimes they need it, sometimes they don't, but it always makes for a better show. This doesn't, and we both know it. What happened, Clausen?"

What could she say? Love? Lust? Stupidity? The latter suggested she'd take it back if she could, and she wouldn't do that. The first two? Those were none of his business.

"Fine." He pushed the paper toward her. "Let's keep this simple. Sign this, we'll call your leaving a resignation, that you left before these pieces were recorded." He waved toward the TV and stereo. "We still use them, and any future footage, but we don't sue Tyler."

Of course not, she thought. They needed their "leading man" for their new hit show. And she had, thus far, been unable to get any footage of Luke with a woman. She could see how they would spin what they had, using the audio recordings as a forecastbite to get the viewers wondering: who's the mystery woman? Then they'd reveal it in the next episode, when they'd show Luke sweeping her into his arms. Someone would do a voiceover explaining who she is. Was. Maybe they would even use one of the moments with Cort addressing the camera and calling her Miss Victoria.

Her eyes blurred. It's what she would have done.

"And if I don't sign?"

He looked at her like she should know better. "You're fired, Tyler's fired, and you're both sued. You probably won't be able to get another production gig. The show's young enough. We won't lose a lot if we can it now, but we gain more if we run it. It was a mega hit out of the gate, but we can't be accused of bias, of leading talent. You, however, have been overstepping bounds. This was a long time coming."

Victoria stared at him. So this wasn't just Brett's revenge, or Ray's for being forced to stop the video feed or Sam's for yesterday, or any of those people whose toes she stepped on. It was also Jerry's, for all the times she'd had him by the balls. And now he had hers.

CHAPTER THIRTY-ONE

Luke grabbed a burrito from the taqueria a couple blocks from the Barn. He sat in the window, letting his thoughts drift, praying a little, and trusting that everything would work out. He thought God might not appreciate being asked for help in getting sex, but Luke figured it couldn't hurt to express thanks for how sex had led to Victoria admitting her feelings. So he sent up a thank you for the good food and an even better woman, and asked for assistance in managing Victoria's job, the show, and a relationship.

His phone buzzed, and his heart jolted with it. He slipped it out of his back pocket to check the screen, and his heart fell to his gut. Dot. His mama'd taken to calling him on both his cell and the landline at the Barn, and he found himself cutting each conversation shorter and shorter. He felt guilty about it without a doubt, but couldn't handle the mama guilt on top of his own right now. He thumbed the Ignore button, promising himself to call her back later.

As he neared the Barn, Luke scanned the street for the white van. All clear. Upstairs, he knocked on Cort's door to see if he'd like to go for a run or grab a game of pool. He could have spent the rest of the day in bed with Victoria, but without her around, his restlessness increased and he needed a distraction. Tessa opened the door to reveal Cort lounging in his easy chair, chatting at Sam, who turned his camera toward Luke. Ray stood nearby, holding out a boom mic. When he caught sight of Luke, he moved the boom in front of him and edged around the back of Cort's leather couch.

Damn. They were getting sneakier. The van must've been around the corner.

Luke said hey to Tessa and nodded at Cort. "Just wondering if you wanted to go for a run or something, but I see you're busy." Luke lifted a hand and was about to leave when Cort's phone rang. He grabbed it from the table and even though he pressed it to his ear, it was loud enough for them all to hear Kristen's voice.

Luke stopped with the door halfway closed.

"Hey, Cort, it's Sunshine. I'm actually looking for Tessa. She's not answering her phone and I'm hoping she's with you on this glorious day. I'm starving and looking for someone to have lunch with. Maybe a hamburger."

Luke's hand tightened on the knob and he looked over his shoulder at Tessa, who had frozen, staring at him like a deer in headlights. She mouthed the word "hamburger," which was one of the codes they'd invented one day away from the cameras. Cort wasn't too bothered, but Parker said his aura had been off since the filming started, Marty worried for Miranda, and now Tessa and Kristen had gotten involved because of their close association with the boys and the show. So they'd all met up to find ways to communicate in code around the crew. If Kristen, a strict vegan, started talking about hamburgers, it was code red. But she'd tempered it with a glorious day. Emergency, but don't panic, there's not enough information available yet.

Luke did a quick scan through the possibilities: Parker was stocking shelves at City Lights Books today, and he had his own codes. He preferred talking about his stock portfolio and baked tofu. So it wasn't him. Marty had a construction gig, and as far as Luke knew, Miranda had a knitting class in the morning, and worked at a cupcake shop in the afternoon. She was eggs sunny side up. They had codes for the crew, too, but Luke refused to let them assign one to Victoria; that stepped too far over the line, even though he knew deep down she'd be hurt if she knew the rest of them had done this in the first place. Another thing to talk with her about. But not yet. He couldn't do that without everyone else's permission; knowing they had something that a camera operator, crew member or viewer wouldn't understand helped them all endure this process.

Luke settled on Kristen needing help from Tessa on a female matter, and he was glad enough not to know about it. He wished she hadn't used one of the emergency codes, though. They might need to have a discussion about that.

Tessa pasted a smile on her face and turned to Cort and Sam. She held her hand out and Cort gave her the phone.

"Hey, honey," she said into the phone. "A hamburger sounds great. The usual place?"

"Meet you there," Kristen said, and hung up.

Tessa handed the phone back to Cort. "Sounds like she needs some girl talk. Maybe you and Luke should go for that run?"

Sam sighed and lowered his camera. "Seriously?"

Cort stood up. "Yep. I'm needin' me some exercise."

He looked like it was the last thing he wanted, but he and Luke had figured out awhile ago the cameramen hated following them when they jogged. They couldn't keep the handhelds steady enough, the mic packs bounced around, and the mics themselves brushed against their clothing and caused irregular noise.

"Either of you know if Victoria is around?" Sam asked. If she had been, Luke knew Sam would ask her to intervene on his behalf. Victoria once said she liked the spontaneity of the show, preferring that to setting up scenes. If she did the latter, the crew could have better equipment in place for recording their run. Sam knew she liked being in control, and would find a way to make the filming happen if she were here. Luke had a hard time holding back his grin at the thought of how much control she'd taken of him recently.

"Nope," Luke said to Sam, and Cort shook his head.

Cort did a quick jog around the apartment, then looked at Luke. "Good to go," he said with a wink. "You coming, Sam? Ray?"

They both shook their heads, but Luke knew they'd have to follow anyway. "We'll see you downstairs," Ray said, giving Luke an up-and-down glance he couldn't read, then pushed his way to the head of the stairs. They heard him clattering all the way down.

"He's gonna break another boom that way," Sam said, and started on a light jog toward the stairs.

Cort stopped in the hall, his arm out. They heard the door close. Luke leaned over to look down the stairs, and said, "All clear."

Cort turned to Tessa. "You'll let us know what's going on?"

Tessa nodded. "As soon as I find out."

Cort looked at Luke. "Know where your girl is?"

"The office. She's fine."

He returned Tessa's look, but neither of them said anything. She nodded again, stood on tiptoes to kiss Cort, and bounced down the stairs.

Cort gave Luke an up-and-down, too. "Someone's wearing the same clothes they left in yesterday morning."

VICTORIA HUDDLED IN her living room chair, dressed in the only pair of sweats she owned and wrapped in an old quilt her mother had made. Normally, she sat on the couch facing the television sets, but looking at them today made her feel ill. She had a lump in her throat, her head ached, and she thought she might throw up any second. Kristen hovered over her, trying to help, but also to find out what had happened. Victoria scarcely noted her presence.

"Teresa's on her way. Do you want some tea or something?"

"Asparagus?" Victoria croaked, head back, staring at the ceiling.

"What?" Kristen sat at her feet, patting her shins. "You want some asparagus?"

Victoria pulled her feet up on the chair and rested her face on her knees. She couldn't stand to be touched right now; she felt so dirty. And she didn't have the energy to explain that Kristen's tea looked and smelled like asparagus.

"So it wasn't Luke?" Kristen asked for the third time.

Victoria shook her head. Then she nodded. Luke hadn't done this to her, but he was definitely involved.

Kristen stood, but kept a hand on the back of the chair. "What did he do?"

Victoria raised her head; it must weigh fifty pounds. "Nothing." She tried to swallow past the lump again. "Can you get me a Dr. Pepper?"

"You might as well ask me to bring you some poison in a can."

Victoria stared at her. "Will you bring me some poison in a can?"

Kristen pursed her lips in a very un-Kristen-like way. "Fine," she said, and loped into the kitchen.

Victoria heard Kristen banging around, and dropped her head with a sigh. It was all over. Everything was over, her job sucker-punched from her, her integrity flushed down the toilet and her sex life available for all to see and hear. She squinched her eyes shut tight.

She heard a key in the lock, but only curled sideways into a tight ball in the chair, tucking the quilt around her hands and bringing the

211

soft material up to her chin. Teresa settled on the couch to her right. "So Kristen calls and says she's looking for me, and uses the code word for an emergency, but she sounds okay and Luke looks okay, so—"

Victoria's head shot up and she looked at Teresa, who looked back, startled.

"—it must be you," Teresa finished. "And you're wearing...sweats."

"Is Luke all right?"

"Same beautiful, brooding cowboy as ever. In fact, he looked happy, not so brooding. So what's going on?"

Victoria dropped her feet to the floor, let the quilt slide away, and stood up, almost bumping into Kristen, who'd come up behind her holding a glass of soda on ice straight out from her body.

"It goes against my karma to even get near this stuff."

Victoria tried to step around her. "I have to find Luke."

Kristen didn't move, and Teresa stood up and blocked her other side. Victoria eyed the coffee table in front of her, ready to crawl over it if necessary.

"Sam's filming him and Cort right now," Teresa said. "With Ray."

"That fucker."

She saw Teresa and Kristen exchange a glance. With exaggerated care, Kristen set the glass on a coaster directly in front of Victoria. "I need to find Luke," Victoria repeated. "I have to tell him what happened."

"If you need to talk to Luke, you're going to need help distracting Sam and Ray," Teresa said. "If you tell us what's going on, we can help."

Victoria gave Teresa what little smile she could muster; everything felt like such an effort. "You'd help me whether you knew what was going on or not, but I appreciate the effort to find out."

Teresa smiled back. "It was worth a try."

Exhaustion flooding her entire body, Victoria plopped back down in the chair. "You're going to find out one way or the other. Better it comes from me first."

Teresa sat on the couch, and Kristen settled on the floor. Victoria took a few swallows of soda, then set the glass down with a noisy exhalation, ignoring Kristen's look of distaste.

She wasn't perfect, she made mistakes—the biggest one now on film—and her worst nightmare had manifested. She'd lost her job. And everyone would be able to see why in a short period of time. So she was damn well going to drink all the Dr. Pepper she wanted. She didn't say any of this, but it must have shown on her face because Kristen changed her disapproving expression to a more encouraging one.

There was no soft introduction to this subject, so she just said it. "Ray left the audio on the night Luke and I...were together."

Teresa gasped, and put a hand to her mouth.

"I don't know how, but Ray got the tapes to Brett."

This time Kristen gasped.

The lump was back in Victoria's throat. She took a deep breath. "Luke came into my office yesterday when Brett was there and Brett...got suspicious. He followed me, and filmed me and Luke kissing." She stopped, brushing her hair from her face; her hands shook, so she gathered the quilt into her lap and clutched it. "He gave all the tapes to Jerry, and they're going to use them on the show." She wrapped her arms around herself and bent forward, rocking. "It was that or they'd sue Luke for breach. At least *he* wasn't fired."

She let out a shuddery breath and dropped her head into her hands.

"What?" Kristen shot out.

"You were fired?" Teresa said.

Victoria nodded and dropped her hands. "They're giving that asshole, watermelon-kisser Brett Soloway my shows." She saw Kristen and Teresa exchange another glance. "So I *have* to talk to Luke. I have to warn him and the boys."

Teresa grabbed her phone from her bag. "I'll call Cort." She stood and walked back and forth in front of the coffee table while the phone rang. Victoria heard, "Landry," on the other end, and Victoria's stomach flipped over at the sight of Teresa's expression going from troubled to serene just at the sound of Cort's voice. This time she let Kristen take her hand; the warmth and strength of her sister's fingers soothed her more than she'd thought they would.

Teresa said, "Hey, baby. It's Tessa. Glorious day, isn't it?" Her voice drifted off as she wandered into the kitchen.

Victoria looked at Kristen, glanced at their linked hands, then back into Kristen's eyes. She couldn't read her sister's expression; it looked like Kristen was studying her, trying to figure something out. "Glorious day?" Victoria asked, remembering what Teresa had said when she'd first walked in. "Is that the code word for an emergency?"

Kristen nodded. "One of them."

Victoria eased her hand from Kristen's and leaned her head back against the chair. "I had no idea."

"It's not a normal way to live," Kristen said. "They needed some coping strategies."

Victoria stared at the ceiling. "Are you kicking me when I'm down?"

"Just explaining."

Victoria straightened and stared at Kristen. "Well, it feels like kicking to me." She stood and headed toward the kitchen.

Kristen called after her, "Crying would be much better for your soul than lashing out at me. But I understand, and I forgive you."

"Crying wastes time and energy," Victoria announced in general as she stamped into the kitchen in time to see Teresa hang up.

"He's calling everyone and we'll meet at the warehouse."

"Using more code words, I suppose?"

"I'm sorry," Teresa said, her shoulders slumping. "They asked for my help. I couldn't say no."

Not so long ago, Victoria wouldn't have understood being so drawn to a man that she couldn't say no to him. Now she was living that scenario, and paying a price for it. She wanted to believe Luke was worth the sacrifice, that being with him justified losing her job. But life wasn't that simple, was it? Victoria leaned back against the counter, bracing her hands on the edge. She hated that her sister and best friend knew a series of codes meant to circumvent the filming for *In Concert*. What else didn't she know? How much of the truth had she really seen when she filmed? Was everything in code?

Kristen stood in the middle of the doorway. "Would this be a good time to tell you all I got a job as a go-go dancer?"

CHAPTER THIRTY-TWO

Luke leaned back against a steel table, crossed his arms, and put one ankle over the other. It was no good; he needed to move. He strode up and down the aisles created by boxes of supplies and equipment.

It killed him not knowing what was going on. Tessa had called Cort and given the code for an emergency meeting, all members present. Until now, none of them had had to say they were looking for a copy of Johnny Cash's "Sunday Morning Coming Down," and even though it gave them a feeling of control over their situation, it also seemed like a lark to talk about hamburgers, stock portfolios and glorious days. As he'd said to Cort early on, "Maybe we think we've got one up on them, but it's like kids in study hall with a secret language. Funny at first, but you get caught or hurt someone's feelings and end up looking like a jackass."

Now they were meeting in a warehouse owned by a friend of Tessa's. Cort said she'd sounded serious, her voice shaking even though she tried to sound cheerful. Had they gotten caught? Couldn't be. Victoria would've said something. Luke lifted his hat, brushed an arm across his forehead and resettled the Stetson. The space was chilly, but sweat still prickled his back.

So far, he and Cort were there. Marty and Miranda had shown up a few minutes earlier and now sat close together on folding chairs, their hands clasped and their heads touching. Parker needed to find someone to cover his shift at the bookstore and he'd be on his way.

Cort hopped up onto one of the tables.

Luke said, "You sure she didn't say anything else?"

"Nope." Cort turned some boxes around. "Arrowroot powder. Spelt flour. Carob chips. What kind of bakery is this?"

"She just said the code words?" Luke persisted.

"That's all, Lucas. Meet at the warehouse ASAP, everyone needs to be there, including Miss Miranda."

Miranda lifted her head, but kept her hand in Marty's. "I like my code," she said.

"Eggs sunny side up," Marty agreed with a shy smile. "Because you brighten my day," he added, turning pink.

Miranda sighed and rested her cheek against his.

Luke tried not to look at them. Their love seemed real straightforward and self-contained, and he wondered if he'd ever find the same for himself. An image of Victoria as she lay sleeping the night before came to mind, the moonlight shining across her face, a curl of hair draped across her cheek.

He'd risked waking her by brushing his fingers over the curve of her cheekbone and sliding the hair behind her ear. She hadn't stirred and he'd wondered what it'd be like to spend forever watching her in the moonlight, learning where to touch her so she came awake wanting him, or how to curl against her without disturbing her dreams.

Cort shoved another box aside, muttering something about egg replacer, bringing Luke out of his reverie.

"Still don't know why my code is turkey bacon," Cort complained.

"Shouldn't be too hard to figure," Luke drawled.

Cort pointed at him. "Grits suits you good, though," he said with a laugh.

Marty and Miranda laughed, too, but their smiles died away when the door opened and Tessa came in, followed by Kristen and Victoria, all of their faces pale and strained.

At sight of her, Luke's heart thumped hard for a beat, then settled into its usual rhythm. Cort jumped down from the table, gave Kristen a kiss on the cheek, and wrapped his arm around Tessa, eyes only for her.

Luke headed to Victoria to do the same, but stopped when she came into the light and he caught a good look at her.

She'd pulled her hair back tight like she'd done in the beginning, but a few strands stuck out, and she wore baggy black pants and a sweater, and boots that didn't click on the concrete floor, but gave low thuds as she walked. Her big blue eyes looked bigger than ever in her pale face, but haunted and miserable instead of bright and snapping.

"What?" was all he could get out as he stood in front of her.

She looked up at him, then at her sister with a pleading expression.

"There have been some changes to the show," Kristen said. "Among other things."

"Wait," Victoria said. She sounded like she'd been crying, but her eyes weren't red or puffy. Just haunted.

Luke's guts tightened.

"I got us into this," Victoria continued. "I need to have the courage to tell you all what happened." She looked around. "Is everyone here?"

"Did someone order baked tofu?" Parker asked as he ambled in, shutting the door behind him.

"We're all here now." Cort gestured to a chair for Parker and led Tessa back to the table and up on the steel counter next to him. She yelped at the cold and Cort pulled her onto his lap.

Luke stayed in front of Victoria, looking down at her. Lowering her eyes, she moved away from him so everyone was in a rough semi-circle around her. He flashed back to when she'd first shown up at Tony's, fire in her eyes, the boys hovering around her. Their circle had doubled, and, it seemed, so had their troubles. Kristen pressed a hand to Luke's forearm, then went to sit next to Miranda, taking hold of her free hand.

Luke remained where he stood, watching Victoria and listening to her explain that some things had shifted at the station and she would no longer be their field producer.

"What things?" Luke asked. "And why not?"

Victoria licked her lips. "Oh, God," she said. "I didn't think this through."

"Did you quit?" Luke asked, a flare of hope shooting off in him.

Victoria looked around the warehouse like a caged animal, finally finding Tessa. "Is there some place we can talk privately?"

Tessa pointed behind them. "There's an office."

"What else do you need to talk about?" Luke asked. "Why bring us all here to go off yourselves?" The bleak expression on Victoria's face turned him cold.

She turned and put a hand on his arm. He felt a jolt pass between them, but she only tightened her fingers. "I need to talk to *you*," she said. "Alone."

He swore under his breath, but gestured for her to go ahead of him. He paused at sight of the tiny office with a long table for a desk and a large plate glass window that faced out on the main floor. Some privacy. But he didn't care at this point, he just needed to hear whatever it was so he could know what they were facing.

Victoria waited for him to come inside before she closed the door. She stayed with her back pressed to it, away from the window.

"Doesn't matter if we give 'em a show at this point, darlin'," he told her, the words light, but not his tone.

"You're right," she said. "It's too late."

From the sound of her voice he thought she might start crying then, and he stepped closer to her. But she held up a hand to stop him, and her eyes stayed dry.

Then what she'd said hit him. "Too late for what?"

"We already gave them a show," she said, her voice flat.

He felt like she'd punched him in the chest. He knew what she was going to say; now it was just a matter of the details. "The cameras weren't off."

"How did you know?"

"Too good to be true." He shoved his hands in his pockets, head down. "God damn it. What happened, Victoria?" His voice sounded loud in the small space, and he started to pace again, head down. If he looked at her right now, he'd be reminded of what they'd said and done that night, how they'd been free of any barriers once they knew they were truly alone. But they hadn't been, had they?

Her voice barely above a whisper, Victoria said, "Ray turned off the video, but not the audio."

"And your friend Ray decided to let your boss listen to it?" His head throbbed and he pulled his hands out of his pockets, clenching them.

"Something like that."

He finally looked at her, saw the hollows under her eyes, her palms flat against the door behind her, as if it was all that held her up. "And they fired you."

"They let me go."

Semantics, he thought. She'd been fired. Because of him. "And I'm next?"

"No!" She held up her hands, took a step away from the door in his direction. "No, that's the good part. You're still on the show."

"The good part?" He gripped the back of the chair tucked under the table. "The good part? There is no *good* part to this, Victoria. It's no damn consolation prize—" he pulled the chair out and tossed it behind him; it clattered against the concrete as it fell "—that I'm still on that fucking show."

"Yes, it is," she said, sounding desperate. "It has to be."

He crossed his arms tightly over his chest; his entire body vibrated. She placed the tips of her fingers on his forearms and his muscles twitched under them.

"Make my having to leave worth something, Luke."

"That show isn't worth anything without you."

"Don't say that. The show is *you*, Luke. I know it, the viewers know it, and the network execs know it." She swallowed. "It's why you're still on and not being let go for breach of contract." Before he could respond that he didn't give a good goddamn about the contract, she went on. "Only they're going to use the footage."

"The audio? How?"

"Believe me, they'll find a way. They...it's all in *my* contract." She shook her head, and looked up at him. "There are two more things: they filmed us yesterday on the street. Kissing. And until they find a new field producer, my replacement is Brett Soloway."

He was still processing the fact that some sneaky bastard with a camera had found them on Sutro Terrace when she said Soloway's name.

"I won't work with that jackass." He looked around for another chair to throw. No way that arrogant asshole would have any control over his life. Or hers. "I'll quit."

She looked horrified. "No! It's at number one, with a huge audience share. BNA has been calling. Radio stations want to start playing 'Return to Me,' there's talk of merchandising—"

Luke stepped so close Victoria ended up finishing her list about the show into his chest. She seemed to lose her train of thought and stopped talking, which was his desired effect.

"Do you hear yourself?"

Her voice rose. "You don't seem to understand the importance of this."

He took a breath through his nose. "I'm trying real hard here,

Victoria." He brushed the tips of his fingers against one upturned cheek, then stepped back to keep her from getting a crook in her neck. She seemed to calm, but he could still see the fire in her eyes, that glimmer that meant she'd closed her jaws on an idea and wouldn't let it go. He'd never been real good with patience, but he needed it now. He cupped her face, thumbs smoothing the rounds of her cheeks. "What I see now is some freedom."

"You can't quit," she said, the frantic note back in her voice. "Breach of contract won't look good to a record company. They're incredibly selective these days..."

"Let us worry about that. And I won't mess up what you worked so hard to build. But there's no more hiding now." He leaned down to her, his voice a whisper, but his heart racing at the silver lining. "The worst happened, and now we can be together. Nothing holding us back." He kissed her forehead, relishing the loss of the weight he'd been carrying for so long. "It'll be like the damn cameras aren't there. They don't matter now." He drew her close, wanting to share this liberation.

Victoria stiffened, pulled her face away, and backed toward the door, bumping into the wall next to it. She shook her head, eyes wide, looking very much like a cornered animal. A low sound came from deep in her throat. "But they capture everything," she said. "I can't, I don't...It won't work...I..."

Someone knocked on the door and it opened just as Luke reached for Victoria's hand. Her fingers were cold and damp. Tessa peered in and Luke could see the others grouped behind her. "Everything okay here?"

Luke scowled at her. "We're not done."

"I don't want my love life on camera," Victoria exploded.

CHAPTER THIRTY-THREE

Victoria lay in bed, staring at the wall, craving Luke's warm body next to hers, and trying to forget how she'd been escorted out of the station with nothing, not even her Blackberry. Her entire world had collapsed from one bad decision. And then she'd gone and made it worse.

If she hadn't told Ray to turn off the feed, she'd never have felt safe enough to sleep with Luke, and none of this would have happened. She rolled onto her back, tucked the covers under her chin, and stared at the ceiling. That wasn't true. She'd felt completely safe with him or she wouldn't have done it at all, cameras or not. And she wasn't sorry.

But none of that mattered now, because she no longer had her job or the show, and she hadn't heard from Luke since three days earlier when he stormed out of the warehouse. After everyone calmed down, she'd given them a quick rundown, feeling no emotion, as if making a presentation at the office. Trying to be reassuring, she reminded them that because of the show's ratings, a good replacement would be found soon, and the boys might not have to work long with Brett.

She stopped herself from saying any more at that point. Part of her hadn't accepted that she was no longer involved in the show anymore, and wouldn't be able to step in. By reassuring them about Brett's replacement, she was still trying to call the shots, without any authority to do so.

She curled up on her side again, pulling her knees to her chest.

Who needed to call the shots, when you had flannel pajamas and a cozy bed to hide away in? It was warm and quiet and peaceful here, soothing.

Until your sister barged in.

"How you feeling?" Kristen asked from the doorway. As a counterpoint to Victoria's mood, Kristen wore a yellow tank top and orange broomstick skirt.

Victoria grumbled into her pillow.

"Ready to get up and see the sun?"

Victoria glared at her. The sun already seemed to be blinding her from the doorway.

"How about all of those phone calls from your friends on *Dress My Best* and *Hairdressers for Hire*? Or that job offer from Archer Productions?" Kristen asked.

Victoria closed her eyes tight. Archer had been trying to recruit her for years, but she wouldn't leave her people. Now, she couldn't bear the thought of telling her cast why she was gone or starting over somewhere as the shamed producer. She just...couldn't. "I don't want to talk to anyone."

"Well, you have a visitor, anyway. Shall I let him into the lion's den or send him away?"

Victoria didn't say anything, but her heart leapt and banged wildly in her chest. *Luke.* She didn't want him to see her this way. But she wanted to see him. She pulled the covers over her head.

"This passive thing doesn't suit you," Kristen said.

"So you've said about five times. Tell him to come back in an hour. No. To wait...just to wait a few minutes."

She heard Kristen sigh, then a male voice said, "You gotta get out of bed and save us from that bonehead producer."

"Oh," Victoria said, when she realized her visitor was Cort and not Luke.

She pulled the covers down to her nose and peeked out. Cort stood in the doorway, arms outstretched, palms pressed against the doorframe, leaning slightly inward, then swaying back toward the hallway. No hat over his buzzed hair, but faded Lee jeans, cowboy boots and a blue t-shirt. "That guy snoots his nose up again like things smell bad in the Barn and I'm kicking him in the nuts."

"Oh," Victoria said again, as it sunk in that Cort was alone. "Oh."

Cort sat at the foot of the bed, leaning against the post. "We can't work like this, darlin'. We're all ready to strangle him by his flashy ties."

"All of you?"

He nodded. "Even Marty."

That was pretty serious for easygoing Marty. Her mind automatically clicked through at least five scenarios she could use to smooth things over with Brett and Marty. Then she remembered that was Brett's job. Not hers. "Oh."

"Your record's skipping." Cort hiked one knee onto the bed, and Victoria felt it shift under her. "You remember 45s? Luke and I had a whole stack of 'em from his daddy when we were growing up, used to play 'em over and over again on this portable turntable. Hank Williams, Elvis, Patsy Cline. We played *Battle of New Orleans* so many times, it started to skip, and 'we grabbed an alligator and we fought another round' got stuck on repeat. We thought it was the funniest thing, me and Lucas." He patted the covers over her leg. "Way your eyes lit up when I said his name, I'm thinking you want to know what's been going on with him the last few days."

"No," she said, shifting up on the pillows and shaking her head. "Not really." She desperately wanted to know, but she figured Luke was done with her after what she'd said in the warehouse, so what was the point of talking about him at all? It would only hurt too much.

He raised an eyebrow.

She lowered her gaze. "Yes," she admitted.

"Stands to reason."

She looked back at him. There was a bit of a grin in his voice, but he only gave her a soft smile and rubbed one hand over his short hair. She now had a better understanding why Teresa felt so special with him.

"Why do you say that?' she asked. "That it stands to reason."

"Well, he's an interesting character, our Lucas. I hear some women find him mysterious and brooding, and that lures 'em in. I expect you saw past that, though, which is the real reason it took you two so long to get together. It sure as hell wasn't on *his* side to keep things slow. He wanted you the second he saw you."

"What?" She scooted farther up on the pillows. "How do you know that?"

Cort shrugged. "Caught him staring at your bra."

223

She burst out laughing. "That's it?"

His smiled widened. "Now, see, that's better." He patted her leg again and stood up. "Now let's go down to the station and get rid of that Salloby idiot."

"Soloway," she corrected automatically, looking away. They'd all seen her with Brett the night of the party last weekend, heard her defend him, and refer to him as her boyfriend. They'd asked if he was good enough for her. She hadn't answered; had some part of her known what he really was? But was she any better, the way she'd treated Luke?

She shook her head, her throat closing up.

"Hey now," Cort said, sitting on the bed again, this time next to her. He eased an arm around her shoulders and pulled her close. "It can't be that bad."

She shook her head again, his shirt soft against her cheek. "I can't go back, Cort. I broke my contract. I'm lucky they're not suing me."

"You had a contract, too?"

"It's standard for this type of work. I broke it, so I'm not only off the show, but out of work. I have no say in what happens." She looked up at him. "I'm sorry."

He gave her a squeeze. "Well, we'll figure something out. But..." He looked across the room. "If you broke the contract and got fired, and Luke broke his contract...why isn't he fired?"

She didn't want to say because Luke was the show's golden boy, the biggest draw. "Because you each bring something to the show, because the four of you together are the show, and the station stands to lose a lot of money if it crashes. Lose one of you, and it won't hold together." That part was true enough; the other three had their share of fans.

"So what's keeping any of us from breaking our own contract?"

She pulled away from him. "You can't do that. You don't know what I...what I had to negotiate to keep them from suing Luke."

She had been about to say that he had no idea what she'd given up, what she'd been through, but she didn't want him to know. She didn't want any of them to know how brutally the situation had cut into her. Even now, she wanted them, and the show, to succeed.

He shrugged again. "We're so big and important to them, they might think twice about suing us." He stood up, rubbing his hands together. "Good. We got a plan."

"We do?"

"Sure we do. We can strike, like the transit folks." He stopped. "I need Luke to get back, though."

"Where is he, Cort?"

He looked surprised. "Didn't I say? Got sidetracked, I guess. He's around maybe five minutes a day, staring at the wall until the cameras get bored and leave, then he takes off and drives."

Cort wandered around the little room, picking up boxes and bracelets and lipsticks. She let him; she didn't want him to get sidetracked again. As soon as he looked like he might go for her underwear drawer, though, she'd intervene.

"He does?" She remembered Luke telling her about his drives, how he couldn't sleep when he and Cort first moved here, so he'd leave in the middle of the night and drive. He'd told her this the day they kissed out on Sutro Terrace. And had been filmed by Brett. The little worm.

"Sure. He doesn't know I know he used to leave when I'd snore up the place we shared. Smaller'n'a shoebox, that place. Damn." He stopped at her dresser across from the bed, picked up a small lacquered box that she'd gotten in Chinatown, then set it down again.

"How do you know where he goes?" Victoria eyed her robe hanging on the back of the door, feeling exposed for the first time since Cort had come in. She was waking up, wanting to answer a call to action, without quite knowing what that action should be.

Cort turned from the dresser to face her, and shrugged. "He's got a restless nature, our Lucas. Just born that way. He's not really a city boy, but he's not pure country either. He gets a wild hair and takes off wherever the wind blows. We'd just be talking and he'd throw in something he saw, some place he'd been, without saying when he'd been there. I just figured it out. He's not saying much these days, though. So I don't know where he's going."

Despite his lighter tone, Victoria thought she heard the anger there, the frustration with his best friend withdrawing. Just like she had been doing.

"I'm sorry," she said, to Cort and to herself. She'd been wallowing, and in the meantime, people around her were hurting.

"For what?" he asked. "You gave me wine, women and song. I'm happier'n a pig in you know what."

"But Luke.."

Cort walked to the back of the door, took down her robe, and handed it to her. "Get yourself dressed and we'll go figure out something with Tessa and Sunshine."

She held onto the robe, calling his name as he headed for the door. He closed it and turned to her, his hand on the knob.

"Why don't I have a nickname like my sister and Teresa?"

"Because I can't sleep with you."

It didn't take him long to read her confused expression and he gave her the charming grin that had brought in hundreds of e-mails to the Reality Strikes studios, asking for his phone number.

"I meet a girl I want to have sex with, she gets a nickname," he explained. "I get within an inch of even thinking about wanting that with you, and Lucas kills me flat dead." He put a hand to his chest. "I'm too fond of my life for that."

"I hope you value it enough not to hurt my sister or my best friend, too," she said, narrowing her eyes at him.

"I said it was for women I *wanted* to sleep with, not ones I was *going* to sleep with. Tessa's a great girl." He pointed down at his feet. "She's even got me tying my shoes. I'm greedy, but I'm not stupid." He gave her a salute and went out the door. She heard his voice booming down the hall. "Tessa! Kristen! She's on her way out."

Victoria shook her head, put on her robe and headed for the shower. No, definitely not stupid.

LUKE WALKED INSIDE the Barn to find Soloway standing in front of the Lounge, lecturing the boys. He wasn't real sure about the lecturing part, but with Cort leaning back and staring at the ceiling, Marty staring at his hands and Parker staring at the floor, it sure looked like they were being talked at.

He'd driven a couple hours north out of the city to go horseback riding, and Sam had dogged him the whole way, then filmed him circling round and round in the corral. They'd probably find a way to turn it into another Mr. LonelyHeart segment, but it seemed like pretty boring stuff to him, which had been his point. If he hadn't wanted to get rid of Sam, he'd have gone riding on the trails. Something had changed, though, because the previous two days, Sam had given up and turned his van around if Luke drove more than an hour away. Had Soloway given orders to follow him no matter what?

And why now?

Everyone turned when Luke closed the door. He expected Soloway to look sour. Most times he wrinkled his nose like something smelled bad. But today he looked smug, which Luke translated as happy. When the boys gave Luke near-identical disapproving looks, it caught him off guard. He'd be damned if he'd try to talk to them in front of the producer, though, so he shoved his hands in his pockets and ambled toward the Lounge, ignoring the two crew members standing behind Soloway; the jackass always brought extra muscle when he talked to the band.

"What's going on?" Luke asked the boys.

In a flat voice, Cort said, "Mr. Salloby here was about to make some astonishing announcement."

"Huh." Luke gave Soloway what he hoped was a bored look and leaned against Marty's chair.

He would've taken the opportunity to chastise Soloway for giving news to the band without everyone present, but it was his fault for taking off so much lately. And he wasn't about to give Soloway the satisfaction. As it was, the muttonhead smirked at Luke in a way that had him straightening and flexing his hands, ready to flatten him if he said anything about Victoria.

"Because of this extra-special news—which I can't, unfortunately, disclose at this point—we will be re-shooting the end of the mid-season episode at Tony's Tavern. There will be, shall we say, a revealing moment at the end."

Luke clenched his fists and took a step forward. "What sort of revealing moment?"

Soloway moved his gaze to a point over Luke's shoulder and did that nose-in-the-air thing. "We really need to keep this close to the vest because we want your genuine reactions on camera. But I can guarantee, it's something you've all wanted a long time, worked hard for, and it will have a huge effect on your careers."

Luke let his hands relax. Not Victoria, then. But what was it?

From his spot on the floor, Parker raised his hand, and after a pause, Soloway said, "Uh, yes?"

"I'm not certain I understand the meaning behind recreating something in a reality show."

Soloway stared at him, then said, "We need to film your reactions to the big surprise," as if Parker hadn't heard him the first time. "We have a tight schedule for this, so the re-shoot is tonight at Tony's Tavern."

There was a general uproar, the boys grumbling about that not being enough time to practice, too short notice to free up their schedules, did he think they could just drop everything for this? Luke kept silent, his blood pressure building. Of course Soloway thought that. He got his rocks off on it, too.

Soloway held up his hands, and Luke could swear he caught another smirk on the bastard's face. "I assume you are all professional enough to be prepared for this. Showtime is at eight p.m."

He turned away and Luke expected him to add, "Be there or be square." Instead, he just gave a wave, shot his cuffs, and walked out trailing his lackeys behind him.

"Asshole," Luke muttered before Soloway was completely out the door. The other man tensed up, then turned and walked to about three feet from Luke.

"Did you have something you wanted to say to me?"

Luke lifted his chin. "I called you an asshole." Behind him, he heard the boys taking their places at his back, just as Soloway's goons shifted their stances to be closer to their boss.

"You have no idea who you're messing with, Tyler."

Luke flexed his hands. He hadn't been in a fight since his teens, but he'd gladly go a few rounds to wipe the smug look off Soloway's face. "Try me."

Soloway took a prissy sidestep and Luke followed his movement, circling.

"You forget your place," Soloway said, shrugging his shoulders. "One word from me, and your show is gone, and your prospects with it."

Luke was about to tell him where he could stuff his prospects when Cort stepped to his side, and said, "Can I punch him in the nuts now?"

"Philistines," Soloway muttered, taking a couple of steps back, then turned and marched outside, slamming the door behind him.

"Damn," Cort said. "That would've been real satisfying."

Luke's blood was still boiling, his adrenaline high. He ran a hand over his face. Needing action, he began pacing around the chairs. Parker settled himself cross-legged on the floor and Cort stood watching Luke, arms crossed over his chest.

"What do you think it is?" Marty asked, looking around. "The big news."

"A recording contract, of course," Parker said.

"You think?" Cort asked.

Luke was surprised by the idea. He'd been so busy figuring out how best to take Soloway down, he hadn't thought about what the surprise could be.

"Something we've wanted and worked hard for," said Parker, "that will have a big effect on our careers."

"Hell, that could be a lot of things," Luke said, not wanting to accept anything from Soloway, even if the boys had earned it and deserved it. He pulled a stool close, but was too worked up to sit still.

"Like what?" Cort asked.

Luke shrugged, but didn't feel very casual. "A raise. Some change in the show. A concert at some big arena." He looked around the Barn, wondering what he could hit.

"I'm going for Parker's idea," Marty said.

"Sounds good to me." Cort crossed his arms over his chest. "And I guess if we're doing this tonight, we'd better get some playing time in. That is, unless you've got somewhere more important to be, Lucas."

In fact, he'd been wondering if he should try to get hold of Victoria, but he knew Cort was needling him about taking off so much, and he'd have to man up about that first.

"No, I do not," he said.

"Where'd you get to today?" Cort asked.

"Sonoma."

"Real pretty up there," Cort said.

Luke just nodded.

"Wineries. Nice views. Fresh air. No cameras. No asshole producers."

Luke pressed a fist to the stool, grinding his knuckles against the bare metal, not bothering to tell Cort there had most definitely been a camera there. He knew Cort needed to get this out his own way.

"No pretty little ex-producers," Cort continued, "so low they couldn't even get out of bed for days."

Luke straightened. "What're you talking about?"

Cort leaned back in his chair. "Don't worry. I helped her out."

Luke shot forward so fast, the stool he'd been pushing on screeched on the concrete floor. He pressed one boot to the footrest on Cort's chair so it collapsed and pushed him upright. Cort stood to face him.

"Explain yourself," Luke said. "Real slow."

"Now, guys," Marty said, standing up, but they ignored him.

Cort said, "That little girl lost the thing that means the most to her because she slept with you, and you up and left with your bruised ego because Sallowface was taking over, leaving us to deal with him and sending Victoria to her bed. Tessa didn't know what to do, even Kristen couldn't talk her out of it, so I went over there."

Luke clenched his fists. "What the hell business is it of yours?"

"Tessa worries, I worry. And you think you're the only one cares about Victoria? Besides, you made it my business when you dropped off the map."

"You saying this is all my fault?"

"Guys," Parker tried this time.

Luke barely heard him. He was still itching for a fight, and this felt bigger than one of his usual "wrassles" with Cort.

Cort said, "Some of it, yeah. In case you missed it while hanging out at the wineries, we got a lot going on here." He threw his arms out to the sides. "You gonna stick around and work it out or are you running some more?"

"I wasn't running," Luke said, thrown off balance by Cort's verdict. They'd faced off on many things over the years, but Cort never passed judgment this way.

"Doesn't answer my question."

"God damn it, Cort, I don't run."

Cort leaned close, watching his eyes. "No?"

Luke didn't blink. "No."

Cort glared at Luke. "Fine. Get the hell out of here and go fix things with your woman. But get right back because we've got some music to make."

CHAPTER THIRTY-FOUR

Victoria sat on the couch staring at a carpet stain.

After Cort had gone to the living room, Victoria charged around putting on makeup, a black pencil skirt with big buttons up the front and a red sweater. She had been slipping on a pair of red pumps with a peek-a-boo toe when Cort got a text from Brett's assistant to show up for a mandatory meeting at the Barn.

"Mandatory," he had snorted, staring at the screen. But he'd given Teresa a hearty kiss and headed out the door with a smile. Then, once they'd seen she was all right, Teresa and Kristen had left to attend to their days, too, leaving Victoria sitting on the couch alone.

"All dressed up, no place to go," she said. "No plan, and no man," she added, then covered her mouth with one palm. Had she officially lost it? No. There must be something she could do. But...what? She looked around the room, found no inspiration, curled her feet up on the cushion, and leaned against the arm, staring at the floor. She felt something inside her struggling against this malaise, wanting to break through and take charge, but after years of focusing everything on production, she honestly didn't know what to do with free time. Where was she supposed to direct her energy?

When the bell rang sometime later, Victoria moved her gaze from the carpet stain to the doorknob. Once the noise had receded, she concentrated on the spot again and the challenge of trying to ascertain its origins: coffee? Dr. Pepper? Kristen's asparagus tea?

The bell rang again.

No. The stain was too dark for asparagus tea.

Knocking on the door now.

Maybe it was Thai chili sauce.

The knocking turned to pounding. "Victoria!"

She lifted her head from the arm of the couch. "Luke?" she said, but didn't think he could hear her over his fist hitting the wood. It reminded her of last weekend, when they'd marched upstairs together to Cort's flat, and Luke had taken charge, hammering on the door with the side of his fist. *"Get your britches on, son, and get out here,"* he'd said. She was used to being the assertive one, and even though she'd witnessed his confidence, his self assurance had a good dose of humility mixed in. His command that night had sent a rush of heat through her, and she felt an echo of that now, trying to make its way to the fore. She pushed up from the couch, her legs and arms leaden, and opened the door.

"Stop that," she grumbled. "My landlady will call the police on you." She looked at his serious expression, then down at his hands. "Hat in hand?" she said, noting the Stetson there.

He nodded. "Yes, ma'am," he said quietly, but she still felt the determination behind his words. "I owe you an apology."

"No," she replied, moving away to slump back on the couch. "You don't owe me anything."

Closing the door behind him, Luke laid the Stetson on the coffee table. "I left without a word. And then I stayed away. That wasn't right."

"You're a grown man," she said, staring at the spot again. "And I'm not your producer anymore. You can do what you want."

If he left now, she might be able to get something on that stain before it became too permanent. Once something got set like that, it was impossible to remove...and it could break your heart as easy as that. She snapped her fingers together, as if she'd spoken out loud and wanted to emphasize her point.

Luke stood in front of her so that his denim-clad legs blocked her view. She was forcibly reminded of their interview in the park, when he walked toward the camera, blocking the lens with his crotch. If she'd had any idea then what was going to happen...would she have done anything differently?

"Victoria," he commanded. "Look at me." When she did, he said, "This isn't like you."

She straightened. "This is exactly like me. After I've lost everything."

"That's just pity talk." He crouched down to her eye level, hands dangling between his knees.

She avoided his gaze.

"Your sister and Tessa still around?"

"Teresa's at the catering company and Kristen is probably practicing her go-go dancing."

She heard him give a chuckle. "Not quite what I meant. Have they abandoned you?"

She studied the frayed seam on his jeans, wanting to run the tip of her finger over it. "Of course not."

"Your other friends still around? Your family?"

She raised her gaze to his; he looked concerned, sympathetic. She hated being an object of pity, but the fire had gone out of her. She shrugged.

He nodded, ran a hand through his hair. Sighed. "You still haven't lost everything."

Was he being dense on purpose? "You have no idea," she said. "What if you could never make music again?"

"I told you once that wasn't the most important thing to me. You saying you can't make any more shows ever again?"

She stared at him. "Not on my own."

"Why not?"

She didn't have the energy to explain financing, running equipment, a crew, and having a distributor for a reality TV show. Networks. Not to mention the green light from a production company. Like the one she used to work for. "Why are you here, Luke?"

He shifted in his crouch, pressing the tips of his fingers to the carpet, and looked down with another expelled breath. When he looked back, his eyes had softened and a sad smile played at the corners of his lips. "Just wanted to remind you you haven't lost everything. I don't plan on going anywhere."

She smiled back at him. Despite all that had happened between them and the horror of knowing their most intimate moment together would be on tape forever, it warmed her to hear him say that. She reached out to touch the pads of her fingers to his cheek. "Why?" she asked, without meaning to. Why would he want to be with someone who was incomplete? Without her job, she felt like half a person. A quarter of one.

Luke stood, brushing his fingertips along her knee. Fully upright, he held out his hand. To reach it, she would have to sit up, to take action. He was right, she was wallowing in self pity, but a hand clenched at her heart and fog surrounded her being.

"You fishing for compliments?" he asked, hand still extended.

She shook her head. "Not my style. But...I need to know. I need to be certain about *something* right now, and you and I are still too new for me to have developed confidence in that." She closed her eyes. Damn it. She might as well have "vulnerable" tattooed on her forehead, and fully expected him to sweep his hat off the table and leave. Or laugh.

Instead she heard him say, in that soft-deep voice of his, "Take my hand."

She opened her eyes. He stood strong before her, his arm unwavering. He hadn't wanted the intrusion of cameras in his life, but had accepted them. Could she accept what had happened to her with the same grace? She felt like she couldn't breathe. "I don't know what to *do*," she admitted.

"Just have a little faith." His hand remained steady.

She shook her head. "I don't believe in God."

With a gentle smile, he said, "Faith isn't always about God."

Taking a shaky breath, she slipped her fingers into his. He waited until their palms lined up before closing his fingers very lightly around her. He eased his arm back but he neither helped her nor pulled; as she stood, he shifted back, in concert with her. Then he dropped her arm, pressed his palms to the side of her head, flattening her hair down, and kissed her temple. When he straightened and took a few steps back, she felt the air move between them, and wondered why he wasn't touching her.

"You want to know why I said I'm not going anywhere?" At her nod, he continued. "I'm not mesmerized by your *job*." He bent his head toward her. "I'm mesmerized by *you*, and it's taking all I got not to touch you right now. But you need to hear this without my hands all over you."

She felt a shimmy along her spine; his hands all over her might not be so bad. But he was right. His words meant more this way.

"You know your job wasn't you. You just did real good at it. And that's because you're strong." He took a step closer. "Capable. Smart." She couldn't take her eyes from his as he came closer with each word. "Passionate. You may not be my producer anymore, but you're still my woman."

She stared at him. "No one's ever called me that before." No one had claimed her that way. "I like it," she told him. "And it makes me incredibly cranky."

Surprisingly, he smiled. "Got your back up?"

She put her hands on her hips. "I do."

"Good."

"Why is that good?"

"Means you're not dependent on a man to complete you. And damn it all...I cannot keep my hands off you." He bent to kiss her.

She lifted her face up, but jumped at a booming knock on the door.

Luke swore more vehemently. "I'll get rid of them." He peered through the peephole, then straightened. "Sam. With a crew."

Victoria shot to his side to look for herself. Another knock, then Sam rang the bell.

"Victoria," he called. "I know you're in there, and I know Luke's with you."

Victoria turned to Luke. "I have to let them in."

"Like hell."

She held her hands up. "I don't have time to explain it all. Let's just say an element of my parting agreement is that they can film me for the show." She hadn't agreed to let them into her home, but she'd trained Sam herself in the art of persistence. His crew could stay on the sidewalk until she left the flat, then follow her to any public place; she had more control over the situation if they came in and all she did was sit around reading about Bundt pans from one of Teresa's *Bon Apétit* magazines. This was Brett stealing her idea of reducing producer involvement, but he was combining it with revenge, and approaching it all wrong.

"What the hell kind of agreement is that?" Luke asked her.

"One that keeps me from being sued," she said. And you, too, she added to herself.

"God damn it, Victoria, how did you get yourself roped into that?"

"It's a long story," she told him, her desperation increasing as Sam's knocking got louder. She wasn't ready to be filmed, but she couldn't say that out loud. Once she let the crew in, Luke would sense her fear and want to protect her, and she didn't want him in any trouble. She needed to do this part alone. "Please, you have to go."

"We need to talk."

"Not on camera."

"When, then?" he asked.

"Later this afternoon. After I get rid of them."

"I need to get back to the Barn. Gig at Tony's tonight. Being filmed." He took her hand. "Will you come anyway?"

She wanted to say no, to hide until this was far in the past. But his eyes were soft, his hands warm, and letting him down wasn't an option. No, she thought, she wouldn't have done anything differently, even if she had known the outcome from the start. "Of course I'll come."

He lifted her hand to kiss the fingertips. "Let's meet at the bakery warehouse right after. Talk this all through."

She nodded.

Sam hammered on the door.

Luke wrenched it open, yelled, "Hold your horses!" and slammed it shut in Sam's gawking face.

Then he pulled Victoria up tight against him, cupped her face with one hand, and kissed her so thoroughly that after he pulled back and led her to the couch, she went without question. "Let me play cowboy and draw 'em off for you."

He bent down, kissed her temple, said, "See you tonight," and was gone, closing the front door firmly behind him.

Victoria let out a shaky breath, listening to the clatter of footsteps on the concrete, gear being gathered and toted down the stairs, and the van starting up and driving away. All sounds she knew so well, and missed with a fierce ache. And tonight she'd have to find a way to face them all from the other side.

CHAPTER THIRTY-FIVE

Luke's boots echoed off the brick buildings as he paced in the alley by the delivery door of Tony's. He and the boys had brought the equipment in earlier, and he waited for Victoria while the others headed out to greet the fans gathering in front. While Kristen set up a diversion, Victoria would go through the side door with him to avoid the crush of crowd and cameras.

He shook his head and smiled at the thought of what sort of distraction Kristen might invent. He sobered quickly, though, looking at the fog rolling in over the tops of the buildings, covering the few stars that had been visible past the streetlights. Even with their smokescreen, he and Victoria would be in the same room with the cameras as a couple. And Victoria would be in the same room with Soloway. It might be in her contract to consent to being filmed, but she didn't have to agree to them following her everywhere, or going into her home. In other words, she could find a way around being filmed. By showing up at Tony's, she was declaring both to the world and to him that she wouldn't hide. Luke's throat tightened at the thought.

He let out a breath at the brisk tapping of high heels behind him. He turned with a smile, forcing it to stay there when he realized Kristen made her way up the alley alone. She wore a bright beaded dress that might as well be a long shirt, and her wild hair floated around her shoulders as she walked. Her impossibly high heels made her taller than him, and he had to brace himself when she flung her arms around his neck for her customary greeting hug.

"You look so yummy," she told him, then stood back to give him a review, her hands on his upper arms.

"You look like multicolored sherbet yourself." Now that she stood under the light, he could better see the beads on her dress made patterns in peach, pink, red, orange and yellow. He was about to ask about Victoria, but she continued her assessment.

"Black Wranglers, slight scruff of beard, black hat. Tall and broad-shouldered. You've really got the cowboy thing down."

"Well, it's pretty much me," he said. "So, where's—" he began, but she squeezed his arms, cutting him off.

"Victoria's running late. She got a call from Maurice, the co-host on *Dress My Best*? He's a scream, have you met him?" Before he could answer, she continued. "He wanted to do a makeover for me, can you imagine? I can't. I have too much fun with my clothes to let anyone change them. Speaking of which, your jaw will drop when you see Victoria. You think I look like sherbet? She's a helping of—"

"Whoa." He took hold of her hands and eased them from his arms. "Let's not give away the surprise there, Sunshine." He liked Kristen and her straightforward ways, but she often stepped too close to the boundaries of his own comfort level. "So she's on her way?"

She nodded, brushing her hair over one shoulder. "Maurice was having a breakdown over her leaving. He said he didn't think the show would be the same, she was his favorite producer, no one else would be able to referee for him and Francesca, not even Jésus , who he has a mad crush on, and he might just have to leave the show. Crazy. I had no idea she was so loved." At his look, she said, "Oh, I know she's really good at her job, but her presence and commanding can really put people off. Her hairdressers for hire feel the same way. LaTanya called me the other day crying because she's leaving."

"One of her people called you?"

"Sure, we're friends now. They wanted to do something with my hair, but I think it scares them." She smiled at him, tilting her head. "I have a lot of questions."

He took a second to adjust to the change in subject. "Just in general, or for me in particular?"

She laughed. "Both, really, but you may not be able to answer why cats like people who don't like them, who really re-elected Bush, or why men are frightened by sexually empowered women. But you *can* tell me if you're in love with my sister."

It took Luke a moment to realize her last question wasn't part of her unanswerable list. "Don't you think that's between me and her?"

"Ultimately, yes, but she's my family..." She stopped, cleared her throat, and continued. "And family is everything to me, so if something ever happened...if you don't really mean it and if you're just leading her on..." Her voice broke and he watched in amazement as she gave a sob and began to cry. And Kristen Clausen did not cry quietly.

Luke raised his eyes to the heavens, asking for a little help here, then took three steps toward Kristen, put an arm around her and guided her to the small bench outside the door.

"Now what's all this about?" he asked, standing over her with his hands on his hips. Crying women made him feel especially helpless, but Kristen also left him stupefied. Did she need comforting or did she need someone to help her snap out of it?

She swiped her fingertips under her eyes and sniffled. "On the surface, I'm worried about Victoria, and I don't want her hurt." She waved a hand at him. "Oh, I don't think you'll hurt her, not on purpose, but she's so very vulnerable right now." She drew in a deep breath and said, "No, I think the biggest problem is that underneath all of that, I'm feeling very sorry for myself, and lonely for a good, strong man."

Luke straightened and took a small step backward.

Kristen let out another laugh, although this one had a touch of sad in it. "Don't worry. I don't cheat *with* people or *on* them—at least not on purpose— so you're safe. But you're a good, strong man, and so is Cort, and I happen to be living with the women you're each involved with. And I find myself simultaneously envious and happy for them. Especially Victoria, who's never let herself have a good relationship. So it would be even harder for me if you hurt her."

"I have no plans to hurt Victoria."

"Well, of course you wouldn't *plan* to. But you're her soul mate, and you're scared, so you might lash out at that, or run away."

Luke sympathized with Kristen's dilemma, and felt she deserved a good man, but at the same time, he thought that man might need a lot of patience. He wasn't ready to deal with the ideas of running away, lashing out or being scared, so he picked what he thought was the most innocent, saying, "You think I'm her soul mate?"

"Of course you are. You have all of the classic signs. Didn't she tell you?"

He nodded. "Well, now, I'm sure she would've gotten to it, but we've had a few other subjects needed our attention first."

She stood and held a hand out, the index finger up. "Well, the first one is instant attraction. The second—"

"I take it you're feeling better now?" He found this a fairly amusing distraction, but didn't feel right discussing his relationship on such a level with his woman's sister.

"A bit," she said, "but, really, the list is important. I mean—"

"I'm glad," he said. Then before she could speak again, he pressed his hands to the sides of her head and kissed her forehead. "But—"

He stopped as her face changed from happier to sad and tears slid down her cheeks again. He put an arm around her shoulders and made some soothing noises, telling her it would be all right, although he didn't know that for sure because he didn't know why she was now sobbing against his chest.

"You're such a nice man," she whispered into his damp shirt. "Why couldn't he have been nice?"

Luke pulled back so that Kristen had to straighten up. "Someone hurt you?"

She nodded, then shook her head. "Not physically, no. But emotionally, yes."

"You talk to your sister about this?"

"No" She wiped at her cheeks. "I'm not ready to yet. I'm not ready for all of the questions." Then she stepped away from him and gave him a brilliant smile. "I'll talk to her. But this is your night. So let's celebrate that." She adjusted her dress, made an apologetic swipe at his damp shirt, and turned at the sound of high heels at the end of the alley.

He turned with her, his heart going into high gear at the sight of Victoria sashaying toward them. Where Kristen was sherbet, Victoria was a scoop of raspberry cream. Her dress showed off her curves, including creamy breasts and luscious hips, and she wore matching platform heels that brought her height up more than he'd thought possible.

She barely heard Kristen whisper with some glee, "It's a bandage dress. Enhances all the good stuff."

He nodded in response, unable to stop staring at Victoria's legs as they moved her closer to him, looking longer in those shoes, with thighs he could picture pressing his lips to, the sway of her hips in a dress that clung so well it reminded him of every bare spot of skin he'd touched when they were together a few nights ago. He may have missed a few sections, now that he thought of it, and as she finally reached him and stood looking into his eyes, all he wanted to do was carry her away somewhere and make sure he knew each inch of her by feel.

Every single thing he could think of saying to her at that moment felt like the worst cliché in the world.

So he started his inventory right then, by running a fingertip from the top of her forehead, down to the delicate curve of her temple, and onto the arch of her cheekbone, where he spread the rest of his fingers and let them rest there. He looked into her bright blue eyes and said, "You're the song I always wanted to write."

She lifted up on her toes and pressed her lips to his, and he pulled her close, wanting to feel her against him. Her breasts pressed against his chest, her lips parted and he brushed his tongue against hers, soft, shivery, and deepened the kiss, demanding more, even as her body yielded.

He thought he heard Kristen announce she was "going inside now, before I burst into flame from the exposure," but he didn't care. The whole world could be there, cameras rolling, applauding, taking notes, whatever the hell they wanted, nothing would take him away from this moment of fully appreciating the woman in his arms. He brushed her hair from her face with one hand and kissed her exposed neck. He felt the shiver down her spine against the palm he had pressed to her lower back.

Luke was so focused on memorizing the dip above her collarbone with the tip of his tongue, he didn't realize at first that Victoria had stiffened in his arms, saying something other than urgent words of encouragement. "Mmm..." he said, declaration and question, as he slid his tongue along the edge of her dress up to her bare shoulder.

"Oh God, stop," she said.

He felt her hands against his chest then, firm, pushing him away. He lifted his head and looked down at her in the warm glow of the light above the door. "What's wrong?"

"I can't think when you do that."

He felt one side of his mouth quirk up. "Me, either, darlin'. And I'm pretty sure you don't *need* to think when I'm doing it."

"You have to play tonight."

He could still hear the breathlessness in her voice, her cheeks had flushed a pretty pink, and all he wanted to do was throw her over his shoulder and take her away somewhere private where they could make love for hours. And then do it all over again.

"Eventually," he said, tracing the edge of her dress right above one breast. "Hope it didn't take you long to get gussied up tonight."

"Why?"

"Because I'm betting I can get that dress off in about two seconds and I wouldn't want you to think you'd wasted all that time."

She stepped back, staring at him, but licked her lips and let out a breathy little, "Oh." Then she straightened and said firmly, "You have an obligation tonight. With the band. For the show."

"Victoria," he said, and tried to take the edge from his voice. "Let go of the show."

She shook her head. "I don't know how."

"Go on a date with me and we'll figure it out together," he said, wanting to distract her.

"I beg your pardon?"

"Go on a date with me," he repeated with a shrug. "Dinner?"

"Isn't that like closing the barn door after the horses have gotten out?"

He smiled. "You said you wanted to get to know me better." One hand splayed against her back, the other caressed the side of her face. "Maybe we should start with the basics. So..."

"Well, you may have to stop touching me like that for me to give you a reasonable answer."

He straightened up, dropped his hands, and took a step back. "It was real hard for me to do that, so I'm hoping you'll make it worthwhile."

He felt the chill in the air on his face and arms when he moved away. She was right; he could think clearer when they were farther apart from each other. Couldn't say he liked it much, though.

"Did you think I'd say no?" she asked.

"Darlin', I gave up predicting you quite awhile ago."

She gave a surprised laugh, then jumped when the back door opened and Tessa poked her head out. She'd pulled her front braids back so they curved along the side of her head, and her eyes looked big in the glow of the light.

"You're still here," she said. "We were getting worried. Kristen's just itching to make her diversion." She looked at Luke. "And it's getting close to eight."

"We'd best be getting inside, then," Luke said, watching Victoria.

"Yes." She pressed her palms to his cheeks, pulling him close for a soft but firm kiss. "*Yes*," she said clearly when they separated, their faces still close. She held his gaze until he nodded.

"Good, then," he said. "I look forward to opening the barn door."

She pulled back as he took her hand to lead her inside. "Wait." He turned to her expectantly. Out of the corner of his eye, he saw Tessa waiting, and Victoria addressed her now. "Go ahead, T." She focused back on Luke's face. "We're going in the front door."

He squeezed her hand. "Are we now?"

She nodded. Before he could ask, she added, "Together."

Tessa looked between them both, then gave a big grin before ducking back inside and closing the door. Luke retrieved his guitar with his free hand and pulled Victoria closer with the other. She nodded at him, and he led her to the mouth of the alley. They stood at the top of the hill, looking at where Tony's Tavern sat at the corner. Luke could feel a slight tremor running down Victoria's arm to her fingers.

"You're sure?"

She nodded again, staring at the crowd in front of the Tavern, at the cameras and bright lights set up outside. "That's my world." She pointed with her free hand. "And *In Concert* is still my show. I won't...I will not let Brett Soloway or anyone else take away my part in it. Or my pride."

Her heels clicked with determination as she charged forward, and his boots thudded as he followed, holding back a grin at her courage. Damn but she had balls.

By the time the cameras and crowd outside caught sight of them, she was striding ahead of Luke, still holding his hand, a big smile on her face. Even then, he could tell she wasn't fully prepared for the bright camera lights, or the crush of people surging at them, phones raised for pictures and video, or for the chattering girls surrounding Luke, touching and petting him, breaking the grip of her hand in his. He knew she was accustomed to being in the background, and watched as she forced the bitter expression from her face when Sam turned to her. Luke had seen their interplay so many times, he knew Sam was automatically waiting for orders from Victoria on what to do next. Luke also knew the cameras on all these shows would focus on the new girlfriend, and he wanted to save her from that as best he could.

"We gotta get inside for the show, boys, and I can't keep my date out in the cold like this." He slipped an arm around her shoulders, lifted his guitar case in a wave, and said he hoped everyone enjoyed the music. He ignored a few sour looks as he led Victoria through the dim opening of the tavern and through the packed room to two tables up front with handwritten Reserved signs on them. Both Tessa and Kristen hopped up and gave her a quick hug.

"There were a lot of heaving breasts out there," Kristen shouted over the excited chatter of the crowd. "We weren't sure you'd make it."

He watched her do a quick scan and followed her gaze, seeing cameramen ranged around the tavern and Soloway at the bar, phone to one ear, hand over the other to Victoria turned to Luke, who couldn't keep his eyes from her as he waited by her side, but he was currently ringed by four women staring up at him as if entranced. One woman looked about to burst into tears, and he felt bad for her, but all he could see was Victoria, a standout with her long wavy hair and raspberry dress. block out the noise, oblivious to everything around him.

Luke gestured with a thumb behind him to the blue room and she nodded. He bent to her and she stood on tiptoes to meet him. "You'll be all right," he said, less a question than a statement.

She nodded again and he grinned at her.

"Never thought otherwise," he said, his lips close to her ear.

He saw her shiver from tip to toes, and didn't know how he was going to get through this set so they could be alone again. He wrapped his free arm around her and lifted her off her feet for a kiss in front of everyone at the club. The kiss was warm and sweet. And he didn't give a damn who saw it.

CHAPTER THIRTY-SIX

While he sang, Luke had to keep pulling his gaze from where Victoria danced with Kristen, Tessa and Miranda. Tessa had suggested he not flirt with Victoria during their set to avoid giving Brett and the cameras any ammo. After Victoria's charge down the sidewalk to Tony's, he didn't worry so much for her, but watching her shimmy in that dress distracted him more than was good for anyone present.

So he gave her a wink, then tossed his head toward the mic, where Cort joined him for the chorus of "Return to Me." The whole audience was on their feet dancing, tables pushed aside, as they'd been that night Victoria first showed up with her crazy notion. Only now, more people than ever crowded the floor, whirling, swaying, and stomping their feet in time.

Luke felt his chest expand with pleasure as Parker joined in on the harmony, the guitars and keyboards rang out the final chords, Marty hit the drums one last time, and it all drifted away.

Parker held the last note, but the roar of cheers and thunder of applause eclipsed it, with much of the audience stamping their boots on the floor. Luke exchanged a grin with Cort, then they both took a bow while everyone continued to applaud. Head still down, Luke noticed the cheering die off at a fast rate, and caught sight of a figure moving toward the stage through the folks still standing.

"Holy Jesus," Cort said next to him.

Luke's jaw tightened.

The cheering stopped completely and was replaced by curious and excited murmurs as the figure advanced—and was recognized. Luke stood rigid on the stage, one hand contracting on the neck of his guitar, the other closing into a fist. He felt Cort move closer.

From the corner of his eye, he saw Victoria shove people aside, walking roughly parallel to the newcomer. A camera followed her.

He couldn't pull his eyes from the man in his signature red leather vest and matching cowboy hat now standing in front of him. A man he hadn't seen in ten years, his last memory of him out back of Bootstraps Bar kissing an unfamiliar woman who had long blonde hair and red talons.

They studied each other, Luke on stage, surrounded by his boys, the other man below, face more heavily lined but still tanned and confident. Recognizable to anyone who turned on a television in the past thirty years.

The man rocked back, nodded at Cort, Parker and Marty, then at Luke. He spoke in a thick, gravelly voice that carried across the now quiet tavern.

"Hello, son."

The crowd let out a collective gasp and the murmurs amplified to a low roar. Victoria moved closer to the stage, looking ready to step in front of Buzz. Tessa, Kristen and Miranda joined Victoria. Kristen held Miranda's hand, and Tessa had an arm around Victoria's waist and was whispering in her ear. Victoria kept shaking her head, but stayed put.

With Cort sticking close, Luke moved to the mic, and spoke into it so his voice reverberated around the room, forcing quiet again. "I'm not your son." When Buzz didn't respond, Luke added, "What the hell are you doing here?"

Buzz looked up at him from under his hat. "Well, now, I came to give you and your band some good news."

"You and good news don't go together, old man."

While another gasp went up at Luke's statement, Buzz ignored it and pulled a crumpled piece of paper from his vest pocket, taking his time to straighten it out. The familiar frustration and anger from Luke's childhood started to grow from its banked embers to a small flame, charring his insides now, the smoke clouding his vision.

"Steady," Cort said next to him, sounding far off.

From the floor, just a few feet away, Buzz cleared his throat and got the audience's full attention. As he'd been doing for years. He had presence and confidence—that could never be denied.

"I'd say a letter from Buzzsaw Productions offering y'all a recording contract is a pretty good piece of news."

A few more outbursts from the audience, a couple of cheers from someone that sounded like Candy and Mandy. Parker and Marty shuffled but kept quiet, and the audience fell silent again.

Luke shoved his guitar to Cort, then jumped down to stand directly in front of Buzz, his boots making a solid thump on the floor. "We don't want your damn news or your damn contract. We don't want *anything* from you."

"Now, son—"

Luke held up a hand, pointing his finger in Buzz's face. "Don't call me that."

Cort stepped down to Luke's right, and Parker and Marty followed suit on his left. Marty took hold of Miranda's free hand. Their support strengthened him, but he also felt alone, just as he had throughout his childhood when faced with Buzz's domineering presence. But he was an adult now, no longer a scared kid in awe of his angry father, and he needed to face the man on his own, without backup.

"You can deny it as much as you like," Buzz said in a mild voice, "but I am your father."

"No!" Luke shouted, stepping closer, his face inches from Buzz's. "You stopped being my father the day you dragged Mama out of the room by the hair and locked me in the closet."

Buzz held his ground. "And that was shameful. It hasn't happened since and it won't happen again."

Luke smelled the whiskey on Buzz's breath, and his temples pounded hard in time with his heart. "You're drunk," he said in a flat voice, pulling away.

"Not drunk," Buzz said in a careful, calm tone, but Luke could hear the slight slur to his words. "Just needed to take the edge off. I've asked your mama for her forgiveness and she's granted it, and now I'm asking for yours."

"You don't deserve it!" Luke said, pushing his face close to Buzz's again, even though his stomach lurched at the fumes. "You'll never earn it. You're a plague, and I'd kick you out, but I'm not going to stoop to your level." He poked Buzz in the shoulder. "You worthless son of a bitch—"

Before he could say more, Victoria put her hand on Luke's arm and pushed in between them, forcing Luke back a couple steps. Buzz didn't take his eyes from Luke until Victoria snapped her fingers in front of his face.

"Mr. Taylor," she said, with what sounded like forced cheer, and held her hand out for Buzz to shake. "I'm Victoria Clausen, producer of *In Concert*. I believe it would be in everyone's best interest if we moved this to a more private location." She gestured toward the back room. "Shall we?"

"Well, now," Buzz said, still holding her hand, all Southern geniality. "You're the little girl called me a few months ago and invited me on your show. It's much appreciated. Couldn't resist the opportunity."

Luke froze. His blood raged so hot through his veins, pounding in his ears, that he barely heard Soloway bleating something about *him* being the producer. He didn't catch Victoria's reply. He only saw her turn to him with a smile, one he'd seen so many times in the early days of the show, when she'd won a victory over his bull-headedness and it got caught on film.

He rounded on her, and her smile froze. "I trusted you," he snarled. "You bitch, have you been planning this all along?" A logical part of him deep inside knew this was wrong, but he'd had one too many blows the past few days and a primitive, protective side was taking over. He was so damn tired of being rational, of doing for everyone instead of himself. And still Victoria hadn't completely stepped up to his side to claim him the way he'd claimed her earlier.

From all around, voices rose in Victoria's defense: Kristen, Tessa, Parker, Miranda and Marty, even Buzz. But Cort made the mistake of stepping into Luke's line of sight, holding up a hand and saying, "Easy there, son, let's all take a breath here and..."

It was the "son" that did him in. All those years he and Cort had played *Smokey and the Bandit*, jokingly calling each other son, but it had really originated from Buzz. Buzz had called them both "son" from the cradle, and Luke had spent the majority of his life denying it. Now it cornered him, all of it, the endearment, his drunken father, how much he'd tried to make everything work, and he'd break if he didn't break out.

He whirled on Cort, shoving him in the chest with both hands. "You sonovabitch. If you hadn't pushed this damn show so hard, we wouldn't be here. This is your fault," he shouted, then rounded on Marty and Parker. "And yours. We could've made it without the show, but look what a fuckup it's turned into."

"You're nothing without this show, Tyler," Soloway said with a smirk. "Just a lying, girl-stealing hack. Who, from the sound of it, isn't even that good in bed. *I* brought Buzz Taylor here. Me. Not your little slut."

Victoria gave Brett a shove, and Soloway shoved back, making her stumble. And that was enough for Luke. He threw his body into a punch that rocked Soloway's head back, then laid him flat with a whump. The impact jarred up Luke's left arm and his knuckles stung; it felt like nirvana.

Amid the uproar and confusion, Luke pushed his way through the crowd toward the blue door, shaking off any hands that tried to hold him back, one of which may have been Cort's.

He didn't care; the blood pounded in his ears, his world turned upside down, and he needed to get out before he exploded. He slammed the door open and stalked past the boxes of supplies to the outer door.

"Luke!"

He paused for the only voice that could get him to slow down, but Buzz's words still echoed in his ears loud enough to keep him moving: *You're the little girl called me a few months ago and invited me on your show.*

He ignored Victoria and slammed the outside door open, not bothering to close it, satisfied by the banging sound it made against the wall.

Victoria called his name again.

The cold outside air did little to cool his rage, but it felt good against his heated skin as he stalked up the alley. He heard the fast click of Victoria's heels as she tried to catch up with him and the steady thud of Sam's shoes as he struggled to do the same with a twenty pound camera on his shoulder.

"Luke, you have to talk to me!" Victoria called.

"No, I do not," he said, as he rounded the corner and headed for his truck.

"Do not run away from me!" she yelled.

He stopped at the back bumper and whirled to face her. She was closer than he'd thought and only had to take a few more steps to catch up to him. She stood with her chest heaving and her cheeks pink in the streetlight. He saw goose bumps raise up on her forearms.

Sam still hadn't come out of the alley, but he was close.

"I am not running," Luke told her. "I'm keeping the situation from going to the dogs."

Victoria put her hand to her side and bent over a little. "Then talk to me. Let me explain."

"No," he said, and stalked to the driver's side just as Sam rounded the corner with his camera light on, followed by Tim with a boom mic.

"You have to," Victoria insisted as he sat inside the truck and closed the door.

He put the key in the ignition and felt the truck jolt. Looking in the rearview mirror, he saw Victoria balancing on the back bumper, her hands clutching the tailgate. She caught his eye in the mirror and shouted so loud it came through the closed windows.

"You *will* talk to me, Luke Tyler. I will climb into this truck bed and go wherever you're going."

Luke started the truck and watched Victoria's fingers tighten on the tailgate even as she lifted one foot to go up and over, pulling her tight skirt high up her thighs, flashing her black panties, the entire scenario illuminated by Sam's camera light.

Leaving the truck running, Luke got out and stepped in front of Sam to stop the lens from recording up Victoria's skirt. Still blocking Sam, who couldn't maneuver because of a car parked behind the truck, Luke put his hands on Victoria's waist and set her on the ground. She turned to face him, but he led her to the passenger door, opened it and set her on the outer side of it.

"Keep yourself covered," he told her.

Leaving the door open, he rummaged behind the seat until he found a tire iron, then turned and smashed the small dash-mounted camera. He eased Victoria into the seat, then shoved by Sam, who was making sounds of protest but still filming, and did the same with the camera on the driver's side.

When he straightened, he looked over the cab of the truck and saw half the crowd from Tony's gathered on the sidewalk, and more coming up the alley, with all of the cameramen now present and capturing everything. And standing in front of them, just on the edge of the curb, Buzz. And right next to him? Luke's mama, Dot.

The fight went out of him and he dropped the tire iron into the bed with a tremendous clang, hearing it reverberate around the street, even its echo loud compared to the dead silence of the crowd. The door creaked open and Victoria stepped out the other side, turning to watch him. Just as quickly as it had gone, heat rushed through him again, shame at how he'd treated her combined with injustice over the entire situation. Luke knew much of the blame rested on his shoulders, but Buzz also had his share, a share he'd never taken responsibility for.

He walked around the back of the truck to stand on the curb facing Buzz, the light from the cameras and cell phones recording so intense he had to squint against the glare. "Soloway deserved the slug I gave him, but I should've gone after you next."

Without a change in expression, Buzz said, "I wouldn't've gone down so easy."

"You're a bastard."

"Lucas Preston Taylor," his mama admonished.

He glanced at her, noting her trademark red boots, jeans skirt and red sweater, a match to Buzz. He clamped his jaw tight against an apology. He wouldn't do that now, not here, not after everything. He'd apologized far too much in his life, with nothing to show for it, and no one else returning the favor.

"No mind, baby," Buzz told Dot. To Luke, he said, "Been saying that to myself every day for the last thirty years or so."

"We don't want your contract." Luke caught sight of Cort, Marty and Parker, standing shoulder to shoulder, with Tessa, Miranda and Sunshine in line with them, all of their expressions unreadable except Victoria's sister. That girl didn't know the meaning of poker face, and she was all kinds of twisted up as she looked between him and Victoria. It wrenched at his guts, but he couldn't go there right now. He pressed his lips together and let out a long breath through his nose. "*I* don't want the contract," he amended. "But it's not up to me. The boys and I'll vote on it." If they were all part of a group at the end of this, he thought.

"I can't change what happened, Lucas." When Luke didn't reply, Buzz added, "But I can change how I behave from now on."

Luke nodded, knowing that somewhere in there was an addendum, something like, "And you can change your behavior, too." He crossed his arms over his chest and leaned back, but he felt far from relaxed. He looked at Dot. "You know he was drinking again?"

She moved closer to Buzz. "He was real nervous about seeing you."

"Don't blame this on me," he said, shaking his head. He saw Victoria ease up to him, holding her hand out as if to touch him or take his hand, and he shook his head at her, too.

"He had a minor lapse, is all," Dot said, swaying in Buzz's direction and looking up at her husband's face. "He'll stop again. He's not perfect. None of us is perfect. We did our best by you, always did."

Luke felt an icy chill go up his back. "What about you, Mama? You lapsing, too?"

Instead of answering, Dot looked at Victoria. "You were right, honey. She's pretty as a Georgia morning," she said, and Luke definitely caught the slurring now.

"I said she was beautiful," he reminded her, "not just pretty."

Victoria did step to his side now, and pressed a hand to his forearm before dropping it back to her side. "Maybe the three of you want to finish this talk in private."

He took in the rapt crowd, the line of his resentful band mates and their girls, all of the cameras and bystanders in the street, and gave her a bitter smile. "You think I have anything to hide at this point? Anything I *can* hide?" By the shocked look on her face, he could tell she'd figured out the rest of his unspoken sentence: *Because of your damn show.* "Well let me be real clear here," he said to Buzz and Dot. "I don't want anything to do with either of you."

And because it had all gone to hell, and there was nothing he could say that wouldn't damn him, he whirled around, slammed a fist into the truck bed, then stomped to the other side and slid in. As he let out the brake, Victoria wrenched the passenger door open and sat next to him. She closed the door on the sudden outbreak of noise as everyone reacted to what they'd just done, but that didn't stop the lights from the cameras as they crowded around the truck, so he pulled away from the curb with a screech of tires.

He kept silent, the knuckles of his left hand pounding in time with his heart. Damn stupid thing to have done, punching the truck, but at least he hadn't used his right hand. Victoria wrapped her arms around her middle and asked him to turn up the heat. He did.

"Where are we going?"

He didn't answer.

She didn't give up, as he knew she wouldn't. "Luke—"

"The heat's all the way up. You want the shirt off my back?"

"I want you to talk to me."

"*I trusted you,*" he snapped, repeating what he'd said in the bar.

"No, you didn't," she snapped back. "You didn't trust me until we slept together."

"That's not true." He slammed on the brakes for a light. He took a quick right, to keep them moving, away from cameras, the judgmental crowd, his accusing friends and dysfunctional parents.

"You're right," she said, and he glanced at her in surprise. "You didn't completely trust me then. Even after I told you the feed was off, you were suspicious, but you knew it wasn't a setup because I wouldn't risk my job."

This time he slammed the brakes on in the middle of the street. Victoria hit the seat belt, throwing her hands up to brace herself against the dash, then fell back.

"You got it all wrong," Luke said. "I slept with you because..." He stopped. It sounded so base to say that he slept with her because he wanted her, because he'd wanted her ever since the first night he saw her. There was so much more to it than that. Was it because he loved her?

He turned. She was staring at him, clutching the seatbelt in both hands.

"Finish your sentence," she said.

He shook his head. He wasn't going to say it until he had some answers. "Why did you ask Buzz to come here?"

She sucked in a breath. "Because it would make good TV," she said, choking out the last words as tears welled in her eyes and spilled over. She swiped at her cheeks with the tips of her fingers. "I know how stupid that sounds now. But it *would* make good television. It *will.*" She gave a strained laugh, then jumped when someone honked a horn behind them.

Luke pulled the truck over to the side of the street in someone's driveway, put it in park and faced Victoria again. She looked down at her lap, tears still sliding down her cheeks. He wanted to pull her to him and wipe them away, to reassure her everything was all right. But it wasn't. And he needed to hear from her that she wouldn't have followed through with bringing Buzz out here for the show.

"I feel so stupid," she whispered. "I know what people want to see, but I didn't know the effect it was having on...on the people in the shows themselves."

"Until it happened to you?"

She nodded. Then she said fiercely, "Some people *like* being on television, love their lives being exposed, all the attention, having it all out there..."

"And some of us don't," Luke said, reaching for her hand.

She shook her head, still looking down, letting him take her hand, the fingertips still damp from her tears, but not responding in any way. "No," she agreed. "Some of us don't." She finally looked at him. "I'm so sorry. I'm so ashamed..."

He stroked the back of her hand with his thumb.

"Brett had all my files. In the confusion of everything else, I'd forgotten about calling Buzz. He and Dot were so determined not to come out until Buzz was further along in his recovery—"

"You talked to my mother, too?"

"Yes. She's a strong woman. And very protective of your father."

Luke stared out the window. "Would you have asked them out again later?"

"Yes."

He let out a long breath through his nose. "Even after we'd slept together?"

Her pause lasted long enough for him to look at her again. She held his gaze as she said, "Yes," and she grasped tightly to his hand with both of hers when he tried to pull away. "Not for the show. Not for ratings. For *you*. But I didn't realize the extent...That was...that was scary back there."

He didn't respond. But he agreed with her.

"Luke—" Her phone interrupted, some annoying pop song. She glanced at her bag, then back at him.

"You going to answer that?"

"No."

The song ended, but started right up again. Victoria sighed, but didn't let go of his hand or look away. "So?"

"I can't think with that thing going off." He knew she couldn't resist the phone's siren call. "Just answer the damn thing," he added. Maybe it would give him a moment to collect his thoughts.

She reached in her bag and looked at the phone. "I don't recognize the number." But she put the phone to her ear, and said, "Victoria Clausen." She cut her eyes to him, then away. "Yes," she said. "He is."

Luke watched her face, unable to read her expression in the streetlight.

"That's not up to me," she said, "but I'll ask."

She put a thumb over the mouthpiece and said, "Your mother."

"Put it on speaker," he said, then added, "Sonovabitch," as he glanced in the rearview mirror.

CHAPTER THIRTY-SEVEN

Victoria turned to look out the back window and wasn't surprised to see a white van trailing them as Luke headed up Broadway toward Divisadero. She pressed Speaker and held the phone up between them, shivering as she waited for the heater to kick in. Or maybe for another scene to erupt here in the tiny cab of the truck.

"Mama," Luke said in a flat voice.

"Lucas, you do not walk out on your mother and father like that."

Victoria watched Luke's profile, saw a muscle in his jaw jump as he clenched his teeth. He had been right, Dot had been drinking, too. Victoria could hear it in the careful way Dot enunciated each word. Luke didn't respond, and after a few beats of silence, Dot continued.

"You do not walk away with such hateful words, and you do not act in a such a manner as you did tonight. I raised you better'n'that." Her next few words were cut off when Luke gave a nasty bark of laughter. "...I brought you into this world, after thirty-eight hours laborin', and that alone earns me your respect."

Biting her lip, Victoria looked out at the still, dark water as they moved across the Bay Bridge and up the freeway. She couldn't imagine ever having a conversation like this with anyone in her family.

"I do respect you, Mama," Luke said, eyes on the road, but his head tilted toward the phone. "I respect how hard you worked to raise me right, and how hard you worked to put up with Buzz and set him straight. But I don't like you very much right now." He clutched the steering wheel and Victoria could see the huge effort it took for him not to add anything else.

"You have no idea, Lucas, none in this whole world what I went through with that man, to keep his demons away and to keep them back from my own self." Her voice didn't break, and Victoria heard the edge in it, the years of postponing her own life, of balancing the needs of her son and her husband with her own, and realizing it had failed. "I love him. Did then, still do. I know you don't understand how I could love someone who hurt me. But he only hurt me when he'd been drinking, and I knew that wasn't really him in there. He wasn't the Buzz Taylor I knew. Not after he'd gotten the drink in him."

Victoria looked at the stretch of freeway ahead of them, then at Luke's profile. She didn't know how he was holding it all together during this speech. "Do you want me to hang up?" she whispered.

He shook his head. "You could've left," he said to Dot.

"No, honey. I couldn't." Her simple declaration said so much. With those words, Victoria knew that Dot Taylor could never conceive of leaving her husband, but even if she could, she wouldn't. She was incapable of such an action. Victoria's throat tightened and she had to lower the hand that held the phone to keep it from shaking too much. "Thing is," Dot continued, "I was just as bad as your daddy. I was caught up in it, too, and I made my mistakes. He drank, I drank. For the same reasons he did, to get rid of those demons. But you can't ever shake them, can you, no matter how hard you try. He cheated, I cheated. I'm not—"

Luke grabbed the phone from Victoria and pressed his thumb to the END button, then dropped it on the bench seat between them. Without a word, he turned on satellite radio to a country station, keeping the volume fairly low. Victoria powered down the phone and slipped it into her bag.

"Luke, I'm so sorry," she said. "No one should have to deal with that. No child should..."

"Shh." He glanced at her and brushed a section of hair behind her ear. "Not now," he said. "Just...not right now." He lifted his arm up. "C'mere."

She shook her head, the issues of the past few weeks heavy in her chest. For both of them. She wanted to talk. They needed to. How would any of this get untangled if they didn't discuss it?

Luke glanced at her, but didn't lower his arm. "Give me this one,

Victoria. Please. Without a battle."

She slid across the seat and felt the comforting weight of his arm across her shoulders, his hand curved around her. She pressed her face to the smooth material of his shirt and rested a hand near the middle button, right where his heart beat under her fingers, steady and strong. She didn't think she'd be able to sleep, but with Blake Shelton murmuring about who she was when he wasn't looking, the heat finally warming the cab, and Luke's chest rhythmically rising and falling under her cheek, she drifted off.

She woke alone in the truck, but saw Luke perched on the back of a picnic bench in front of a wide expanse of grass that sloped gently up to a row of low buildings. He sat with his hands wrapped around a cup, hunched over, his boots resting on the bench seat. She glanced behind her and saw the Dolphin Club; beyond that, a low concrete wall led to a stretch of sand, the gentle waves of the bay creating a line of white froth as they advanced and receded. Farther out, she saw the pier that formed this small lagoon, and past Black Point, like a beacon, the north tower of the Golden Gate Bridge. She didn't need that as confirmation they'd returned to the city, but its presence smoothed some of the jagged edges in her heart. They were home.

She straightened, yawning, feeling stiff and as if she'd never be warm again. A bright pink sweatshirt with a cartoon map of San Francisco on it lay in her lap, and a cup of steaming coffee sat in the holder near the shattered camera.

She'd been on a relentless roller coaster ever since the morning Jerry fired her. No. Before that, really. From the night she and Luke made love. Things had moved at such a rapid-fire pace, she hadn't had time to absorb any of it, much less react beyond any immediate need, or make any decisions. But looking at the man who sat on the bench in front of her and stared out at the rising sun sparkling on the gentle waves that created shimmering patterns in the fog, she knew one thing without question: she wanted to be with him.

She pulled on the tacky sweatshirt, slid the warm cup out of its holder, and went to join Luke. He didn't turn until she'd reached the bench, where he gave her a brief smile and held out his hand. She took it and squeezed, stepping between his legs, then set her coffee on the bench. "Thanks for that," she said, gesturing at it. "And for this." She ran a palm over the gaudy sweatshirt, which reached almost to her knees. "I think."

His smile broadened. "Only one the coffee shop had." He sobered again, and she wondered what he was thinking. "Couldn't have you freezing," he added, watching her.

She resisted the temptation to smooth her hair down and her eyebrows in line and held his gaze. "I guess we lost Sam and the cameras along the way."

"Mmm." Their hands still linked, he pulled her closer. He put his own coffee down and reached for a tendril of hair, curling it round and round one of his fingers. "I've got some straightening out to do, some things to fix. At some point, I'll have to deal with Buzz and Dot. For now, I don't want them in my life. But more important...I want things to be right with you."

"What do you mean?"

"It means I'm sorry. Sorry about what I called you last night, what I said to you at Tony's. I had no call to do that. And sorry I was so hotheaded, fighting you every step of the way with the show, making things hard for you. I put you in a bad spot that night, getting you fired..."

"There were two people in that room."

"I should've walked away, figured another option, something that wouldn't risk your job."

She shook her head. "I don't think I would've let you walk away. I didn't know it then, but I wanted it to happen as much as you did."

He laughed. "I don't think that's possible." Then he grew serious again. "But afterward, the..."

"The fallout?" she suggested.

"Like that." He dropped his hand in his lap. "You lost the most important thing in your life, you said yourself. And I feel responsible."

"You're not. I was my own undoing." She really had thought it was the most important thing in her life, but now she wasn't so sure. And what was she—*who* was she—if not a reality TV producer? She didn't know, and it left her mute, unable to voice her pain and confusion. She didn't do therapy, damn it, she didn't know how to express any of this. Now she shook her head, and took a couple steps back, feeling her lips trembling and hating herself for it. Because not only was she no longer a producer, but she'd also lost her edge. Her world was shifting under her like the tectonic plates along the San Andreas fault line, everything breaking apart, and she no longer knew how to respond to anything.

"No," he said, jumping down from the bench and reaching for her. "Don't..."

He tried to draw her close to him again, and she resisted at first, not even sure why. Maybe because the old Victoria only relied on herself, not on a man, for comfort, and that was a familiar pattern, so she automatically turned in that direction.

"Please let me be sweet to you," Luke said, sliding his hand around her neck, and easing her toward him. She finally let him wrap his arms tightly around her so she could press her face into his shoulder and wet his shirt with her tears. She clung to him, crying for so many things she couldn't name, but glad for his warmth and strength. That steadiness that seemed to come from his core eased her own instability.

Eventually she wore out, shifting from sobs to sniffles, and finally to long, shuddering exhalations. When her breathing evened out, she heard Luke's heartbeat against her cheek, strong and constant as usual. With the backdrop of waves and an early morning jogger pattering by, she rested in his arms, more peaceful than she'd been in a long time.

BACK AT VICTORIA'S flat, Luke scooped her out of the passenger seat and carried her up the stairs. She'd taken off her shoes in the car and let the heater blow over her toes on the drive back. It had been a quiet ride, with her leaning against Luke's side, but the atmosphere was less tense than when they'd driven away from Tony's the night before. She felt warm and safe in his arms, and even though it seemed unrealistic, for the moment her optimism led her to believe all of their problems could be easily solved.

She opened the door to see Teresa and Kristen sitting close together on the couch, expectant looks on their faces, T's cell phone on the table in front of them.

"Oh, thank God," Teresa said, one hand to her heart.

Kristen popped up. "Where have you been?"

Teresa followed her up and they stood side by side. "We were scared to death. Five minutes," she added. "You couldn't have spared five minutes after everything that happened last night?" She gestured at Victoria's bag. "You have a brand new phone. I think we tried to call you every half hour, but it went straight to voice mail."

Luke's fingers twitched around Victoria's side, and she looked up in time to see him hiding a grin.

"We had things to do." Victoria bridled at how much their parental tones made her feel like a teenager.

Kristen's eyes widened. "You didn't get married!"

"What? No. My shoes got damp." She looked up at Luke again. "You can put me down now," she said with some regret.

He lowered her until her feet touched the floor, and she set her bag and shoes by the chair while he laid his hat on the coffee table. When he straightened, he slipped his arm around her waist. Kristen and Teresa watched them closely.

"I'm sorry, okay?" she told them. "I turned off my phone. What happened?"

Teresa goggled at Victoria. "You always have your phone on."

"You weren't having sex," Kristen said. It was a declaration, not a question. "That's the only reason important enough that I can think of for you to turn off your phone."

"You always have your phone on," Teresa repeated in an awed whisper.

Victoria looked at Luke, who smiled down at her. "Maybe my priorities have changed."

"Oh my God," Teresa said again, and dropped back onto the couch.

Kristen smiled. "Well, it's about time."

Victoria ignored that, and asked Teresa, "So what happened last night after we left?"

"Chaos," Teresa replied.

"Pandemonium," added Kristen.

"Sam and Tim drove after you all in one of the vans," Teresa said. "Cort wanted to, but Parker stopped him. Marty got Miranda out of there. It was too much for her."

Victoria stifled a yawn; her limbs felt heavy and she leaned into Luke. She really wanted to know what had happened, but she'd barely slept in the past few hours, alternately dozing and being jolted awake with the movement of the truck. "Why?" She knew Miranda was quiet, but didn't think of her as especially delicate.

Teresa and Kristen exchanged a look.

After a pause, Kristen said, "She's pregnant."

Victoria gasped mid-yawn. "What?"

"Almost four months. She was so stressed out, they didn't want to risk anything."

Victoria looked at Luke. "Did you know this?"

He met her gaze, his expression chagrined. "Yes." He took a breath and said, "They're married, too."

"What?!"

Victoria turned to look fully in his face, stumbling as she twisted around. "You *knew* about this?"

Luke led her to the chair and took her on his lap. She struggled, angry that he'd kept this from her—that they all had—and kicked him in the ankle. Which did no harm since he wore cowboy boots. She sat rigidly upright.

"They didn't want cameras," Luke said, his hands still light on her upper arms.

"We would've paid for it," she said in a voice that sounded pitiful even to her.

Gently, Luke told her, "It wasn't worth it to them."

"I don't understand," Victoria said, but she did. It was part of her new perception of what life was like when lived on camera. A life without her in charge of things.

"I know, darlin', but this was important to them. That's what matters."

Victoria gradually relaxed back against his warm, solid chest and he wrapped his arms around her. She really was too tired to think about it now.

"Why are you wearing a tacky tourist sweatshirt?" Teresa asked.

"We drove around. It got cold," Victoria said, still distracted. How much more? How much more was she in the dark about? "What else happened? After Marty and Miranda left."

"Well, everyone was pretty much yelling and running around like chickens with their heads cut off," Teresa said. "No one knew what to do. Both Cort and Buzz shouted for everyone to calm down. It was actually sort of funny, watching them competing to take charge. Parker went inside and got help putting the equipment away, a few people helped Brett, and when things calmed down, Cort and Parker took Buzz aside to talk to him." Teresa glanced at Luke, then away.

"To calm him down," Kristen said. "He wasn't mad, just upset."

Victoria felt Luke shift, and put her hands on his forearms.

"Your mom talked to him, Luke, and she calmed him down. But then she got in a cab and went back to the hotel or something."

"She called us," Victoria said. "My phone. Anyway, Luke talked to her."

"Oh. Well, Buzz hung around for a long time with Parker and Cort. The crew cleared everyone out except the staff, who had to clean up. And Candy and Mandy, who now have their sights set on Parker."

Victoria looked at Teresa, who nodded, her smile too grim. She would have to deal with that later, too. She wanted to ask about Brett, but not in front of Luke. Knowing how malicious Brett could be, she was worried that he might retaliate.

"They filmed their conversation," Kristen said. "In case you want to know what they said."

"I don't have access to that anymore," Victoria reminded her, and noticed it didn't sting quite as much as it would have a few days before.

"I'm sure Brett will distort it," Teresa said.

Luke's breathing remained steady. "Should've hit him harder, then," he said, "if he could actually get up to finish producing." The rumble in his voice reverberated through Victoria's spine. She shivered and slid her legs sideways along the tops of his thighs. His arms tightened around her waist and she pressed her nails into the flesh of his forearms. He made an almost imperceptible groan, then sighed when Victoria stopped moving.

"That's debatable," Teresa said and her smile looked more cheerful this time. "You laid him pretty flat. He was out for a few minutes even after you drove off."

"I wanted to toss a glass of water in his face, but T wouldn't let me," Kristen said.

"Only because he's easier to take when he's passed out on the floor," Teresa told her.

Kristen shrugged. "True."

Victoria couldn't wait anymore. "What happened when he came to?"

"Oh, he whimpered about his nose never being the same," Kristen said, "then sulked in the corner with an ice pack for awhile. Jamie made Carl take him to the ER."

That would be like her director, Victoria thought. Tolerant but firm, with an ease about him that convinced people to agree with his instructions. As much as she wanted to be with Luke, she was sorry to have missed the events at Tony's the night before. She would have loved taking charge and socking Brett in the nose herself.

"Things calmed down after that," Kristen said. "The crew packed up, Parker left with Candy and Mandy, and Cort and Buzz left. But not together."

"Buzz probably went to the hotel," Luke said, and Victoria wondered if that was true, but kept quiet. "But if y'all were so worried about us, where's Cort?"

Teresa looked at the floor. Kristen watched her, then sat up straight and looked over Victoria's shoulder at Luke. "He said he knew you'd turn up like a bad penny and that at the moment, he didn't much care where you were." She shrugged. "Paraphrasing, but..."

"He was mad," Luke said.

"More than a wet hen," Kristen said.

"I'll talk to him."

"You may want to wait."

Luke asked why and Teresa said something about Cort that Victoria missed because she was yawning so hard. She covered her mouth with her palm, and snuggled against Luke, her eyelids getting heavy. Maybe she could just close them for awhile, to rest a bit, before tackling all of the things that needed her attention.

She had so much to do, she thought, turning sideways and resting her cheek against Luke's warm, firm chest. So much to do...but she was so comfortable...

CHAPTER THIRTY-EIGHT

Luke felt Victoria slump against him as Tessa told him about Cort. He'd called Cort a sonovabitch, but he had to own up to the fact that he'd been one himself.

Tessa whispered, "She's asleep."

"Hmm?" Luke inclined his head toward Victoria and in the quiet heard her slow, steady breathing. Her grip had relaxed, too. "She didn't get much sleep last night."

"Is my radar off?" Kristen said. "*Did* you have sex last night?"

Tessa gave a shocked laugh, but Luke didn't mind Kristen's bluntness. "No," he said with a chuckle. "We were a touch busy for that pleasure."

"Too bad," Kristen said.

"Indeed," he said with a nod. "But I should probably get her to her bed now and let her sleep. Then I'll go talk to Cort."

Tessa had stood up while he was talking, and she turned to him. "You don't want to let him cool off?"

Luke shook his head. "Won't do much good. If he's mad at me, he'll just get riled again when I show up, no matter how cooled off he was before."

Kristen tilted her head at him. "That's very perceptive."

Luke gave her a nod, then shifted Victoria to get an arm under her legs, and stood with her balanced against his chest. "Thanks for the information, ladies. I'm sorry we troubled you. We'll call next time."

"Unless you really are having sex," Kristen said.

Tessa turned toward the door. "I need to get to work. Are you all

265

okay here?"

"We're fine," Kristen said, giving her a squeeze. "We'll all meet up at some point and figure out what to do about..." She waved a hand around. "All of this."

Luke nodded at Tessa, then turned the corner and went up the short hall toward Victoria's bedroom.

"Wait," Kristen called from behind him, keeping her voice low. "I'll get the door for you."

Luke stopped in the hall while Kristen slipped past him and inside. He settled Victoria on the bed and covered her with the quilt while Kristen drew the curtains, then stood at the bed's foot, clutching the post and staring at him.

Luke brushed the hair back from Victoria's face, then straightened up and said, "Something I can do for you, Miss Kristen?"

"No," she said with a bright smile. "I'm just taking in the aura." She pointed to him and then her sister. "Of your intense attraction. You're both pumping out pheromones like crazy and I think I'm high on it." She let out a happy sigh, glided over, and kissed him on the cheek, one hand on his upper arm. "Don't hold back with her," she whispered, then twirled out the door, closing it behind her.

He smiled after her, amused at her turn of phrase and little-girl actions, but then the smile slipped and he sagged against the edge of the bed. He gripped the bedpost, watching Victoria's face, smooth and at ease in sleep, and felt not just his smile slipping, but something inside him. It had started to crumble the first time he saw Victoria, and kept breaking apart the longer he knew her. At the same time, he'd been building up the strength to face his parents, to finally step away from the shadow of their lives and to live his own.

Still. It wrenched at him, and as he curled his body around Victoria, one arm on the pillow over her head, the other laying over her torso, the dam finally broke and his tears soaked into Victoria's hair and rolled down his cheeks to her forehead. He had felt on the verge of this earlier at the picnic table, but she needed him then, so he'd held it together. But now that she lay open and vulnerable to him—and her sister had basically given him permission—he released everything.

A few minutes later, Victoria's sleepy voice broke through. "Luke?" Her hand tightened on the arm he'd rested over her. "What is it?" When he didn't answer—he couldn't answer—she pulled him to her and wrapped her arms around him, holding tight.

When he felt like he could breathe again, he shifted back, brushing at the tears on his face, then kissed away the ones that had slid to her forehead. "It's nothing, darlin'," he whispered to her. "Go back to sleep."

"No." Her eyes met his in the dim room. "What's wrong?"

He shook his head. "Nothing now." He smoothed the furrows on her brow with his thumb.

"Something now," she insisted, sounding like the old commanding Victoria Clausen, but with a tender quality that almost did him in again.

Don't hold back with her.

"I need to see Cort, straighten some things out."

"Can I help?"

"You already have," he told her. "More than you know." He got off the bed and took her face in his hands. "But you can be here when I come back, so I can make love to you and fall asleep here proper."

He drove on autopilot to the Barn and climbed the outside steps to the apartments. He stood in front of Cort's door for a few minutes, feeling unbearably tired. He pressed his forehead to the wall, hat in his hand, remembering how he'd shown up at Victoria's place in a similar fashion just the other night. He felt much more weary this time around. Since last night, he'd played a show, confronted both Buzz and Dot, driven all night, carried Victoria to her bed, and cried like a baby. His eyes felt dry and scratchy, his stomach rumbled from caffeine and hunger, and his head felt hot except where it touched the cool wall.

He didn't necessarily want to be in bed, or even sleeping, but facing Cort's anger right now wasn't high on his wish list, either. But he'd been mighty hateful in front of and to a lot of people the night before, and he had some making up to do. That started with his best friend.

He might not know where he would go next—Parker, Marty, Tony—but he'd always known where he needed to go first.

Before he could talk himself into giving Cort time to cool down some, he straightened and knocked. Some shuffling inside, then footsteps and the clatter of shoelace ends on the hardwood floor. His heart thumped hard.

The door opened and the bright, expectant look on Cort's face disappeared as soon as he caught sight of Luke. Neither one spoke, and when it became clear to Luke that Cort wasn't going to, he said, "Bet you were thinking you wouldn't see me for awhile."

Cort dropped his gaze. "Nope," he said, and started to close the door.

Luke held up a hand. "Wait."

Cort stopped, but didn't look happy about it. "Why?"

"Because I'm sorry." He rested a forearm against the doorjamb, leaning toward Cort. He slapped his hat against his thigh, looking at the floor. "I was an ass last night. I messed up. I'll apologize to the boys, too, but..." He stopped, not knowing how to finish that sentence without sounding like an idiot. He wanted to say Cort was more important than the other guys, that all that mattered was working it out between them. Things automatically set themselves right if Cort was in his corner, and he needed at least one normal situation right now.

"You were," Cort said. "An ass, I mean. I fed Frog, by the way."

"Aw, hell," Luke said, not sure where to go from there. He could add forgetting his cat to his list of crimes. "Thanks."

"Tessa's not too sure about me right now," Cort added. "On account of how unstable you are. Guilt by association or something."

Luke stomped in a half circle, banging his hat against his thigh out of frustration now instead of worry. He turned back to Cort, pointing to emphasize his words. "I'll make it up," he said. "I'll talk to Tessa." Damn. Another thing to fix.

"Don't know if there's any making up with this one. Besides—"

"I will." He had to. He started to walk away, then shifted back, pointing at Cort again. "I will," he repeated, then headed to the stairwell.

"She's at the catering place, setting up for a wedding," Cort called out to him. "What you gonna do, go in with guns blazing, mess up her job?"

Luke froze, his hand on the door knob. He tried to count to ten before turning around, but that never worked for him. He strode back to Cort, who now stood leaning in the doorway. "What're you saying?"

"Charging in there's not a real good idea right now."

He didn't think Cort was blaming Luke for messing up Victoria's job, but he felt the sting of the accusation just the same. "The camera guys around?"

Cort finally looked Luke fully in the eye. "It's Saturday, Lucas."

Luke slapped his hat against his thigh again. So it was. "Damn," he muttered, wondering when his head would get set right again.

"Anyway, they're all probably resting up from last night or still over at Parker's, hoping to catch him with the twins."

"You mad about that?"

Cort shrugged. "Not so much. The girls were great, but Tessa..." His voice drifted off, and he straightened. "No comparison."

Luke nodded his agreement. "You need me to say something to her, I'll do it. Listen, I hear you talked to Buzz last night. How'd that go?"

"Same old bastard," Cort said.

Luke nodded, unsurprised. "That's what I figured." He glanced at the cameras in the corner of Cort's living room, then eased past his friend and stood in front of one, staring into its red light. "Same old bastard," he repeated for its benefit.

"We don't want his contract," Cort said from behind him.

Luke let out a slow breath of relief. Still looking at the camera, he said, "He's not changing any time soon."

"Nope," Cort agreed.

"Neither is Dot." Luke realized it didn't hurt as much to say that as he thought it might. She'd stood behind him many years, but he knew for certain now that her main support would automatically go to Buzz. He wouldn't live with that anymore.

"Lucas..."

Luke inclined his head at the loyalty in Cort's voice, but declared for the cameras—and the world: "They're both out of my life." He finally turned to his best friend in the world and held out his hand.

Without hesitation, Cort clasped Luke's wrist. Normally, they would pull their hands back, letting the palms and fingers slide against each other before stepping away. This time, Cort pulled Luke forward and they pounded each other on the back with their free hands. They nodded in acknowledgement of the gesture, then Cort said, "I'm still not real pleased with you right now, but there's something you should know. The boys and I were talking after you run off." He held up a hand when Luke opened his mouth to object. "I know. You didn't run. Doesn't matter now. We got to talkin' and come to a conclusion, but we won't settle it until we've got your go ahead."

"What is it?"

Cort gave the cameras a big wink, then gestured for Luke to follow him into the hall and shut the door behind them. Cort tilted his head toward the back stairs. "Let's go for a walk and have ourselves a little discussion."

CHAPTER THIRTY-NINE

That afternoon, Victoria paced around her living room, picking up random things and setting them down again a second later, much like Cort had done in her bedroom the day he came to rouse her from her depression. With all that had happened recently, she needed to find a way to wrap her mind around it.

She'd had mind-blowing sex with Luke, faced off against Brett, lost her job, watched Luke confront his parents, spent the night driving with him, baring her soul while he did the same, fell asleep in his arms, and held him while he cried.

Relief, exhaustion and restlessness coursed through her, sharing space with feeling right with the world and completely turned around at the same time. She thought she might be in love. And she liked it. Intuition told her Luke was close behind, if not already there, but his frequent inscrutability left her in some doubt.

She didn't need intuition to know her behavior toward Brett bordered on appalling, despite his being a complete asshole. She'd used him, she knew that now, and she needed to apologize to him, for her own integrity. He probably wouldn't accept her apology, much less her explanation, but that wasn't the point.

However, it was clear that attempting this right now would be a bad idea. He'd had his ego bruised twice, once when he found out she'd slept with Luke and again last night when Luke hit him. Going to see Brett now would just remind him of those two incidents. Better to let him cool down first.

So what else could she do in the meantime? She hated being

without a purpose or plan.

She looked in the corner, at the small dining table Kristen had salvaged after she first moved in, refinishing it and proudly announcing the three of them could now eat dinner together. This was before she'd learned that Victoria and Teresa were hardly ever home at the same time, much less for dinner. Now, books, magazines, purses, and Victoria's new phone charger cluttered the lilac table. She may not have been able to take anything from her office the day she was fired, but she'd made a practice of backing up all of her files and had transferred everything to her new phone. She studied its shiny surface; so much of her life had revolved around her phone. But it was so *quiet* right now.

She turned away from it. Time for some action.

She showered and dressed in a suit she normally would have worn to her job, a pink sweater, dark gray blazer and matching skirt. She even put on her pink and gray platform heels, but when it came to pulling her hair back in its usual clip, she paused. She shook her head, letting the locks settle around her face in soft waves. Luke liked it, she liked it. Old and new, she thought. She'd still be the shark, but she knew the softness Luke had coaxed out would only enhance her, not work against her as she'd always thought.

The same contract that led to her firing also prevented her poaching anyone from her shows for two years from now. But they could come to her. Was that what needed to happen? She didn't know, and pressed a hand against the panicky flutter in her chest. For the first time in many years, she didn't know what would happen next, either with a show she produced, or with her life.

She scrolled through the texts and e-mails on her phone, the solid weight of it a reassurance in the midst of so much insecurity. A text from Teresa: "My first meringue!" captioned a picture of rows of gorgeous swirled multicolor cookies for a couple celebrating their sixtieth anniversary. A text from Kristen, using Teresa's phone: "Melt in your mouth decadence!" with a few smiley faces after it that visibly reminded Victoria of smiley face condoms. And Luke.

An e-mail from Robin Archer, CEO of Archer Productions, outlining how much they wanted her to work for them, and what they could do for each other. It sounded like a dream job: field producer, creating new shows, just as she'd done for Reality Strikes. But how would they treat someone who'd broken one of the Ten

Commandments of reality television?

She thought of Jerry and Brett. Of Rita, whom she'd known for eight years, but never knew she was writing a play. Of Teresa, quitting to follow a dream, but also because Victoria had chosen job over friendship. But what a job it had been. It suited her, and she suited it, and she missed it with a shattering pain that left her fragmented. She didn't know how else to reconstruct the pieces except to continue doing what she knew best.

With a deep breath, she dialed Archer Productions. After a long conversation, she took another steadying breath and called the catering company Teresa worked for. While waiting on hold, the doorbell rang. She answered and even though she returned to her spot leaning against the table and held a hand up to indicate she'd just be a moment, Luke moved with deliberation in a straight line to her. His gaze shifted around the room, to the phone at her ear, and finally to her eyes. He caught her uplifted hand in his and ran his tongue up the length of her index finger, then sucked it into his mouth. With his other hand, he started undoing the tiny buttons down the front of her sweater.

He released her finger and said in a throaty whisper, "Hang up," just as the receptionist came on the line and chirped, "I apologize for keeping you on hold so long. How may I help?"

Victoria hitched in a breath, grasped the edge of the table, then said as firmly as possible, "I needed to...ahh."

Luke moved his kisses along the tender flesh at the inside of her wrist, pulling her body close to his with his free hand. She shifted the phone to keep from dropping it when he purred against her other ear, "*Hang up.*"

"I apologize," she said with a gasp. "I was going to make an appointment to come in, to...*oh.*"

Luke grasped her hips and lifted her onto the table, stepping between her legs. Her skirt had already shifted, but when she wrapped her legs around his, she felt it slip higher up her thighs. The denim of his jeans rubbed against the sensitive skin on the inside of her legs and the vee between as Luke slid his hands under her bottom and lifted her closer.

This time, Luke growled, "I'll make you come here," and Victoria gasped, "I'll have to call back," into the phone and hung up.

She dropped the phone and said, "There's something *I* need first."

Luke took her face in both hands and kissed her soundly, lips cool from the outside air, the side of his face rough with stubble. Her hands automatically slid around his neck and she warmed his mouth with hers, pressing her body against his solidness.

In between kisses, his breath coming in gasps, he said, "condoms?" and she leaned to the side and he shifted with her, holding her close and placing kisses down her neck while she shivered and dumped her purse. She grabbed a condom and held it up for him.

When he set her back on the table, she undid his belt buckle and pulled his jeans open, then pushed them down his hips, saying, "I'm going to have to stash these around the house."

"Whatever you want, darlin'," he said, concentrating on the condom, then pulled her close to him again.

He slid her sweater off one shoulder and ran the tip of his tongue along her collarbone, then held her with one hand while shifting her underwear aside, and settled her over his erection. She wrapped her arms around his neck and slid onto him, slowly, her eyes on his. He pushed into her all the way, then lifted her up and drove into her again, rocking her against him. Her back arched and her head fell back as he moved faster, grasping her tight, his breath coming in harsh gasps. He leaned down to encircle her nipple with his lips and as he tugged on it, and thrust into her, the desperation built for that point of no return, and she molded to his body to accelerate it until she exploded in a sharp release that left her gasping and clutching him hard, even as he followed. His breathing ragged, he eased her down to the table. She slid her hands down his arms and held onto him.

"Now I can sleep," he murmured against her neck.

"I don't know," she said into his chest. "I feel like we're just getting started."

He chuckled, then straightened to look in her eyes. He took hold of her shoulders, and bent down to kiss her.

She grabbed the bottom of his shirt, then slid her fingers to his back and clung tight.

His lips now warm, his velvety tongue brushed against her mouth, then across her own tongue. She pushed against him, greedy, wanting more despite the orgasm she'd just had.

His back muscles shifted against her fingers as he wrapped his arms around her shoulders. He held her so close she couldn't breathe, and didn't care. When he shifted her, she lifted her legs and wrapped them around his waist so he could slip his hands under her bottom and hold her up that way. She could inhale again, but thought maybe he'd taken her breath away with his kiss.

He pulled her to him and carried her to the bedroom where they made love again, and fell asleep nestled together.

LUKE WOKE WITH Victoria pressed against him, her head resting on his chest, and a strange humming sound filling his ears.

"What the hell is that?" he said aloud to the dark.

Victoria stirred and he felt bad for waking her. "Kristen," she mumbled. "Meditating." She snuggled closer to him, her breathing deepening again. Luke glanced at the bedside clock. Four in the damn morning, he thought. He took a breath, trying to go back to sleep, but was too keyed up. He wanted to charge right out and take over the world. He also wanted to lay here with Victoria forever.

His chest tightened and he let out a cough. Damn. Forever. Did he mean that?

He looked at the top of her head, her hair spreading over his arm and chest, her delicate hand resting on his stomach. He thought of when they'd first met, such a small woman charging into a roomful of men and having them eating out of her hand without flashing a lot of skin. Well, he'd caught that glimpse of her bra and it heated it him right up, but her courage, her no-fail attitude grabbed him first. Then her stomping around in that orthopedic boot, the day she came to the Barn and he fixed her hair for her, loosening it when she insisted it needed to be pulled back. The way she'd proposed her show idea to the boys, there in her high, high heels and his red t-shirt, professional and gutsy at once. He'd hated the idea, so much it burned inside him. But he'd never hated her. He admired her.

That first kiss in the Barn, to finally know what she tasted like, and realizing it wasn't enough, would never be enough. But then filming took over. And she started seeing that asshole Soloway, and it was all he could do not to shake some sense into her.

His mind drifted along to the wrap party at Tony's and afterward, when she showed up at his place. Didn't matter that she was there for Tessa and Cort, his heart had thudded hard in his chest when he saw her at the door, and all he could think of was getting her inside. Well, he'd gotten his wish, and it had all gone sideways. Until that day on Sutro Terrace when he walked away from her, and it sucked all the breath from his lungs. He couldn't breathe again until she called his name and he could hold her in his arms.

Then the re-shoot, Buzz and Dot, letting himself fall to pieces in front of Victoria.

Yes, he thought after that review, forever was about right. But they needed to get through right now first.

Her voice came soft through the darkness. "What are you thinking?"

"You," he said.

Her fingers splayed on his chest, stroking. "I'm fascinated."

He smiled, edging down on the bed until they lay face to face. He couldn't see much in the dark, just her outline from the glow of the alarm clock on the bedside table. But he could feel her breath warm and gentle on his face, her body pressed close. "So am I," he said. "So fascinated, I can't stop."

She leaned forward to kiss him, and he let her take it to the next level until she knelt over him, the kisses growing more enthusiastic, their hands everywhere, skin on skin, and then he was inside her, and he knew with a confidence like no other that he loved her. But beyond their mutual gasps and moans, he stayed silent. He wouldn't say it the first time when she might think he was just out of his head from sex. The damn mind-blowing sex. He wanted to hold her tight and purr it into her ear, but he'd wait for the right moment.

Afterward, as they lay close together again and the first rays of sun slanted around the curtains in her bedroom, she asked him how things went with Cort. He told her everything, from beginning to end, as he'd wanted to do for hours, including how he realized he had no desire to talk to Buzz again. Lord knew how that would all fall out. It was only a temporary solution, but for now, Buzz and Dot didn't need to be in his life.

Then he said, "There's one more thing we need to talk about," and filled her in on Cort's plan. She surprised him by saying she'd already heard Cort wanted to strike, that the idea had come up when Cort visited a couple days earlier trying to cheer her up. She didn't think he'd actually do it.

Luke felt her struggling against her former producer self,

obviously wanting to warn him against the pitfalls of such an action, the dire consequences, how they would most likely be sued. He and the boys had talked it all through for hours before settling on a course of action.

Victoria started and stopped more than one sentence before flopping onto her back and pressing her palms to her face. She was quiet for a long beat, and he waited, giving her some time. Finally she whispered, "I love that show," and the pain in her voice stabbed clear through him.

He leaned over to kiss the back of one hand, then the other, holding himself up until she lifted her hands and swiped quickly under each eye. He waited for her to look him in the eye before whispering back, "I'm sorry."

She nodded, blinking, then pressed her lips together before blowing out a long breath. "Change sucks," she grumbled. She pushed up on her elbows and kissed him. "Most change," she added with a smile, and he found himself holding back another "I love you" when she slid down his body and took him in her mouth. Warm and wet, her full lips enveloped him, and he lost the ability to think for a few minutes.

After returning the favor, he collapsed next to her, his head propped on her stomach, and dozed off until her voice brought him back.

"There's something I want to tell you about, too..."

CHAPTER FORTY

Victoria set two big picnic baskets on a bench and sat with a groan, startling a red-faced parrot from a nearby tree. One of the infamous birds of Telegraph Hill whose territory had expanded to her Russian Hill neighborhood, it flew off with a loud screech, and she apologized to it in her head. She had no breath for spoken words. In the chocolate brown boots she bought the day her blouse ripped and Luke loaned her his t-shirt, she'd lost track of how many steps she'd climbed to reach the park, and sat breathing heavily, one hand to the stitch in her side.

But when she raised her head to the view—sunlight glinting on the Transamerica Pyramid, the Bay Bridge, and the water of the bay itself—she sighed in satisfaction. The trek had been worth it. And as she heard her sister's bright laughter and the breathless response of her best friend, she smiled in anticipation. In the past six months, her job had brought her that same anticipatory flutter countless times. But she knew exactly how many times the thought of hanging out with these two important people had delighted her the same way.

Zero. And the realization shamed her.

So when Kristen bounded up the path in her white leggings and flowing yellow blouse, followed by Teresa in purple skinny jeans and a matching halter top, Victoria popped up from the bench and trotted over to meet them. She looped an arm around each of them, and tugged both toward the long green bench.

"You appear to be a friendly alien," Kristen said, "but I'm pretty sure you've done something nefarious with my sister."

Teresa stood staring at the baskets, which bore the logo of the catering company where she worked.

Victoria lifted the lids and swept a hand through the air like a magician about to perform an amazing feat. "I present to you: Picnic in the Park. No cameras, cell phone on silent, both vegan and carnivore fare...and me," she ended lamely, not sure how to read the expressions on their faces.

They'd both gone still, and while they seemed curious, Teresa also looked doubtful. Kristen looked slightly bemused.

"What's the occasion?" she asked.

Victoria had planned on satisfying them with food before delving into the main reason she'd asked them here. Still on shaky ground these days, she wasn't sure if she'd be taken seriously. Or how they would respond. But she'd always been one for directness, so she said, "The occasion is my sincere apology, both in person and via delicious cuisine. I've been..." She stopped, her chest tight. "I haven't been a very good friend for awhile. Or a good sister."

When Teresa opened her mouth to respond, Victoria held up a hand so she could finish. Then she took a deep breath, lowered the hand and said, "Sorry. Go ahead."

"I was going to defend you," Teresa said, "say no, that's not true. But..." she glanced at Kristen, then looked at Victoria again. "It is true."

Kristen nodded. "But we knew that wasn't your entire being. Or we wouldn't still be here."

Victoria couldn't help laughing, although it was tinged with pain. "At least you're both honest. So..." She took in Kristen's big blue eyes and welcoming smile, and Teresa's lovely, exotic features, both women here despite her poor behavior the past few months. "Can you forgive me?"

Until she said it and watched them pause as they took the question seriously, she didn't realize how important their responses were. But she'd promised herself she'd pay more attention and not take control of every situation, so she waited. At the same time, she couldn't help wondering who might respond first. She would have bet on Teresa. And would've lost the bet as Kristen smothered her in a tight hug.

"There's nothing to forgive, big sister."

Despite having her face pressed against Kristen's breasts, Victoria heard the hitch in her voice. "Are you crying?" she asked, trying to step away.

Kristen tightened her hold. "No," she sobbed.

Victoria managed to disentangle herself and stood holding Kristen's hand while waiting for Teresa's response, letting her initiate rather than pulling T along as usual. The longer Teresa hesitated, the more Victoria knew what a jerk she'd been.

Teresa pressed her lips together, then nodded, the beads in her hair clinking together musically. "Me, too."

Victoria nodded back, blinking at the sudden tears that filled her eyes, relieved more than she'd thought by Teresa's forgiveness. Watching Teresa struggle over the past few months to express herself, quitting, asking for her job back, and quitting once more, Victoria knew she had extra making up to do for her part in that struggle. One moment of forgiveness wouldn't clear the slate, but it was a start.

With a sniffle, Kristen pulled them into a group hug, and when they separated, Victoria got them settled on a large blanket on the grass to dig into their picnic. They oohcd and ahhed over the stuffed Portobello mushrooms, fried calamari, bruschetta, fruit salad, chicken skewers, and pasta primavera. Before they got to the dessert of cannoli, lemon bars, and vegan cupcakes, Teresa announced she was done with TV. "No more, ever, no way." She stared down at the half empty containers around them. "That pasta primavera is my recipe. I want to do catering. That's my future."

Victoria glanced between the cannoli and the lemon bars. "I'm not done with TV. Not yet." She picked up a cannoli, but didn't take a bite. "I'm really excited," she admitted, looking back and forth between them. "I got a distribution deal with Archer to film the boys recording their album, maybe even a tour." She'd shared all of this with Luke the other night, warm in his arms after he'd told her about Cort's plan for the boys to strike. "We've already talked a little, and the band still might not agree to it, but...either way, my future is still in film."

Kristen swallowed a bite of vegan cupcake, and licked frosting off her upper lip. She gave them a serene smile. "Well, my future is mommyhood."

Victoria choked on her cannoli and Teresa let out a squawk as Kristen's smile turned into a grin and she patted her belly.

"You are such a scene stealer," Victoria croaked, then took a swallow of her drink to clear her throat.

Kristen gave her a very mom-like look that spoke volumes and left Victoria feeling very small. "I'm not one of your TV people."

"Kristen, it was just a..." Victoria stopped herself. Kristen was right. She was her sister, not someone to be set up as a "type" on a reality show. And she was...

"Are you serious? You're pregnant?"

Kristen nodded. "That's why I've been so moody." She grinned. "Hormones of the baby-making kind."

Amidst the food and drinks, they came together in another group hug, both Victoria and Teresa throwing questions at Kristen in a rapid-fire manner. She was about two months along, she told them, the father knew, but he was a shit and she didn't want to talk about him, but she was thrilled to her bones about everything else. "I love being pregnant," she said. "I can't wait to get huge." And she picked up another cupcake.

Victoria wasn't sure she could take in all of these changes. Even if Kristen seemed unconcerned, Victoria felt a clutch of concern for her. She realized this wasn't the time to discuss it, but she wasn't going to let too much time pass before they had a long conversation. "Well, I can't wait to get going on the next phase of my life," she said. "And spend more time with you all. And Luke."

Teresa looked at her watch. "Well, you won't have long to wait for that."

Victoria lowered the lemon bar she'd been about to devour. "What do you mean?"

"The strike," Teresa said, sounding surprised. "Just about now. I thought you knew it was today—"

"What?" Victoria dropped the bar into the grass and stood up. "They can't do that." The realization that Luke and the boys could have already issued their ultimatum struck her hard in the breastbone. "We have to go. I have to stop them." She started scooping up picnic items.

"I thought you were okay with them doing this," Teresa said, standing and brushing at her pants. "Luke said you talked—"

"We did. You don't understand." She randomly tossed items into the baskets, ignoring the dismayed expressions on Teresa and Kristen's faces, as if she'd rapidly reverted back to her old self and didn't want the boys to ruin the show. Her show.

As Victoria charged down the steps double-time, her boots

clacking, Teresa and Kristen tried to talk her out of going to the Barn. She knew they didn't understand, and for once words failed her. "I can't...I need to...damn it, it'll ruin everything. We just have to stop them."

She had to get there in time.

She shoved the baskets in the trunk, they piled into her car and she sped along the now-familiar route from Russian Hill to the Barn. Turning onto Folsom, she didn't even search for an open parking space, but parted the small sea of gawkers in front of the Barn by pulling straight into the small driveway and stopping the car behind Cort's Ford Ranger.

Without waiting for Teresa and Kristen, she jumped out of the car, and ran up the drive, pushing through the groupies to the front door, only to be stopped by two of Brett's henchmen.

"Rob, Joseph," she said with a nod, unconcerned that Brett had probably shared her "sex tape" with them, her focus solely on reaching Luke. She would not allow anything to ruin this moment, one she'd planned on happening a very specific way. She started around them and Rob held up a hand while Joseph shifted to block her.

"They're filming," Rob told her.

"Clearly," she said, with a nod to the two white production vans spilling crew members out the back and the array of fans surrounding them on the sidewalk. She took a step closer until she could feel Rob's breath on her face and added, "I need to get inside. Now," then stared at him without blinking.

In tandem, Rob and Joseph folded their arms over their chests. "No admittance. Soloway's orders."

She refrained from rolling her eyes at their Brett-esque superior attitude, even as relief washed through her. The cameras hadn't left; production continued, if just for the moment. "I'm part of the production," she said in a tone that should allow no opposition, "and I'm needed inside."

Teresa and Kristen flanked her now, her own henchwomen, and the crowd of fans moved closer to observe, a few even filming the encounter on their phones. God bless her show's supporters. Victoria smiled, and Joseph's expression turned wary. Ignoring him, she turned on her heel to address the women—and a few men—in the crowd, her smile broadening as she caught the expressions on their faces. These were true fans, practically camping out at the Barn for a glimpse of the show's stars, or to be part of a television show's production.

"Hello, everyone," she said, positioning herself so that Kristen and Teresa stood behind her, blocking Rob and Joseph. In a voice meant to rouse the group, she asked, "How would you like to be part of a segment of *In Concert*?"

They responded with cheers and a "hell, yeah," here and there, and even as Teresa hissed, "What are you doing?" Victoria tossed out a few more questions, encouraging volume in the enthusiastic responses. She gestured for everyone to follow her and charged right past now powerless Rob and Joseph and into the Barn. All of its familiar scents assailed her, from the faint gasoline and oil residue, a reminder of its service center days, to the musty smell of the old chairs in the Lounge to the intensity of men, musky, heavenly, addicting.

For her, one intense man in particular, who now strode toward her across the floor, past his band mates, Brett, and the camera crew, ignoring the steady stream of fans flowing in behind Victoria, eyes never leaving hers. Everyone involved in the production had already turned toward the cacophony outside the Barn, and they now concentrated fully on Victoria's entourage.

Brett huffed, "What the hell...?" but Victoria barely heard him, all of her being focused on the black boots, muscled thighs, broad chest and five o'clock shadow of Luke Tyler. That and the way his eyes lit up at sight of her. He tossed his hat to one of the girls in the crowd, swept an arm around Victoria's waist, bent her backward and kissed her long and hard.

When he finally raised her up, he said, "Thank God you're here."

"Why?" she asked, breathless.

Hand still firmly on her back, he leaned close and said, "Because when all of five minutes goes by without you, my heart breaks just a little bit."

Victoria heard a few sighs from the crowd behind her, and even though her knees had gone weak, their response reminded her why she'd come here. She turned to the camera crew and saw Brett nearby, hands on hips, looking so ineffectual she could cry over the time she'd wasted mooning at him. Ignoring him, she asked Sam and Gary, "Are the cameras on?" as if *In Concert* were still her show and she called the shots. Brett huffed something, but Gary nodded.

"Good," Victoria said, motioning Tim to move his boom mic closer. "Keep filming."

She turned to face Luke, taking his hands in hers, and opened her mouth to speak, but Brett interrupted. "What the hell is going on here? I have a production to run, and if you and your mob aren't out of here in five seconds, I'm calling the police."

Victoria laughed. "Call them." Then she faced Luke again, unable to suppress a smile just being near him. "I want everyone to hear this." She squeezed Luke's hands. "I have been terrified every single day since I met you. First because I so desperately wanted you on my show, and then because I was afraid you'd find a way out of it. And I was more attracted to you than I could ever admit. But now..." She couldn't read the look on his face, some sort of combination of amused, interested and expectant. "Now, I'm terrified because you're the one..." This time she knew the happy sigh behind her came from her sister. "I don't want to waste another minute hiding behind a camera, or behind my fears, and I want the whole world to hear this." She gestured toward the cameras, but her eyes never left his. "I love you, Luke."

He froze for a second, and Victoria's heart stopped. Had she made a mistake by announcing it to the world the same time she told him? She'd wanted to prove that nothing else mattered, she wouldn't let anything come between them now, and she had no fears about everyone knowing it. But his face had gone blank, and he straightened, letting out a sharp breath at her words.

Luke's hands slipped from hers, and she took a shaky step back, staggering in her boots as the blood rushed out of her face. Then Luke leaned toward her, his face near her chest, and swept her up so high she had to not only grasp his shoulders for balance, but also wrap her legs around his waist. She let out a whoop of surprise, then laughed in delight and shivered in ecstasy as he trailed kisses up her neck to the edge of her jaw, finally finding her lips again.

A round of applause from the assemblage didn't stop her from brushing her tongue against his and squeezing her thighs hard at his waist.

He pulled back to look in her face. "Awhile back, I told you music wasn't the most important thing to me. You remember asking me what was more important?"

She nodded, her heart beating hard, but not fluttering quite so much as it had when he'd pulled away from her. She lowered one hand to his chest, watching him.

"I knew there was *something*, just not what. You were so sure about what was important to you, my saying I didn't know yet seemed foolish."

She shook her head. "I was crazy for making work the most important thing in my life."

"No," he said, shifting her closer, his hands firm and strong. "You had a lot of conviction. I envied that. But now I'm certain, too."

She leaned farther forward, feeling the steady beat of his heart under her palm, every other person in the Barn completely forgotten. "What is it?"

"Well, she walked in on these real high heels..."